BLOODY EISTEDDFOD

Bloody Eisteddfod

Myfanwy Alexander

Whilst the area represented in this book is real,
all characters are fictional.

First published in Welsh, A Oes Heddwas? in 2015
First English edition: 2017

Published by Gwasg Carreg Gwalch,
12 Iard yr Orsaf, Llanrwst, Wales LL26 0EH
tel: 01492 642031
email: books@carreg-gwalch.com
website: www.carreg-gwalch.com

ISBN: 978-1-84527-630-0

Cover design: Design Dept, Welsh Books Council

Published with the financial support of the
Welsh Books Council

'To the six best girls in the world, Myfanwy, Eleanor, Amelia, Lucia, Henrietta and Gwenllian and in loving memory of my dear father, J Mervyn Jones.

I would like to thank all those freinds who helped me in the creative process, especially Ann Lowther for her essential and unstinting support.'

Glossary

This is not the place for an essay on Welsh pronunciation but readers may like to be aware that 'f' in Welsh is pronounced as 'v' in English, so our hero's name would rhyme with 'chav'. The following list contains words commonly used untranslated from Welsh in conversations held in English but it is worth remembering that, in this story, everyone speaks Welsh unless stated otherwise. I have also included a few cultural references which may be unfamiliar. It should also be noted that farm names are frequently used as unofficial surnames and these do not always change when someone moves house.

Ann Griffiths	Great Methodist hymn writer (1776–1805). From Montgomeryshire. Like Jimi Hendrix, she added to her creative mystique by dying young
Bach/bech	Literally meaning 'small' in Welsh, it is used as an endearment and in Montgomeryshire, some people pronounce it with a flat 'a' written as 'bech'
Bing	A small farm building
Bodo	Aunt (North Wales)
Cariad	An endearment, meaning 'my love'
Carrying clecs	Telling tales or betraying someone's secrets
Cerdd Dant	A technically challenging form of singing where the voice and harp follow different melodies
Clec	A blow or slap
Clic	The catch-up service for Welsh language TV channel S4C
Cog	A boy, often used as an endearment in Montgomeryshire
Cont	An obscenity used as a term of address in Caernarfon
Cymanfa Canu	A hymn-fest which is the first major event of the National Eisteddfod
Cyw	The brand of S4C's programmes for young children
Duw/Duwcs	God, used as a mild expletive

Eight Inch Nails	The great and the good, the big shots
Eisteddfod	A cultural competition, which can be local or national, in which the desire for artistic expression combines with an all-consuming will to win
Eisteddfod Cylch	The local opening round of the Urdd (see below) Eisteddfod
Flower Dance	A ceremonial dance performed to honour the winners of the major prizes at the National Eisteddfod. Involves elfin children and wild flowers/garden weeds
Golwg	A weekly magazine which represents almost the entirety of the Welsh medium National Press
Lanc	Lad, a term of endearment
Lodes	Literally 'wench', it is a very warm term of endearment used in Montgomeryshire and has no sexist connotations
Nain	Grandmother (North and Mid Wales)
Noson Lawen	A light entertainment format where the audience no longer sit on bales of straw, alas.
Maes	The Maes is the field on which an Eisteddfod is held
Merched y Wawr	'Daughters of the Dawn' like the WI but even more formidable
Pl@tiad	The smart eating place at the National Eisteddfod. Everyone wears linen, even their socks, and almost everything is garnished with dill
Plethyn	A Montgomeryshire folk group, huge in the 80s
Sali Mali	The main character in a universally read series of children's books. Also on TV. Often
Smic	A small amount
Smithfield	Local name for the livestock market in Welshpool
Taid	Grandfather (North and Mid Wales)
Urdd	The Welsh League of Hope, a vast youth organization giving opportunities for young people to participate in many activities but noted for its highly competitive Eisteddfod

Virgin of the Vale A ceremonial role for a young woman who presents the prize-winners with a vast basket of flowers

Y Brawd Houdini A 70s song. Like 'Come on Eileen' or 'I would walk Ten Thousand Miles', any collection of drunk people always contains a few people singing it

Ych a fi! Yuck!

Ymryson A fiercely contested poetry competition for teams. Half way between the TS Eliot Prize and bear baiting

Ymgom A short play, mainly performed by children

Chapter 1

Sunday, August 2nd 2015

There was no doubting that it was a good idea, to move out of the snug bungalow to rent it for the week to visitors to the Eisteddfod. Any number of local people had done the same, and today Daf Dafis should have been relaxing in Greece instead of unpacking his shaving kit in the en-suite off one of the spare rooms at Neuadd, the home of his brother-in-law. Daf thought with rueful envy of Dr Mansel and his wife sunbathing on the island of Ithaca, having rented their house out to a group of academics from the University of Swansea and flown off to the sun on the profits. When Daf's wife Falmai heard this, she was furious.

'Shame on them, renting from people who don't speak Welsh, spending public money like fools,' she spat, speaking to her husband as if he were one of the less promising pupils in a year three class. Daf sighed. For several reasons, not unconnected with her being unimpressed with Welsh language and culture, Dr Mansel's wife was not exactly popular with Fal and when Daf had murmured that there was something to be said for the idea of escaping to a distant island during the Eisteddfod, he received a hen's bum face as the first reply, before Falmai gradually came to accept that it might not be such a terrible plan after all. The process of finding the best possible Eisteddfod tenants for their home became a subject of dispute between them for months. According to Falmai, the bungalow on the land at Neuadd, the large farm on which Falmai and her brother John had been raised, was perfect in every particular, only four miles from the Eisteddfod Field and less than a mile from Llanfair Caereinion, which offered all the amenities any Eisteddfod-goer might wish for. There was a garage, a Londis, a cash point and, above all, three pubs and a wine bar. The weekend between registering the house on the appropriate site and getting the first enquiry was an absolute nightmare, Daf remembered. Falmai insisted on checking the answering machine every half hour and when no-one had been in touch, it was Daf who was to blame. He hadn't given enough details or had asked for an exorbitant rent or had omitted to stress just how convenient the house was.

'Everyone always likes having an immersion heater to heat the water then they're on holiday, Dafydd. Why didn't you mention the immersion in the particulars?'

Daf held his tongue. He could have included the smell in the details. When John, who had inherited the whole farm and a fair chunk of cash when his father had retired, gave Falmai and Daf a piece of ground on which to build their home, he made sure it was far enough from the farmhouse to ensure that everyone had a bit of privacy. But the site wasn't quite far enough from the Neuadd muck heap to be exactly fragrant.

Daf was perfectly well aware of the load Falmai was carrying on her shoulders: she was the deputy head teacher in the local primary school, where three members of staff were absent because of stress and after a weekend of the edge of her tongue, Daf wondered if he could take time off from his marriage for the same reason. He had had a bellyful of her complaining ceaselessly about things he couldn't care less about, like Post-Inspection Action Plans and joint assessment. It was a rule in their house that Daf's career was not sufficiently respectable to be discussed over the family hearth so Daf seldom got a word in edgeways. That suited Daf: his job as an Inspector in Dyfed Powys Police was challenging and sometimes tragic so he had no desire to bring his work home with him. So, the system was that Daf was had to listen quietly as Falmai moaned about the unfair judge who took against her *cerdd dant* party in the Eisteddfod Cylch, about the lack of support from parents, about the fact that someone had nicked the triangle before the retirement concert for Mrs Evans, Hafodwen who had been training the school's folk dancers since the 90s. But sometimes, as the torrent of words fell over him, Daf did think about the difficulties he faced on a daily basis, problems like knocking on the door of the parents of a fifteen-year-old girl to tell them their daughter had died after taking a legal high, or trying to persuade a young man with a twelve-inch kitchen knife to not slit the throat of his unfaithful wife. But these were nothing compared to Falmai's troubles, because they were part of his unrespectable job and because they were concerned with the doings of unrespectable people, they counted for nothing. Falmai simply did not understand his decision to go into the police force. With his good joint honours degree in English and Welsh, he could have taught in a high school and aimed to be a head, instead of spending his days in the company of the poor, sinners and people suffering from mental illness. But Daf was glad that, every day, he could at least try to create a little bit of justice amidst all the chaos. That meant any amount more to him than any adulatory article in the local paper.

Falmai wasn't long in getting suitable tenants for the big week: an independent TV company that was perfectly willing to pay a pretty substantial rent, so Daf and Falmai spent a number of unusually pleasant evenings browsing the web in search of hotels and villas. According to Falmai, southern Spain was too common, northern Spain too Catholic and after the business with Madeleine McCann, Daf knew better than to suggest Portugal. After over twenty years of marriage, he knew there was absolutely no point in drawing attention to the fact that their children were much older than the little girl who disappeared, or that it was more likely that their children would be out and about on the pop whilst they stayed sedately in the villa. Italy had been the favoured holiday destination for the Neuadd family for many years but Daf was reluctant to, yet again, follow in the footsteps of his bloody brother-in-law.

They were on the point of paying the deposit on a villa with a pool in Greece to secure their Early Bird booking discount when Carys received a call from the Eisteddfod Executive committee. Elin Cain Parri, 'Virgin of the Vale', a bouquet-toting role essential to the Eisteddfod's pageantry, had broken her leg in a skiing accident. According to the specialist at Gobowen Hospital, there was not a canary's hope that she would have recovered fully in time to endure the rigours of the ceremonies in August. As a result, there was an opportunity for Carys to step into the breach. She agreed without a second thought.

'But what about our holiday?' asked her brother, Rhodri.

'We have to think of everything with a positive approach,' his mother answered quickly, shutting down any possibility of argument. 'Looks like you'll be able to take part in the Children's Choir after all.'

'I'd rather not,' Rhodri answered under his breath. 'The Children's Choir is literally the most lame thing on earth.'

'That's enough, Rhodri Dafis. It's an honour for Carys to be selected.'

'But she wasn't selected! She's only Reserve Virgin.'

'Rhods would be a bit old for the Children's Choir anyway,' Carys clarified.

'I've got a bit of influence, you know: they wouldn't turn any son of mine away,' responded Fal, stretching her neck like a peacock.

'No thank you very much, Mum. Everyone would rip the shit out of me. But anyway, where can we stay, if this place is let?'

'I'm sure there will be a very gracious welcome for us over the yard at Neuadd, as always.'

Daf coloured a little to hear his daughter described, even ceremonially, as a 'Virgin of the Vale'. For over a year, Carys, who had just finished her A level exams, had been courting Matt Blainey, a lad a bit older than her. Daf was not an unreasonable man: he realised that a normal, attractive young girl like Carys would be bound to attract a bit of male attention.

Even though there was no specific reason to hate Blainey, Daf was struggling to come to terms with the two of them being together. Using his professionally-honed reasoning skills, Daf came up with any number of reasons to hate the lad, including the fact that he was a distraction from her school work and her singing but, at heart, Daf knew he would feel the same about anyone who was her boyfriend. She was still his baby girl and definitely too young to go out courting. Like clouds, a number of unsuitable images floated through Daf's mind: Carys in the back of Matt's car, Carys on her back in the heather up above Llyn Hir, Carys responding as a woman to the touch of that bastard Blainey. Once and once only he had shared his concerns with Falmai. Her response was to remind Daf of their own courting days, of late nights and endless afternoons in the dunes at Aberdyfi. Falmai failed to see the vital difference, which was, of course, that Carys was their child and therefore, like almost all of their discussions these days, it ended in a row. The following day, when Falmai was safely ensconced in her classroom, and her brother was in the Smithfield, receiving his rightful tribute as owner of one of the largest farms in Montgomeryshire, Daf raised the point with Gaenor, his sister-in-law, John's wife.

'The truth of it is, Gae, I don't want Carys to end up caught like me. I settled down way too early. Very often, I feel just like a fox caught in a trap.'

'Please don't talk bollocks, Dafydd,' was Gaenor's reply. 'You've got great children, a career which suits you perfectly and enough books to make even you happy.'

'Fair enough, but I really have had enough of living in this bloody yard.'

'Move, then.'

'You know we couldn't afford to buy a chicken coop. And don't even dream of suggesting I get any more money off John. He's got a mortgage over my body and soul already.'

Gaenor laughed like a teenage girl. 'Oh, Daf, don't trouble

yourself for a moment about John. We've found a grand way of paying that stiff-legged old heron back, haven't we?'

Thinking of John standing grey and lonely on the bank of the brook, Daf had to laugh with her. He wrapped the duvet over both of them.

'Oh, Gae,' he whispered in her ear.

'Don't be soft, Daf. This is a bit of quiet fun and nothing more.'

So now the Eisteddfod had arrived and he was unpacking: Daf looked about the room. Even though he was reluctant to accept John's invitation to stay at Neuadd over the Eisteddfod, there was no choice: it was way too late to find anywhere else. Carys turned it into a joke.

'We're just like Mary and Joseph looking for a place to stay,' she declared and Daf couldn't argue with that, even though he couldn't recall any verse of the Bible which suggested Joseph had an improper relationship with the inn-keeper's wife, and it had to be admitted that the spare room at Neuadd was a good deal more comfortable than a stable. The door opened and Gaenor came in.

'Welcome to Hotel Neuadd,' she pronounced. 'Breakfast between seven and eight and I'll leave it to your imagination to work out what kind of room service is available.'

'We are going to have to act tidy this week, Gae.'

'Tidy? I intend to go a good deal further than tidy: I'll be the perfect wife. For example, I've only just filled no less than seven Thermoses for John to give to the parking stewards.'

'Are you going to the Cymanfa?'

'Two hours of hymn singing? I'd rather scratch my eyes out with red-hot scissors.'

'But Siôn's playing for Carys, isn't he?'

Siôn, John and Gaenor's only child, was a pretty good harpist and Carys had honoured the family tradition at Neuadd by winning the solo under 21 at the Urdd Eisteddfod the previous year. Gaenor had once said, after knocking back a whole bottle of Chablis by herself that the women of Neuadd always had to push three times when they were in labour: once for the baby, the second time for the placenta and the third time for the harp which always followed.

'Oh, Daf Dafis, how many times do you think I've heard their pieces? By now, I couldn't give a flying fuck if the Great Redeemer guides them to Ibiza. I've got a bottle of white Burgundy and I'm going to need help emptying it. I think you're just the man for the job.'

'I have to get the tenants sorted in the bungalow. After, maybe.'

'Oh yes, these media types! Any chance that the bungalow will be the ultimate party venue all week?'

'A quiet place for a member of staff and his family, they said they wanted. An elderly couple, in their seventies, their son and his partner.'

'I'm disappointed now. I was looking forward to a bit of glamour on this yard for once.'

'And am I not glamorous enough for you by now, Gaenor? Fifteen months ago, you were all over me like a rash.'

'Ah, but you were the famous detective in the Plas Mawr murder case back then, remember? On the news every night ...'

Fifteen months ago, just before the Urdd Eisteddfod, a girl's body was discovered in the grounds of a local manor house. She was naked, her bloodstream full of drugs and her head had been blown away. She was engaged to an aristocrat but she also had a local lover, a farmer. The press, both local and national, gave a good deal of attention to the story and Daf had to work very hard to ensure that the real perpetrator was caught instead of the man the press had in their crosshairs. Naturally, Daf's priority at the time was to concentrate on the case, the little matter of someone going about with a twelve-bore and shooting people's heads off, rather than giving all his attention to the Urdd Eisteddfod. Falmai hadn't forgiven him for this at the time and it looked highly unlikely that she ever would.

Daf felt a touch of guilt, like a cold shiver over his skin, before he recalled Falmai's icy sourness. Daf thought of himself as a man who was pretty easy to please and he had enough self-awareness to know exactly how any woman could attract his attention. A bit of fun, talking nonsense, the odd word of flattery, something approaching banter and, more than anything, the impression that she enjoyed being in his company. Which was exactly how Falmai used to be, back in the day. The words of that Kate Bush song came into his mind, the one describing a wife as having frozen on her husband or something. Talk about the middle-aged man straight from central casting.

'Mum! I'm taking the Outlander, OK?'

Like many houses of its era, Neuadd was constructed around a vast oak staircase. Anyone yelling up the stairs could hear their voice re-echoing throughout the whole building. Gaenor decided to kiss Daf before answering her son.

'Siôn's getting more like his father every day,' she whispered. 'Calling after me like I was a sheepdog bitch. Do come for that Burgundy, please Daf.'

'I'll do my best, my blue best'

Gaenor raised her voice to answer Siôn. 'What's wrong with the Suzuki?'

'I can't get the Salvi in the back of the Suzuki, in the name of reason!' Even from afar, there was a note of impatience in the young man's voice.

'Fine. The keys of the Outlander are on the dresser. Need any help?'

'I'm good, thanks.'

Gaenor turned to the window. She watched Siôn move the Outlander, then Matt emerged with the music stool. The two young men packed in the harp, the stool, the music stand and the case full of sheet music with practised ease.

'Of course I don't mind lending him my car,' she explained

softly, 'but sometimes, well, quite often, I get the feeling that nothing belongs to me. The car I call mine is really one of the Neuadd cars, just like I'm part of the fucking livestock.'

'Pay no attention. They don't own us.' Daf showed his support for his sister-in-law with a long kiss and he thought about making a firm promise about the Burgundy.

'Sometimes,' Gaenor whispered, 'I'm just longing to have the chance of telling them about us. John Neuadd isn't a man of flesh and blood like you are, Daf. If he walked in on me giving you a blow job, the only thing he'd say would be 'Have you seen my hi-vis jacket?' or something like that.'

At that very moment, John's voice thundered up those oak stairs which Cadw had decided were worthy of Grade II listing.

'Gaenor, you haven't seen my hi-vis jacket, have you? I could swear it was on the hook last night.'

Daf had to chew the back of his hand to keep his laughter under control. Gaenor was shaking from head to toe.

'I'll have a look now, John. Sure you haven't put it in the Defender already?'

'Could be. Don't rush now: make sure Daf's got everything he needs.'

Daf tried not to meet Gaenor's eye but it was beyond him. They were like a couple of daft children. With a remarkable effort, Gaenor managed to get her voice under control.

'I'll get you some soap now then, Daf,' she said, as if it were a line from a farce. Daf jumped back onto the bed and pulled the pillow over his head to muffle the idiotic laughter. He heard, from far off, the sound of a heavy door closing. Still shaking, he went into the en-suite to wash his face. He looked at his reflection in the mirror: looking back at him was a man with plenty to lose who didn't seem capable of preventing himself playing with fire.

Daf went back to the window to open it: the baking August heat had even penetrated the strong, thick walls of Neuadd. From this vantage point above Llanfair Caereinion, row after row of shapely hills stood, as if the topography of Montgomeryshire was a series of distinctly female curves. Nearer to the house were good fields, every one a carpet of rich green and the meadows by the river were almost ready for their second, or perhaps even their third, cut of silage. The only thing detracting from the perfection of the scene was the bungalow. It was a very ordinary little house, suitable for Defi the Shop, the policeman from a far-from-wealthy background who was so far above himself that he had dared to raise his eyes up to Falmai Neuadd.

A car was winding along the lane, above the surgery, up the slope. Daf glanced at the clock on the wall: it was almost five. That would be them, the tenants. He had better go over and greet them, especially as it was for their benefit that he was obliged to spend a whole week under his brother-in-law's roof. Under his roof but not under his duvet, Daf promised himself, without thinking for a moment that he was going to be able to stick to his resolution.

At least they had a decent car, Daf considered, proud for some reason that the people who were moving into his house, even if only for a week, were not too shabby. But who was he trying to fool? He needed them to be nice. The last thing he wanted over the Eisteddfod was a constant flow of complaints coming over the yard to Falmai's ears. Suddenly, he thought of another aspect to the business. If the tenants were too nice, an invitation to Neuadd was sure to follow. To one of their barbecues, more than likely. It's pretty difficult to create a stiflingly formal atmosphere at a barbecue but John managed every time. Still, at least in a week as busy as the Eisteddfod week, there would be plenty of credible reasons for Daf to stay away. Immediately after Carys' news made the family change their plans, the Chief Constable had issued an 'all leave cancelled' statement, reminding Welsh-speaking officers in particular that their presence was required.

Daf opened the gate for the visitors. A man of Daf's age was driving, his daughter beside him. In the back were the grandparents. And the grandfather was the first of the faces Daf recognised, a face which was very familiar from many different contexts. Professor Talwyn Teifi: historian, poet, member of every significant committee or movement in Wales for decades. Which meant that the driver must be ...

'Geth?' Daf called, remembering a moment too late that yelling his tenant's name across the yard was not exactly what his mother always used to call party manners. Gethin Teifi jumped out of the Mercedes M-Class to shake Daf's hand.

'Daf! What are you doing here? Is there another sensational murder for you to investigate?'

'I live here, Geth. I'm your landlord over the Eisteddfod.' By now, the whole family had climbed down from the car, stretching their legs after their long journey.

'Dafydd Dafis,' the Professor recalled. 'How have things been with you since the days of Noah? We see your name in the paper often enough. Who would have thought so much crime and danger would be bubbling under the verdant surface of these gentle hills?

'I said to the Professor, if Ann Griffiths knew the half of it, she would be turning in her grave,' contributed Gethin's mother, a little brown wren-like woman. It was typical of her to express her concerns for the feelings of a hymn-writer who had been dead for two hundred years. Daf recalled spending many a pleasant weekend in their Georgian house in the middle of Llandeilo, which was an excellent place for students to escape for a while to enjoy comfortable beds and healthy meals not involving kebabs or Pot Noodles. Mrs Prof, as the students called her then, had tended to remain in the background, popping in every now and then with another bottle of wine or some good French cheese. Before meeting Geth's family, Daf had never tasted exotic food or taken part in abstract discussions which could last all night. Ever since, despite his own circumstances, that was the kind of life he had longed for which meant that there was a fair bit of irony in the fact that the Teifi family had come to Neuadd, to spend a week a little too close to John's slurry pit. Daf's time in Aber had been educational in every sense of the word. As the only child of older parents and as a member of a family deemed too respectable to mix with the rougher elements in the town yet too poor to mix with the big people, Daf had lived in a state of permanent uncertainly before getting to uni. There, amidst the poetry and the booze, the politics and the gigs, he found himself. He arrived in Aber as a shy young lad, Defi Shop, and returned to Montgomeryshire as a man.

'People get killed everywhere,' said the young girl. 'Why should Montgomeryshire be an exception?'

Daf, as a man who made his living observing the responses of other people, thought that he saw a hard edge in the Professor's eye as he framed his reply.

'Very likely, Manon dear, very likely.' But the look in the old man's eye was not full of love such as might be expected from an affectionate grandfather towards his beloved granddaughter. A second later, Daf understood this lack of warmth from the Professor: Gethin put his hand on Manon's backside. It was a simple gesture which said a great deal. Gethin and Manon were lovers not father and daughter and it was obvious that the Professor was not willing to offer his blessings on a relationship between his son and a girl barely in her twenties. Like a cloud of dust blowing up from a hayground, suggestions, words and half-formed sentences came into Daf's mind, forming into a story he had heard with little interest. Gethin Teifi had left his wife and moved into a flat in Penarth with some girl. Daf had only met Gethin's wife once or twice: she was a tall and beautiful actress but somehow troubling, more likely to be cast as Medea than Desdemona. And who was the girl? A presenter, an actress, a researcher? No-one with a proper job, as John Neuadd would have said. Manon was, of course, strikingly pretty but Daf was pretty sure Gethin would regret his choice before too long. It was as if the owner of an E-Type Jaguar had decided to trade it in for a brand new Suzuki Swift. Fewer miles on the clock, perhaps, but surely not better?

'The house looks very different to the pictures on the website,' Mrs Teifi ventured in her uncertain little voice. 'Pretty difficult to keep warm, I would think.'

'Warm? Isn't it warm enough for you already, Derwenna?' replied her husband dismissively.

'Neuadd is my brother-in-law's house,' Daf explained, feeling that the shadow cast by the late afternoon sun falling on the bulk of the vast building was metaphorical as well as literal. 'The bungalow's over here.'

Daf took a quick glance at Gethin's face. He was his old friend and had no reason to belittle him, but Daf was certain a sly smile had been shared between Manon and Gethin. As a rich man's mistress, Daf was sure she was used to accommodation a good deal more luxurious than the bungalow in the Neuadd yard.

The landscape around the characterless little house was second to none, everything inside had been polished and scoured and the plug-in air freshener was, thus far, keeping the slurry at bay. Somehow, this made Daf feel worse: to him, the message which was being put across was 'We've made every possible effort and the place still looks like a chicken coop.' The process of showing everything, the switch for the immersion, the little cupboard full of cleaning equipment, added to this feeling, reminding Daf of the days of the shop, when his dad had to bow and scrape to every customer to stay in profit. Decades had gone past and yet here he still was, Defi Shop, doing his best to please.

'I don't know what your plans are for supper tonight,' he offered, 'but there's a curry in the freezer. Falmai's not that keen on the idea of our guests having to rely on eating chips in the square. Pop the curry in the microwave and you'll have a meal in ten minutes.'

'Lamb curry?' Gethin asked.

'Straight from the fold to the freezer,' replied Daf, feeling a little guilty as it was a matter of principle with him to avoid being roped in to help with work on the farm. Falmai often said, like a mantra: 'We are Neuadd and Neuadd is us' and if that was the creed, Daf was an atheist.

'We had a good lunch on our way, thanks. After the Cymanfa, perhaps?'

The Professor's readiness to attend an evening of hymn singing was scarcely surprising but what about Gethin, the unrepentant adulterer?

'I've arranged to go to see Meic Stevens tonight,' Manon declared. There was suddenly a discernibly awkward atmosphere amongst the members of the family and Daf felt it was high time he disappeared.

'I'm home alone on my first night at the 'Steddfod then,' Gethin laughed. 'What are you doing later, Daf?'

My sister-in-law if my luck holds, was the first answer which came into Daf's mind but, of course, no such reply emerged.

'Not quite sure at the moment.' Daf was certainly curious to find out more about the domestic arrangements of his old friend but desire had him in its grip. He decided to keep his options open. 'I'll knock the door later if I get a free moment.'

'Don't tell me you're expecting any trouble to kick off after the Cymanfa?'

'Oh, I don't know: what if they don't sing enough Ann Griffiths hymns? I predict a riot.'

Like in the old days, the sessions in the Cŵps, the evenings on the Pier, Gethin quick to appreciate his friend's humour. They had been close friends once, friends who somehow failed to keep in touch, but that closeness was still there somehow. There would be plenty of chances to catch up over a glass or two during the week. For the first time, Daf was thinking of the week of the festival with something other than dread.

Before that, he would have the pleasure of taking all the gossip back to Gaenor. As he walked over the yard, under observation by sheepdogs who seemed to have passed their hatred for him down the generations for over twenty years, Daf considered the vast difference between Gaenor and Falmai. Duty and respectability were the most important things for Falmai, not pleasure. She was always on a diet, always asking for a contribution to some good cause or another. She was more interested in Merched y Wawr than love these days and Daf had reached the point where he struggled to recall their days of passion, when they were both longing for each other. By now, sex was nothing more to her than a part of the pattern of life of a woman in her forties, something done out of duty, like buying a raffle ticket, and because it would be noteworthy and weird to refuse. Worse than anything, Daf could not remember the last time they had shared any kind of joke, let alone the kind of explosion of merriment he had enjoyed with Gaenor earlier. His phone rang.

'How's things, Dafydd?'

The voice of Tom Francis, one of John Neuadd's friends. Older than Daf, old-fashioned in his manners and, naturally, thought of very little but farming. Daf had come to know Tom the previous year when a woman with a twelve-bore came to his farm with the intention of killing him. In the course of that investigation, Tom, who was a bachelor knocking on for fifty, had come to meet one of Daf's colleagues, Sergeant Sheila Bowland. Before Tom had started courting Sheila, Falmai had held no particularly high opinion of her. 'What kind of woman chooses to make her career out of all that nastiness? And she doesn't have a word of Welsh,' was her dismissive opinion and she didn't make much effort to hide it. But in a wink Sergeant Sheila had become engaged, with a diamond the size of a guinea pig on her finger, and old Mrs Francis, Tom's mother, had bought herself a big house in Llanfair, making room for her new daughter-in-law to become the undisputed mistress of the farmhouse at Glantanat hence Falmai had found herself a new best friend. It was with Falmai that Sheila had gone to Chester to get those lovely Italian tiles for the new utility room at Glantanat and it was with Falmai that she chose her tasteful and very expensive dress for the wedding which had been arranged for November, not the most romantic season perhaps, but a quiet time on the farm. Daf was infuriated by Falmai's hypocrisy; Sheila deserved better. Yet in the last few months, Daf had managed to avoid reminding Falmai of her original opinion of Sheila and a little social group of six came into being. For the first time, John included Daf in his social plans, not because of his role in the family but because he was the boss of Tom Glantanat's girlfriend. So that's how it was: Daf had to 'enjoy' himself, by making joint bids at charity auctions, sharing a table at every marquee Sunday lunch and even spending the day in their company at Ludlow Races. The ladies got a bit silly on Pimms and Daf felt his life ebbing away as the conversation amongst the men turned once again back to farming. Tom's next sentence therefore came as no surprise:

'Fal said you didn't much fancy the Cymanfa?'

'Too busy here: got to get these tenants sorted.'

'Of course.'

The Francis family also had Eisteddfod tenants, in the house in Llanfair, and they had been settled in for almost a week. That was how things always worked out for the Francises somehow: they were always very well organised.

'But these girls are mad keen on going out after. They don't want to miss the buzz of the 'Steddfod.' Somehow, Tom Francis' voice could suck the energy out of the word 'buzz' and Daf did not feel the slightest temptation.

'Sorry Tom, but I've said I won't go further than the other side of the yard tonight, in case anything goes wrong in the bungalow.'

'Fair play. We've got the whole week ahead of us for a bit of a spree.'

The thought of having a spree with Tom Glantanat made a big smile rise to Daf's face. When Gaenor opened the door to him, another part of his anatomy rose as well and the cork stayed in the Burgundy for another hour.

'You know what's grand?' Daf asked, doing up the buttons of his shirt. 'We've got the whole evening ahead of us. We can sit down all cosy on the sofa, listen to a bit of music, talk for hours.'

'If you don't nip over to see your old friend, that is. I can't wait to meet him.'

'Well you can't. Geth's a good-looking bugger.'

'Don't get jealous.'

'I'm not. But don't forget, Gae, I spent three years playing second fiddle to him and that fiddle has been firmly put in the attic.'

Gaenor was changing the bedclothes and Daf went over to help. He pulled the corner of the sheet tight and felt the fabric slightly rough beneath his fingertips. Pure Egyptian cotton: polycotton would never meet the Neuadd standards. When he raised his head, Gaenor was looking at him.

'Do you know what else is grand?' she said. 'The two of us can actually be ourselves for once, instead of being things belonging to Neuadd. I know it may sound a stupid thing to say, but on times I can almost feel the tag in my ear.'

Daf went round to the other side of the bed and took her in his arms. 'There's nothing in your ear except my tongue, *lodes*.'

'Can you bear to hear a dull story?'

'Depends how dull.'

'Do you remember May last year, Daf? When the weather was so nice?'

'I remember it very well. There was that little business of a body in the garden at Plas Mawr, Carys won the Urdd and, if I recall correctly, you'd taken to walking about the place with not much on.'

'I was only doing the garden in my swimsuit, Daf – practical in that hot weather.' The humour in her eyes went out like a flame. 'There were a few of Siôn's mates from school calling by just then ...'

Daf decided a joke might raise her spirits but could only come up with a feeble one.

'Don't tell me you've got a Mid Wales version of *The Graduate* to tell me about! Didn't think any of the lads in the sixth form would be handsome enough for you.'

Gaenor shook her head. 'Nothing sexy, sorry. Tea time one day, Siôn got a text and after that he was a bit weird about his phone. I was worrying about ... well, we've all heard stories about what these young people send each other on their phones and ...'

Daf had to shut his eyes for a moment to rid himself of the image in his head of the sort of image Carys might sent to Matt fucking Blainey.

'I took his phone when he wasn't looking and I found he'd been sent a picture of me, in my swimsuit, pulling up weeds.'

'They're just lads, don't worry.' Daf was confident in offering his comfort. 'It's what they call banter.'

'I couldn't give a damn about the picture itself but whoever took it had done a bit of a Photoshop job on it.'

'What do you mean?'

'They'd put a big blue pitchmark on my thigh: a big letter "J" to show I belong to Jones Neuadd.'

Daf understood at once what an insult this was to her so he took her in his arms and kissed her with fierce affection.

'You remember, Gaenor Morris, every time you feel like one of the livestock, that we're putting two fingers up to every one of the eight inch nails, the respectable people. You couldn't be more of a rebel! John Neuadd's wife fucking in the matrimonial bed whilst the man himself is stewarding the car park for the Cymanfa Ganu in the Royal National Eisteddfod of Wales? Result!'

Once again they were laughing and Daf was enchanted by the pleasure of walking hand in hand with Gaenor down the oak staircase, settling on the sofa, remote in his hand as if he owned the fifty-inch screen. Gaenor came in with a tray bearing all that was required for what Carys would call 'a big night in'. Daf swallowed a glass of wine and allowed himself a blasphemous smile. What was it that St David had said about doing the small things?

Like everything else on the farm, the front door bell at Neuadd was heavy and old-fashioned. Half a century ago, John's grandmother would have rung it to call the servants in from the fields for their dinner, served in a room called the back kitchen. As a member of the family, albeit a rebellious one, Daf had never had occasion to pull that thick chain and therefore he was not familiar with the sound. Gaenor leapt to her feet, her face full of anxiety.

'Bit late for Jehovahs,' observed Daf. 'But don't you fret, *lodes*: I've got a legitimate reason to be here.'

It was Gethin Teifi, with three bottles of wine in a Londis bag.

'I was just about to drink the lot by myself but I'm not quite that sad yet. Let's have a party instead of the Cymanfa.' When Gaenor went into the kitchen to get another glass, Gethin bent over and whispered in Daf's ear. 'What was that quote from Laurie Lee: "Quiet incest flourished where the roads were bad"? This looks pretty damn convenient, Dafydd Dafis, pretty damn convenient.'

'We're not related. At all. Gaenor's married to my wife's brother, that's all.'

'I'm taking that as a confession.'

The two old friends began to laugh. Daf was rather pleased with Gethin's half-envious response which confirmed his own view that Gaenor was a seriously attractive woman. It would give Daf a bit of status with a man like Gethin who had always been so easily successful with women. Daf had been a very faithful student in his college days, with his first love waiting for him back in Montgomeryshire but it was impossible, even for a settled chap like Daf, not to feel some jealousy when on nights out. Somehow, girls seemed to appear out of nowhere wherever Gethin showed his face. Daf observed something else about these girls: like dogs smelling fear, some girls could smell success. Gethin was a pretty remarkable young man, knowing everyone, winning at every game he cared to try and his father was well respected. Whoever could land Gethin Teifi would be the wife of a successful man. In comparison, Daf had nothing much to offer. Which explained why, after all those years, he was rather proud to notice Gethin's eyes sliding over Gaenor's shapely arms and saw no reason to deny there was a relationship between them: if Gethin said anything to anyone else, Daf could pass it off as a misunderstanding. As the three of them relaxed, chatting and drinking, Daf realised yet again how easy it was to be with Gaenor. She was sociable, always ready with a smart, funny reply to any comment or question, showing a lively interest with her gorgeous smile. Daf thought how strange it was that he knew very little about her background: Falmai and John belittled her roots on a routine basis. He recalled asking Falmai, many years ago, when John and Gaenor had first started seeing one another, who she was and receiving a very abrupt answer:

'She's nobody. Some little nobody from nowhere in Dyffryn Tanat.'

Wherever that nowhere in Dyffryn Tanat was, Daf considered, at least Gaenor had been raised to be courteous there, to be kindly and to make everyone feel comfortable. Falmai might have been brought up in the splendour of Neuadd but the lessons she had learnt there included sourness and prejudice.

About eleven o'clock, a family procession entered through the back door. Falmai paused for a moment in the parlour doorway and Daf knew from experience that she was preparing a bollocking for him. The old, old story. 'Why didn't you come with us? Everyone was asking after you; it looked odd. It's not a nice experience for Carys to perform in front of so many people when half the audience are talking about her family ...' And so on, to bloody infinity. But before she opened her mouth, Daf saw that she had observed who was sitting on the sofa, pouring Gaenor another glass of wine. Gethin Teifi, a wealthy man, next door to being famous, owner of one of Wales' biggest TV companies and, more importantly, Daf's only social connection of any significance. Her frown melted and she threw herself across the room to greet Gethin.

'Gethin! How lovely to see you? Where are you staying? You must stay here with us, mustn't he, Gaenor?' Daf felt his cheeks redden: did she have to be so bloody obvious?

'Neuadd is pretty full as it is,' Gaenor replied.

'I'm sure we can squeeze Gethin in somewhere.'

Gethin stood up to shake hands with John. Before John or Daf had an opportunity to introduce him to Sheila, Tom Francis, Siôn, Carys or Matt, Gethin put his arm round Falmai's shoulders in a gesture which looked a bit patronising to Daf.

'You can squeeze me anytime you like, Falmai but I'm staying across the yard, in your bungalow.'

Bungalow. A narrow little word with no romance or history to it. More like a cowshed than a proper house, just a place to shelter.

'No!'

'Honestly. We'll be neighbours throughout the Eisteddfod.'

Falmai's next question was rather rude, Daf thought.

'Who have you got with you?'

'My parents, of course, and my friend Manon.'

Behind Gethin's back, John raised his eyebrows. Gaenor responded with a confidential little smile and for the first time, Daf was seized with passionate jealousy. Of course John had the right to share secrets with Gaenor, he reasoned, and he just had to keep his mouth shut and accept the situation. Daf did feel rather grateful to Falmai when she started up again.

'Gethin, you must meet Carys, our daughter. She took the Solo in the Urdd last year and she would have had it again if she hadn't concentrated on her exams. She's recording a CD and there's talk of TV appearances. She gave a beautiful solo tonight, *'Wele'n Sefyll'*, really lovely. Do you think the Cymanfa's on Clic yet, Siôn? Why don't you check?'

'I didn't want to go to the bloody Cymanfa,' Daf interrupted, 'so it's a safe bet that I don't want to watch it on catch-up.'

'You don't have to be spiteful, Daf.' Falmai turned back to Gethin but all that Daf could see in his eyes was sympathy for his old friend. Gaenor, as so often, save the situation from getting any more awkward.

'We're forgetting Tom and Sheila! Come in, you two: sit down and have a glass of wine.'

'I won't but Tom will,' answered Sheila in her halting Welsh, taking the keys of his Audi out of Tom's jacket pocket. It was a small action but full of meaning: by now, Sergeant Sheila was on the farm insurance policy at Glantanat. 'I'm very interested to meet you, Gethin,' she continued. 'I work with Daf so I would love to hear some dreadful stories of his college days.'

Tom Francis' pride in his partner was evident to everyone and the contrast between Sheila and Falmai was evident to Daf. Even in her second language, Sheila was making an effort whilst Falmai's voice was droning on in the background like a pneumatic drill.

'... Carys has always had an interest in the media and she's a natural in front of the camera as well by now.' Daf saw the embarrassment in his daughter's red cheeks and Daf felt as if he must do something to cut across the moment.

'I know I'm a jibber, but what about a coffee?' he suggested.

'You bloody well are a jibber, Daf Dafis. There's plenty of wine left,' was Gethin's response. 'Lock-in!'

'I've got the case I bought in the Royal Welsh, that's a good drop of stuff,' John offered.

'We're not half drunk enough to drink that horse piss,' Daf retorted. 'I'll put the kettle on.'

'I'll give you a hand, Dadi.'

In the kitchen, Daf relaxed at once.

'There's no reason for you to be spiteful to Uncle John, Dadi.'

'I know, Carys. Sorry.'

'You'd better apologise to him.'

'I will, later on. Your mother was getting on my nerves a bit, making a show of herself.'

'That's what she's like, Dadi. You can't change people.'

'It's her who's changed. Sometimes, it's like I don't even know her. You're talented enough to get any job you want: there's no reason for her to go ... fishing about like that. True to God, I need all my patience.'

'You're not a saint yourself, Dadi: remember that when you're busy judging Mum.'

'What do you mean?'

'Do you want me to go right down the list for you? What's her name, that stuck-up trendy lawyer, Aunty Gae, even Chrissie Berllan.'

'Don't talk rubbish.'

'I know, it is hard to believe that Chrissie would look twice at you when she's got a man like Bryn Gwaun in her bed but ...'

'It's not funny talking like that, Carys. Not funny at all.'

'I'm not joking, Dadi, just trying to put a bit of balance into the conversation, that's all.'

'I could do with a bit of fresh air.'

Daf couldn't see the stars when he stood outside the back door: there was too much light flooding out of the bungalow where it seemed that every bulb was switched on. There was a sound of low weeping from the room he shared with Falmai. Without wishing to eavesdrop, Daf heard the voice of the Professor trying to comfort his wife.

'But poor Peredur, what about him?' she was asking, time after time.

Daf walked away, into the shadow of the vast barn, a place where he spent hours, looking for the peace he seldom seemed to find in his own home these days. He decided to forget about the complications of his personal life and concentrate on the professional challenges which would face him in the coming week. Thousands upon thousands of people were coming to the area. Tens of thousands of bottles of wine would be drunk, there would be waccy baccy being smoked by the Guinness Bar, unsupervised children would be running wild on the caravan site and badly organised gigs would draw audiences to places that were far from ideal. To say nothing of the traffic. In only a few minutes he was feeling better, thinking clearly and on the right track. He was no longer a man coping with a marriage under strain but an effective and professional policeman.

He heard the sound of a car on the lane. He opened the door in the furthest corner of the barn. He heard two car doors shutting, then voices.

'You don't have to go back to him. In five years, he'll be an old man.'

The voice was familiar to Daf but he couldn't recognise it as it was so far out of context.

'Very likely, Gwion. A very rich old man.'

'You're living in a fool's paradise, Manon. Whatever he's got, he'll have to share with his wife or his ex-wife or whatever she is.'

'You're wrong there, Gwion *bach*. Any money he has made since their marriage broke down, that's safe.'

'Is that right? And just how much money has he made lately? He's more likely to be fucking than filming these days.'

'One bit of work's enough.'

'Enough for what?'

'Enough to make a fortune.'

'It's late, Mans. Come back with me.'

'No way, Gwion. I'll see you tomorrow, on the Maes.'

'But what about tonight?'

'You know exactly what I'll be doing tonight, good boy. And you know why. If you'd managed to offer a better way, fair enough, but I'm not prepared to hang about until you've finished having your fun.'

'I've made every effort. Truly, I have.'

'Oh, have you, really truly? Did you go to that place?'

'I did. It was a right odd place. Full of monks.'

'What did you expect in a Buddhist retreat? Fucking clowns?'

'Please. I love you. It's only fun, that stuff, and I could stop it tomorrow.'

'You still don't understand. I don't care what you do to get a buzz and if Gethin was putting thousands of pounds up his nose every week, that would be fine. He can afford to treat himself to a bit of snow. You're still living in a place that's like a squat, with no proper career, no proper future. If you put yourself into any proper recovery programme, the first thing they would ask you is: is it costing you more than money? Say the truth, Gwion, you had the choice. Me or the charlie. You made your decision and everyone is moving on.'

Daf heard footsteps heading towards the bungalow then the door opening and closing. For several minutes there was perfect stillness, as if Gwion was standing still, following Manon with his eyes. Then came the sound of footsteps going in the other direction, a car door, the car engine starting, the sound of the car disappearing into the stillness of the night. Daf had time enough to process what he had heard, as Gethin's friend, as a landlord and as a policeman. However these people chose to live their lives, Daf was not going to allow anyone to cut lines on his washbasin, in his bathroom. Who was this man Manon had left for Gethin? Whoever he was, he certainly seemed to regret losing her. Could that regret turn into a police problem at some stage?

Daf decided it was high time he went to bed. He climbed the stairs without encountering anyone. He woke when Falmai came to bed and took his hand under the duvet.

'Please don't be difficult this week, Daf. We're not at home and I can't bear it when I know people are judging us. There's nowhere for us to hide for the next seven days.' Her voice was soft and small.

'OK, Fal. Why don't we make a deal? If I try to be nice, can you try not to be so pushy?'

'I'm only looking for opportunities for Carys. She's so talented and so beautiful: she could be the next Alex Jones or Katherine Jenkins.'

'She's a girl, not a lump of Play-Doh. She needs a chance to be Carys Dafis before trying to be some second-rate version of someone else.'

'You've got no idea how talented she is, Daf. Perhaps if you had been bothered to turn out to see her perform a bit more often, you would realise.'

'I know my own daughter perfectly well, thank you.' He turned his back on her. In the darkness, it was clear that Falmai was struggling to hold back her tears, but that was her own business.

Chapter 2

Monday

Half past five. Daf swore under his breath. He opened the curtain – outside, all was quiet. Walking barefoot down the corridor in the dawn light he was reminded of sleepless nights when the children were babies. The first moments of every day can be full of potential and romance and he had almost liked the floor walking, whispering and singing to his little scraps until they fell asleep in his arms, but there was no magic whatsoever in the sound of the Neuadd stock truck moving about the yard, preparing for an early morning in the Smithfield. As he passed the large window opposite the top of the stairs, he saw John and Siôn working silently, completing their accustomed tasks like robots. As good farmers, it was important to them to arrive at the Smithfield early, never mind how much wine had been downed the previous night. In terms of his clothing, his movements and his way of speaking, John Neuadd had been an old man since he was fifteen but today Daf noticed something different about his way of moving, tight and full of tension. Before long, he thought, Gaenor would have a genuinely old man in her bed.

He returned to the spare room and dressed; there was little point in attempting to sleep. There was no point in going back to share the warmth of his wife's body either: after her behaviour last night, touching her skin would be a lie. Before returning to the wide window in the stairway, he watched the stock lorry drive down the lane. As he would have foreseen, the sound of the lorry had awoken someone in the bungalow. The light came on in the largest bedroom: the Professor or his wife. Daf watched for a while but no-one turned the light off. One of the inhabitants of that room struggled to sleep or had too much to think about, perhaps; Daf knew exactly how that felt.

He walked out quietly through the back door to fetch a book from the car. He shivered in the cold: the air was perfectly clear. Another fine day, reminding him of the last time the Eisteddfod had come to Meifod. 2003. Carys had been the youngest of the participants in the Flower Dance, a tiny elf in her green frock, hair full of flowers.

The book was lying on the back seat of the car, a heavy hardback novel Daf had borrowed from Haf Wynne, whom Carys had described the previous night as 'that stuck-up, trendy lawyer'. Daf picked the book up without much eagerness: a poignant novel which had won the Booker, written from the standpoint of a woman, yet again. In his years in the police, Daf had seen plenty of evidence of the cruelty of men, scars on little children and terrified women insisting there was nothing wrong in their happy family and he wasn't sure he wanted to read about that kind of stuff in his downtime. He also knew pretty tidy men as well, men who were tender, kind and caring but Haf Wynne, who was not far off being a feminist jihadi, was reluctant to admit that such men existed. To her, the world was black and white.

Yes. Haf Wynne. Last year, for about a week, Daf had felt himself to be in a dangerous situation. During the investigation of the Plas Mawr murder, they had worked closely together and Daf had begun to seriously admire her intelligence, her strength, her persistence. As he grew closer to her, and under the strain of his family's absence at the Urdd Eisteddfod, Daf was captivated by her. She made no special effort to attract him but he began to be very curious about her, about who she was and why she had decided to live by herself in an untidy cottage full of books in an area where she knew no-one. She was representing Bryn Humphries, the local man suspected of the murder who just happened to be the local Romeo. Bryn, who regarded himself as a bit of an expert on the subject, had described his lawyer to Daf in his own particular fashion: 'Fine-looking, I'll grant you, Mr Dafis, but if you look in her eye, there's no fun to be seen there.' Recently, when they had been working together, Haf had told Daf a little of her backstory and Daf had felt an unexpected relief. His conversations with Haf gave him reasons not to love her: her distance and coldness were carefully stage-managed and she threw all her warmth into her good causes. They regularly lent books to one another but there was a difference: he lent her books because he thought she would enjoy them whereas she sent him away with reading matter which felt like homework. She wanted him to learn, to change. Daf glanced at the cover and decided he couldn't be arsed with a lesson this time. He threw the book back into the car and resolved to read anything else, even one the volumes of agricultural reminiscences he had seen on John's shelves. Or he could pick up a book from one of the many stalls on the Maes.

In the kitchen at Neuadd, the phone rang and the kettle boiled at the same moment.

'Neuadd.'

'John?' Daf was unsure of the voice; it was not the voice of an old man but it was certainly the voice of someone who had lost a fair few teeth.

'John's gone down the Smithfield. Can I give him a message?'

'It's Dewi Dolau here. I was going to ask John for the phone number of Falmai's husband, the policeman.'

'Dafydd Dafis speaking.'

'Oh, thank goodness for that.' Dolau. A farm about a mile from the Maes.

'Bother overnight?'

'No. Well, yes. I've got people camping here and there's one girl right sick, by the look.'

'Have you phoned for an ambulance?'

'I don't want no bother, Mr Dafis,' Dewi muttered. 'Mum didn't agree with the idea of making a bit of money on the side. There hasn't been an accident, just she's in a deep sleep and I can't wake her.'

'OK. I'll be over there now.'

'It's real early ...?'

'You said it was an emergency.'

'Yes, but I don't want to put you to no trouble.'

'Trouble's my business, *lanc*. I'll see you in a tick.'

That's a good expression, Daf thought: trouble is my business. He had a broad smile on his face as he turned to see Gaenor in the kitchen door in her nightdress.

'What time is it?'

'Just before six. I've got to go.'

'Of course. "Trouble is my business", hey? Any chance that anyone around here thinks a bit too much of themselves?'

Old friends, family, lovers: only a few people can put your feet back on the ground without any type of spite. Gaenor was one of those, those people who would never take any shit from him. Daf had to give her a long kiss before going.

Dolau. A small house dating back to the 1950s, looking like a council house dumped in the middle of the countryside. It was an arse of a place, like Daf's own home in many respects but adding neglect to its original lack of charm. Nearby was a cluster of farm buildings of various periods which also needed serious modernisation. In the hayfield, Daf saw about thirty tents, a couple of Portaloos and a water bowser: not much in the way of glamping going on at Dolau. Daf didn't have to knock on the door: Dewi was on the threshold waiting for him.

'Thank you indeed for coming over, Mr Dafis. I didn't know what to do for the best.'

About ten years younger than Daf, Dewi was a perfect example of the kind who 'stopped at home to help dad'. More than likely, Daf considered, looking at his thin, dirty hair and the clothes he had bought from the feed-merchant, he didn't leave the yard from one week to the next. Perhaps another family would have sought some treatment for his squint, but as an eye like that was part of his genetic inheritance, they had done nothing about it. Daf felt a good deal of sympathy for him – even with a farm to come his way after his mother's death, he had a life little better than slavery from day to day. No money, no freedom, no friends. Daf was almost certain there was no girl in the picture either: under the icy glare of his parents, any tiny spring of romance would have been blasted into nothing.

'Are you on your own, Dewi?'

'Yes indeed. Mum's in Gobowen, having a new hip. And we lost the boss back in the spring, of course.' Daf saw something unexplained in his eye, some kind of guilt.

'Where's this girl then, *cog*?' He used a word he would normally use to a younger man, but it seemed appropriate.

Dewi grew red.

'In ... in the parlour.'

Daf walked through the chilly kitchen to a dark room which was crammed full of furniture and cheap ornaments. Several model bulls, of course, but also more fanciful choices, a Pierrot with a single tear on his ceramic cheek, a slender little lady in Victorian costume.

'Open the curtains, Dewi.'

Lying on the wooden-armed settee was a girl in her late teens. Her face was pale and her hair clumped into strands. She was wearing a T-shirt adorned with a yellow smiley and one word: *Hapus*. Her denim skirt was short. On the carpet were a pair of bright pink cotton pants. Daf took her pulse: running a bit quick. Her breathing was shallow. He shook her gently before checking that her windpipe was clear then rolled her onto her side, into the recovery position.

'What's her name?'

'I haven't got a clue. Stopping in the meadow she is, with her friend.'

'What did she take last night?'

'I don't know.'

'Well, if you know so little about her, what is she doing unconscious on your settee?' Dewi made no reply. Daf took his phone out of his pocket and pressed the buttons of a familiar number.

'And good morning to you, Steve,' he began, speaking in English. 'Give Sheila a ring and tell her to get down to the station to get the rape suite ready. Get onto the out of hours service and tell them we may need a mild detox, a bit of charcoal maybe, nothing heavy ... Yes, from the Eisteddfod. Looks like some little shit had his fun with her when she was off her face. I'd like a bit of back-up, SOCOs and a paramedic, preferably with an ambulance. Send Nia up with the back-up and if she's not available, get any Welsh first language PCSO you can find. Dolau Farm, half a mile from the Maes, in the Meifod direction.'

Daf had chosen his words with care in order to alarm Dewi Dolau and he certainly had been successful. But everything needed to be done properly and there would need to be a Crime Scene Officer appointed because that was what the parlour at Dolau had become, a crime scene. Daf turned to face Dewi.

'Dewi Griffiths, I am arresting you for the rape of this girl. You have the right to remain silent but ...'

'That wasn't how things were, Mr Dafis. She was right keen.'

'And how did you know that?'

'Well, she never said "no" when I started to ...'

'To do what?'

'Touch her and that. I thought she was enjoying it.'

'Did you ask her?'

'No, I couldn't begin to ask such a question. She was the one doing the asking.'

'What?' Daf found it very hard to believe that a pretty young girl could fancy a creature like Dewi Dolau.

'Well, she was obviously up for it. Skirt right up to her arse and top that tight.'

Daf was struggling to hold it together.

'And you are such a fucking expert in how girls feel that you don't need to talk to them, because you can just read the vibes, yeah?'

'Like I said, Mr Dafis, she didn't say no. She was laughing at times ...' A great wave of rage built up inside Daf. How could a stupid twat like that think he could do what he pleased with a young girl?

'You won't say anything to Mum, will you, Mr Dafis?'

'Your mum is bound to notice when you get sent to prison.'

A knock at the door. Dewi stood perfectly still, as if he were frozen. Another knock.

'Answer the door.'

A girl came in, the same age as the girl on the sofa. She was wearing pyjama trousers and a sweatshirt with the logo of a hockey team on it and, naturally, she reminded Daf of Carys.

'Gwawr!' she exclaimed.

'Do you know her? I'm a policeman, Inspector Daf Dafis.'

'Yes, she's my friend. We're camping here together. What's happened to her?'

'Had a bit too much of this and that, I suspect. Dewi, you go wait in the kitchen: I want a private word with this young lady.'

'Right you are, Mr Dafis.' His voice was flat and he seemed glad to be able to retreat into the kitchen. When Dewi was gone, Daf looked straight into the girl's eyes, realising that his face was just like that of a teacher about to give a row to a pupil.

'What did you take? Ket? Es for dancing, but what after?'

The girl looked down at her feet in their dew-drenched Converses.

'I can guess. A couple of bottles of wine, then a bit of hippy flipping?'

'We ... we've been so stupid. Is she going to be alright?'

'I'm a policeman not a doctor but I reckon she'll be fine. Enough sleep and plenty of water, and she'll be grand.'

'I'm so sorry.'

'Where did you get your 'shrooms?'

The room was perfectly quiet except for the sound of Gwawr's breathing.

'What's your name?'

'Dyddgu.'

'It would be,' Daf could not resist remarking. A name favoured by the upper middle classes, the sort of people who love the Eisteddfod. 'So, Dyddgu, where did you get your 'shrooms?'

A moment of silence. The clock in the corner ticked.

'Fair enough, keep your secret. I'm going to charge you with possession with intend to supply, I reckon. A criminal record won't help you when you're looking for a job after graduating and you can forget about getting a clean DBS check.'

'A local lad, I think. Outside a pub in Llanfair. We went over to get ourselves a tidy Sunday lunch and we started chatting to a couple of people over a pint. That's the great thing about the 'Steddfod, yeah?'

Looking down at Gwawr, Daf couldn't think that there was that much great about the Eisteddfod at that precise moment.

'If you saw Mr Mushroom again, would you know him?'

'I think I would.'

'OK, Dyddgu.'

He checked Gwawr's breathing again: her condition hadn't changed. He'd seen any number of ODs in his time and it didn't look as if the girl was in serious difficulties but he wished the paramedics would hurry up.

'Listen to me, Dyddgu. You're a girl with a grand future ahead you and so is Gwawr. You don't need to get involved in shit like this.'

'I know. We've been so dull.'

'Because of how Gwawr is, plenty of policemen wouldn't think twice about charging any friend of hers with possession with intent to supply.'

'It wasn't like that. We bought the stuff together, to share, like we did with the wine.'

'You've seriously overdone it, whatever. Do you know what happened to her last night?'

'No. We went back to the tent together.'

'So how did she end up in here?'

'No idea.' Trying to avoid Daf's eye, Dyddgu caught sight of the pants on the floor. She flushed, then turned pale.

'Has that fucker ... has he done something to her?'

'Could be. Did she mention him to you at all?'

'No, except saying, like all the girls staying say, that he's a creep.'

'Nothing more?'

'Well, things did kick off a bit yesterday morning.'

'Kick off?'

'Between him and the guy with showers.'

'Showers? I didn't see any showers? Only a field and a couple of toilets.'

A warm smile spread over Dyddgu's face.

'Every morning, a man comes by with three shower cubicles on the back of a trailer. We pay three pounds a time.'

'What kicked off then?'

'Well, the showers guy said to him, the farmer, the creep, to keep away.'

'Why?'

'He thought the creep was trying ... trying to perv on us. But the creep said he could do what he liked on his own land.'

'What happened next?'

Dyddgu started to laugh softly and suddenly Daf had a good idea who the gentleman with the mobile showers might be. There was only one man in his square mile who was capable of making girls react like that.

'Well, he picked the creep up and flung him right over to the other side of the yard.'

'And nobody thought it might be a good idea to tell the police about this scrap?'

'No-one wanted to get him into any trouble. He was looking out for us, after all.'

'And he's that fine-looking, isn't he?' Daf remarked,

somewhat wearily. Sometimes, being a policeman who knew his area almost too well generated a feeling of boredom in Daf. Who else had that impact on the ladies? Including Carys and, especially, Haf Wynne. Even Sheila wasn't immune and Sheila was usually pretty level-headed. Sometimes, he thought to himself, the job of a policeman in this type of district is like being the director of a rep theatre company – it's the same old people all the time, just playing different roles.

'Listen, Dyddgu: if you help me sort out the big trouble, we'll forget the small things, shall we?'

'Of course, sir. Thank you, sir.'

'But I want to know where you got your stuff. I don't have any clear idea what happened to Gwawr last night but it doesn't look likely that she enjoyed it.'

'Did the creep ...?'

'We shouldn't discuss that now. But you look at her, flat out on his settee and her pants on the floor. Look at her and wise up, will you?'

'I will, sir.'

Daf stood up. They were girls like Carys, exactly like Carys.

'And don't bother with the man with the showers either. The woman who owns him would eat a girl like you for breakfast.'

For the first time, Dyddgu gave a proper laugh and Daf was sure she was sharp enough to learn her lesson.

'Is every policeman a mind-reader?' she asked.

'Is every student so obvious? Write your number down here; you're a witness now and I'm going to be in touch pretty soon.'

From the kitchen came a totally unexpected, shatteringly loud sound, an explosion. The house shook and several of the ornaments fell from the mantelpiece. Before he opened the door, Daf knew what was ahead of him. Dewi Dolau's body had fallen across the chair, his twelve-bore in his hand. There wasn't very much of his head left. Flesh, bone fragments, brain and blood everywhere. The kitchen at Dolau had been turned into an abattoir. Daf pulled out his phone again.

'Steve, me again. Got ourselves a suicide up here at Dolau now to go with the rape. Might cut down on the paperwork a bit. Get Jarman on the phone and I could do with at least another two Welsh speakers up here to take the witness statements. And if Nia hasn't left, can you get her to stop by the bakery and get me a bite of breakfast?'

He waited for Steve, who was rather defiantly monolingual to make some remark about all the Welsh-speaking witnesses being perfectly capable of giving their evidence in English but he didn't: the message must be getting through. Daf turned round to see Dyddgu by his elbow, staring into the appalling scene in the kitchen.

'How ... how can you stand there so quiet in front of that?' she asked.

Daf took hold of her shoulder and led her into the parlour, shutting the door behind him.

'I've seen plenty of suicides over the years, *lodes*. Some hang themselves, some drown, some fill their cars with exhaust fumes but around her, in the famous gentle beauty of Montgomeryshire, most of them are shooters.'

Dyddgu sat down on the wooden arm of the chair.

'You need a cup of tea for the shock,' Daf suggested. 'When the team get here, they'll have a flask. I don't want to leave you but there are a couple of things I've got to get done at once.'

'OK. I'm OK.'

Daf took off his jacket and put it around the girl's shoulders. As he reached the door of the parlour, Gwawr woke up, perhaps in a delayed reaction to the explosion.

'What's going on, Dydd? Where am I?'

'In the farmhouse. You crashed on the creep's sofa.'

'Who's that?'

'A policeman.'

'Oh fuck, no!'

'He's a nice policeman, not a knob.'

Daf was rather proud of this description.

'Listen, ladies, I have to step outside for a minute. Stay here please and whatever else happens, don't even think of going through into the kitchen.'

It was clear that the front door hadn't been opened for years: the rain of any number of winters had warped the wood. Daf had to use his shoulder to open it, another of the skills he had picked up in his years in Dyfed Powys Police.

Outside, the sound of the gunshot had awoken all the campers. Some dozen of them had already reached the yard and others were moving purposelessly about in the field, like ants when hot water is poured into their nest. Daf looked at his watch: a bit after seven. Far too early for people on their holidays, especially after a late night.

'Now then, everyone, there's no need to worry but a couple of ... unexpected things have happened here overnight and this morning. I'm Inspector Daf Dafis from Dyfed Powys Police and other members of my team are on their way over to help. The police officers will have to ask all of you a couple of questions and I'd be grateful if no-one left the site without giving their statement, right?'

A smart little man, like a bantam cock, stood up straight and coughed to clear his throat.

'What has happened?' he asked, in a loud voice. Teacher, minister or actor, Daf guessed: someone who was used to his voice being heard.

'It's better if I say nothing till the other members of the team arrive. I'm sure you understand.'

'That's totally unacceptable,' answered the little man. 'I've got my family in the tent over there which gives me the perfect right to know what has been going on.'

'Unfortunately, whilst I am here alone, I don't have enough time to discuss matters,' Daf countered firmly, pulling a roll of incident tape out of the boot of his car. In the background, he heard the sound of an engine – he hoped it was the ambulance or the team from the police station in Welshpool, but no. It was a tractor.

'What has happened here?' the bantam cock man cried out again, louder. 'We have paid to stay here and we have every right to know.'

Daf fixed the tape across the back door of the farmhouse. The other campers seemed uncertain. Crowds, Daf thought, nothing worse. After one's raised his voice, they'll all be bleating in a minute, just like sheep. A dark liquid appeared on the concrete, seeping under the back door.

'Great Jesus – blood!' It was a young girl who noticed it first.

'Like I said, we have an investigation to undertake here. The best thing would be if you all went back to your tents to wait for the other members of my team to get here.'

'Which will be before the flow of blood reaches the field, we hope,' responded the little man. 'I'm going to speak to Mr Griffiths, to see if I can get any more sense out of him.' He stepped towards the back door.

'You can't speak to Mr Griffiths,' insisted Daf.

'Really? And who is going to prevent me doing that, may I ask?'

Once again, a feeling of boredom blew through Daf's mind like an autumn wind through an orchard. For half a minute, he considered opening the back door to give the little bloke the fright he deserved but immediately reminded himself of all the complications that might cause, satisfying though it would be.

'Me, if I have to,' he replied, standing by the back door without treading in the little pool of blood which was collecting on the uneven surface of the yard.

The tractor arrived in the yard with a flat-bed behind it: the showers. Bryn Gwaun jumped down from the cab, wearing, unsurprisingly, well-fitting jeans which made his long legs look even longer and, despite the early hour, a tight vest which didn't warrant being described as a T-shirt. Displaying his extensive muscles was clearly more important than defending himself from the morning breeze, and the impact of this impressive flesh was visible in the eyes of the girls, and in a good number of the mothers as well. Daf had to admit that with his toned and well-proportioned body, his plentiful black curly hair and his wide smile showing any number of gleaming teeth, Bryn was a pretty good specimen of an attractive man. But the previous year, Daf had been obliged to learn far too much about Bryn and, partly as a policeman but also as a father, he had lost patience with him. A man that good looking with no innate sense of morality and precious little common sense was a man with the potential to do a good deal of harm. And since the case, Bryn had gained something like celebrity status, as his appearance and romantic story had appealed to the tabloids. Every now and again, some superficial story would emerge as an excuse to publish a picture of Bryn with his shirt off. He was all right at heart, Daf thought, but the effect he had on women was very wearying.

'What's up, Mr Dafis?' Bryn asked

'Had a bit of bother overnight, *lanc.*'

'And he isn't willing to answer any of our questions,' the little man interjected.

'Mr Dafis is the boss,' Bryn declared. 'He's a policeman.'

'But ...' the man began.

'But nothing. Mr Dafis is a busy man and he'd much rather you all fucked off out of it.'

Daf smiled. No-one could put in an official complaint against Bryn Gwaun. For half a minute, there was an uneasy quiet: the campers were unwilling to back down but when it became clear that no further information was likely to emerge, they returned to the field to share the story with the others.

'What the fuck has Dolau done?' Bryn asked. 'Hurt one of them girls?'

'Thanks for your help, but I can't talk about it just now.'

Bryn took a deep breath, filling his nostrils like a hound.

'This place stinks like an abattoir. Is that blood there on the concrete?'

'Yes.'

'So, he hurt one of the girls then blew his ugly head off. I should have said something to you before, Mr Dafis. I could see the look in his eyes.'

'God in heaven, Bryn Humphries, you're not to blame: you can't get the police in every time you see someone eyeing up girls.'

Another annoying thing about Bryn, in common with many farmers Daf knew: he didn't keep to normal rules about personal space. He was now standing so close that Daf could smell not only his sweat but something else, the scent of a woman.

'You're up early, Bryn.'

'No more lie-ins for us, not when there's money to be made.'

An image rose up behind Daf's eyes. Three months previously, Bryn had married his twin brother's widow. His bride, Chrissie, was the sexiest woman Daf had ever met so it was impossible for Daf not to imagine exactly what Bryn had been doing half an hour ago. There was something very special about Chrissie, she was honest, smart and blissfully happy in her own skin. And she also chose to wear her T-shirts very tight over her remarkable breasts. She had lost her husband in an accident: he had cut through a power line when hedge-trimming. Even though it was a terrible blow, Chrissie had not wasted her time, despite her grief. She bought a new tractor and a JCB with the life insurance and the compensation from the power company so she could set up as an agricultural contractor. Chrissie was also second to none as a mechanic but, thus far, Daf hadn't taken full advantage of her offer of a full service. Very often, when Falmai was sitting comfortably in her armchair, complaining how hard her life was, Chrissie would be out cutting silage by starlight to feed her family. She had four children and very fine children they were too, in Daf's opinion: her eldest son was good friends with Rhodri. Taken as a package, Chrissie was a woman and a half.

'Good business, the showers?' Daf asked, eager to erase images of Bryn's wife from his mind.

Bryn laughed aloud and, of course, the bugger's laugh was warm and generous.

'You know Chrissie, Mr Dafis – always got some new idea to get the cash rolling in and this is a little goldmine. Everyone gets five minutes, three cubicles, three pound a go. Fettled them herself she did, the cubicles. Comes to near on a hundred pound an hour. Three hours in the morning, four in the evening. We're taking the kids to Disney Florida in the autumn.'

'Not in term time, I hope.'

Bryn laughed again.

'School doesn't do much good to people like us, Mr Dafis. They need to learn enough book stuff to make sure no-one can rob them and after that, the best lesson is what they'll learn from hard work.'

There they were, chatting about this and that as the pool of blood spread near their feet. Daf considered ringing Steve again but there was little to gain by being impatient.

'Grand weather, Mr Dafis.'

'Very nice, Bryn. How was your silage?'

'Champion, thanks, Mr Dafis. Good enough to get a fair load of hay in as well.'

'Yes, I saw the sign – you've got in enough to sell some, then?'

'Chrissie again. She reckons these horsey people are made of money: we're making some heck of a margin on our hay.'

'I bet.'

At last, the blues and twos came up the lane. Ambulance first, then two cars. There was no time for further conversation and the tractor needed moving but Daf still didn't quite understand why Bryn left without a word, as if he had no more time to waste. He was polite enough to Daf but saved his charm for the opposite sex.

'Right then, friends,' Daf announced. 'There's a man who's killed himself in the kitchen and a girl who I reckon's been raped in the front room. We've got SOCOs and the pathologist on their way. Nia, can you go in to see the girl? We need to decide if she needs to go down to Welshpool in the ambulance. I haven't got much interest in what happened here this morning because I was in the house when it happened and I'm enough of a witness, but I need to know anything anyone can recall about what went on the site from half ten, eleven last night onwards.'

'Are you sure the suicide's dead, Inspector?' asked one of the ambulance men.

Well, he hasn't got a head any more so if he's still alive, we're breaking new ground, in terms of science.'

Those who were familiar with Daf laughed; the second ambulance man looked uneasy. Daf and Nia went back into the house. The place stank, the metallic reek of blood. Gwawr was sitting up on the settee, staring into space.

'She's hardly said a word,' whispered Dyddgu. 'Can we go outside? A bit of fresh air might do her some good.'

'I'm WPC Nia Owen,' Nia said to Gwawr. 'Come with me for a minute.'

With Nia and Dyddgu's arms around her, Gwawr got to her feet. She was shaking. Dyddgu put Daf's jacket over her friend's shoulders.

'Come on, flower. There's a cup of tea for you out there.'

In the fresh air, the difference between the two girls grew more marked. There was no colour at all in Gwawr's face and she couldn't stand without support.

'I don't want to go in the ambulance,' she breathed.

'Sit in the back of my car then,' Daf offered. The book Haf Wynne had lent him was still on the back seat, expensive, bulky and good for nothing: Daf put it in the boot. Nia sat beside

Gwawr and, not for the first time, Daf considered how lucky he was to lead such a team. The back door of the car was open and Dyddgu reached in to hold her friend's hand. In the background, Daf could hear the sound of the little generator heating the water for the showers and high above everything, buzzards were distant spots in the blue of the sky. A cold shiver ran down Daf's back: the blood had summoned the birds of prey. What if he left the back door of the house open and let them, the buzzards, the kites, the magpies and the ravens, have their feast? That was only natural and looking at Gwawr, Daf didn't think Dewi deserved being anything better than food for the birds. But he knew very well that everything had to be done properly, even for Dewi Dolau. Someone would have to go to the hospital in Gobowen, to tell Mrs Griffiths. For half a minute, Daf considered telling the truth to the old witch: if she had raised her son to be a decent man instead of thinking of him merely as cheap labour, perhaps Dewi would have had a chance of treating others better. But, of course, that wasn't how things went. Daf have would pretend to be courteous to her, just as he used to when helping in the shop: 'Yes, Mrs Griffiths, no, Mrs Griffiths.' One of the buzzards landed on the doorstep and, walking heavily on its feathery legs, moved to the pool to taste the blood.

'PC Nia is asking for a blanket please,' Dyddgu asked. She lowered her eyes before adding: 'and a ... a pad to go between Gwawr's legs.' This simple request reminded Daf of the reality behind the word 'rape'. His throat filled with vomit which he choked down: he had to keep a grip on himself. As he went over to the ambulance to fetch what was needed, he saw that a magpie had joined the buzzard at the pool of blood. Following the superstitious tradition of his family, he raised his hand to his forehead to salute the magpie. He had made this gesture tens of thousands of times without thinking of its meaning but today, in the yard at Dolau, he was delighted to see the magpie and to give him a respectful salute.

After doing all she could to help her friend, Dyddgu came back to Daf, her face still full of anxiety but anxiety of a more normal range, like a sixth former who hadn't completed her coursework rather than a witness to a brutal suicide.

'I saw through the window, sir, you were talking with a man by the back door ...'

'Bryn? Don't worry, he's not one for chatting over other people's business.'

'No, I didn't mean him. Short man, brown hair.'

'And?'

'He's Eifion Pennant. He knows my dad.'

'I haven't told anyone anything. I don't.'

'But my dad's a head teacher. If he gets to hear about the Es and 'shrooms ...'

Pity the head teacher didn't find time to teach his daughter the simple lesson about avoiding illegal drugs, was Daf's immediate thought but he realised he was being unfair: how much did he know about what Carys did on a night out?

'I've said before: confidentiality is one of the key skills in the job I do. You help me find the people selling the stuff and it can all remain private.'

'I've got the number of the boy who sold the Es to Gwawr. He's around and about on the 'Steddfod Field.'

'That would be a great help.'

'I've never met him.'

'Fine. Can you come down to Welshpool later, see what we can do about getting hold of this Mushroom Man?'

'I can, but wouldn't it be better if I went back to Llanfair? He's sure to be there tonight.'

'OK. And when you see him, send me a text.'

'I will. And thank you for being so nice.'

'Listen, *lodes*, you're a young person who's done some dull things on a night out – who hasn't? It's not as if you're a major threat to law and order, not as if you were a member of Islamic State.'

'Yes, but we did break the law. And we come from tidy families: there isn't any excuse.'

'Maybe the tidy families are party of the reason, Dyddgu. It's not always easy to live with people's expectations of you, is it?'

The girl took Daf's hand for a moment.

'You're a very strange man, I have to say. I don't think I've ever met anyone like you.'

'Rubbish, *lodes*. I'm just a policeman trying to do his job, that's all.' But he thought he understood what she meant: perhaps she hadn't met many people in positions of authority who also remembered what it felt like to be young. And if growing up meant behaving like John Neuadd, Daf was happy to stay a bit immature.

'Is it OK if I go for a shower now? I don't think I've ever felt more like I need a wash in my life.'

'Go on.'

Dyddgu ran back to her tent like a child to fetch her towel and the money to pay Bryn. Daf remembered parties at Aber where hash cakes or stew enriched with magic mushrooms were going around but he'd avoided them for two reasons. He could barely afford beer let alone any more exotic stimulants and he had seen several friends slip into being rather boring about their stimulants, whether they were stoners or beer boys, talking about little but their last session or some great stuff they had got hold of. And he also remembered weekends full of poetry and endless wonderful evenings with Falmai: his life was pretty full back then. He'd be more likely to turn to something stronger these days to fill the gap left inside him by the quiet death of fairly ordinary dreams, but he smiled when he thought of his drug of choice: Gaenor.

Nia was anxious to get down to Welshpool as soon as possible to give Gwawr the care she needed. Daf was fine about leaving the site and everything seemed to be pretty well under control. As they slowed down to cross the cattle grid, Eifion

Pennant hurried over. Daf opened the car window.

'They say that Mr Griffiths has killed himself.'

'That's true, unfortunately.'

'I can't allow my family to stay here.'

'I understand perfectly but I don't have any idea how I can help.'

'You must know of another camping facility.'

'I'm a policeman, not TripAdvisor. The girl in the back's right poorly: we've got to get going.'

'Do you know who I am, Dafis?'

'Well, I certainly know you're not a happy camper.'

'Ffion Pennant, my sister, is editor of the *Daily Post*. My wife is a lecturer at Aberystwyth University. I have a first cousin who is a Member of the National Assembly and I am not accustomed to being ignored.'

'I'm delighted to meet you but I've got to get on. Have you contacted the Tourist Information Centre in Welshpool? They might help.' Daf was no fool. He knew exactly what kind of trouble people like Eifion Pennant were capable of causing if they didn't get their own way. But in the rear-view mirror, he saw that Nia had a broad grin on her face. Over the years, Daf had developed quite a name for taking no nonsense from bigwigs, empire builders or eight inch nails and he had to keep up his reputation. But he wasn't being awkward for the sake of it and when he passed Bryn Humphries' home, he had an idea. He turned into a lay-by to dial the number: even with a handsfree, there were some calls he couldn't make when driving.

'Hello?' Falmai would have thought that the voice Daf heard at the other end of the phone was extraordinarily common but that was not how he would have described it.

'Chrissie? Daf Dafis here.'

'Mr Dafis! And where have you been? I've been sitting here waiting for the phone to ring for months.' It was an old joke between them. Daf knew perfectly well that it was a game but it was still a game which did wonders for his self-esteem.

'Listen, Chrissie, I've just come from Dolau.'

'I've heard. Can't say I'm surprised: the little bastard watched some filthy stuff on his Sky.'

'How do you know that, *lodes*?'

'I went over to scan his ewes for him one day when his mum was off on some trip with the Merched y Wawr. He wanted me to watch porn with him and offered me two hundred pound if I would. Cash.'

'What did you do?'

'Little short legs like I got, Mr Dafis, they're champion for kicking. I'm like a fierce little Section A, I am. I gave him some heck of a kick in his meat and two veg and I took the money, like a fine.'

'Fair play to you, Chrissie. I can't say I'll be mourning him much.'

Chrissie's voice changed and there was a tender note in amongst the banter.

'Nor will anyone else. That's how they kept him there, on his own, like. If I hadn't pushed my way in, that's how Bryn's mum and *nain* would have kept him, and Glyn as well.'

'Get on with you, Chrissie. They're totally different to Dewi Dolau.'

'Don't be so sure, Mr Dafis. I won't be doing that to my children, anyway.'

'Never mind about that now. I've got seventy people who were camping at Dolau and they can't stop there. Do you fancy opening a campsite at Berllan?'

'Haven't got the paperwork for it, Mr Dafis.'

'It's an emergency, Chrissie. I'll sort the paperwork for you.'

Half a minute passed as Chrissie weighed up hassle versus financial advantage.

'Right then. But I'll have to take the Portaloos from Dolau: there isn't a spare one to be had this side of Chester.'

'Good girl.'

'You come by with that paperwork, Mr Dafis. I'd be right glad to see you.'

'I will.'

'You promise?'

'I promise. Cheers, *lodes*, and thank you very much.'

'See you later, Mr Dafis. I've got something to show you.'

It was only natural that there was a broad and rather smug smile on Daf's face.

'You're hopeless,' Nia declared, from the back of the car.

Chapter 3

Later on Monday

Daf, as often happened, found himself relaxing as he reached the doorstep of the police station. There he could be like a king looking out over his kingdom, unless a member of the top brass had decided to drop in. But he considered he was pretty safe from that today – the Chief Constable wasn't expected to make an appearance on the Eisteddfod Field until the following day, together with the Police and Crime Commissioner. She, a Labour appointment, had known nothing about her job until she was appointed to it and therefore, being sensible, hadn't done anything revolutionary or indeed very much at all. The official reception for the Justice Department had been arranged on the Maes and when the invitation, in its bulky envelope, fell onto the front mat of the bungalow, Falmai had gone a bit crazy about it.

'We've received a very special invitation,' she boasted. 'I'd better get up to Chester at the weekend to get a dress that's smart enough.'

'I don't intend to go,' was Daf's response. 'A room full of people we don't know chatting shit – no thanks.'

'But they're offering us a meal and everything.'

'I'd rather have a burger and be left alone, thanks.'

Falmai's eyes had filled and as Daf remembered the incident, he felt just a bit guilty.

'People we know will see us going in and they'll say that we're mixing with all the big shots. That's what they'll say.'

'I couldn't tell you how few fucks I give about what people say.'

'But you're doing well in that peculiar career of yours, Daf. It's only fair that you get invited to events of this sort.'

'I've had more than enough attention lately, because of

some of the cases I've been on. But if you think that I've dealt with things like the death of a girl like Jacinta Mytton or a lad half drowned after taking ket just to get a bit of notice, then you're a total fool, Falmai Dafis. I'm not wading through blood and violence to get to some fucking finger buffet.'

That was a perfect example of the gulf which had opened up between them. To Falmai, a swanky buffet in the National Eisteddfod was a pinnacle at which to aim, a sign of success the world could see. To Daf, it was just a nuisance. As he was thinking about the reception, Daf tried to calculate how often they had disappointed one another but there were too many examples to count. And perhaps that was why he felt as if he was on solid ground when he was in the police station, his crew around him, and sinking when he was in the bungalow.

Nia had settled Gwawr in the Sexual Assault Referral Centre to wait for the doctor. Daf saw the familiar car arrive: there was only one light blue 1950s Volvo Convertible in the district and it was owned by Dr Hugo Meredith. Daf drew up a list of reasons for his dislike of the doctor: the car was just the beginning. His voice was too English for his background, he wore coloured chinos, his hair was irritating and he went shooting at weekends with his friends. The truth was that Daf had taken against him months ago and not changed his mind; it was nothing to do with the fact that Dr Hugo had asked Haf Wynne out a couple of times. As far as Daf was concerned, odd people like them deserved each other.

'You've got a rape for me, Inspector?'

'That's right. Mixed things up a bit last night, she did, so she's not that straight yet.'

'I see. WPC with her?'

'Yes, she's in the SARC with WPC Owen.'

Professionalism in a doctor is one thing, Daf thought, but being clinically cold is another: this was the root of his dislike of a man who spoke as if his patients didn't matter, as if they were animals to be treated by a vet. Perhaps he didn't yet know what rape was, perhaps he had yet to learn the nature of the crime which left its victims hurt in soul as well as body. There was nothing else he could do for Gwawr but Daf felt it was a personal failure on his part: no girl should be injured like that in his square mile.

He turned his mind to a number of other matters needing his attention, including how to catch whoever was selling drugs on the Maes. The phone on his desk rang.

'Dafydd Dafis?' The loud voice of Gwilym Bebb, County Councillor and Chairman of the Eisteddfod's Organising Committee.

'Good morning, Mr Bebb.'

'What have you been up to down at Dolau? I've had any number of people on the phone complaining that you burst into the place, throwing your weight about and acting like I don't know what. There are some pretty influential people staying there.'

'Mr Bebb, a girl was raped there last night after taking a mixture of drugs. I've been trying to keep things a bit quiet ...'

'For the sake of the Eisteddfod? Well done you.'

'For the sake of the rape victim, Councillor Bebb. I couldn't give a damn about the Eisteddfod.'

'Was there any need for you to be hostile ...?'

'To Eifion Pennant, you mean? That little bantam cock was ...'

'That bantam cock as you so rudely describe him has very significant contacts.'

'He's an interfering little fellow, that Mr Pennant. He tried to push into the crime scene. He was lucky I didn't fancy the paperwork or I would have done him for obstructing an officer in the execution of his duties.' There was a little silence as the Chairman of the Organising Committee considered the implications of such a prosecution.

'Have you caught the offender?'

'Yes.'

'One of the men who was staying on the campsite? A student, I expect?'

'Dewi Dolau.'

'You've made a mistake. Mrs Griffiths Dolau is the Secretary of the County Committee of the Merched y Wawr.'

'That's a problem for the Merched y Wawr, not for me. But anyway, he's killed himself by now.'

'Rape? Drug? Suicide? In our Eisteddfod?'

'Bad things happen everywhere, Councillor Bebb. We didn't give much of a priority to drugs education or fostering healthy sexual relations before the Eisteddfod, did we? We were too busy raising funds and selling bunting.'

'Who do you think you are talking to, Dafydd Dafis?'

'To you, Councillor Bebb. I'm only trying to say that stuff can happen without people blaming the 'Steddfod.'

'I sincerely hope you're right, Dafydd. We don't want any kind of scandal. And what is to become of all those innocent people who were staying at Dolau?'

'I've sorted another place for them to go.'

'A good place, I trust?'

'To be perfectly honest with you, Councillor Bebb, assessing campsites doesn't come within my job description but I've asked a favour from an old friend who's got some ground near Dolau.'

'I don't believe for a moment that you have friends who are local landowners, Defi Shop.'

The old insult struck Daf like a blow but, remembering Chrissie's warm voice on the phone, he managed to laugh.

'Oh, I'm a bit of a man of mystery, Councillor Bebb. We have to get a permit sorted out in a hurry but then we're cooking on gas,' he answered, smiling as he spoke.

'Fair play, Dafydd. You're not planning any more of your heroics this week, I hope?'

Daf's father had taught him to count to ten under his breath before replying, which was what he did.

'It wasn't me hurt the girl, nor sold her the drugs. I intend to catch whoever is selling illegal drugs in our area because that's my job and I'm right keen on maintaining the standards of Dyfed Powys Police.'

'But you don't need to do it … in the public eye, Dafydd. Softly, softly catchee monkey.'

'What if the next overdose dies? What kind of scandal would that cause for the Eisteddfod after? I'll do what I think fit.'

'We understand each other, I think, Dafydd. Just try to act smart, can you?'

'Of course, Councillor Bebb.'

'I'll see you and Falmai at the reception tomorrow.'

'We aren't going.'

'I was almost certain the authority had sent an invitation to you …'

'They did and I turned it down. I'm too busy for small talk and canapes, sorry.'

'Don't be an enemy to yourself, Dafydd. You don't always need to act the martyr.'

'I'm not a martyr, sir, just a busy man.'

'Very likely, Dafydd.'

Daf had to chew a piece of gum to clean his mouth after talking to the old bastard. He decided to go straight to the Maes to start his investigation to see if he could put a stop to the supply of Es before nightfall. He didn't want anyone else to suffer like Gwawr had suffered. He knocked on the door of the SARC.

'How's it going, Nia?'

'OK. The doctor's been and gone, I've done all the swabs and we're just waiting for the results of the blood tests to make sure Gwawr's OK to go.'

'Is she going home?'

'She'd rather stay with Dyddgu. She doesn't want to tell the story to anyone.'

'I understand, as long as she's safe. I'm planning to go up to the Maes right soon: I could give her a lift.'

'That would be a big help. She's taken a liking to you, which shows she's not in her right mind yet.'

'Glad to hear it,' Daf replied, ignoring the dig. Then he added, under his breath: 'I'm that glad the fucker had a lead shot breakfast, Nia.'

'You shouldn't talk like that, Inspector. And speaking of breakfast, I didn't get you anything to eat for two reasons. The first is that I've gone a bit scatty since having the baby so I forgot but the second reason is that I'm not keen on running about after you. Sheila's way too soft with you. You'll never grow up into a big boy who can look after himself if we keep on looking after you.'

'But I'm starving.'

'As luck would have it, they haven't moved Tesco – it's still round the corner.'

'Fair play. I'll go round for a Danish: can I get you anything?'

'I'm fine, thank you.'

'Don't say you're back on the bloody Weight Watchers?'

'Just go, please, Inspector.'

Banter in the workplace – nothing like it. Sharing a joke, pulling people's legs, talking bollocks – these skills weren't mentioned in any management guide but to Daf, they were vital to running a successful team. He strolled over to the supermarket, past the Gorsedd Stones. It was great to see flags everywhere: Welshpool was rejoicing in its Welsh identity, for once. Signs welcoming visitors were everywhere. Even the DIY store proclaimed its enthusiasm for the great event though Daf wondered just how many Eisteddfod visitors would need putty or grout during their stay. He bought his breakfast and six bottles of decent wine: with Gethin in the bungalow, he would need them. When he returned to the station, Gwawr was ready to leave. She was holding a bottle of water tightly.

'I've got one phone call to make, then let's go and see how

Dyddgu's getting on, shall we, *lodes*?' Gwawr nodded her head.

'Do you want to go back to see WPC Owen or stop here with me for a couple of minutes?'

'I'm fine with you.' Her voice was weak and distant, as if she were speaking from the bottom of a well. Daf noticed how dry her lips were.

'Are you sure you don't want to go home to your mum and dad?'

'Dad went off years ago. I'm better off with Dyddgu.'

'Your call.'

Daf picked up the phone. 'Nia, can you put a call through to the Council offices: Arfon John in the Licensing Department, please.'

Whilst he was waiting, he gestured Gwawr to sit down but she decided to stay standing.

'How are you, Arfon? Grand, grand. Can you prepare a temporary licence for a 28-day camping site for me, and do it right away? Well, not for me. What it is, is, a couple of right ugly things have happened overnight at the site at Dolau which means everyone stopping there will need to move and there's nowhere for them to go. I've managed to talk one of the neighbours to provide a place for them, if I can get the paperwork sorted ... Mrs Christine Humphries, Berllan ... Yes, that Chrissie Humphries ... I bet, but luckily everyone else doesn't think quite like you, you old ram... No, I'll give it to her ... No, no, the licence, I'll give her the licence ...Thanks, Arfon, we've all got to do all we can to make sure the 'Steddfod goes well. I'll see you by the Guinness Bar on Friday evening, yeah.'

This conversation made him think, yet again, about Chrissie. Without breaking any rule of confidentiality, he could ask her to keep an eye on the girls. With Chrissie, they'd be totally safe.

'Come on then, *lodes*.'

Gwawr moved like a person walking in their sleep. They had to call by at the Council offices on the way and Daf took pleasure in parking in one of the spaces reserved for the cars of councillors only. He dashed into the reception area to fetch the large brown envelope and when he returned to the car, Gwawr had locked herself in. Daf smiled at her through the window and she opened the door. There was an embarrassed look on her face but she didn't say a single word all the way back to Dolau.

There was a fair bit of toing and froing at Dolau and, in the lane, the car of Dr Jarman, the pathologist.

'Not much for me to do here, Dafydd. Bit of a mess.'

'We'll need a DNA sample from him.'

'Your officers said. The SOCOs have almost finished in the front room.'

'Great. Many thanks, doctor.'

'No problem. I didn't see you at the Cymanfa: Carys was outstanding.'

'Carys is always outstanding but I'm not a big fan of hymn singing.'

'Shame on you, then, Dafydd. These hymns are a significant part of our heritage.'

'If you're trying to persuade me to go to the Cymanfa, you can't have ever heard me singing.'

'Next time. Good morning to you.'

'Bye then, doctor.'

Daf had endless respect for the pathologist and was even prepared to take a lecture from him. They always met in circumstances like this, where Jarman's old-fashioned Welsh attitudes were a comfort somehow, amidst the blood and trouble.

The ambulance had gone and the SOCOs were almost finished, as Jarman had said. A girl in a white suit came out of the front door with one of the cushions from the sofa, wrapped in plastic, in her hand. Daf frowned. Plenty of evidence but what was the point of a court case without a criminal.

Sometimes, as he tried to cope with some horrendous case, Daf longed to make an example of the criminal, to send a clear message out to anyone who might be contemplating doing anything similar. But without a criminal to put in the dock, he couldn't secure justice for Gwawr.

'Almost sorted, boss,' Darren called over to him. 'Three, maybe four, more interviews and we're done.'

'And?'

'Not much of anything. A bit of coming and going last night amongst the youngsters and several of the girls said they didn't care for Dewi at all but nothing specific, apart from the fight yesterday between him and your friend Bryn Gwaun.'

'Bryn Gwaun is no friend of mine, Darren. I got to know him during that business at Plas Mawr, that's all.'

'Oh, I forgot, you're a friend of his wife's, aren't you? I wouldn't mind being friendly with a woman with a pair like that. Never seen anything like it since I bought the last packet of Dry Roasted one time.'

'DC Morgan, you are very familiar with the rules of Dyfed Powys Constabulary concerning prejudice and unsuitable language.' Daf smiled, knowing that talk like this wouldn't bother Chrissie in the slightest. 'OK then, *lanc*.'

'The one problem we've got here ...'

'A little man called Eifion Pennant?'

'Well, yes, but fair play to him, he has got a point. Even after we put a pressure washer over the place, Dolau's not going to be the place for family holidays.'

'I've sorted that. I'll go have a word with them now.' Daf returned to the car. Gwawr looked at him with shy gratitude – she hadn't opened her mouth to speak since leaving the police station. She was still too weak to walk more than a few steps so Daf drove into the field.

'Which one is your tent, Gwawr?'

She pointed to a little pop-up tent which had been decorated with strings of pink and yellow bunting, the sort of thing Daf expected to see on a stall at a primary school summer fair. The anger rose in his chest again to see this visual evidence of the kind of innocent delight in life which had been wrecked by the lust of a creature like Dewi Dolau.

Like a rabbit emerging from its burrow, Dyddgu's head appeared from the tent next door and Daf was very glad to see her. She had sobered up and Daf saw before him a confident and kindly girl, able to do her bit to care for her friend. A young girl ran towards them, a large chrome flask in her hand.

'Mami's made too much coffee, would you like some?' Further up the field, a woman in her thirties raised her hand in greeting before returning to the shelter of a vast blue tent.

'Please say thank you very much to her, would you?' Dyddgu answered as she fetched three plastic mugs from the back of her car. Gwawr sat down gingerly on the grass and though Dyddgu pulled a colourful blanket out of the boot of her car, she didn't move. Dyddgu settled herself and crossed her legs like a little girl on the floor of the school hall.

'I'm way too old to sit like that,' Daf explained, letting himself down rather stiffly, legs straight out in front of him.'

'You ought to do yoga,' Dyddgu suggested, 'to keep yourself flexible in your old age.'

'No, I'd be too afraid of breaking wind.' Gwawr smiled for the first time since Daf had met her and though it was a tiny smile, it was real.

'I've found another place for you to camp, OK? It's half a mile nearer the Maes and the lady who owns the place is a friend of mine. She's the wife of the man who comes with the showers.'

'Oh, don't say he's got a wife!' cried Dyddgu. 'My heart is in splinters now.'

'I said he had a wife,' said Gwawr. 'I remember the pictures in the papers.'

'Why was he in the papers?' Dyddgu asked, puzzled.

'Bryn was one of the suspects in the murder of Jacinta

Mytton,' Daf explained. 'Because he was having a relationship with her, the papers made a big thing of it.'

'And you were the policeman!' Dyddgu suddenly remembered. 'My mum started to get a bit of a crush on you, said you solved it too quickly because she missed you on the news.'

'I'll take that, given that every other woman on earth seems to have a crush on Bryn.'

'You can't blame us,' Dyddgu replied. 'He's so hot and he's such a nice man as well, so polite to all us girls.'

'Oh, Bryn's got all the moves, *lodes*, but he's also got Chrissie so you'd best forget all about him.'

'No harm in looking.'

From the corner of his eye, Daf observed the effect of their stupid talk on Gwawr. She had begun, very slightly, to relax. In his experience, the nonsense of everyday life was sometimes something of an antidote to horrific memories. He finished his coffee, and a good cup it was too.

'You get packed whilst I explain what's going on to everyone else, then I'll go with you to the new site. I want to introduce you to Mrs Humphries, see you settled, right?'

Eifion Pennant was nowhere to be found but Daf was able to get his message across in a brief chat with his wife, who just happened to be the thoughtful woman who had sent the coffee down to the girls. In Daf's opinion, Eifion Pennant did not deserve such a wife. Life was just unfair at times.

'You don't have to tell me anything, Inspector, I get it. The girls went over the top last night and Mr Griffiths took advantage – horrible business. And I'm very glad you've found another place for us; you didn't need to go to so much trouble with so much else on your mind.'

'End of the day, Mrs Pennant, you are guests, guests of the people of Montgomeryshire.' Daf could not believe that such words had come out of his mouth. It was as if he was subject to demonic possession, haunted by the spirit of Councillor

Gwilym Bebb. 'And ... and we wouldn't want anything to cut across the welcome,' he finished, lamely. He was glad to get on to the next tent, to escape from his stupid words. Except that, for some reason, he gibbered on about the people of Montgomeryshire and the duty of welcome to every other person on the campsite.

In under half an hour, Daf had spoken to them all and was on his way over to Berllan, with Dyddgu following in her little Suzuki with the expected stickers in the back window: Cymdeithas yr Iaith and the Eisteddfod. As he turned into the gateway at the bottom of the Berllan lane, he noticed that the paint marks he had left when he had misjudged the width of the opening were still there. Perhaps Chrissie, who usually liked things neat, had left the scrape mark to remind her of him, he thought, and then dismissed this as a fantasy: if she was practical enough to panel beat the dent out of the damaged wing for him, she was unlikely to go in for sentiment. He caught sight of her as soon as he entered the yard, shaking hands with a rather bemused looking man with a clip-board under his arm. As he walked towards them, Daf saw the mixture of desire and nervousness in the eyes of the jobsworth from the Council – the Chrissie effect.

'I was just saying to Mrs Humphries, if she gets that field fenced off where the brook is a potential drowning hazard, we're all good.'

'My husband'll do that before he gets his dinner. When the job's done, I'll take a picture on my phone and send it you, save you coming out again.'

It was impossible not to admire her. Three hours ago, the idea of creating a campsite at Berllan hadn't crossed her mind but by now, it was all sorted. And she'd found time to put a good bit of mascara on as well, which Daf was hoping was for his benefit. She saw the council man off and turned to Daf with a wide smile.

'Your first customers, Chrissie. Dyddgu and Gwawr.'

'OK, girlies. That's the field. I got a Portaloo for you by there but it's the one we use when we're contracting, so don't expect too much. I'll get my hands on a better one by and by. Bryn's just getting a bowser for water. Pitch up wherever you fancy an' if you need me, I'll be in the house or over there in the workshop.'

'What about paying?'

'I'll have to chat that over with Inspector Dafis, *lodes*. I got no idea how much to charge.'

'We were paying ten pounds a night at Dolau.'

'That'll do me champion. I'll call by to see for you later, yeah?'

'Any chance of a cup of tea? Been one heck of a morning,' Daf asked as the girls set out to find the optimum pitch for their tents. The children were kicking a ball about, the yard was tidy as a pin in paper and a fresh breeze blew the faint scent of gorse down from the tops. Chrissie paused on the doorstep.

'Big plans on the go here, Mr Dafis. We've just got our planning for a fair bit of a new barn and an extension on the house. I wouldn't mind a conservatory, to keep the summer a bit for us, but we'll need an extra bedroom whatever.' Daf ran his eyes over her tight T-shirt. Her stomach was rounder than usual. In the kitchen, she pulled a small folder out of the drawer in the table and passed it to him. He opened it to find the image of a baby scan, showing twins. Daf remembered that Chrissie's eldest son, Rob, had been a twin but his brother had died before he was a week old.

'Congratulations, Chrissie.'

'Fair play, Mr Dafis, this bull's done his job as good as his brother. Honeymoon babies they are.'

It was good news, of course, but Daf couldn't help obsessing a bit, looking at the wedding picture on the wall. In the photo, Chrissie was sitting in a chair and behind her were both brothers, each with a hand on one of her bare shoulders. The brothers had been very close and had shared everything, including Chrissie, before Glyn's sudden death. But, if the look in her eyes in the picture was anything to go by, Chrissie had no complaints whatever about being shared.

'So we'll be like sardines in this house before long, Mr Dafis. Bryn's *nain* is losing the day and we've seen the will: we'll be able to sell Gwaun next spring.'

'What, sell the farm?'

'No, no, Mr Dafis, sell that old chicken shed of a house.'

'I believe it's a perfect example of a Welsh longhouse.'

'It can be a perfect example of a Quality Street tin as far as I'm concerned: I don't want to live in such a place. By the back end there'll be enough room down here for Bryn to bring the cattle into our new shed and it'll be right handy all round.'

Daf drank his tea, the best tea he'd had in a long while, made with spring water. She looked over the papers and they went through a few details about the campsite but Daf was distracted by a question he was longing to ask, a question he would never dream of asking anyone but Chrissie. He knew she wouldn't be angry with him for asking it and would only answer it if she felt like doing so. He took a deep breath before starting.

'Chrissie, you recall last year, we were talking about how things were with you and Bryn and Glyn and you said you'd ... you'd understood one another real well for a good long while?'

'I do recall Mr Dafis but, *Duwcs*, you talk real odd on times. We didn't "understand" each other, we fucked each other.'

'And you were ... happy with that, were you?'

'Happy as a cuckoo. Most girls would count themselves right lucky to have one of the Gwaun boys, let alone the both.'

'Well, I've been thinking about the business right often since then ...' Daf began but Chrissie interrupted him, licking her lips slowly before she spoke.

'Have you now, Mr Dafis? I'm that glad.' It was obvious that she was delighted to be the subject of his fantasies. She was unlike any other woman and Daf was not surprised that the respectable local wives, like Falmai, hated her. It wasn't just her lovely body or the flash in her eye which was attractive. There was something fresh in her attitude, the suggestion that a feast of experiences could be enjoyed with her. Since he'd got to know her, Daf had tried many times to define what was so special about her and he had come to the conclusion that it was the fact that she seemed able to decouple sex and romance. Like a man, Chrissie seemed able to separate physical lust from the need for a relationship and she was the only woman Daf had ever heard who could speak openly about sex without the need for a context of love.

'Listen, I know I'm being ... well, asking questions I shouldn't but how did it start? Did they ask you if you would ...?'

She laughed and ran her small, strong hands through her black curls.

'Got to say, Mr Dafis, I like your question because I was half thinking you'd forgotten all about me. Suppose I've not got much to interest a chap like you.'

'Don't be daft, Chrissie. You'd interest any man on earth.'

Chrissie paused for a moment before answering. 'Do you remember I said Glyn got a bike when we were courting? And not just any bike but a Norton Commando 1973, bike and a half it was. Might have been old but there was plenty of go in her and we went all over, even to the Isle of Man one time, for the TT Races.'

'But there's a down side to a bike, when the weather closes in?'

Chrissie smiled and winked at him. 'You're ahead of me now, Mr Dafis! So, well, you know what kind of a place Gwaun is. Not room for nothing so the lads had to sleep in the old hayloft above the stable. No stairs, just a ladder, no ceiling just the beams and the slates. In the winter, I'd climb in through the little window in the gable to meet with Glyn – you know I can climb like a monkey, Mr Dafis. Whatever, one night, Glyn had come over to our place so I could cut his hair for him because he was going to the bank in the morning to see about a business loan, so he'd got to be smart. Then we went back to Gwaun. As usual, Glyn went in, I waited ten minutes and climbed in. I stripped off in the dark and got into bed. Everything was going right well in the right direction and I was happy as a cuckoo then I put my hand in his hair. Long hair, it was, so it was Bryn. "Hey," says I, "what's going on?" and Bryn answers, full of cheek, "What's your problem? We've done it time and again before tonight."'

'What! You mean you'd ... had Bryn any number of times without knowing?'

Chrissie smiled again but now there was a hint of longing in her lively eyes.

'They were that alike to each other, Mr Dafis, like one man with two bodies. But after that, I took a little torch with me so I could see who I was loving.'

'And you weren't mad with them?'

'How could any woman of flesh and blood be mad with them? They're that grand.' Then she remembered. 'Were that grand, the both of them. We were right happy altogether, us three.'

Daf was seized with sudden guilt.

'Sorry, Chrissie, I shouldn't have asked. I'm nothing but an old pervert.'

'You're not, Mr Dafis. I like to think on good times, even good times gone. And, I got to say, the worst thing you could do is not to think of me at all.'

'You're a woman and a half, Chrissie Humphries.'

'Why d'you think I said yes to all the hassle of these campers? Just for the chance to flirt with you a bit, Mr Dafis.'

Daf tried to think how to broach the subject of Gwawr with her but he wasn't sure how to being. He needn't have worried.

'The little blondy, she was the one Dewi Squint had, yeah?'

'Yes.'

'Ugly fucker. Want me to keep an eye on her?'

'Please. She doesn't seem keen to go home for some reason ...'

'You know was it is when a girl's been forced, Mr Dafis? It's when heed hasn't been paid to what the girl says. She's got to have a fair bit of her own way for now, OK?'

'You're spot on, Chrissie, as ever.' Daf felt very glad to share some of his responsibility with a woman as wise as Chrissie.

'Stopping for your dinner? There's a chicken in the Stanley.' She gestured towards the gleaming red range.

'With all you've had to sort this morning, you've had the time to do a roast dinner?'

'Children always peel the potatoes and that's the worst job. And Bryn had to get up early to start on his round with them showers. It's right important to me he keeps his strength up, Mr Dafis.' Daf was filled with jealousy and not for the first time. Like an actor in a play, Bryn entered on cue.

'You got to put a bit of chain link over the corner of the Dol, *cariad*,' ordered Chrissie.

'Cup of tea first? It's like a furnace out there.'

She ran her fingers through his sweat-damp hair.

'A glass of squash will cut your thirst better than tea, and take less of your time.' She put a glass of Ribena in his hand. Bryn gulped down the purple liquid and vanished like a boy obeying his mother's orders. Daf smiled to think of his friend Dr Mansel's theory that every family was a system and operated in a unique way. Behind every door, he said, there was a different pattern and Daf felt that his job was to keep order, not to interfere with how people chose to live. But he couldn't conceal his interest in this particular domestic situation.

'Are you stopping for your dinner or not? I got to know how many carrots to do.'

'Thanks for the offer, Chrissie but I've got to go. I need to find whoever sold the stuff to the girls before something else bad happens.'

Just before opening the door for him, Chrissie put her arms around Daf's neck. Because she was so short, she had to stand on tiptoe. She rubbed her body against his chest.

'When I was little, I loved Westerns. There was always a sheriff who got everything sorted, a chap right like you, Mr Dafis. I always fancied the sheriff and I don't reckon I've changed.'

'Better get myself a white hat then, Chrissie.'

'Back last year, you said you couldn't come to see for me because I was a witness in a case. I'm not a witness now, Mr Dafis.' She put her hand on Daf's backside and squeezed it hard.'

'You're another man's wife, Chrissie, and he's the father of your little twins.'

'You don't need to remind me, Mr Dafis. I think the world of Bryn, but variety is the spice of life, they say.'

'You know what, Chrissie Humphries, you pick your moments. I've never had more on my plate than now.'

'I won't let you go unless you tell be you'll be coming back to see for me sometime.'

Daf had to give her a passionate kiss.

'Wait till the kids are back in school. Send Bryn off on a contract the other side of Newtown, then give me a ring, Chrissie.'

'I will too.'

'I'll be back later anyway, see how things are settling down here.'

Chrissie started to laugh.

'I got to say, Mr Dafis, I'm a bit crazy about you. I can't stop asking if what you've got in your trousers is up to what you've got in your head.'

'Only one way to answer that, but not now.'

'But sometime?'

'I promise.'

From the threshold of the house, Daf could see the girls' tents: Gwawr's pop-up had popped up and, with Bryn's help, Dyddgu's tent was almost ready. Daf was conscious of the tears in his eyes as he saw Gwawr pull the bunting from her bag. Chrissie squeezed his hand.

'You don't have to take care of everybody, Mr Dafis. They'll be grand here with me.'

'Thanks, Chrissie.'

'You know what my problem is, don't you?'

'What?'

'I got a lot of people depend on me. I think the world of Bryn but ... I got seven lads on the payroll by now, Bryn and the kids to care for and Mum isn't that champion. Everyone comes to me to sort their shit for them, just like they come to you. And like me, Mr Dafis, there's no-one standing behind your shoulder with a chequebook ready to sign all your worries away. We're the grown-ups, Mr Dafis, that's the truth of it.'

'And what've I done this morning? Loaded a lot more worries on you.'

'I'm grand. But you make sure you think of a nice way to say thank you to me.'

'I promise, Chrissie.' She hadn't let go of his hand and as the scent of the gorse filled his nostrils, the words of an old song came to Daf's mind:

The gold I have to share

Grows on the gorse so fair...

Without his realising it, he had been humming the tune quietly and Chrissie had picked up the song. She pressed his hand.

'What does the song say, Mr Dafis? Summer's the season to love ...?'

'Don't call me "Mr Dafis" all the time: I'm not a school teacher.'

'OK, Mr Dafis.'

'You're a hopeless case, Chrissie Humphries.'

As he drove down the lane, window open, Daf could hear birdsong, a song by Swnami coming from Dyddgu's car radio, the voices of children as they played and, from the corner of the field, the sound of a hammer. There was another sound too, a man whistling. Daf laughed. That was the Chrissie effect, Bryn whistling like a tone-deaf blackbird and he himself, Inspector Dafydd Dafis humming the Plethyn back catalogue. It was a very nice thing for any man over forty to think that any woman had an interest in his body, let alone a woman as attractive as Chrissie. And it was grand to receive such an offer, though Daf was far from sure he was confident enough to take her up on it. After years of experience with the perfect bodies of Bryn and his brother, how would Chrissie respond to a middle-aged man with a weakness for Danish pastries? Daf had to admit that he wasn't that confident about his sexual technique. Perhaps it would be better to stay in Chrissie's fantasies, the sheriff in the white hat, rather than fail in her bed.

Given that thousands of cars were arriving at the Eisteddfod every day, the traffic system was nothing short of a miracle. From Berllan, Daf arrived at the Maes in a quarter of an hour. At the entrance of the car park stood Hwyel the Fridd, one of the members of the team that was managed by John Neuadd, Chief Parking Steward for the nation's Chief Festival. For Daf, it was childish to feel pure pleasure as he pulled out his ID.

'Sorry to cut across your system, How, but I'm in a bit of a hurry.' That was a bare-faced lie: he wasn't in the slightest bit sorry to drive past all the Hi-vis Hitlers to the corner of the Maes which had been set aside for emergency vehicles and neither was he in any real hurry. He thought of himself as a real rebel, but didn't use the emergency entrance: he went through the main reception area, getting his infantile buzz from flashing his ID to the respectable stewards.

He paused for a moment outside the reception area, consulting the map he had picked up. He checked that he knew exactly where Carys' stall was and the Food Court: he would pick the rest up as he went along. As in every Eisteddfod, half the crowd were rushing to attend some event or ceremony, the rest dawdling. The fine weather and convenient location had drawn a good crowd: Daf wondered what the heck it would be like by the end of the week. He was folding up the map to slip into his trouser pocket when it was taken from his fingers.

'Mr Davies?' asked a rather gentle English voice. 'I was wondering if you could tell us what we ought to be doing?'

Eager, overdressed, and wearing shoes which no Eisteddfod-goer would ever risk on uneven ground, Daf recognised the mother of one of the Flower Dance girls. Her daughter, an exquisitely pretty child of nine, was standing nervously by her mother's side.

'Big day, Polly *fech*,' Daf remarked. The Harpers, whose children were baby sat by Carys from time to time, were staggered when their daughter had been chosen for a ceremonial role at the Eisteddfod. Though Polly had been educated through the medium of Welsh, her family had more idea of what went on the surface of a distant planet than on the Maes. They were joined by Polly's father, a senior manager in a high-tech company in Newtown.

'Out of our depth, that's what it is, Mr Davies,' he began. 'Pol here knows her dance but we know nothing. I don't even know what's happening today.'

'The big prize today is the Crown,' Daf explained. 'Polly will be dancing to celebrate the success of whoever wins the *pryddest*, which is a competition for a long poem in free metre.'

'But why the dance?' Mr Harper's voice held an edge.

'Why the Trooping of the Colour? Why a medal for winning a race?' Daf felt defensive and rather cheap: he was championing traditions he did not greatly respect.

'So, what do we do?' Mrs Harper asked. We'd like to watch Polly, of course … but it's all so puzzling.'

'You know what time you're needed to change, Pols?' Daf asked. The girl nodded, big eyes gleaming. 'Well, you stay to sort the flowers for her hair and that, then get into the Pavilion to watch.'

'Is it in all in Welsh?' asked Mr Harper, the edge buried under a faint hope.

'Of course. But you can get headsets to have everything translated.'

'It is rather a shame that everything's in Welsh,' Mrs Harper opined. 'Gavin's parents are coming up from Somerset for the big ceremony on Friday and it would be so much nicer for them if they could understand.'

Daf bristled but decided to subdue his desire to snap at these very decent people. They had moved to the area and chosen to educate their daughter to be bilingual: they didn't deserve a telling-off from a sweaty policeman.

'That's what the headsets are for,' he repeated.

'I'm a marketing man,' Harper confided. 'And if it weren't for this Welsh language, this could be bigger than Glastonbury. It's Hay meets Glyndebourne meets the Edinburgh Festival meets Lord of the Rings and it could be huge.' He paused and, noting that this suggestion had not inspired much enthusiasm in Daf, he added: 'We love it. The hymn singing last night was unbelievable.'

'The "language" is what the 'Steddfod is all about,' Daf explained, patiently. 'May I ask you, Mr Harper, do you ever have a week when you only speak English?'

Harper laughed and Daf reminded himself that this was a decent man who just knew nothing about the land in which he had made his home.

'Every week: I don't speak any other language, except schoolboy French.'

'Right. So can you imagine how you would feel if, in ten years' time, you couldn't hear English anymore in the place where you grew up?'

'It would be very odd.'

'So, how would it be, and you're a Somerset man, I think, if once a year, people who wanted to speak English all got together for a festival, at Glastonbury, maybe? And the only time you could get back to having your language all around you was at the festival?'

There was a silence.

'I've never thought about it like that,' Mrs Harper said, in her quiet voice. Daf decided to press home his advantage.

'In our house, we speak Welsh all the time but when we go out the door, we've got to think twice, check our words, translate, like I'm doing now. Here, on the Maes, it's our chance to relax.'

Harper looked at Daf as if seeing him for the first time.

'Do you think in Welsh?' he asked.

'Mostly. Think in English at work on times.'

Harper reached out a hand and Daf shook it.

'You think we're idiots, I know,' he began, 'but before we moved here, we knew nothing about how different things are here.'

'And we like it,' his wife added.

Daf laughed and patted Harper on the shoulder.

'So, what happens is, the poets have written their pieces with no names attached, using a false name. The judge talks about the work, then names the winner, who stands up and they come down to get the Crown. Then there's the ceremony.'

'And what is Carys' role?' Mrs Harper asked.

'She's the Virgin of the Vale: represents all the young people of the area.'

'Then Polly does her dance.'

Harper had been quiet for a while.

'Why don't we even learn anything about this at school?' he mused. 'I grew up in England and I think that I'm pretty well-educated but we never hear about Wales.'

'We like to keep it like that,' Daf replied, joking.

'Will we see you in the Pavilion?'

'Not today, no: I'm on duty. Taken Friday off so I'll go to the Chairing.'

'Which is another poetry prize?' Mrs Harper asked, with a smile that implied she was just about getting the hang of things.

'Yes, but strict-metre rules poetry this time. You get your

headset, make sure Polly's where she needs to be and you'll go along fine.'

As he watched them wandering away in a state of enthusiastic puzzlement, Daf did wonder why, if the Eisteddfod was such a wonderful thing, he had never taken his family there for the week. He was as Welsh as the next man but it had never been a part of their year. So he'd been a bit of a hypocrite as he talked to the Harpers but if it helped them enjoy their week, perhaps it didn't matter.

He strolled between the stalls, looking for a familiar face, for a person he could ask to help, someone who wouldn't ask too many questions. One weakness in his team: apart from Nia, none of them could make any kind of a fist of undercover work. He'd need outside help.

Carys had found a job on the Maes without any difficulty, selling 'quality Welsh gifts' on a stall called 'Nain's Dresser'. To suit their vintage style, Carys was dressed in 50s dress and Daf had a shock when he saw her: she was so like his mother, from the images he had seen of her before she became a mother, let alone Nain Shop. The Neuadd lineage wasn't visible at all when he looked at his daughter and that was a significant victory as far as Daf was concerned, even though he knew her beautiful voice came from her mother's side. He wandered into the stall pretending to look for a gift but, like most men in similar places, he had to feign his interest. After she had wrapped a mug for a customer by the till, Carys came over.

'Are you looking for something in particular?' she began, using the formal form of 'you' as if to a stranger. 'O, Dadi, it's you.'

'Hello, *cariad*. I was just looking for something for Aunty Gaenor, to thank her for welcoming us, something for the house, perhaps?'

'Hmm. Let's look for a little something, then.'

'Not too little. We don't want to look cheap.'

'What about a Welsh tapestry cushion? Or, for a lot less money, one with a message on?'

On the top of the pile of cushions was one with the words Nos Da meaning 'Good Night' was way too suggestive, Daf thought. Every one of the cushions reminded him of the pillows on John Neuadd's bed, way too redolent of his adultery.

'Something for the kitchen, maybe?' Daf picked up one mug then another. *Cwtch. Hiraeth. Cariad.* Hug. Longing. Love. Almost every one of the gifts was a trap of some kind and Daf felt a kind of panic rising in his chest – was there any way he was going to get away from the stall without his daughter learning the nature of his relationship with her aunt? He recalled the story Gaenor had told about the picture Siôn had received, the one with the pitch mark on her thigh. She loved gardening.

'What about that slate planter?' he asked.

'It costs a fortune, Dad, and its heckish heavy.'

'It'll do. I'll come back for it later.' There was a broad smile on Carys' face.

'You don't have to, Dad. There's plenty of other stalls, you know.'

'*Twt lol* – you've saved me potching about half the day trying to find something suitable. You deserve your bonus.'

'Not much chance of me getting a bonus – I've got to spend half the afternoon in the bloody Crowning. But Dadi, honestly, don't think you've got to spend like this every day: you'll be bankrupt by the end of the week.'

'Can you wrap it up nice for her?'

'For them. Uncle John's invited us as well.'

'Yes, but he doesn't do the housework.'

'Nor does Aunty Gae, not the cleaning anyway. But I'll try to wrap it, if we've got paper wide enough.'

'I'll bring the car over to pick it up, at the end of the day.'

'You can't drive on the Maes, Dadi.'

'I'm a policeman: I can drive through the Pavilion with my blues and twos on if I like, *lodes*.'

Carys took his card and pressed some buttons on the reader by the till.

'You should have asked me to enter my code.' The paper came out of the machine. 'That's way above my contactless limit, Carys.'

'O Dadi *fach*, I know your PIN better than I know my own. We'll be closing up about six tonight, or later if there's lots of people about and I'm on shutdown, since I'm taking time off for the Crowning.'

'OK. Is Siôn on the Maes?'

'Everybody is on the Maes. Heck of a gang by the Guinness Bar and I saw Aunty Gae sitting on the deck outside *Pl@tiad*, drinking Sauv Blanc like it was water.'

'Was your mum with her?'

'She's your wife as well, Dad, and no, she wasn't: she's in the Churches Together tent, cutting sandwiches all day.'

'She's what?'

'The vicar asked her.'

Daf managed not to make a scornful noise. Church in Wales was the faith of Neuadd, and had been for generations but to Daf their religion was just nonsense. He came from chapel stock and had been taken to Sunday school by his grandfather. Of course, to avoid a fuss, Daf's family had followed the religious tradition of Neuadd but it was just a custom, as far as Daf could see, without passion, charity or evidence of the Spirit. So there she was, Falmai Neuadd, cutting crusts off sandwiches for Pharisees whilst there was a wide world full of tears to dry, of heart-broken people needing comfort. Who was the Christian, he wondered, Falmai with her sacred sandwiches or Chrissie with her tender care for a rape victim? The heat was getting to him: he needed a pint.

'Don't work too hard, *lodes*.'

'Don't spend too much time at Berllan, Dadi.'

'What?'

'I've heard the whole story from Mair. But I'm not worrying Dadi dear: no-one's going to choose you over Bryn Gwaun. Not in a million years.'

'I don't suppose for a moment you've heard anything like the real story, Carys *fach*. And thank God for that. You stick to your nick-nacks and leave your dad to deal with the dark stuff.'

Another customer had come to the counter with a question about one of the tasteful Welsh gifts. Daf raised his hand in farewell but her patronising words hung between them like a curtain. A curtain made of Welsh tapestry with an appropriate motto embroidered on it.

By now, Daf's thirst had grown in the baking heat; the tea at Berllan seemed far distant. There wasn't a cloud to be seen but the heat was turning the blue sky white. Underfoot, the dust was rising, settling on the canvas of the stalls until they looked like features in old sepia pictures. The Syched bar wasn't far but Daf wanted to take advantage of every available corner of shade as he made his way there. It was the perfect weather to be lying on a bed of heather up on the tops, preferably with a likely girl, but it was not ideal for a policeman with an investigation to pursue. After walking only a few yards, he paused in the shade of the next stall for a moment.

'Water?' asked a man Daf did not know, offering him a plastic cup.

'Oh, thank you very much.' This stall was very different to the one where Carys was working – it was large, open and filled with mountain bikes. Above the pictures of fit people racing down mountain paths was a bright sign: 'Over the Tops'.

'First visit to the 'Steddfod?' Daf ask the good Samaritan.

'I'm sorry, I don't really speak Welsh, just the odd word. Garmon!' A young man in a wheelchair emerged from the back of the stall. He was about twenty-five years old and remarkably good looking with a wide smile, long golden hair like a lion's mane and the skin of someone who spends most of his time outdoors. Like Bryn Gwaun, he wore a vest that showed the muscles of his wide shoulders.

'A bike – that's a grand way to get after people stealing

sheep up on the hills,' he said to Daf. 'Six bikes and five training sessions – it'd be the best investment Dyfed Powys Police ever made.'

There was a brief silence as Daf tried to recall where he had seen the young man's face before, in a totally different context. Garmon, on the other hand, obviously knew just who Daf was.

'With the cuts going like they are, we'll be selling our cars by the end of the year and I'd rather have a bike than a donkey.'

'When that day dawns, you know where to come for the best bikes!' He extended his hardened brown hand to Daf.

'I will. I'm Daf Dafis.'

'Garmon Jones. Or Garmon Mountain Bike as they call me by now.'

Garmon Jones. Daf remembered the story. World champion at mountain biking, he had travelled to ever corner of the word competing. The irony was that it was in his own square mile he had his accident, on the familiar paths of Snowdonia. He injured his spine and, after being taken to hospital in Stoke by air ambulance, the diagnosis allowed no doubt. The world champion would never walk again, let alone ride a bike.

'Sold a lot of bikes today?'

'More than you'd think, Inspector Dafis, but I don't expect to be that busy until the end of the week when everyone will be sick to death of culture and looking for something different to do.'

'And every parent who's been blind drunk since the Cymanfa will be willing to pay any amount just to keep their children quiet.'

'Very likely, Inspector.'

As he was talking to Daf, Garmon was keeping an eye on his stock. One boy in his early teens attempted to put his leg over one of the bikes.

'I've told you, you can go on it after you've paid for it. That's not some trashy little present from Santa, that's the Superfly FS 9.9 SL.'

'I know,' answered the boy.

'Where's your money then?' demanded Garmon.

'I've got almost five grand.'

'And what does it say on the label?' The boy scratched at the back of his hand. 'You come round here sounding off about all the money you've got but you're not smart enough to read a price label. Seven thousand is the price of the Superfly FS and kids who waste my time do my head in.'

'I'll have five grand for you tomorrow.'

Daf saw something stubborn in the boy's attitude, as if he were used to having his own way.

'Right, I believe you, thousands wouldn't. Won the lottery, have you?'

'My dad's given it me, over the years.'

'Well, aren't you the lucky little chap to have such a nice daddy, but do me a favour and fuck off. There are people here who actually want to buy bikes, not just hang around shooting their mouths off.'

The boy pulled a plastic bag from the pocket of his jeans. He offered it to Garmon.

'Just shy of five grand, cash.'

'Are you dull, or what? How many times do I have to say, for that money you get the Zesty, which is a grand bike, not the Superfly.'

'Why's that, then?'

'Because the Superfly is a better bike, so it costs more pennies, yeah?'

'You don't get to speak to me like that, crip.'

Whatever damage Garmon had sustained to his nervous system, his reflexes were impressive. In seconds, he had picked up a metal water bottle and thrown it towards the boy, with a true aim. The boy ducked and the bottle fell after smacking into the canvas wall of the stall with some force.

'Get out of here, now, you little bastard.'

'Why, what are you going to do – run over my feet?' sneered

the boy as he stalked off. Daf hastened after him and caught hold of his elbow.

'What do you think you're doing, boy?'

'And what do you think you're doing?'

'Where did you get that money?'

'From my father, like I said to the crip.'

'You are not to speak to people like that. What would your dad say, if he could hear you speaking like that?'

'He's fucked off anyway.'

'Right then, *cog*. Wise up, or you're going to regret it, yeah?'

'And who are you to tell me how I ought to behave?' the boy retorted, sniffing.

'Inspector Dafydd Dafis, Dyfed Powys Police. And I'm on the Maes to keep a bit of order. Mr Garmon Jones does not deserve to be spoken to in that way, do you understand?'

The boy nodded and ran off, sniffing as he did so. Odd time of year to have a cold, Daf thought. Perhaps the lad was allergic to something – the Eisteddfod, possibly. Back at the stall all was well, the man who had offered Daf the drink was selling a helmet and Garmon was signing pictures of himself for an admirer.

'Don't pay any attention to the little fool, Garmon.'

'I won't but I'm not selling him the Superfly at a loss either. No way, José.'

'No-one expects you to do anything like that. If you have any more bother with him, pick up the phone.' Daf gave him a card.

'I will, Inspector.'

Daf swore under his breath as he walked over to the bar: he should have asked the boy for his age. With his wad of cash, his aggressive attitude and his unseasonal cold, if the lad had been eighteen, Daf would have been on the look out for a bit of charlie but the boy wasn't more than fourteen, younger, perhaps. His voice was still high and his skin bore the marks of adolescent eruptions. Underneath his aggression, there was something pathetic about him, like a dog which has been neglected. That having been said, Daf's sympathies were with Garmon Jones, a young man who had worked so hard to reach the top of his highly competitive field only to lose it all in a moment. Life was nothing but random, Daf considered.

Carys was right: plenty of people were seeking a drink. Daf passed the Syched bar without seeing anyone he knew but there were several hundred people in the horseshoe-shaped space surrounded by the food caravans. At once, Daf saw a host of familiar faces: some he knew from their television appearances, some were local and others again fell into a category of being vaguely familiar. Children were running wild like deer around their boozing parents, whilst the grandparents geared up for babysitting later. Every now and again, like lava bursting out of a volcano, a song rose up into the sky, a hymn or a folk song, lasting for a verse and a chorus, every song drowning in the bottom of a beer glass. Every song, that is, apart from the seventies classic 'Y Brawd Houdini' which seemed to be being sung without a break, like a round. Daf could smell the perfect Eisteddfod: a mixture of sweat, beer, onions and dust.

As he approached the edge of the crowd, Daf spotted a familiar face. A tall boy, slightly stooped as if his height were an embarrassment to him, as drunk as a skunk. It was Siôn Neuadd, John and Gaenor's only child, the same age as Carys though he behaved as if he were five years younger. He was not an unhandsome boy, with his mother's even features and deep-set blue eyes but, somehow, Siôn was always a bit off target. His choice of clothes today was a case in point. From his waist down, he was fine for a day at the Eisteddfod in his surf shorts and flip flops, though sandals on feet which spent fifteen hours a day in heavy work boots are less than ideal. The T-shirt, by contrast, was both tasteless and in the wrong language: at the Royal Welsh Show, Siôn's choice would have been fine but at the Eisteddfod, the logo of a chocolate bar and the legend 'She asked for a chocolate bar so I gave her four fingers', was grossly inappropriate. He had topped the outfit off with his white cricket hat. On his chin was a spot which shared with the Great Wall of China the distinction of being visible from space. For fuck's sake, Daf thought. It made matters worse that he had been sober when he had got dressed.

'Hey, Uncle Daf!' Siôn called. 'Good timing – Bebb's just gone to the bar.'

'How's life, Siôn?'

'Champion, thanks, Uncle Daf. Any chance of a lift back to the Black after?'

'No problem. I'm staying on the Maes for a while, mind.' He had to offer the lift: this was Gaenor's son, even if he did need a personal stylist.

'That's grand, no hurry. I fancy going to Llanfair later but it's great here too.' He waved his hand around as if he were conducting a choir. A girl, and a sexy girl at that, arrived with six pints of beer on a cardboard tray. She knew the dress code of the Maes far better than Siôn, in her short denim skirt and her T-shirt which proclaimed that she was a Welsh Wild Flower, short enough to show the ring through her navel. She was every bit as drunk as Siôn, though hiding it better, her rather lumpy face showing no lack of control. She was what Carys would describe as a prawn: nice body but ugly head.

'Three pints for you, Siôny Boy, and three for me.

'Fair play to you, Megs, fair play. This is Uncle Daf.'

'Were you the policeman on the murder case, on the news?'

'Very likely. Nice to meet you, Meg; having a good Eisteddfod?'

'Cracking, Uncle Daf, craca-fuckin-lacking. I'm on a week-long serious spree.' Siôn cut in, admiration in his eyes.

'Megs hasn't eaten since Friday.'

'Eating is cheating, Uncle Daf. And there's lots of goodness in beer.'

'But we can have chips in the Black later if we like, Megs. Uncle Daf's offering us a lift.'

'I'm in love with you, Uncle Daf, I really am. We've been mad keen on going over to Llanfair but we hadn't got a way.'

'Right you are. I'll give you a ring when I'm ready to go. Did you say Arwel was about, Siôn?'

'By the bar,' answered his nephew. 'Some bit of a crowd of people there. If you see him, Uncle Daf, remind him it's his round. I'm a pint down on him by now.'

A family stood up from the table nearest to Siôn and the boy sank down onto it clumsily.

'Take care, *cog*.'

'I'm grand, Uncle Daf.'

He was a decent young chap and Gaenor's son but Siôn could really be a lamb's cock at times and Daf was rather glad he wasn't his son. He wondered if Megs had worked out that he might be a lamb's cock, but he was a wealthy one.

Daf found it impossible, after his encounter with Siôn and his new friend, not to think about Gwawr and the fun which had turned so sour. When Daf was young, he was always rather anxious. He had more worries than money so he didn't very often let himself get completely hammered. If young people chose to wander about in such a condition, shouldn't they expect bad things to happen? But there was freedom in the air, a spirit of innocent fun Daf associated more with Ireland, or Wales before the Methodist Revival: all about him people of all ages were drinking, sleeping, dancing and singing. There were exceptions to the revelry, of course: the Professor and his wife were sitting nearby, eating sandwiches from Tupperware and drinking tea from a flask in the heart of the bacchanal. Daf had to stop to talk to them, even though their respectability seemed to impact somehow on the atmosphere of hedonism.

'Having a good day, I hope?' he enquired politely.

'A very satisfactory day indeed, Dafydd. The bungalow is very convenient, apart from the early morning traffic.'

'They moved that lorry before dawn,' agreed Mrs Prof.

'It's only on a Monday they make such an early start, to go

down to the livestock market.' Perhaps Daf was imagining things but he was almost certain that the Professor was being just a shade patronising.

'Of course, of course. You know, Dafydd, we tend to live in our little academic world, forgetting that everyone else has to earn their bread and butter. And of course, it's wonderful to see the farming sector thriving. It's in our agricultural communities that the Welsh language is really kept alive, isn't it?'

Daf sympathised with Mrs Teifi: even on his holiday, he had to keep on lecturing.

'Would you like to have a cup of tea with us, Dafydd?' she offered, in her dry voice, the sort of voice a bowl of pot pourri would have, if it could speak.

'Unfortunately, I'm on duty.'

The Professor laughed like a character in some old-fashioned drama.

'Don't tell me that you're investigating crimes here on the Maes, Dafydd! You should have been in the Literature Tent at lunchtime: there were enough crimes against poetry being committed there.'

'I'd rather be a detective than judge the poetry, thank you, sir.'

After leaving them, Daf came across their son, in the heart of a cluster of media types. Gethin was sitting on the end of a table, rather than on the bench, his legs splayed apart and Manon was standing between them. Apart from being an appalling example of what Carys called 'manspreading', it was a rawly sexual stance, even though Manon's back was turned to her lover. Daf heard a sentence or two of the discussion before he was close to the group: it was clear that Gethin was leading the debate.

'The days of the little companies are long gone. Big is beautiful these days: the game is all about combining and cutting costs these days.'

'But what about the good ideas which emerge from the

small companies, Gethin?' asked a tubby little man with small, round spectacles which made him look like Mr Pickwick's body double. Though he wasn't yet in his thirties, his clothes were old-fashioned and there was a coffee stain on the sleeve of his shabby linen jacket, a total contrast to Gethin in his Versace jeans and his Ralph Lauren polo shirt.

'My door's always open, Elwyn. Pick up the phone, send an email ...'

'I won't be such an innocent fool again, sorry, Gethin. How many ideas of mine have you stolen in the last five years? Seven? Or is it eight?'

'If you hadn't gone to live in some cave in Pembrokeshire, Els, you would have some idea about what I mean when I talk about the zeitgeist. There are ideas about, everyone is discussing them, then the first man to the mill gets his corn ground. It's as simple as that.'

'Fuck your zeitgeist, Gethin Teifi. You've taken every one of my ideas without a *smic* of acknowledgement, let alone any fee.' Daf had seen Gethin win arguments many times before. Every chat with him was liable to turn into a debate, every debate into a victory for him, but Daf had never before heard this note of cruelty in his voice. Elwyn's face showed his anger and disappointment but Gethin had another blow to strike.

'Are you about to burst into tears, mummy's boy? I don't usually bother discussing things like this with kids.' Like other bullies, Gethin knew where to find the weak spot. Daf saw Elwyn's eyes, behind the thick lenses, well up with tears.

'You've got no right ...' he began.

'I've got every right. I bought the right to every idea when I bought the company, when I bought you.'

'How dull could an afternoon in the 'Steddfod get?' asked Manon, with a noise which was halfway between a yawn and a sigh. 'You heard the man, Elwyn *bach*, pick up your little red spotted handkerchief on a stick and fuck off, can't you?'

Elwyn stood still for a moment, unwilling to leave the

battlefield. Manon pulled a tissue out from her pocket and waved it in front of his nose. Gethin smiled at her and Daf suddenly realised what was responsible for this new cruelty in his old friend – Gethin had found himself a girl who was willing to back him up in his bullying. Eira, his wife, was a strong woman but far too dignified to lower herself to that degree.

'Oh, blow your nose before you go, Eli *bach*,' Manon concluded, with a smirk.

Elwyn's head sank onto his chest but before going, he threw his pint – thick, dark Guinness – over Gethin and Manon. Unfortunately for him, his aim wasn't very good and only a few splashes reached their target. A weak gesture by a weak man. The group around them understood the dynamic. To succeed, you needed to be on the same team as Gethin Teifi. Daf regretted than he had witnessed this little drama: it was going to make it a good deal harder to socialise naturally throughout the week with the friend who had developed into such a bully. Daf wanted to melt away into the crowd but he was spotted.

'Hey, come over here for a pint, Daf!'

'Sorry, Geth, I'm busy.'

'Bloody landlord class! You're not willing to share a glass with a simple tenant like me, are you?'

'Far from it. I'm working. What are you up to later?'

'We thought of going to see the Theatr Bara Caws show tonight.'

'It doesn't start till tomorrow,' Daf informed him.

'Then we'll hit Llanfair then, and hit it hard, hey boys?' Gethin announced and his toadies all agreed.

'May see you there, then.'

It was a strange feeling but Daf was longing to escape from his old friend with his superficial, sneering girlfriend, his flatterers and his insignificant influence. High time to concentrate on the case: he had to find someone who could contact whoever it was who was selling the drugs.

'Hello, Dafydd.'

Daf turned to see Arwel Bebb, a friend of Carys and Siôn, a student at Aberystwyth and one of the very few sober people to be seen. He hid his strong character behind his trendy image, never revealing the troubles he had endured. Arwel's case was a perfect example of the reason why, at times, Daf hated the area he was supposed to defend. Whilst Arwel was going through his own personal hell, which started but did not end with drugs, his mother was in a flap about whether the installation of underfloor heating would be worth the trouble, his father was chasing every woman he came across and his important grandfather, Councillor Gwilym Bebb, was far too busy arranging the Eisteddfod to notice the fragility of his grandson. Respectable people who were too snobbish to look after their own children. Daf thought the world of Arwel but every time they met, a cloud of memories gathered. By now, one of the bastards who had hurt Arwel was dead and the other in prison but this was a failure not a triumph as far as Daf was concerned because of the scar which had had been left on the lad. A good policeman would have succeeded in protecting him, not clearing up the mess afterwards.

'How are you, *lanc*? Have you seen Siôn?'

'He's on a spree on double time after starting so early: he tells me he was in the Smithfield before six this morning.'

'Going to a gig later?'

'I reckon on going with some of my college friends but Siôn reckons paying to hear a band is a waste of good beer money.'

'Well, I'm glad to see you're in a tidy state, whatever.'

'As you know, Dafydd, I took a right hard lesson. I haven't been really off my face once since then.'

'I remember it all too well. Listen, *cog*, I need your help, to solve a case which is like your case in lots of ways.'

Arwel swallowed the spit which had gathered in his mouth, as if vomit had risen in his throat. 'Do you reckon I'm the one to help you, Dafydd? I'm real shit at standing up to people.'

'I only want you to make one phone call for me. Last night,

there was a girl the same age as you ... well, she made a bit of a night of it and then some bastard decided ...'

'I get it, you don't need to spell it out.'

'We know who raped her but I need to know who sold the stuff to her as well.'

'Hey, steady on Dafydd. I'm not at all sure I can ...'

'You remember, back in the day, you used to say that you got your stuff from Jacinta and she took care of you, right?'

'Yes, but I've been clean for months now.'

'Whoever sold to that girl sold her a cocktail of shit. I don't want anyone else to have the same trouble tonight.'

'Alright, alright. Just the one phone call, you said?'

'Yes. Ring him and ...'

'Or her. There's enough girls selling.'

'Whatever. You ring, ask for something, arrange to meet him and I'll get him. Or her.'

'But what's going to happen to the bastard who raped her? Because I'm not going to be a part of shifting the blame from whoever ... hurt her to someone who just sold her a bit of grass.'

'He's killed himself, so you could say he's paid the price.'

'And I'm not going to use my own phone, in case it turns out to be someone I know ...'

'I've got a Pay as You Go for things like this. Come on, *cog* – it's five minutes of your time.' Daf gave him the phone after entering the number Dyddgu had given him. Arwel turned his back on Daf to make it easier for him to play his role.

'Hello mate ... Yeah it's great weather, real party weather ... bit of bath salts, drone maybe ... Sorry, mate, I can't afford any snow, I'm only a student. Yeah, yeah, that'll be great ... well, I know where I am with Es. Half an hour? No worries. OK, OK.'

After making the phone call, Arwel's attitude changed.

'His voice was that young, Dafydd. Way too young to be part of that scene. He's going to leave the stuff for me behind the S4C tent, after the Cyw show.'

'However old he is, he's certainly got plenty of nerve, choosing such a public place.'

'He's probably heard about the safety of hiding in plain sight. Far better than skulking in the shadows.'

'Thanks, *lanc*. I should be alright now.'

'You've got to be joking, Dafydd. Whoever he is, he is bound to have seen you on the telly talking about some case or another. And, if you don't mind me saying so, you don't look like you're in the market for any party drugs. Ovaltine, maybe.'

'If I get to the rendezvous....'

'He'll vanish at the sound of your size tens and there won't be a scrap of evidence. I'll make the mark, OK?'

'Fair enough, if you're willing. You've changed your tune a bit.'

'Yes, after hearing his voice. We've got to do all we can to get him out of that world: he's only a kid.'

'Shall we have a cup of tea in the meantime?'

'To make sure as many people as possible see us together? The best thing would be for you to give me a bollocking, as if you were concerned about what I was up to. Then, I'll see you by S4C.'

'I can't get on with the idea that people recognise me. I'm just doing my job.'

'Yes, by solving the most notable cases in the area. OK, you're not an A-lister like Bryn Gwaun but people do remember you. See you later, Dafydd.'

Daf realised he had time to look for a book to read, something to enjoy instead of the literary preach-fest he had borrowed from Haf Wynne. He strolled over to the Welsh Books Council stand, conscious of a strange sense of freedom: he could find a book he wanted to read without needing to impress anyone. There were several novels which caught his eye but he decided on a literary fiction set in the First World War. By the till, he encountered the local MP, Mostyn Gwydir-Gwynne, with a large coffee-table book in his hand. He was just the type to attend the Justice Department Reception, which was reason enough to keep away.

'Good afternoon, Inspector,' intoned the MP, in his dry, upper-class English.

'*Prynhawn da, Mr Gwydir-Gwynne.*'

'The weather is ideal.'

'*Debyg iawn.*'

As a man who firmly believed in breaking all rules as long as no-one got hurt, Daf never usually gave a damn about the rule which insists that Welsh is the only language to be spoken on the Maes. Daf knew it was childish to speak Welsh to him and would not do anything to alter the fact that, just as they had for centuries, Gwydir-Gwynne's family and their friends owned an unhealthily large slice of Montgomeryshire but it still felt like the right thing to do, a rebellion which followed at least one rule.

Twenty minutes to go. Enough time to quench this thirst. There was a delicious breath of air-conditioned coolness emerging from the *Pl@tiad* restaurant. Outside on its veranda, tastefully dressed people were drinking wine and sheltering under the large umbrellas, quite a contrast from those boozing by the Guinness Bar. There was a sea of linen adorned with rocks of chunky jewellery and in the midst of the crowd was Gaenor, enjoying the company of a gang of old friends. There were no less than seven empty bottles on the table. Daf could not resist gazing at her for a few moments: after all her years of loss and compromise, she still knew who she was, and how to have fun. He raised his hand in greeting but walked quickly on. A burst of laughter followed him and he was sure they were talking about him but he felt no concern at this thought: any comment from that lot was more likely to be benign than spiteful.

With a bottle of rather costly water in his hand, he went straight to the S4C building and arrived in the last minutes of the children's show. On the stage were a handful of young people in sweaty suits dancing rather listlessly in front of a packed crowd of children, many of whom looked sulky to the point of mutiny. There was a familiar man in their midst, his face recognisable even under its burden of whiskers. Daf knew at once where he had heard the voice of the man in the rabbit costume before: he had been in the yard at Neuadd on the previous night, pleading with Manon. That was why his voice had rung a bell with Daf: he was a well-known presenter of children's programmes. For a young woman like Manon, there was not much competition between Bunny-Boy Gwion and Gethin Teifi. Daf recalled the conversation about Gwion's cocaine habit: could there be some connection between the young voice on the phone and the troubled TV presenter? At the front of the stage, Fireman Sam and Norman Price were laboriously having fun with a giant chicken, all in their bulky suits. Daf wondered what the health and safety assessment of this performance might be: if he was sweating in his shirtsleeves, whoever was in those suits must be close to melting point. He glanced at his phone. Less than ten minutes to go. The final song came to an end, some of the children who had been sleeping through the performance awoke and the exhausted performers staggered off the stage. Daf left the building, using his phone as an excuse to keep his head down, as he often did. There was a text from Chrissie: 'Girls are grand – all sorted here.' He was a bit disappointed that there were no 'x's at the end of the message. Two minutes to go. One by one, the performers emerged from the rear door of S4C, most of them wiping their faces with large pieces of blue paper. They threw the paper into an old oil drum which was being used as a bin. Arwel came round the corner and made straight for the bin. He pulled a small packet out, wrapped in the same blue paper with which the performers had been wiping their faces. Daf took a picture of the scene whilst pretending to take a selfie with a row of flags behind him. Arwel put a small envelope in the bin and, without a word to Daf, strolled off in the direction of the Pavilion. Daf looked into the bin after he had left: apart from the envelope, it contained nothing but the pieces of blue paper. Daf sat on the grass, pulled his book from his pocket and waited. Nothing to see here, just a middle-aged man relaxing in the shade behind the S4C building.

After seven and a half chapters, just as Daf was beginning to think the dealer wasn't coming, he received a message on his Pay as you Go phone: 'Got it?' He replied, politely: 'Yes, thank you, and I left the money as arranged.' This was a good sign: the dealer would surely arrive before long.

'Dafydd Dafis, his head in a book, as ever.'

Daf leapt to his feet to greet Eira Owain Edwards, actress and former wife of Gethin Teifi. She was wearing a long dress of some light fabric and her bare arms were displaying an exotic suntan. She had a firm policy about make-up, only wearing it on stage, but then, why would she? Her skin was perfect, like that of a girl in her teens. Daf noted, as he did every time he met her, how exceptionally tall she was, not far off six foot.

'Eira, how are you? You're looking great.' She seemed to demand praise, her deserved tribute.

'I went out to Australia for a month. A long journey did me the world of good.'

'But you came back for the 'Steddfod?'

'I have a project here.'

'Of course.' Daf racked his brains to think of all he had heard about the cultural side of the Eisteddfod but failed to make any connection to Eira.

'You're an open book, like you always were, Dafydd: you haven't heard of my show.'

'There's a lot on ...'

Eira took his hand for a moment in a gracious gesture to show she bore no grudges. Her fingers were cool and smooth as if she were one of the porcelain ladies from the front room at Dolau.

'There'll be a ticket by the door for you tomorrow night, and I know you will give me an honest verdict.'

'Sounds great.'

'And we'll share a glass afterwards.' It was an order, not an invitation. Passing years had added to her dignity and she was now queenly in her manner. Two women walked past, growing very excited when they saw Eira. Daf remembered that she was quite a celebrity these days: no matter how incisive and ground-breaking were her theatre projects, everyone remembered her eleven-month stint on *Coronation Street* as the gutsy barmaid, Gwen. One of the women decided to venture over to Eira.

'Sorry to moither but were you Gwen on Corrie?'

'I was.'

The excitement on their faces startled Daf: this was only a soap opera actress, not the Messiah launching his Second Coming from Meifod.

'Would you sign this for me, please?' the woman asked, pulling a leaflet from the Cerdd Dant Society from her bag.

'Of course.'

Daf couldn't quite work out why the women hadn't noticed how patronising Eira was being. She was delighted, she told them, that they had enjoyed her performance in *Coronation Street* and perhaps they would also enjoy her current project? Daf couldn't walk away without being very rude so he stood there, dumb as a post, his unease increased by the speed of Eira's transformation when the fans had gone. She simply picked up the conversation she had been having with Daf as if the interruption had not taken place.

'Dafydd, you are my ideal critic,' she began. 'Very rare indeed: lovers and students of literature who have not had their enthusiasm blunted by decades of teaching. Besides, I have an ulterior motive.' She was a very attractive woman but the last sentence alarmed Daf. He was self-aware enough to know that there could be no idea of any romance between them and the last thing he wanted was to be dragged into action as a weapon to use against her ex-husband.

'Gethin is staying in your bungalow with that prostitute, I hear. I need a spy! How is the Professor welcoming Little Miss

No-Knickers? And I hear the old lady is having to rely on prescription tranquillizers to get through her days ...'

It was obviously a joke and the two of them were laughing like the old friends they almost were when a boy approached Eira. He was drinking a can of Coke but the moment he lowered the can, Daf knew him at once: the lad who had caused the fuss on the bike stall. Despite being a policeman, Daf was not one for telling tales and therefore he decided to not report to Eira on her son's behaviour.

'Peredur, this is Dafydd Dafis, an old college friend of your father's.' Peredur's face was a deep red, perhaps from the heat. 'Peri's been working very hard on the Maes today.'

'Plenty of work needing doing.'

Peredur went over to the bin to throw away his can but he pulled his hand out quickly.

'You know perfectly well what the rules are about recycling.'

Modern morals, Daf thought: the boy had been raised to believe that putting a can in the incorrect container was a serious sin but no-one seemed to have told him that it was unacceptable to goad and torment a man in a wheelchair.

'You promise you'll come along tomorrow evening?'

'I will, unless anyone gets murdered in the meantime.'

'The person most likely to be murdered is staying with you, Dafydd: almost everyone has got a reason for killing Gethin Teifi.'

Daf laughed before considering the effect this joke would have on Peredur. A van pulled up some yards away from them and the driver jumped down to empty the contents of the oil drum into the back. Daf decided to do nothing: the dealer was likely to be close at hand and if Daf went to collect the money, he would see. The plan had failed but at least the connection had been made: the hook was in the dealer's mouth even if Daf had failed to reel him in. It would be easy enough to contact the Maes management team to retrieve the envelope from the rubbish. There might be fingerprints on the packet Arwel had received but if the dealer was as young as they suspected, his details were unlikely to be on the database. These thoughts ran through Daf's head whilst Eira was still talking.

'What about Valerie? Would you like a ticket for her as well?'

'Valerie?'

'Your wife. Navy blue, are we so easy to forget, us wives?'

'Sorry, I misunderstood: my wife's name is Falmai.'

'Of course, of course, Falmai. Well, she's very welcome to come along if she fancies.'

'I'm not certain.'

'Oh, Dafydd, do forgive me. I am so selfish. I have been so locked into my own little tragedy that I have forgotten anyone else exists. Have you parted, you and ...?' It had taken less than half a minute for her to forget Falmai's name again.'

'No indeed,' Daf replied, not sure if he was telling the truth or not. 'But she's that busy this week, I can't swear she'll be free for anything.'

'Two tickets by the door then.'

'I'm looking forward,' Daf lied, glancing over at the silent boy. There was something about him which led Daf to believe that Peredur was well used to spending time with adults who were not telling the truth.

'I've got to go Eira; been lovely to see you.'

Eira frowned a little. It was normally her role to bring an end to every conversation and to give her permission for people to leave her presence. Consummate actress that she was, she managed the parting with grace. As he walked after the van into which the bin had been emptied, Daf imagined casting her in the perfect role. Lady Macbeth, perhaps? No, with her son sulking by her side she was more like the Duchess of York in Richard III, a casting which boded ill for Peredur.

It was simple enough, after waving his ID, to persuade the lad on the bin van to go straight to the waste bulking centre. Daf borrowed a pair of thick gloves to rummage through the refuse but the envelope was not there. Very odd. He left his phone number with the bin boys in case anything turned up but Daf wasn't particularly hopeful. There were only two possible options: either Arwel had failed to put the envelope in the bin or the dealer had collected it unseen. But Daf had been sitting opposite the bin for over half an hour without seeing anything. He couldn't do more. He suddenly remembered that he had said he would collect the slate planter from Carys' stall before it closed around six and the afternoon was gone.

Strangely, no-one tried to stop Daf driving his car onto the Maes. He drove straight over to Carys' stall but she was not there. No-one had closed the stall and Daf saw no reason why he shouldn't simply walk in. He had nearly reached his car, carrying the trough, when he heard a strong voice, full of authority.

'What do you think you're doing?' Daf had not known how fast a wheelchair could move. In less than a minute, Garmon Jones had sped around Daf's car and taken the keys from it.

'You're not going anywhere, mate.' He looked up into Daf's face and grew red.

'Inspector Dafis, I am so sorry!' he exclaimed, holding out the keys to Daf who could not take them because his hands were holding the slate planter.

'No worries, *lanc*. Perfectly natural to be a bit suspicious if you see someone helping themselves.'

'Can I help? Looks like a heavy old thing.'

A young girl emerged from Garmon's stall, a bottle of lager in each hand: it was Carys.

'Dadi! We thought the place was being robbed.'

'Well, if you hadn't mitched off, I could have asked you to officially hand over the bloody trough.'

'But,' Garmon put in quickly, 'Carys deserves to quench her thirst after a hard day's work, Inspector.'

'Fair play. Want a lift home, Carys?'

'I haven't closed up yet.'

Daf almost thought that a look had passed between Garmon and Carys, a look which signified that there was what his mother would have called 'something between them.' But that was a stupid idea. After all, Carys was going steady with Matt and as for Garmon, well, he was not quite like other men. Daf was quietly very proud of Carys: she was always friendly and courteous to everyone, in total contrast to Gethin Teifi's son.

'See you later then, *lodes*. Glad you're so vigilant, Garmon: we could do with a few more good citizens.'

In the rear-view mirror of the car, he saw Carys turn back to Garmon's stall. There was a drop of lager on her lip and as she licked it away, Daf saw Garmon's eyes soften. Daf was normally very defensive when he saw any man admiring his daughter but poor Garmon was no threat.

It was harder to have sympathy for Siôn. Daf parked by the Food Court and rang Siôn several times. From the step at the side of the small stage, he finally caught sight of him, lying in the dust in front of the vegetarian food stall, No Bones Jones, with Megs tucked under his arm. People were tripping over them, sometimes anointing them with stray bits of falafel. For a second, Daf considered that he could just walk away because Siôn was not his problem but then he remembered Gaenor's tender eyes and the delicious taste of her skin. He went over and knelt down beside them, receiving a chunk of halloumi down the back of his collar for his pains.

'Siôn? You asked for a lift back to the Black, remember?'

'I did, Uncle Daf, but I got dead sleepy somehow.'

'On your feet, *lanc*.'

Shakily, Siôn rose. He followed Daf to the car and collapsed onto the back seat. Daf was surprised to see how much shape there was on Megs: she rose unaided and made her own way to the car, opening the other rear door and settling herself beside Siôn. Daf drove past *Pl@tiad* to see if Gaenor needed a lift: she was nowhere to be seen.

Daf managed to settle Siôn and Megs on the sofa at Neuadd. No-one else was at home. He considered a coffee but Gaenor's Tassimo machine was too complicated for him so he made tea all round. When he opened the door of the sitting room, mugs in hand, it was obvious that tea drinking was the last thing on the young peoples' minds. Somehow, they had managed to get undressed and Daf instantly developed a new respect for Siôn. He could not stand or speak but he had enough stamina to create a remarkable impact on Megs, who was screaming like a wildcat. Hard to say which one was taking advantage in these circumstances, Daf considered, and, even if they did regret it in the morning, they were both certainly enjoying the experience, totally different from what happened to Gwawr. After shutting the door quietly, Daf decided to pick up the phone.

'Chrissie?'

'Mr Dafis?'

'How's things going?'

'Champion, thanks. Dyddgu's gone off down into Llanfair to meet you after and Gwawr's come here to watch *Frozen*. Anni Mai and I have wanted to watch it for months but the bloody boys in this house reckon anything without cars in it is crap. With Gwawr here, we're not so outvoted.'

'Site OK?'

Grand thanks, Mr Dafis. Everyone from Dolau's settled right well and we've picked up three caravans and four tents extra. I'm doing bacon sandwiches for the morning ... Where are you, Mr Dafis, and what's going on there?'

'Neuadd and Siôn's brought a girl home from the Maes.'

'Sounds from here like he's doing a grand job, Mr Dafis. Here's hoping his uncle's just as good.'

'Ah, but I'm an old man, Chrissie.'

'Bollocks. Whatever, I've got chips in the fryer – thanks for calling, Mr Dafis.'

Chrissie was a one-off, a real star. The best possible therapy for Gwawr was an evening in the company of such a warm family. Time he was heading down to the town to see Dyddgu, to search for Mr Mushroom. He had reached the foot of the stair when he heard someone let themselves in through the back door. Not Carys, way too heavy. So, not Carys' Vans, Gaenor's heels or Falmai's Crocs: handmade, old-fashioned shoes with leather soles, the sort of shoes which were repaired twenty times before being thrown out: John.

'God, Dafydd, I'm knackered. Where's Gaenor?'

'Still not back from the Maes, I suppose.'

John washed his hands in the kitchen sink. After getting up at four, he was almost on his knees by now. He opened the fridge and, just as he was choosing between cheese, ham and cold beef as his sandwich filling, he heard a loud and unrestrained voice:

'Oh yes, yes, yes boy, just like that.'

Daf did not have time to restrain him: John opened the heavy oak door. On the wooden floor, Siôn was on his back whilst Megs demonstrated her equestrian skills. John stood still as a statue. Daf took a hold on his elbow and led him back to the kitchen.

'Would you take a little whisky with me, Dafydd?'

'It'll have to be a very little one: I've got work to do tonight.'

John nodded as he reached for a bottle from the cupboard which must have been his secret stash because in the sitting room at Neuadd, there stood a black oak corner cupboard which officially housed all kinds of drinks.

'Who is she, Dafydd?' John asked, having taken a good slug of his whisky.

'Megan is her name. Siôn seems to have met her on the Maes and they've been on one hell of a spree. I had to take them somewhere: Siôn's better off here than wandering around, given the state he's in.'

'I should say he's better off, Dafydd.' The little joke broke the tension. John had another drink. 'Well, well,' he said, after a while. 'Fair play to the lad for having a go, even if he is doing it wrong.'

'Wrong?'

John grew redder than ever. 'I haven't had ... The Talk with him, I wasn't bold enough, somehow. I feel that bad about it now, because I should have taught him that it's the chap goes at the top, the girl below. Don't they have lessons ...? You know the sort of lessons, in school, I mean? You're a school governor, so ...'

Daf came to his brother-in-law's aid, cutting across the voice which was trailing away into silence.

'I'm not sure how much detail they go into but I wouldn't worry about Siôn; looks like he's doing a grand job to me. Meg is having a fair old time of it, by the looks.'

'What kind of a girl is she?'

'Likes a bit of fun, I'd say, but I only met her today.'

'I wouldn't want her to think my lad didn't know how the business should be done, Dafydd. What if she told people? Siôn could get himself a bad name before he starts looking for a wife.'

'Like I said, she's having a good time: she won't say anything against him, I bet.'

'You sure? It looks right odd to me.'

'Lots of girls are keen on getting on top, I'm told. Matter of taste.'

'Well I never.' John laughed. 'Very educational event, the National Eisteddfod.'

Daf joined in the joke but found himself thinking of poor Gaenor. Over twenty years always on her back looking over John's bony shoulder. Then Daf realised something he had never considered before: John Neuadd had assumed that his wife's body was part of the bargain he had struck. Defi Shop had to work hard to persuade any girl to share his bed, which didn't come wrapped up in a black and white house and however many fruitful acres of moneymaking ground. Daf rather smugly calculated that Gaenor might have experienced more pleasure in the last few months than in all the years of her marriage but he couldn't help also feeling rather sorry for John. He would almost certainly never learn, unless chance threw him in the path of a woman who both fancied him and was confident enough to teach him, which didn't seem likely.

The men had not noticed Gaenor coming into the room. Her cheeks were red, her voice rather loud and, from the look on her lovely face, she had laughed until she could laugh no more. To Daf, there was nothing in the world quite as attractive as a pretty woman on a spree.

'What are you two doing in here, roosting like a pair of old hens?' she asked them both. 'Settle yourselves down in the sitting room and I'll sort out a bit of something to eat.'

'Siôn's in the sitting room with a lady friend,' Daf explained.

'And they're ... a bit busy, like ...' added John with an uncharacteristic grin.

'Not on my upholstery, I hope?' Gaenor asked, looking as if she were uncertain whether she should laugh or be angry.

'I reckon your sheepskin rug is going to have to go to the cleaners,' John responded.

'Fair play to them, you're only young once,' Daf remarked, conscious of his own bald hypocrisy – if he had seen Carys in such a situation, he would have killed the man with his bare hands.

'So, it's a cosy kitchen supper for us, then,' Gaenor replied. 'What sort of day did you have, John?'

'Oh, not too bad, considering all the coming and going there was. How about you, *cariad*?' Daf had never before heard John call his wife anything other than her name, or, too often for Daf's liking, 'Mother'. The tender word seemed bulky in his mouth, like a pebble.

'Oh, I went of a fair old spree with the old gang from the Forestry Commission – Siân, Meinir, Ella, the whole lot. I couldn't do the same again tomorrow, not got the staying power.'

Daf tried to restrain his laughter but failed. The situation was farcical.

'So Siôn gets his stamina from his dad then, does he, Gae?' he asked. For the first time ever, he felt as if he was really one of the family at Neuadd, a proper member of the team. Perhaps he had found his role at last, his function being to keep Gaenor cheerful. When John offered him another Scotch, it was hard to refuse.

'I've got to get down to Llanfair, look for some fellow who's selling drugs round the place.' As if seeing Daf for the first time, John nodded his head.

'I shouldn't fancy your job one bit, Dafydd, to tell the truth,' he remarked. 'I've heard a bit of what went on at Dolau.'

'Horrible business,' Gaenor said under her breath before looking from John's eyes to Daf's as if looking for agreement. 'I'd rather have a lad like Siôn for my son even if he were a thousand times more wild, rather than a creature like Dewi Dolau.'

'It's right important to give a bit of freedom to them,' John declared. 'The world stretches further than the corner of the rickyard, to tell the truth.'

On cue, Siôn came into the kitchen, breathing like a man who has just completed a marathon.

'Any chance of a coffee, Mami?' he asked, like a little boy, his childish words sounding strange from a young man who stank of sex and hormone-loaded sweat.

'Of course. Would your ... friend like one?' There was a suppressed giggle in the brief pause before Gaenor uttered the rather arch phrase and Daf's feeling of warmth towards her was like a tide of blood in his veins, a kind of venous Severn bore.

'Thanks. White and no sugar for Megs. When are you going down to Llan, Uncle Daf?'

'Right away, lad.'

'I think you'd better have a bit of a break before hitting the bright lights,' Gaenor suggested. 'Dad can give you a lift down later if you like.'

'I am knackered,' Siôn admitted.

'Get upstairs then. I'll bring your coffee up.' She used the plural form of 'you'.

'Right you are.'

There was a moment of silence after Siôn had gone before John started to laugh again.

'Is that girl going upstairs with him?' he asked.

'Hope so,' Gaenor replied. 'I want my sitting room back.'

Looking at Siôn's smiling parents, Daf realised that there was just about enough material between them to create a potentially happy marriage, if Gaenor was always drunk and John always in very high spirits.

'I got to go. See you later.'

Gaenor, with no attempt at an excuse, followed him to the car.

'You do us all the world of good, you know, Daf,' she whispered. 'I always have trouble getting off to sleep after a sesh. D'you fancy going for a bit of a walk? There'll be a fair moon later.'

'We'll have to see, Gae. You know I'd love to, if I can.'

'Good luck.'

She was close enough for him to smell her skin, her expensive perfume and the wine on her breath.

'I'll see you later, Gaenor. I can't keep away from you, you know.'

'Stay here now then.'

'I can't. We've got to act tidy.'

'Do you want to act tidy, Dafydd?'

Daf jumped into the car before he changed his mind, and opened the window.

'I've got some heck of a story to tell you later.'

'What kind of story?'

'A heckish funny one. Later.'

As Daf saw Gethin swaggering up the path to the bungalow accompanied by Manon in her short skirt, he didn't feel an ounce of jealousy. Gethin Teifi wasn't the only middle-aged man to have fun.

Chapter 4

Monday night

Held in a cup of rising green ground, Llanfair Caereinion seemed to have gathered like a pool running off the hills. As he drove down the lane, car window open, Daf heard an unusual sound, as if a vast beehive were around the next corner. Over the fields, on the gentle breeze, music was blended with the buzz and for the first time, Daf loved the Eisteddfod. It was as though the little town had been given a generous transfusion of life, of money, of fun.

First question: where to park the car? The town was full of people, cars and music. He remembered the reserved place by the old police station. The police station itself had been sold years ago and turned into a house but there was a parking place outside it, kept for police use. Daf was rather surprised to find it empty and backed neatly into it. He scribbled a small, bilingual note to put in the windscreen, since his car was unmarked: 'DI Dafydd Dafis, on duty' and off he set into the vast party. He decided to have a quick look round before contacting Dyddgu, partly to enjoy the atmosphere but also to be able to make an educated guess as to exactly what form of trouble might kick off later. The smell of barbeque was everywhere, like a mist, and Daf realised how hungry he was. He was considering the choice between anything involving a sausage or a lamb burger but he changed his mind when he saw the queues: at least fifty people waiting before each meaty altar. He did not have the time to spare. His phone rang: the station.

'Boss,' Sheila began in English, 'you are going to have to speak to the mother of the suicide.'

'What about Nia?' he replied in Welsh. If he always spoke English to her, her Welsh would never improve and he didn't mind at all waiting whilst she selected the correct words for her response.

'Nia went there but the mother is not happy. She asks to see you. She is in the Orthopaedic, you know.'

'Not tonight!'

'The hospital will be paining me until you give them a time for tomorrow.'

'OK, how about ten in the morning?'

'Very good, boss. Having fun tonight?'

'Still working, Sheila.'

'I'll see you in the morning.'

'*Ta-ta, lodes.*'

'I don't think *ta-ta* is very good Welsh.'

'If it comes to good Welsh, you buggered up the mutations in that last sentence, my girl.'

'*Hwyl fawr.*'

Her vocabulary was developing daily, fair play to her. Or perhaps, nightly: Daf had heard that the best way to learn Welsh was in bed. An image came into Daf's mind: perhaps Tom and Sheila played a grown-up version of 'Head and Shoulders, Knees and Toes' in bed, to learn the parts of the body. He would share the joke with Gaenor later: it was just the kind of thing which made her crack up.

Outside the Black, eating a large packet of pork scratchings, was Arwel.

'On your own, *lanc*?' Daf asked.

'Mair went to the loo over twenty minutes ago: there's some heck of a queue. The place is mental tonight. Scratching?' Arwel's girlfriend happened to be Carys' best friend.

'Too old for scratchings, sorry: my teeth aren't up to it.'

'Sure?'

'Five minutes' worth of scratchings, five hours in the dentist.'

'Did you get the big man, then?'

'Not yet.'

'Because just before you came out of S4C, I had a quick look in the bin and there was nothing there then.'

'And only the cast of the show came within a yard of the bin.'

'You're the detective but it looks to me as if one of the cast is our dealer.'

'I came to the same conclusion. Maybe if he's an actor, he can make his voice sound young.'

'Could be, Dafydd, but he sounded dead young to me. Can I do anything more to help?'

'No thanks, *lanc*, but I'll need the stuff back, ok?'

'Of course. It's safe in my car.'

'Give me a ring when you're at the car, then. Are you driving?'

'Yes. I was thinking of going back to go to the gig in COBRA but Mair's shitfaced, been on it serious.'

Daf had heard that the best gigs were being held in there, in the Rugby Club.

'Can't be as shitfaced as Siôn and Meg. They're safe in Neuadd by now.'

Arwel laughed aloud. Daf was glad he could still enjoy his life, share a simple joke, after the hellish experiences he had undergone.

'Megs is the Ultimate Party Animal: what does Mr Jones make of her?'

'Well, she seems to suit Siôn and that's what matters.'

'Oh Dafydd, what an old romantic you are! It's a "Friends with Benefits" thing, nothing more.'

'You youngsters have some heck of a lot of options these days, *cog*.'

Mair emerged from the front door of the pub, accompanied by a couple of her friends.

'Where's Carys tonight, Mr Dafis?' she demanded.

'Still working when I left the Maes.'

'Hmm.' Mair made a sceptical noise. 'And where is Matt?'

'No idea.'

'You know the song "My Humps" by Shakira, Mr Dafis?'

'Yes, but...'

'It saying in the song about not needing drama. We don't want drama over the 'Steddfod, Mr Dafis.'

'Black Eyed Peas,' Arwel interrupted.

'What?'

'Shakira – "Hips Don't Lie". Black Eyed Peas – "My Humps".'

'Shut your head, Bebb.' Mair pulled her phone out. 'No signal at all. I'll have your phone please, Mr Dafis.'

'Sorry, Mair, but it's a police phone.'

'This is an emergency,' Mair insisted. 'If I can't check that out on Shazam this minute, I'll have to kill this twat.'

Being a sensible young man, Arwel silenced her with a kiss and Mair forgot the dispute for a moment. As Daf was walking away, she called after him:

'You tell Carys, Mr Dafis. No drama.'

Daf was totally confused. He thought his daughter's life was pretty straightforward. She had just finished her exams, had applied to several collages and had been going out with Matt for over a year. So why was Mair trying to warn her? What kind of drama did she mean?

He turned and was startled to see Mostyn Gwydir-Gwynne, MP drinking a half of lager from a plastic glass. He was sitting on the bench outside the chip shop and beside him was Haf Wynne.

'Hello Dafydd,' she greeted him, in her smooth voice. 'Business or pleasure?'

'Work,' he growled. He had no idea why she was in Llanfair at all, let alone why she had decided to choose the company of the MP.

'Thought one should sample the atmosphere, Inspector Davies. Miss Wynne was good enough to volunteer to accompany me.' His English words seemed exotic, out of place.

'You're the native guide are you, Haf?' Daf replied, using his Welsh discourteously. 'You're Tonto and he's the Lone Ranger?' He tried to fill his tone with spite but she smiled as if it was a splendid shared joke.

'I was looking for an excuse to come along, actually,' she answered in her unaccented English. 'So when Mostyn rang ...'

'Like I said, I'm working. Enjoy your evening.' Unreasonably, Daf hated Gwydir-Gwynne for not understanding and, as he walked away, he knew his abrasive attitude was embarrassing: he had let himself down in front of the bastard.

Disappointment, that's what is was. Daf was disappointed in Haf for being the person she always had been, and disappointed in himself for ever having considered that something might have developed between them. She had been a great help to him as he had struggled to solve Jacinta Mytton's murder and when they grew to be friends, Daf knew he was in some danger. He admired her because of her principles; she was extraordinarily clever and sometimes she made Daf feel that his opinion on some subject or another was the most important thing in the world. She herself admitted that her nature was cold. They were particular friends at that time and, when Haf confided in him, he grew to understand her loneliness and the nature of her sexuality. Given that they were intellectually so close, Daf did feel that is was rather cruel to be told that she was starting to thaw, but that it was her client's perfect body which had sparked her dreams and fantasies. In Bryn's opinion, she was a nice girl, and long-headed beyond, but hadn't a bit of go in her, which meant he was not interested in her in the slightest. Daf felt he knew too much about her and not enough: in the past six months, he had been looking for excuses not to visit her in her chaotic, book-filled black and white cottage in Bettws Cedewain, yet he felt guilty to be drawing back from her, given that she was so lonely. He had stepped back from a friendship he felt was not working for either of them and now Mostyn Gwydir-Gwynne had decided to move in. Fucking Tory.

Having a laugh with a friend outside the chip shop on a fine night at the Eisteddfod was a perfectly natural thing to do but Daf, hearing their laughter, assumed he was its target. Bastards. He was so irritated that he almost passed Dyddgu without recognising her.

'How are you, sir?'

Daf had to admit that her use of the word 'sir' went a long way to restoring his equilibrium. A succession of cheerful thoughts ran through his head: he was Daf Dafis, the effective policeman. He recalled the first faint smile on Gwawr's white face and the taste of Chrissie's lips, a woman with Bryn in her bed already who still carried a torch for her sheriff hero. Haf Wynne, Daf decided, could fuck right off.

'Champion thanks, *lodes*, and you?'

'The new campsite is ace. The lady boss is something else, isn't she?'

'She's grand. How's Gwawr?'

'Chrissie's invited her round to watch a film with the kids. I have to say, sir, I'm very glad to have someone to share the responsibility with. She was so flat this afternoon, I didn't know what to do with her. And she's determined not to go home ...'

'Don't worry. Chrissie'll help.'

'I don't have any experience of anything like this ...'

'Experience isn't important, Dyddgu: friendship is.'

Daf was glad to see how sober she was: a hard lesson had been learnt, for the moment, at least.

'You know the guy who was selling the 'shrooms? He's been sitting on the bench by the war memorial for an hour and a half. I've been in the Goat, so I can see through the window: every now and again, he's been going for a bit of a walk in the graveyard.'

'Selling?'

'What if you put a wire on me and I go over and pretend to ask for some more of ...'

'*Lodes*, I haven't got a wire: this isn't *Breaking Bad*. Just go up to him and ask for some more of what you had last night.'

The high wall around the churchyard could be useful at times. If Daf entered the graveyard by the lower gate, he could reach the war memorial, which stood on the outer side of the wall, without being observed. In order to have a credible reason for being in the churchyard, Daf stood like a man about to piss. He heard voices from the other side of the wall.

'Thanks for the stuff last night.'

'Pleasure, *lodes*.' It was a melodious voice, local, and young. Daf was angry.

'Any chance of a bit more?'

'You come for a wander with me now, *lodes*. We'll have a look at that old holy well, always right quiet down there.' Daf hated to hear the delightful local word '*lodes*', a word full of comfort and affection, used in this context.

He heard the upper gate click as it was opened. He opened his flies to pretend to pee but, at once, he heard a loud voice yelling at him.

'And what do you think you're doing, you dirty beggar? This is a churchyard, not a toilet.'

Nev appeared, in his uniform, the perfect image of PC Important catching the bad man.

'Can't you keep quiet, Nev? It's me.' As this was happening, Dyddgu and the mushroom man had slipped out of sight.

'Well boss, you shouldn't be peeing in the graveyard, Eisteddfod or no Eisteddfod.'

'I wasn't having a piss.'

'Then why were your flies open? Is there a girl about somewhere?'

'I was not having a widdle or a shag, I was trying to do a bit of a drug bust.'

'With your trousers open?'

'I was attempting to look natural.'

'Very natural,' said Nev, with a perfectly straight face. 'Not Jewish, then?' Daf did up his zip.

'Oh, ha ha ha. In case you had forgotten, we are Dyfed Powys Police, not *Live at the* fucking *Apollo*. They went that way, a young man and a girl.'

Daf ran flat out through the churchyard towards St Mary's Well. He switched on his torch and saw little things floating on the surface of the dark water, mushrooms which had been thrown into the well. He looked up. A couple were strolling past the public toilets, walking naturally, arm in arm but Daf recognised the girl. Over the years, Daf had needed to chase wrong-doers in the churchyard often enough so he didn't need to worry about where to put his feet on the uneven ground. Fifteen seconds later, he had taken hold of the arm of the young man walking by Dyddgu's side. Nev was following, at a steadier pace.

Daf was looking into a very familiar face. A lad of twenty, a prominent member of the local Young Farmers' Club. A likeable character, full of humour, well known for his performances in every type of light entertainment.

'OK, Ed Mills, don't start up giving me any old bollocks. I was behind the wall when you were having your chat with Dyddgu here.'

'Dyddgu? Fuck of an odd name, Mr Dafis.'

'You ought to know by now: the customer is always right.'

'Very likely.'

'Right you are. You're going to have a little trip down to Pool with me.'

For a second, Ed looked straight into Dyddgu's eyes. 'Why's that, Mr Dafis?'

'Because, *lanc*, you've been selling magic mushrooms. You know it's against the law. I remember you sitting in the back row when I came to give the drugs talk to year eleven.'

'Do you have to charge him, sir?' Dyddgu asked, as if in response to the look Ed had given her.

'I've at least got to have a good long talk with him. You understand that, don't you?'

Dyddgu nodded and stepped back into the shadows.

'Tidy girl, that,' Ed remarked, as if he had just met her at the County Field Day.

'She is, so why have you acted so dull? Selling that crap to a girl like her?'

Ed frowned. 'You know how much those bastard supermarkets are paying for milk, Mr Dafis?'

'Come with me for a chat.'

'What if I don't want to?'

'PC Roberts, can you arrest this lad and take him down to the cells in Welshpool? I've had enough buggering about for one day: I'm going to get myself a lamb burger.'

'Yes, boss. Possession with intent to supply?'

'That's it. Class As. You'll miss the Young Farmers' Entertainment Festival this year, *lanc*. What a shame.'

'OK, OK, Mr Dafis: take me down to Pool then.'

From the door of the Black Lion, music was blaring with a strong bass beat. It felt to Daf like the rhythm of his own failure. He had come to the town that night to catch a powerful drug dealer, and instead he had Ed Broniarth on his hands. Just to put the cherry on the cake, when he returned to his car, someone had clearly had a piss against his back wheel. The Eisteddfod was supposed to be a blast, not a pain in the arse. Daf heard footsteps behind him.

'Do you want me to come down with you, boss? Because there's only me and a couple of PCSOs from Newtown here and ...'

'I'll be fine, Nev, you stop here.'

'Because, if you're reckoning on charging him tonight, you're going to ...'

'Nev, I know how to charge someone, in the name of God! I'm just looking at a bit of a chat tonight: we can sort the paperwork in the morning.'

'OK then.'

Halfway down to Welshpool, he remembered Arwel. The

lad said he had not altered his mood with anything other than alcohol for months, but was it wise to leave him overnight with the Es? But for the moment, Daf had to focus on Ed.

'You're right quiet, *lanc*.'

'I'm better not saying anything, I reckon.'

'Ed, you know me. I've never made a fuss just to have something to keep me busy: you've really landed yourself in the shit.'

'I know, Mr Dafis.'

They lapsed back into silence which lasted until they reached the station; Sheila was still there.

'I didn't know you were working tonight,' Daf remarked.

'Swapped with Nia. She'd got tickets for last Friday and for tonight: Tom and I are doing to the folk thing tomorrow.'

Daf remembered: the Noson Lawen was on tonight and on the previous Friday, the show presented by the local youth theatre. These, together with what Sheila so aptly described as 'the folk thing' were the sell-out shows so it was little wonder that Eira was trying to give tickets away for her theatre performance. Carys had turned down the starring role in the youth theatre production, to Falmai's fury. It was pure hypocrisy, Daf considered: normally, Fal wanted her daughter to concentrate on her A levels but the potential bragging rights generated by Carys' involvement in such a high-profile project were irresistible. Daf smothered a little sigh as he recalled the weeks of rows and grim silences. Falmai was too used to getting her own way but her daughter was developing a strong character of her own. Rhodri, who had a gift for such comparisons, described his mother during this time as being very like the dragon Smaug from *The Hobbit*, willing to destroy everything in order to get her own way. This image lodged in Daf's brain to the extent that, every time Falmai opened her mouth, he was half expecting a burst of flame. Once again, he tried to remember the girl he had fallen in love with but couldn't manage it, somehow. When he saw Sheila, ready to spend hours in a sweaty tent being 'entertained' by things she barely understood just because it was a chance to spend more time with Tom Francis, he was filled with envy. Then he remembered the scent of Gaenor's warm skin when they had kissed by the car: life did move on.

'Sheila, can you do a cup of tea for me and one for the lad as well?'

'Right you are, *cog*.'

'Don't call me *cog*. I'm your boss, so it sounds weird.'

'OK. I am doing my blue.'

'"My blue best" is what we say in Welsh.'

'What you said. I'm doing it.'

When he opened the door into the interview room, Daf relaxed at once. He took off his jacket before sitting down.

'I'm not sure if I should say anything to you before I get a lawyer,' said Ed, still on his feet.

'Fair enough, if that's how things are, I can wait till your 'torney comes, then I'll charge you and you stand a very good chance of a very stiff punishment. Or we can have a bit of a chat now so I get a chance to think overnight which bit of the paperwork I'm going to be doing.'

'Are you saying there's a chance I won't be charged?'

Daf looked directly into his eyes. 'You've been heckish dull, Ed. I didn't think you could be as much of a twat as this. You do understand, don't you?'

'Yeah, I do.'

'If drugs are called Class A, it means they are the most serious type.'

'But they're only 'shrooms.'

'Sit down and tell me the story, *cog*. I'll decide what to do after.'

'Right you are, Mr Dafis.'

After he had settled in his chair and taken a good drink of his tea, Ed looked better. He was still anxious and shaken but there was a trace of the usual spark back in his eye. Daf recalled the last time he'd seen him on the stage, doing a comic song in the Young Farmers' concert. Carys was a rather semi-detached member of the Club, dropping in now and then to sing for them but Ed Mills was the backbone of the club. Daf attempted to remember all the times Ed's name had come up in casual conversation: nothing but good reports.

'I'm going to start with a bit of background, Ed. How old are you, where you live and that.'

'You know me, Mr Dafis.'

'Listen, Ed, I meet thousands of people in this job of mine and I can't keep all their CVs in my head.'

'OK. I'm Ed Mills, Broniarth. I'm twenty years old since last back end and I live with my mum and dad.'

'How do you get on with them?'

Ed grew red. 'This is my shit, Mr Dafis. It's got fuck all to do with Mum and Dad. They've not done nothing wrong.'

'Fair play. Work at home?'

'Yes. And I help over Groeslon right often.'

'You've got enough money in your pocket then?'

Ed started to rip up a scrap of paper which had been left on the desk. 'You know Dad's bad, don't you, Mr Dafis?'

'Yes. MS, isn't it?'

'Yes. Can't barely walk by now, let alone do any work.'

'You do the farm work, then?'

'I try, like. We weren't doing that bad but we haven't a penny free to put into the place. That parlour of ours, it's fit for the Folk Museum down St Fagans. Then the fuckers cut the price of milk, time and again. We're up against it now right enough.'

'But you get a bit of cash from Groeslon?'

'Enough to keep the pick-up on the road, that's all. But I'm not making no excuses. I'm a fuckwit and there it is. What's the worst penalty I could get, Mr Dafis?'

'Class A Possession with Intent to Supply is a real serious charge. Where did you get the stuff?'

'Home. They grow on the *boncyn*.'

'Bit early in the year?'

'Everything's early this year. We had primroses at the bottom of the Crib before the end of the Little Month.'

'Why did you decide to do such a dull thing, Ed?'

Ed scratched at his ear, as if to take attention away from his words.

'Mum's shit with money. She makes a mess of things and in the spring, she got one of them payday loans. Three hundred it was, to pay the electric. Gone up to over two grand by now and they're putting some heck of a lot of pressure on her.'

'That's her responsibility, not yours, *lanc*.'

'I've learnt a lot from Mum and Dad, Mr Dafis. Before Dad was bad, it was grand. Dad chose his wife with his eye, not his brain and she can't manage nothing. I got to keep Dad as well as I can. Stress makes him real bad. So, it's down to me to bring in a bit more money.'

'But there are other ways to make a bit of cash, Ed. You don't have to set yourself up as a drug dealer.'

'I've tried, Mr Dafis. There's no more hours to be had at Groeslon and I asked everywhere else. Tried grading eggs at Dolfadog but I can't do that and milk at home. I had a couple of day's contracting off Chrissie Berllan but she pays shit and docks your wages if you stop for a piss.'

'What?'

'The lads work for her regular say they've got to just open the cab door and piss whilst they're driving. If you stop, she'll dock half an hour off your pay.'

Though Chrissie did have a bad name for being a tough employer, Daf smiled to himself. It was grand to be the only weakness of a tough woman.

'When did you get the idea about selling the 'shrooms, then?'

'I went down to COBRA on Saturday, to the gig they had there. I got to talking with a gang up from Carmarthen and one of them said that if I farmed round here, I'd probably got a kitchen full of 'shrooms. I went on the net when I got home, check up on prices and it was then I reckons I'd got well over a thousand pounds' worth up on the *boncyn*. A few sandwich bags from the Londis, and job's a good 'un, Mr Dafis.'

'So, Sunday night was the first night you were selling, yeah?'

'Yes.'

'And you sold some to Dyddgu?'

'Yes. Her and her friend were going to make some special tea, she said.'

'Do you know what hippy flipping is, Ed?'

'Not a clue.'

'It's when you mix Es and 'shrooms. Some people reckon you'll always have a good trip on the 'shrooms if you take them with Es at the same time.'

'I don't know anything about the business.'

'Which is one good reason not to be so dull as to potch with this type of stuff, Ed.'

'I know.'

'Whatever. That's what Dyddgu and her friend did, a bit of hippy flipping. Her friend was off her face when some man found her.'

'Not Dewi Dolau?'

'How do you know?'

'Everyone's talking about it.'

'I'm not going to talk about that with you but you need to learn what you've done. If she hadn't taken the 'shrooms, that girl wouldn't have been hurt like she was.'

A silence descended like a thick blanket. A nerve below Ed's eye began to twitch.

'It wasn't me who, who ...'

'But it was you gave the stuff to her. Same age as you, she is.'

'Is she alright now, Mr Dafis?'

'No way. And, say the truth, she'll never again be the girl she was before last night.'

'Is that why you're coming after me, then?'

'I'm coming after you, *lanc*, because you're a danger to yourself and to other people, that's why.'

'I never thought about a thing like that ...'

'Don't take me for a fool because I'm speaking tidy to you, Ed Mills. You're nobody's fool. You know very well that people do dull things when they're full up of drugs. Last year, a young man drowned in Welshpool after taking three tabs of acid.'

'But acid is heavy stuff, Mr Dafis. 'Shrooms are just a laugh.'

'They contain a strong hallucinogen. After taking them, people don't know who they are or where they are. That's why they're Class A.' There was no reply. 'How much did you sell, last night and tonight?'

Ed pulled his wallet out of the back pocket of his jeans. 'Eight bags last night, six so far tonight. Here's the money, Mr Dafis. Seven hundred quid. Not enough to ...'

'To pay your mum's debts?'

Ed nodded.

'I still don't get it. Can't your mum go to the bank to get a loan?'

'She never sorts things tidy. She saw some dull advert on the telly when she was watching *Emmerdale*. She rang the number and she was all full of herself because everything had been sorted grand.' Ed's voice had gone quiet: by this time, his voice was not much more than a whisper and tears were not far away.

'You know you can say anything to me, lad, right? Whatever else I do, I'm not one for carrying *clecs*.'

'Mum got an idea, a fucking horrible idea, about the debt. She wanted to loan the money off one of the neighbours.'

'I can see that wouldn't be good for your pride, but it's not that bad an idea.'

'You don't get it, Mr Dafis. Evans the Rhyd has offered her the money, any time. But there's ... terms to the loan.'

'Evans the Rhyd?'

'He's always half-fancied Mum. Dad used to laugh about it but that was before ...'

'Before what?'

'Before he got ill. I been on Google, Mr Dafis. When you got MS, you can't always ...'

'I get it.'

'OK, Evans isn't half the man Dad is but he's sniving with money. So if Mum isn't getting want she wants from Dad ...' He hid his face in his hands, shaking.

'Ssh, *cog*, don't you worry. Your mum is a nice woman: she won't do anything to hurt your dad.'

'But on times, when they're fighting ...'

'Like every man and wife fight.'

'Of course, but lately they're only rowing over one thing, about what happens in bed. It's heckish hard to hear them, Mr Dafis. Then Evans stops by to borrow some bit of kit and they're laughing, him and Mum ...'

'And dealing drugs was your way out of the situation, was it?'

'I didn't reckon I was doing anything that bad. Just selling a bit of local produce to people who'd come the Eisteddfod, that's all.'

'Don't you dare take the piss with me, Ed Mills. Who were your consumers?'

'Students, I reckon. I didn't ask them for ID.'

'They're young people, just like you. Some of them have got shit at home, just like you. And you decided to exploit them.'

'I didn't plant the 'shrooms.'

Daf rose to his feet. 'You know what, Ed? I've heard just about enough. All I'm getting from you is dull excuses. I'm right sorry things aren't grand at home but you got no right to solve your problems by turning someone else into a victim. I'm going to charge you.'

'Please, Mr Dafis. I never been in trouble before.'

'I know that, but I haven't heard a word from you which makes me sure you wouldn't do the same thing again. You're angry about the situation in your family and you're willing to ruthlessly exploit other people to sort things out. Class A Possession with Intent to Supply it is.'

'I'm sorry. I am right sorry.'

'You should be sorry.'

'Say the truth, Mr Dafis, I didn't think it through at all. I saw the things growing wild and I got the dull idea.'

'And what do you think about it now?'

'I can't believe what a wanker I've been.'

'Because you were caught?'

'No. Well, that as well. But what you said, about the girl ...'

'I'm not blaming you for that, Ed but if she hadn't got the 'shrooms off you, she wouldn't have been so wasted.'

'I get it.' A short silence. 'Perhaps, Mr Dafis, the best thing would be if I went to prison for a bit. High time I did a bit of growing up. Can I ring Mum before I go?'

'In the name of reason, *cog*, don't you know anything about the system? Even if I wanted to send you straight to gaol, I can't. The CPS would have to prepare a case, then they'd be a trial, all sorts. And, you know what?' Daf concluded, making his decision.

'What, Mr Dafis?'

'It's all going to be way too much paperwork. I'm going to give you a lift back to Llanfair and in the morning, I'll send the details off to the CPS with a recommendation that we deal with you by giving you a caution. I'm too busy to waste my time standing in a court in Mold telling some judge that you're a fuckwit: that's clear enough already.'

'Thank you, Mr Dafis.'

'But I am going to talk to your parents. They've got responsibilities. Their troubles caused all this hassle.'

'No, Mr Dafis, you can't. Dad can't deal with stress.'

'And how much stress would he have if you got sent to prison? You've got no right to tell me how to deal with a situation like this. I could get your parents pulled in for questioning now, if I like.'

'Sorry ... sorry.'

Daf was furious, with Ed, with himself, with the lack of justice in the world in general. He didn't have much real choice in the matter: a young man like Ed, of previous good character, wouldn't be likely to be given much of a sentence anyway. And, if Daf showed a bit of understanding, Ed would learn that authority was not always a bad thing. Which only added to his fury: the raising of Ed Mills as a decent citizen was not really not his responsibility.

'It's after half nine. Where's your car?'

'I got a lift in. I fancied a couple of pints and I'm not totally dull.'

'Could have fooled me. Right. I'm taking you home and I want you to go straight up to your room, I'm going to speak to your mum and dad, OK?'

'Right.'

Daf had another quiet journey. There was an empty look on Ed's face, as if he'd used up all his words. When they reached Broniarth, there was no car in the yard. The house was in darkness.

'Mum's gone out then,' Ed remarked. 'She was half talking about going to see some film tonight with a couple of her friends. And Dad goes to bed right early these days.'

'I'm glad to hear your mum's got the spare cash to pay for little outings.'

'You know what, Mr Dafis, she's not a bad woman in the bone. Just weak. If she'd married someone like ... Tom Francis Glantanat, or John Neuadd, she'd've been grand.'

'Hmm. Well, you tell her I'll call by to see her tomorrow, right?'

'OK. And ... thanks, Mr Dafis.'

'You've got no reason to thank me, *cog*. And you behave yourself, right?'

'I promise.'

Ed went into the house. Daf caught sight of a Zimmer frame amongst the work boots in the back porch. Dave Broniarth had been five years below Daf in high school. Life, Daf concluded, was a bitch.

Not far off half ten. If Daf stopped by in Llanfair on his way back to Neuadd, he might run into Arwel and get hold of those Es. He drove carefully through the busy street. He stopped for a moment outside the Black but no-one there had seen Mair or Arwel for some time. He turned back to his car; there was someone sitting in the passenger seat. Carys was a little tipsy but nothing in comparison with most of the people enjoying their big night out.

'Any chance of a lift, Dadi?'

'Of course. Good night?'

'I've only just got to Llanfair. I was on the Maes till then.'

'Good company?'

'Great, thanks.'

In the car, with the windows closed, Daf could smell something he did not want to associate with his daughter. That morning, standing close to Bryn, he had smelt it on his body and now it was on the body of his daughter. He had to ask:

'Lot of local people on the Maes?'

'Not that many.'

'Bryn Humphries?'

'They're flat out with the new campsite from what I hear. I had a real good laugh with a gang of people from the stalls. There's a couple of girls from Pwllheli working on a soft toy stall and they are total nutters.'

But, Daf thought, Carys wouldn't have gained that scent on her skin through hanging out with girls from Pwllheli. Carys' phone rang and when she saw the number, her smile widened.

'Hello. Yes, and me ... No, I'll sort that in the morning ... And me: I'm so stoked.'

Stoked? What kind of a word was 'stoked'? Carys had never

used that word before, the English word intruding into her Welsh. Daf recalled what Mair had said about not wanting any drama. He had to ask another question.

'Where was Matt tonight?'

'No idea.'

'Oh. I just thought that maybe ...'

'Dad.' The happy expression on her face had vanished. 'I know what your job is but there's no need for me to get interrogated all the time.'

'Fair play.'

Daf was glad to reach Neuadd. Carys vanished straight up to her room. In the kitchen, Falmai was just finishing making herself a cup of tea: she didn't offer one to Daf. She looked exhausted and low spirited. And why, Daf asked himself? For the good of the bloody vicar? Or to make sure as many people as possible saw her doing what was right?

'Good day?' he risked.

'No, not at all. It's a horrible thing to be working hard in killing heat and hearing so many vile stories about your husband.'

'What kind of stories?' Daf's conscience wasn't clear, of course. All he could think of was how bad the timing was: if they were going to have a massive row, where would he stay? In his car? In his office in the station? In the Eisteddfod Pavilion?

'Oh, and Rhodri's fine, thank you for asking.'

'What do you mean?'

'I was so busy today, too busy to keep an eye on Rhodri but you left me no choice.'

'I was working.'

'Oh yes, your important work.'

'Nobody, not even you, Fal, could expect me to take the lad down to the rape suite with me, especially when you're not doing anything more important than cutting bloody sandwiches.'

'What did you do down at Dolau this morning?'

'It's confidential.'

'Everyone is saying that you decided to close down the campsite there to give a chance for your bit of stuff to make a bit of easy money.'

'What?'

'You kicked the front door down, then you took the computer, to frighten Dewi, but you didn't expect him to kill himself. But that doesn't matter: what matters is that you had a chance to make a bit of pocket money for Chrissie.' For a moment, Daf could not frame any sensible response. 'They say that she's a nymphomaniac, used to having two men in her bed. I didn't expect much of you, Dafydd, but I would have expected some scenario that you could fool yourself was a bit more romantic than being the second man in the orgies at Berllan.' Her eyes were burning with spite and Daf, for a brief moment, wanted to slap her.

'Two things, Fal,' he began, trying to keep the emotion out of his voice. 'Last night, Dewi Dolau raped a girl a few months older than Carys. A nice girl, from a nice family and she'll live with the scars of that crime for the rest of her life. After that happened, I had no choice but to close the campsite. And the second thing – it may be that our relationship has come to an end, but there's no need for you to be so full of spite.'

'You admit to it, then?'

'Admit what?'

'That you've been fucking Chrissie Berllan, like half the parish.'

Conscious that he was at risk of sounding like Bill Clinton, he answered: 'I've never fucked Chrissie.'

'I don't want to imagine what other filthy things you may have got up to with that whore.'

Daf felt angry with Falmai and her prejudice. She clearly didn't know that Chrissie and Bryn, whatever the weather, spent at least an hour a week standing by the grave where Glyn, her first husband and Bryn's brother lay with his eldest son, the weaker twin who died after four days in the special care baby unit. And because Chrissie had survived, had managed to not only live but enjoy life despite the burden of her grief, the respectable women like Falmai hated her.

'You know what, Falmai Jones, I haven't fucked her but have no fear, I will. And this morning, when I was on the lookout for someone kind enough to give a bit of care to a girl who had been hurt, your name never crossed my mind. Whilst you were trimming the crusts off your sandwiches in the name of Jesus Christ, it was Mary Magdalene who was helping.'

'Oh, that's the fantasy, is it? You're the Jesus saving everyone and she's kneeling down and drying your feet?'

'Oh, shut up, Fal. I've been busy. And I know that Dewi Dolau's mother is a big noise in the Merched y Wawr, but her son was a disgusting criminal. Perhaps you could ask her to give a bit of a talk, with slides: How to Raise a Psychopath.'

Fal slapped Daf's face, hard enough to leave a mark. Daf suddenly noticed that Rhodri was standing in the doorway of the kitchen. The boy had a weary look on his face.

'Is it OK for me to have a lift down to the Maes before ten tomorrow, please?' he asked.

'No worries,' answered Daf, remembering immediately that he had agreed to see Mrs Dolau in the hospital.

'I'll be going down before nine,' answered Fal, competitive on even the smallest point.

'I'll go with Dad. And not just down to the Maes. If Dad's off to Berllan, I'll go with him.'

'What do you mean, Rhodri Dafis?'

'You know what, Mum? I'm big mates with Rob Berllan. And Rob is allowed to be himself; no-one pushes him to practise for stuff he never wanted to do in the first place. He's got a trail bike, he shoots clays: he's got a life any amount better than mine.'

Daf could not avoid seeing the effect these words had on

his wife. Her face fell, quivering. Rhodri vanished and a small, hopeless sound escaped through Falmai's pale lips, like a small dog whimpering.

'I'm not going to Berllan, Fal. I don't want to go anywhere.'

'But we can't carry on like this.'

'Fair play. After the 'Steddfod, I'll find a place to live, rent somewhere in Llanfair, maybe.'

'How did this happen, Daf?'

'People change. We got wed when we were only children and as we've grown up, we've grown apart.'

'Cliché, Daf.'

'Something can be a cliché and still true. You think I'm an embarrassment to your family and I don't share your way of life.'

'I've seen a lot of change in you this last year, I have to say. The things which were important to you, like family, don't seem to matter anymore.'

'And what family is that, then? Clearly doesn't include Rhods, does it? You spend all your time running after the eight inch nails, and I've got no interest in your snobbish little games.'

Fal pushed past Daf on her way to the kitchen door and for half a second, he felt the warmth of her body, perhaps for the last time. Through all the passion, he could not help thinking of his major practical problem which was where would he be able to sleep that night? The car would be cold, even in the heat of August. He couldn't think about asking to sleep on the sofa in the bungalow because that would break every law of landlord–tenant relations. He decided to help himself to the Scotch John had offered him earlier and when Gaenor came into the kitchen, Daf was perched on a stool, gripping the glass in the way a drowning man would grip a rope.

'Did you hear ...?'

'I heard enough, Daf. She's so stressed out about the bloody 'Steddfod. You know what the problem is, don't you? She hasn't got any status in the business and she's always in the heart of anything around here. You changed your plans and she feels out of it, as if everyone is running her down for not doing her share.'

'Yet again, all she cares about is what other people think. I've had enough of it.'

'It's a strange time: it affects everyone.'

'Rhodri came down. He's had a bellyful as well.'

'You look so tired. Get to bed.'

'I can't sleep in Fal's bed.'

'And you can't share with John and me. What about cwtching on the sofa? I'll find you a duvet.'

There was plenty of room on the wide sofa. The room was rather cold so Gaenor put a match to the woodburner. Like a man in a trance, Daf watched the flames catch the wood. Gaenor returned with bedclothes and several large pillows – Daf had to admire her purposeful movements. Without saying a word, she left the room. Daf pulled off his trousers and settled down under the duvet. In less than ten minutes, Gaenor returned with a tray and the room filled with the scents of coffee and whisky.

'You need a little nightcap.'

Daf sat up to take the cup from her.

'John was in a strange mood tonight,' she remarked in a conversational tone. Through all the shit, Daf sensed a flash of fun.

'Don't tell me he suggested a different position?'

'How on earth did you know that, Daf? Even the best detective in the world can't know everything.'

The day came to an end in laughter and a long kiss.

'We'd better not make things worse,' muttered Daf.

'What's a drop of petrol, if the house is on fire?' whispered Gaenor in his ear.

Chapter 5

Tuesday

About seven o'clock, it became clear to Daf that Gaenor had decided to raise everyone's spirits with a good breakfast: bacon, eggs, beans, the works. Around the table, everyone was rather quiet. Siôn was still pretty ill but Daf observed Meg's eyes flicking about, taking in the kitchen, the oak dresser, the corner cupboard, the American fridge, the four-oven Aga.

'I am sorry for turning up without an invitation,' she said, giving John her best smile.

'You didn't have a lot of choice in the matter,' Daf said. 'There was no shape on either of you.'

'Where do you come from, *lodes*?' John asked.

'Swansea. Dad teaches art and my mum is the school secretary.'

Falmai lifted her eyes from her plate to glance at Gaenor; even though, in Falmai's opinion, Gaenor wasn't half good enough to have married John, there were occasions when she was obliged to recognise the status of her sister-in-law. Fal was eager to establish what the opinion of Neuadd was towards this new girl – were they, as a unit, to welcome her or give her the cold shoulder? By reputation, Siôn was a bit of a slow starter with the girls, which worried his father, but after hearing about the previous night's gymnastics and Meg's middle-class parentage, Fal could spot potential in her. Daf saw nothing in Gaenor's eyes but her usual kindliness which would, he knew, infuriate Fal.

Falmai only uttered a couple of words at the table and her eyes were red. She didn't look as if she had slept well whereas Daf had enjoyed an unbroken seven hours on the sofa. He had a twinge of guilt which did not last long: it was her decision, not his, to have a row. By contrast, Rhodri was full of life, looking forward to his training session with the Ospreys later. Carys came into the room as everyone was finishing their food, sports bag in her hand.

'No bacon for me, Aunty Gae.'

'Don't you dare say you are on a diet!'

'I've got to keep a bit of control over myself since I'm eating rubbish all day on the Maes.'

'Have you tried those nuts they're selling?' Rhodri asked his sister. 'Candied cashews? They are seriously nice.'

'Yes, and there's about a thousand calories in every nut.'

'You and your calories!' exclaimed Gaenor. Daf observed, not for the first time, the close and easy relationship between Gaenor and Carys. Falmai didn't realise the damage she had done to her relationships with all those around her by her years of nagging and complaining.

'Who fancies an early barbeque tonight, before the Folk Evening?' John offered.

'That would be very nice,' answered Falmai. Daf saw the strain in her eyes: normally, she would be the first person to be making arrangements but she was sitting in passive silence.

'I'm staying with Meilyr tonight,' Rhodri announced.

'Sorry, Uncle John,' added Carys, 'but I'm going off for the afternoon so I don't know what time I'll be back.'

'Off?' Daf asked. 'Off where? And what about the stall?'

'I worked Sunday, so I'm allowed one afternoon off. And I'm not quite sure where. Down to the sea perhaps. Or up Cader Idris.'

'I forgot to say last night, Car: Matt phoned.' Gaenor was usually very good at passing messages but then, Daf recalled with a smile, she had been pretty drunk the previous night.

'Yes? What time?'

'About nine-ish.'

Daf looked at Carys. Her tone of voice was leisurely, like Matt was just one amongst her number of friends, not her boyfriend. Fal seemed to notice nothing. Daf decided he needed to ask Carys a bit more, but not over the breakfast table at Neuadd.

Unexpectedly, there was a knock on the back door and before anyone had a chance to answer it, Gethin strolled in.

'Take pity on me, dear Gaenor. I'm starving to death and the bungalow is full of the smell of your bacon.'

'I seem to recall your mother used to do a grand breakfast,' said Daf, rather irritated by this presumption.

'But only for good boys: she hasn't a crust to share with a sinner like me. And Mans isn't prepared to make me a fry-up because she says I'm fat enough as it is. Bad enough to love an old man, she says, but an fat old man ...'

'Sit down there, you're very welcome, Gethin,' John announced. 'Get him a knife and fork, Gaenor.'

Gaenor obeyed, as if she were the farm maid but she knew how much Daf hated it when John spoke to her like that so she tried to avoid his eye. Daf had had enough of the Neuadd breakfast so he rose to his feet.

'Well, I've got plenty to do today so I'd best crack on. See you all later. Coming with me, *cog*?'

'Yes please.'

'You can wait and come down with me if you like, Rhod,' Carys offered. Once again, Falmai was silent.

'I want to go with Dad, Car.'

Carys bent down to pick up her bag and Daf could not help noticing Gethin admiring her backside. For many reasons, Daf was longing to get away.

'What evening would suit you for a barbeque, Gethin?' Daf heard John's question as he was walking out through the back door, Rhodri at his heels.

'Sure it's not too early for you to go now, *cog*? I've got to be in Gobowen by half ten.'

'It's fine.'

Walking to the car, Daf felt he had to say something. 'Sorry about last night.'

'Mum's so hard to please. She's always pushing us and praising someone else. I never feel she's on our side, or on your side, come to that, Dad.'

'Fair play.'

'Last year, Rob's dad was in some heck of a lot of trouble, but his mum stood by him, didn't she?'

'She did, but Bryn's not Rob's dad, remember.'

'Oh, he is in every way that matters. Anyway, it's not just them who're like that. Think of the care Aunty Gae takes of Siôn. And Meilyr, well, Meilyr's mum is always trying to help him, not bullying him into being someone he isn't.'

'I don't know Meilyr's family.'

'You don't, because I can't have friends over, because of Mum. She runs me down in front of people all the time.'

Daf nodded his head. He found it hard to find suitable words. When they were sitting in the car, Daf suddenly noticed how tall the lad was getting.

'We weren't just talking about Berllan last night, Dad.'

'I'm not going to Berllan.'

'Well, wherever you go, we'd all be better off without her.'

'Thanks for being plain with me, *lanc*. I've got no idea what to do next but of course you can come with me, wherever I go.' There was a short silence.

'Have Matt and Carys finished?'

'No idea, Rhod. Why do you ask?'

'He phoned several times last night. I like Matt.'

'And me, but we don't have to do the courting with him, remember.'

As he left his son by the Maes, Daf could not help feeling positive. At last, the iron framework of the Neuadd family had started to crumble and, as a result, anything was possible. Yet the sourness of his conversation with Falmai the previous night seemed to run through his veins as he travelled to the orthopaedic hospital. How many people, over the years, had been poisoned by the traditional values, the tight net of rules which was administered by the mothers of the district, people like Falmai and Mrs Griffiths Dolau? How many people had been crushed? Those who weren't lucky enough to be as tough or bloody-minded as he was himself, people like Dewi Dolau. He was ready for a battle when he reached the hospital but, when he saw the little woman in the high bed, his anger dissipated. She wasn't a symbol of oppression but an old woman who had just lost her only son.

'Mrs Griffiths?'

'Defi Shop? I remember you very well. You've grown tall.'

'Dafydd Dafis. I've come from the police.'

'Your grandfather was a tall man, if I remember right.'

'How was the treatment, Mrs Griffiths?'

'A lot more painful than I expected. They say I'm nearly ready to go home, but how can I go from here without anyone at home to do the work?'

'Social Services will put a package together to ...'

'Are Social Services handy at second cut of silage?'

'They're there to help you get back on your feet.'

'And what then? Boots on, and straight out to the yard?'

'You'll have to find someone to help you with the work.'

'And how can I come across a farm labourer when I'm as lame as this?'

'I know a right steady lad in need of a bit of work. Local to you, he is.'

'Who, then? I'm not willing to give a minute of work to that lot at Berllan: they work all through the night, their pop music blaring out.'

'What about Ed Mills?'

'Ed Broniarth?'

'Yes. I heard on the grapevine that money's a bit tight there since his dad's been poorly.'

The old woman shifted her weight in the bed. Her skin was like paper. Her face gave no indication that she was about to change the subject completely. 'I wasn't young having him, you know. Over forty.'

'I see.'

'You don't see at all. Hard to have him, hard to raise him. His dad said one time, if he'd had a calf like that, the calf would have met the shovel in no time. Like the English say, put it out of its misery.' A cold shiver ran down Daf's spine. A woman speaking of her son without any smic of tenderness in her voice. 'His father used to make an account every quarter: how much he'd cost us in food and clothing and how many hours of work we got out of him. Most times, he just managed to pay his way.'

'Mrs Griffiths, do you know what happened yesterday?'

'Of course I know. You sent some girl over to tell the tale.'

'How much of the story have you heard? You do know Dewi's dead?'

'Shot himself in my kitchen, I was told.'

'What did the PC tell you about what had happened earlier?'

'Some nonsense about a girl. Dewi had never been near any girl.'

'Unfortunately, Mrs Griffiths, that isn't true. When I arrived at Dolau yesterday morning, there was a girl on the sofa, completely out of it and Dewi had ...' Daf saw no shock or pain in the eyes of the old woman so he decided to speak bluntly. 'Dewi had raped her, Mrs Griffiths, and I arrested him.' No response. 'It's not a nice story, I know that, but you have a right to know the truth. Especially when your home is the crime scene.'

Mrs Griffiths coughed like a cat with a fur ball in its throat. 'It isn't a nice story at all, Defi Shop. And that's your job, is it? Going round looking for trouble?'

'The other way about, Mrs Griffiths. I try to stop the trouble happening, if I can. This time, I couldn't.'

'Hmm. Whatever, you've been courteous enough to come to see me to tell me face-to-face that my son was a rapist. Are you sure he did it?'

'I'm sure, Mrs Griffiths. And after we had the report back from forensics, there's no doubt at all.'

'I'm surprised – I wouldn't have said he had enough go in him to attempt any such thing.'

Even after hearing the whole dreadful story, she would neither defend her son nor grieve for him and Daf was reminded of Rhodri's description of his mother's attitude, always wanting him to be someone else, never on his side. Mrs Griffith's observations didn't warrant any reply.

'I've got to go, Mrs Griffiths.'

'Is there a mess in the house?'

'After we are sure there is no more evidence to be had, we'll arrange to have the place cleaned.'

'Get out of here, Defi Shop; I've had enough of your nonsense.'

Relieved to be able to escape into the open air, Daf repeated her words. His nonsense was bothering her? At least she hadn't attempted to put any blame on Gwawr. Daf considered Dewi's family and his upbringing: was it enough to create a rapist? That self-satisfied old bitch wasn't willing to take any responsibility and people like her were the public face of the area it was his duty to protect.

Unfortunately, another mother who wasn't shouldering her family responsibilities was the next person on Daf's list. He had to go to Broniarth to have a talk with Ed Mills' parents. As he drove past, window open, he saw a busy scene in the field at Berllan and smelt bacon and good coffee. Daf knew himself well enough to know that he was just making an excuse to drop by and have a word with Dyddgu after the events of the previous night in Llanfair. The moment he turned over the cattle grid, he saw what he had wanted to see: Chrissie. She was wearing her overalls and was running down to the stand-pipe in the corner of the field, her tool bag swinging from her hand. When she saw Daf, she yelled over her shoulder:

'With you in a minute, Mr Dafis – just got to get this water sorted.'

Enchanted by her competence, Daf gazed at her as she changed the tap, not noticing that Bryn was standing by his elbow.

'Bloody great, isn't she?' Bryn observed. 'She can sort any shit under the sun.'

Daf smiled, without admitting that more than the tap had been fixed; after quarrelling with Falmai and sampling the family poison of Dolau, Chrissie had managed to raise the black cloud of negativity which had settled over him.

'Mr Dafis,' Bryn began, in a low voice. 'I know Chrissie fancies you. She's a grand girl, champion, and if you feel like going with her, don't think twice about me. She's been that good to me over the years, she deserves a bit of a spree.' For the second time in a few hours, Daf was groping without success to find words. 'We had a right nice night last night with the girl ... Gwawr last night. Watching films with the kids first, then she and Chrissie went through into the back room and had a fair bit of a talk over a bottle of Baileys.'

'All OK?'

'Never going to be OK, is it, Mr Dafis, but as good is it can be, maybe.'

'Oh, I haven't had a chance to congratulate you on your good news.'

'Grand, isn't it? Twins as well.'

'You've got make sure Chrissie spends enough time resting, putting her feet up.'

'I'll do my blue best, Mr Dafis, but she's not much of a girl for resting.' On cue, Chrissie approached them, wiping her wet hands on the body of her boiler-suit, which had several of the front poppers strategically unpopped.

'Just checking all is well with our campers, Chrissie.'

'Champion, Mr Dafis. I'm not expecting to see Gwawr too early: she had a good old sesh on the Baileys last night.'

'Thanks for keeping an eye on her.'

'She's a grand girl, lovely.'

'Glad to hear it. Now, I've got to be off.'

'Not stopping for a cup of tea, Mr Dafis?'

'Not this morning, Chrissie.'

'See you soon then, Mr Dafis.'

The Broniarth farmhouse stood on a choice spot on a shelf of land above the valley floor, which kept it clear of floods whilst still within the shelter of the rising ground. Even though he did not have a scrap of interest in agricultural topics, Daf had spent enough time in the company of men like John Neuadd and Tom Francis to know at first glance that Broniarth was not a successful farm. The place needed both money and care, though Daf could observe that someone was still making an effort. The yard, for example, had been recently scraped and several sheets of corrugated metal had been delivered, destined to repair the roof of the *bing*, which looked as if it would not see another winter through. Last night, if Daf was honest about it, he had been looking for a living person to blame for what had happened to Gwawr but now, in daylight, surrounded by the evidence of Ed's lonely hard work, he was glad he had not been too heavy-handed. Ed was a young man who had made a mistake under the pressure of responsibility.

Daf knocked on the door. He had to wait for several minutes before the door was answered by a woman of his own age, good looking but rather on the skinny side, in Daf's opinion. From her choice of clothes and her heavy make-up, she did not look like what Daf's mother had always referred to as a 'handy woman on the yard'.

'Mrs Mills? Dafydd Dafis, Dyfed Powys Police.'

'Is Ted alright? Has he had an accident?'

'No-one has had an accident but I've got to have a bit of a chat with you, about your son, Ed.'

'Ed? What has he done?'

'I'd rather not discuss the matter on the doorstep, Mrs Mills.'

The interior of the farmhouse had been neglected rather

more than the yard and buildings. Daf thought, perhaps rather unfairly, that if Mrs Mills had chosen to dedicate all the hours she spent every week painting her face to painting the walls instead, the effect might have lasted a lot longer. She opened the door of the office for him, which was little more than a cupboard with a desk and computer in it, with files all over the place. Daf expected to be offered a cup of something but no such offer was made.

'Last night, in Llanfair, we caught Ed selling mushrooms.'

'Without a licence to sell food? I would have thought that was a food safety issue, not to do with the police.'

'They weren't ordinary mushrooms: they had powerful hallucinogens in them. They are sometimes called magic mushrooms.'

'Sorry, Mr Dafis, but you have made a mistake. Ed has never gone within a mile of any type of drugs.'

'I'm not saying that he took them but he was selling them.'

'It doesn't make any sense at all. There's definitely a mistake somewhere.'

'I heard him offer mushrooms to a girl of his own age and since then, he has confessed.'

Mrs Mills shut her eyes for long moments, as if she hoped to open them and find that the whole situation was only a dream.

'I ... I'm not very good in situations like this. We'd better wait until Ted gets back from his physio.'

'No-one is good in a situation like this, Mrs Mills.'

'But Ted is that much more ...'

'According to Ed, your husband is a sick man and stress makes his condition worse.'

'And what about the effect the strain has on me?'

'You don't suffer from MS, Mrs Mills. And whatever, I don't have enough time to wait for him: I intend to discuss Ed with you now.' Daf observed a change in her attitude as she saw there was no way to avoid the reality any further.

'Is he ... going to prison?'

'I don't intend to charge him. The Crown Prosecution Service will make the final decision but I reckon he's learnt his lesson.'

'I hope he has. What a dull thing for him to do. Has he told you why ever he did such a thing?'

'He needed money.'

'To buy a new car?'

'No, Mrs Mills. To pay your payday loan.' Again, she changed her expression completely and guilt filled her eyes.

'What did ... what did you say?'

'Ed is a tidy lad. He would never do such a foolish and dangerous thing without a very good reason. Your money troubles had frightened him and he was prepared to go to prison to help you.'

'I don't know ... I didn't...'

'We're talking about your son, Mrs Mills, not you. If I decide to recommend an official caution instead of prosecution, I have to be sure that he's not likely to do anything like this again.'

'I'm certain he's learnt his lesson, Mr Dafis.'

'And how can you be so sure, given that you haven't discussed it with him? To make sure he doesn't go down that line again, we'll need a close relationship between the authorities and your family. So, this is the question I'm asking and I'm expecting an honest answer from you, Mrs Mills: are you willing to help Ed or not?'

'Of course I am.'

'There's no 'of course' in cases like this, Mrs Mills and I have to say that I'm not that impressed with your response. Just now, you were mad keen on passing the responsibility for Ed onto his dad who isn't in a fit state to care for him. So, I'm going to ask the question again: are you personally ready to work together to help Ed?'

'I'm glad to have the chance to help him.'

'And you should be glad, Mrs Mills. In my opinion, the first step would be to get your finances into a bit of shape.'

'But since Ted's been ill, things have been ...'

'I've heard the whole story. I'm not a debt counsellor but there is plenty of help available. You've got to make Ed less anxious.'

'I understand. I've got a friend who could help, maybe.'

'What about a member of the family? Ed's right worried about ... well, about the strength of your marriage under all this strain and if you try to sort things out by asking for money off some man, the lad will be frantic.'

Mrs Mills rose to her feet and attempted to gather together every last scrap of dignity and self-respect.

'You've got no right to come into my house and lecture me,' she announced.

'Mrs Mills, I couldn't give a damn about your private life but the way you act affects your son and he's likely to be selling Class As in my patch again if you don't listen to me and change your ways. That's all. I don't care if you lend money off half the parish but can you please make sure your lad acts tidy, please?'

Her mood changed again and black mascara-coloured tears ran down through the powder on her cheeks. Daf had the strong impression that she was expecting him to put his arm around her but he was too familiar with attempts to influence him to feel the slightest temptation. He was more attracted to strength and competence than slightly staged weakness.

'Oh, Mr Dafis,' she breathed, in a voice he was supposed to find sexy but didn't. 'I've got so much on my plate and I'm so alone.'

'Talk things over with your family, Mrs Mills: I've got work to do.'

Crossing the yard, Daf laughed as he thought of her trying to flirt her way out of trouble, and not for the first time, he suspected. He'd have to come back to talk things over with her husband at some point: MS or no MS, Dave Mills would be of more use to Ed than his mascara-streaked wife.

Daf heard an unexpected sound: a tractor moving on the *boncyn*. It was too late for first cut silage, too early for second cut and too steep for fodder crops or rape. He glanced up: someone was turning the sloping ground with a deep plough, the furrows tracing the contours. Peculiar time to be ploughing, Daf thought, especially turning grassland. He screwed up his eyes to focus in the strong morning sun and recognised the shape of Ed in the cab, ploughing the mushrooms deep into the brown earth, putting temptation out of his way. On the lane, Daf opened the car window and raised his hand and the tractor's horn hooted a response. Daf seldom felt like he was doing his job well but as he watched the rich soil cover the 'shrooms, he marked down one little victory.

His positive feeling didn't last long: he had to sort out the other supplier, the person who had somehow managed to make his connection under Daf's nose the previous day. It was no good being glad to see the 'shrooms buried if there were still Es to be had. He pulled over into a gateway and sent the dealer a text: it was easy enough to make the second bargain. He asked for something a bit stronger this time, two hundred pounds' worth of snow. The same pattern as yesterday was suggested, with the goods to be collected after the final Cyw show. Daf decided he needed to speak to Gwion very soon, but not until the second exchange had been accomplished.

Flashing his ID at the entrance wasn't such a buzz this time. The stewards in the car park were expecting him and the reception area was so busy that the volunteers barely glanced at him, leaving him with the feeling that he hadn't really challenged the authority of the Eisteddfod at all. He reached into his pocket for the little butterfly badge: for months, a local group had been selling them in memory of one of the most well-loved figures in the district, to be worn on the Eisteddfod Field. He pulled it out and put it on his lapel with pride, despite the bent wing, a symbol not just of a man like no other but also of all that was good about his square mile.

On days like this, when the sun was strong before ten o'clock, Daf easily lost track of time, relying on his stomach to tell him the hour. He was starving when he reached the Maes so he assumed that it was lunch time but when he checked on his phone, it was after two. Late enough to catch Arwel by the bar, perhaps. On his way to the Food Court, he passed by Carys' stall and happened to hear the owner chatting to a friend:

'... No, she's taken the afternoon off, gone off somewhere. And, of course, I have to let her go for all the ceremonies.'

'But don't forget, Enid,' the friend replied, 'it's such an honour to think the Virgin of the Vale works on our little stall – top notch PR.'

'Definitely, and she's such a great girl, as well.'

Daf's mum had always said that you should never eavesdrop for fear of hearing something you wished you hadn't heard but he was delighted to hear them praising Carys. She'd always been a good girl and perhaps, by now, she didn't always have to tell her dad just where she was going.

As on the previous day, the bike stall was busy. Three men of Daf's own age were seriously examining expensive bikes and half a dozen children were hanging about, trying to fill up a long day on the Maes.

'Where's Garmon?' a boy in his early teens asked the man who had offered Daf the drink the previous day.

'Gone for a little spin. He's got a new wheelchair, the ATW Extreme X8, and he fancied going up Cader Idris.'

'You can't go up Cader Idris in a wheelchair,' the boy responded, somewhat cheekily.

'Garmon doesn't know the meaning of the word "can't",' came the reply, as if it were a slogan. That was a co-incidence, Daf thought, that Garmon and Carys had decided to go for a jaunt on the same afternoon. Fair play to the lad: Daf would be out of breath before he got to the top of the mountain, never mind about getting up there in a wheelchair. He had just turned round the end of the row of stalls when he heard the end of the conversation from the bike stall.

'Has Garmon been up Cader before?'

'Never. He was very stoked about it this morning.'

Stoked. Carys had used the same word last night. Another co-incidence. But of course, language was contagious amongst young people. Easy enough for Carys to pick up a bit of vocabulary from the gang on the stall next door.

Yesterday, Daf had not even noticed the North Wales Police stall but it was a substantial presence on the Maes, with eye-catching boards telling parents about the tell-tale signs of drug use and warning about the death toll on the area's roads. Just coming to the end of a talk on the use of new technology in modern policing was an old friend of Daf's from Caernarfon, Meirion Martin. Daf immediately thought about Falmai: she had prejudiced views about gays and therefore, to wind her up, Meirion tended to turn his behaviour dial to maximum camp when she was around. Meirion was a highly effective officer but, like Daf, had a tendency to be a bit of rebel. In his hand was a tiny camera.

'What you got there, Mei?' Daf asked him.

'Great little bit of kit, *cont*. Wi-fi camera. You set it up somewhere, then you can watch the pictures on your laptop, or even on your phone.'

'Can I lend it off you?'

'What for?'

'I want to get a hold of whoever's selling Es on the Maes. I did a shit stakeout yesterday and the dealer got away.'

'Sounds good to me – proper police work: I've had a bellyful of show and bloody tell. Shall I record your pictures on my laptop?'

'Spot on. And we can have a pint later?'

'Definite. Remember though, Daf, a nifty thing like this doesn't come cheap and buying a replacement would probably be a year's total budget for you sheep shaggers.'

'I'll take care.'

It took five minutes to hide the little camera in an old chip box and to put it in place. Daf nipped back to Meirion to check it was working and the pictures of the area behind the S4C building were visible on the screen of his laptop.

'Thanks for this, Mei. Can you put the pictures on a memory stick?'

'Yes, or you can borrow the laptop if you like. But don't look too closely into the pictures in my folders. I've just got back from Stiges and there were sights worth seeing there, I can tell you. I wouldn't want your good lady wife to see the pictures I had taken grooving down amongst the party boys.'

'I didn't think you'd got a colour like that in Tywyn.'

It was great to be working with Mei, Daf thought, as he headed to the Food Court. It was also great to think how unlikely it was that Mei would ever suffer from Falmai's spite and prejudice again. How many of his friends, colleagues or neighbours had suffered her scorn over the years? From now on, Daf would not have to apologise or try to explain her unforgivable conduct. He filled his lungs with the pure air of freedom. Well, freedom, stale beer, dust and onions, anyway.

Just like the day before, Lord Gethin was holding court, with his followers heaping flattery and praise upon him, as he deserved. Daf raised his hand from afar: he was keen to stay well clear of that atmosphere. He would rather spend his time with those who were buying and selling drugs than spend time with Gethin and his followers. And, as he had said, Arwel was waiting by the lamb-burger van.

'I'm not happy wandering about with a pocket full of Es,' he said.

'Give them to me.'

Arwel swallowed the last mouthful of his burger, put the paper napkin into his pocket, pulled it out and offered it to Daf. Daf put the paper in his pocket: he did not need to look to know what was inside because he could feel the little plastic bag.

'Mair's worried about Carys,' Arwel declared, changing the subject radically without a thought. 'She reckons a big break-up is in the offing.'

'I never stick my nose in things like that.'

'Nor me, but Matt keeps ringing me, asking if I know what's going on. Where is she today, for example?'

'I don't know but I do know that it's not a good idea for Matt to keep moithering her.'

'Good advice, but I can't see him listening to anyone.'

'Thanks for your help, Arwel.'

'Fine but I don't like being mixed up in shit like this. I've changed. I was thinking about that last night when I heard people saying that Ed Mills had been caught selling. It's a mug's game and there's plenty enough fun to be had in life with girls and beer and a bit of music: like the song says, the Drugs don't work.'

'Ed'll be OK, don't worry. He's a tidy lad in the bone.'

'You can see people right clear, can't you, Mr Dafis?'

'That's my job, *lanc*, but I've buggered things up time and again by getting people wrong. Big style at times. It's part of life.' And he was thinking of the mistake he had made by not realising that the sexy, bright girl from the big farm he married would turn in time into a snobbish version of the dragon Smaug.

Five minutes later, he saw his biggest ever misjudgement coming out of the Churches Together tent, three large cake tins in her arms.

'Fal,' he called, in the gentlest voice he could muster. 'You're looking busy.'

'Yes. I've got a lot to do.' Daf looked at his watch: there was still half an hour to go before the end of the Cyw show. He had to say something.

'Have you got time for a cup of tea?'

'No. I can't drink a cup of tea whilst I'm cutting cakes.'

'OK. But I want to talk to you. Talk properly, I mean.'

'I'm not sure what we've got left to say to each other, to be honest, Dafydd. You said it all last night: we've come to the end. There's not much point in going further.'

'Do you remember that time when we took Carys down to the rehearsal for the Young Farmers' National Choir in Builth? You saw the No Through Road signs but I thought I knew better. Had to stop the car when we got to a river with no bridge though, didn't I?'

'I remember.'

'There wasn't any way of going ahead but I turned into the field, found a place we could ford the river and off we went. Well, maybe it's like that now. There's no clear road ahead but maybe we can find another way around? Another, different way of moving on?'

'I honestly don't know, Dafydd. I'm trying to be positive but ... it's as though you decided a couple of years ago to give up on your marriage to look for things you found more exciting. Your face was always in the paper and everyone always saying how clever you are. And me? I was trying to teach years three and four, like I always do. Looking forward to the Urdd Eisteddfod every year because there's nothing in my life more exciting or interesting than that. I thought you might be more contented, things might be better if we had some more fun together, like we did going about with Tom and Sheila but ...'

'If you're depending on Tom Francis to save our marriage, I'm going to have to disappoint you on that one.'

'There's always such an edge in your voice when you're talking to me, had you noticed? You're so kind to everyone else and people say that you're so patient and honest and full up to the top of wonderful principles but I get nothing from you but scorn.'

It suddenly seemed very surreal to Daf to be having this conversation with a woman with three cake tins under her arm.

'OK, OK, fair enough. By now, I reckon we know each other

too well. We know just how to hurt each other.'

'And do I deserve to be hurt, Daf?'

One thing Daf couldn't stand was self-pity.

'Oh no, Princess Neuadd, bad things should never happen to you! You should just sit in your great big house, feet up on a pile of subsidy cheques, talking about nice things with nice people and drinking your tea from a cup and saucer while everybody else is dragging themselves through the shit, covered in sweat and blood. You deserve the best, then go back to it and leave me in peace.'

It wasn't Fal who had been widowed at thirty in a stupid accident. Fal wasn't the woman from Neuadd weeping her years away as baby after baby slipped out of her womb. Even her bloody grandparents were still alive. Compared with many other people, Fal had enjoyed a fortunate and privileged life but she was still complaining all the time. The only thing they had in common, by now, were the children. And the fact that they were both wearing the little butterfly badges.

In purely practical terms, a row took up less time than a reconciliation, and Daf had to get after this dealer. After his failure the previous day, he decided to keep his distance and watch the whole thing on Meirion's computer. He went round to the S4C building and, studiously calm, he dropped the two hundred pounds in the rubbish bin. On his way back to the North Wales Police stand he saw several familiar faces: it was clear that the Chief Constable's Official Reception had been a big success. That was a nice irony: all the big cheeses sipping wine, nibbling snacks and talking policing whilst people like Daf and Meirion were actually out there doing the job.

At the back of the stand, Mei had prepared things very well for him, with the laptop on a little table, chairs and, better than anything else, two mugs of good tea.

'If you want another cuppa, ask Betsan.' A WPC came in through the canvas partition, a young woman with a lovely smile and a spark in her eye which lit up her face.

'No-one gets to ask me for a cup of tea just because I'm a girl. Sexist, that's what it is, plain sexist.'

'I can't be sexist,' Meirion protested. 'Gay people can't be sexist.'

'Help me out, Inspector Dafis. The fact that he's the Only Gay in the Police Station doesn't mean he can get away with disrespecting women, does it?'

Daf grinned before answering. 'Even though the code of conduct doesn't allow for such things, almost every word which comes out of his dirty mouth is an insult to someone.'

Outside, the number of children between the rows of stalls had suddenly increased. That could only mean one thing: the Cyw show had come to an end. Daf looked at the screen. Clearly, he could see a member of the cast leave the back of the building through the back door dressed as Fireman Sam's friend, Norman Price. He strolled over to the bin, threw something into it then, as though he had made a mistake, reached in and scrabbled about for a moment. He picked up a little envelope and moved out of the narrow range of the camera shot.

'Norman Price selling charlie on the Eisteddfod Field?' sighed Meirion. 'Is life worth living anymore?'

'You make sure everything here's been saved: I'll get after our little friend.'

It doesn't take much to create panic by running through a dense crowd of people so Daf strode quickly, cursing the fact that he was surrounded by people moving at a snail's pace. It took him several minutes to reach the bin. Taking care not to leave finger prints, Daf picked up the packet of white powder. He tasted the contents. Not just coke, but good coke. He followed the direction Norman Price had taken but he hadn't gone ten yards before he tripped over half of a foam suit. Even inside out, it was easy enough to recognise them for what they were: the trousers of Norman Price.

Arwel's words came back to Daf: hiding in plain sight. No face, no voice: anyone might be hiding behind the familiar smile. Daf picked up the costume and noted that the sweat had soaked deep into the spongy fabric: enough for DNA, perhaps? In the meantime, it was high time to have a little talk with Gwion.

The lad who was selling plastic nick-nacks in the S4C building had clearly had a bellyful of the crushing heat.

'We're closed' he mumbled, not raising his head from his bucket of Sali Mali key rings.

'Dyfed Powys Police. I want to speak to a man who works here: Gwion.'

'He's gone.'

'Where?'

'I don't know. Gone for a pint maybe? Or back to his B and B.'

'Have you got a mobile number for him?'

'Yes.'

The phone rang several times before a tired voice answered. 'Gwion Morgan.'

'Mr Morgan, Dafydd Dafis from Dyfed Powys Police here. I need to have a word with you.'

'What?'

'I want you to come round to the North Wales Police stand right now. Where are you staying?'

'Pandy Newydd Farm. But why do you want to talk to me?'

'In connection with a number of serious crimes we are investigating. I expect to see you within the next ten minutes.'

Next, he rang Nev.

'Nev, can you get a couple of people to go over to Pandy Newydd? Nothing to do with the family there but one of the presenters from S4C is stopping there and I reckon there'll be more snow there than you'd find in St Moritz.'

'Right, boss. And we've had a call reporting that someone's left the Maes after six pints, driving.'

'Got the reg?'

'Yes.'

'Blues and twos then, Nev. Zero tolerance, Eisteddfod or no Eisteddfod.'

As he told Meirion the tale of Norman Price's trousers, Daf saw the funny side. Betsan wrinkled up her nose as she picked up the costume.

'Nice,' she remarked, sealing the trousers in an evidence bag.

'Handy that you've got evidence bags. Were they a prop for a talk or something?' Daf asked.

'Yes,' Meirion replied. 'Thank God we were here because you sheep shaggers can't manage without us.'

'You know what, Meirion Martin? We may be a bit fond of our livestock round here but if you look at the police performance figures, year after year, we knock you boys right out of the park.'

Gwion walked in, treading lightly as if walking on glass. Betsan showed him into the back of the stand and closed the canvas flap.

'Right then, Gwion Morgan, what's this?'

'I don't know.'

'I'm Inspector Dafydd Dafis, Dyfed Powys Police and this is Detective Sergeant Meirion Morgan from North Wales Police. We think this is cocaine and we also think you're going to be looking at five years inside.'

'I've never seen it before. What is it? Some bag of white powder?'

'Charlie. C. Snow. Peruvian Marching Powder. Coke. I don't care what words you use to describe it. I would describe it as Class A, which means you're facing the most serious type of Possession with Intent to Supply.'

'Possession? It doesn't belong to me. I haven't ...'

'OK, Mr Morgan,' Meirion broke across in a gentle, caring voice. 'What if Mr Dafis tells the story and you just listen for a minute, hey?'

'What story?'

'You received a phone call yesterday afternoon, from this number,' Daf explained, showing his phone to Gwion. 'Verbally, you agreed to sell Es to a young man and arranged to leave them in the bin outside the rear door of the S4c building.'

'Es? I don't know anything about Es.'

'You put the Es in the bin and someone came to collect them, leaving the money there instead. Somehow, you managed to pick up the money without me seeing you and then sent a text, checking with your customer that all was fine. If I ring the number I used yesterday, we'll hear your phone ring.' Daf pressed the button. There was no sound.

'Put your phone on the table, now.'

Gwion pulled his phone out of his pocket. Daf called the dealer's number again. No sound. Meirion picked up Gwion's phone and pressed a couple of buttons.

'07773057661.'

Daf closed his eyes for a moment. The wrong bloody number.

'Give me the number, Inspector,' Betsan put in. 'I'll get it traced now.'

'OK, Gwion,' Daf began, taking another tack. 'How long have you been taking coke?'

Daf saw the shock spread across the young man's slackly handsome face and he answered in a very low voice: 'Since I was in 6th Form, at Taff Castle.'

'And how much of a habit have you got by now? Three hundred a week?'

The young man's astonishment had faded into a limp acceptance that Daf knew everything about him, somehow.

'Less than that. Two fifty, less very often.'

'Less because you can't afford to buy all you want to use?'

'Yeah, all right.'

'And what is the best way of keeping yourself happy? Doing a bit of selling instead of always being the one doing the buying, right?'

'I can't do that.'

'Oh, don't you take me for a fool, Gwion *bach*. You're not the angel in the school nativity play now, you know.'

'I'm telling the truth, Mr Dafis. I can't sell because ... because no-one trusts me. I would be lying if I told you that it hadn't crossed my mind but I'm not well organised enough to sell Sali Mail sun visors, let alone coke.'

Looking at Gwion shaking in his chair, Daf began to take pity on him.

'How old are you, *lanc*?' he asked. Meirion glanced at Daf in surprised: he had never before heard him use the word '*lanc*' when talking to a suspect.

'Twenty-six.' Young enough to change, old enough to have done a fair bit of harm.

'High time you said goodbye to the charlie then, isn't it?'

'Very likely.'

'There's any number of people who can help you, you know. People who know their stuff.'

'Yeah, I know that.'

'But you've got to want to change, you get that, don't you? And you can promise me that it wasn't you who was selling?'

'I've never sold in my life.'

'OK. We're going to need a bit of DNA and your finger prints.'

'No worries.'

Daf's phone rang.

'Boss,' Nev declared, 'there's enough snow in the front bedroom at Pandy Newydd to run a fair old downhill slalom.'

'Thanks, Nev.' Daf set his phone down on the table in front of him. 'One of my colleagues has just found a shed load of cocaine in your room.'

'I said to you, sir. I do use coke. But using and dealing's not the same thing.'

'But why did you need so much?'

'If you can do ten nights at the Eisteddfod without any form

159

of artificial stimulants, fair play to you. I can't.'

'There's another reason for you needing a bit of extra money, isn't there, Gwion?'

'What are you talking about?'

'Manon's a girl with a taste for the good things in life.'

'Manon?'

'Don't act dull, Gwion. You're dull enough without putting it on. Your girl left you for a rich man.' No reply. 'So, if you could make a little fortune on the sly, you could be the one buying the nice things for her, the world's gold and little pearls?'

'Maybe, except, like I said, I can't deal. And I've never been able to.'

'Were you sweating in that Norman Price suit?'

'Yes, I hate the bloody thing.'

'So, after the show, you pulled it off at once?'

'Whenever I have to wear it. I haven't had the Norman Price kit on since the Christmas show three years ago.'

'You were wearing it this afternoon.'

'No I wasn't. I'm Hoppy Happy Hare.'

'What?'

'Who's the hare who's kind and good, Who's always dancing through our wood?' interrupted Betsan, singing rather sweetly. 'My nephew's favourite character.'

'Well done, girl, you're a loss to the stage,' responded Meirion.

'So who was in the Norman Price suit, then?' Daf asked.

Gwion frowned. 'Gethin Teifi's little bastard. Peredur Teifi.'

'How old is he?'

'I don't know. Year seven or eight, something like that.'

'Why did you call him a bastard?'

'Because he is a little bastard. I've never met such an arrogant child. Insolent little fucker.'

'Why did you give him the job, then?'

'Oh, Mr Dafis, it's not the Hoppy Happy Hare who makes the decisions on staffing.'

'But Gwion, we've got footage of whoever was in the Norman Price costume leaving the bag of cocaine in the bin.'

'He's an annoying kid, not a dealer.'

'Someone could have borrowed his suit. You, for example.'

'With the greatest respect, Mr Dafis, you've seen the size of that costume and you've seen the size of my arse. My Norman Price days are long gone.'

'Point taken. I think it would be a good idea if you backed away from the children's programmes for a bit.'

'Why?'

'Because you're coked up to your ears, *lanc*.' There was a long silence. 'Did you see the Teifi boy getting changed?'

'He went straight out in his costume. I stayed to get a drink of water.'

'How well do you know Peredur?'

'Not at all.'

'So you wouldn't have any idea who could be pressuring him into doing things?'

'No idea, but if anyone has managed to put the frighteners on the nasty little shit, I'd like to get a chance to shake their hand.'

'Who are his friends?'

'Like I said, I've got no idea. I've got no interest in him at all.'

'OK. Bets, can you take Gwion down to the station in Welshpool for prints and DNA?'

'Of course, if the boss lets me go.'

'Oh, just go, miss, you get on my nerves something serious by the end of the day,' responded Meirion

'Inspector Dafis?' Betsan asked, wisely ignoring Meirion. 'Do you want the ownership details of that phone?'

'Please. Have you got a name, Bets?'

'Not a person's name. The phone belongs to a company called XTreme Team Films.'

'And who are they?'

'They shoot a lot of outdoor stuff, mountain biking, climbing and that. They belong to a group of companies operating under the name of Tei Fi TV.'

'Thank you very much, Betsan. Do you know how to find the police station in Welshpool?'

'Just opposite the train station, isn't it?'

Daf nodded then turned to Gwion. 'Wise up, *lanc*. That stuff won't help you build a decent life for yourself in the future, right?'

Daf wanted a chance to chat things over with Meirion, so he suggested a pint. The stall was quiet enough to allow him to shut up early. The pictures were safe on Daf's memory stick and Meirion closed the laptop and fitted it into its bag.

'Lads in year eight don't sell cocaine,' Daf began, as they strolled through the lessening crowd.

'Maybe someone else is doing the business and he's only acting as the mule.'

'He's certainly stubborn enough.'

'Do you know him?'

'His dad is an old college mate of mine but we're not close. I saw the boy yesterday, causing a fuss on the bike stand.'

'What sort of a fuss?'

'Wanted a discount. Not listening to anyone. Being insulting to people. But his parents have just split and his father's parading his new fancy round the Maes.'

'Since when did a bit of family bother become an excuse for dealing drugs?'

'But how could a young lad get involved in this sort of shit?'

'They do grow up quick these days.'

'We're going to have to go to find him.'

'Who are these 'we' of which you speak?'

'C'mon Mei: we're a good team. And you have got less than fuck all else to do.'

'Good point. Pint first?'

'Better have it after.'

'Why?'

'If you knew the mother of the boy, you wouldn't ask that question. It's going to be hard enough to discuss this with her as it is, without her noticing that we stink of beer. I am not looking forward to this discussion with Eira Owain Edwards.'

'Eira? I remember her from her time with Theatr Gwynedd.'

'And how do you think she will take to the idea that her beloved only son has been involved in drug dealing?'

Meirion paused for a moment. 'You don't by any chance carry stab vests in your car, do you, Daf?'

'Nothing thick enough to cope with the edge of Eira Owain Edwards' tongue.' They were laughing together as they walked along the road to the entrance of the caravan site.

In Daf's opinion, no form of animal life was lower than a jobsworth and in the Caravan Site Office was the winner of the World Jobsworth Championship, 2015. From his little cabin, he had managed to create an atmosphere which was positively Kafkaesque: outside, groups of people had formed and every now and again, the jobsworth, in a totally arbitrary manner, selected whose enquiry he would satisfy. After waiting for over ten minutes and observing three people who had arrived after them receiving attention, Daf pulled out his ID and showed it to the little man.

'We've waited long enough,' Daf said, in a loud voice. 'Do you want a quiet little chat or shall we talk about confidential matters out here?'

'Please come in, gentlemen.' After shutting the door carefully behind them, he whispered: 'What's the problem?'

'Where is Eira Owain Edwards staying?'

'Rule 54 in the Caravan Site Rule Book: the Office will under no circumstances share personal details of residents.'

Meirion leant heavily on the little desk. 'We aren't stalkers, we're police officers.' He turned to Daf. 'I've had enough of this bullshit: I'm going to arrest him.'

The little man's voice grew high and piping. 'Arrest me? What for?'

'Shall we start with Obstructing an Officer in the Execution of his Duties?'

'Don't forget about Wasting Police Time.'

'But, especially with people who are well known, like Ms Owain Edwards ...' the jobsworth started.

Daf saw the anger in Meirion's eyes and decide to make the situation perfectly clear to the little man before his colleague started emptying filing cabinets onto the floor.

'We're investigating a number of serious crimes, including rape and drug trafficking. Just tell us where her caravan is.'

The little man pointed a trembling finger at a diagram of the Caravan Site.

'Over there. Plot 357.'

Out in the sunlight, Daf could see drops of sweat on Meirion's forehead.

'Don't let wankers like that get to you, Mei.'

'I'd rather have a lad with a knife than a prat with a clipboard. Live in a bubble, they do, and cause trouble for all the rest of us.'

It wasn't an ordinary caravan, of course, but a beautifully restored vintage VW camper van. By its side stood a teepee with a vast fire pit. This was glamping.

'Even my Damian isn't as high camp as this,' Meirion remarked. He was always making some flippant remark about his husband but from what Daf could see, they were very well-suited.

Daf knocked on the door of the VW. Eira opened the door wearing nothing but her bra and pants, as if she had been in the middle of dressing. She showed no trace of embarrassment and Daf could not help observing that her body was as firm as that of a twenty-year old.

'Dafydd, you're too early!' she exclaimed. 'And who have got with you? Mei Martin? What a treat for a lonely old lady! Shall I put the kettle on or open a bottle of Sancerre?'

'Unfortunately, Eira, we're on duty,' Meirion replied.

'On duty? Oh, how exciting! And you going to arrest me?' Behind his mother, in the shadows, Daf caught a glimpse of Peredur playing on his tablet.

'Could we have a bit of a word, Eira? Outside, please?'

'Of course.' She stepped out into the fresh air without any kind of covering but there was nothing provocative in her manner: her lack of clothing seemed factual, not relating to anyone but herself.

'Put something on, can't you, Eira?' Meirion asked. 'Otherwise, you're going to burn like a Pop-Tart.'

'Takes one to know one,' she responded in a teasing tone but she did pick up a light muslin shirt and threw it over her shoulders. For some reason, the light fabric combined with her shapely arms to create an impact of Daf which was more than psychological and he had to turn to one side as he spoke to her to hide the degree of his interest. He found it hard to find the right tone of voice, given that he was not sure if he wanted to run away in terror or ask her for a quick, no-strings fuck.

'Since yesterday morning,' he began, 'we've been looking for people who have been selling drugs, on the Maes and in Llanfair Caereinion.'

'I take no interest in things like that, Daf. Intellectual stimulation and sex are my drugs of choice. Any artificial stimulants play havoc with my chakras.'

'Even Sancerre?' Meirion asked.

'You've been to the Eisteddfod before, Mei. You know that every middle-aged woman is obliged to drink a minimum of three bottles of wine a day. More if their child is competing.'

Daf saw his opportunity to discuss Peredur. 'Is the lad competing?'

'Dafydd Dafis, you disappoint me. He won the under 16 Folk Song Solo.'

'I haven't been following the stage competitions much, to tell you the truth.'

'Shame on you, with your own girl competing as well.' Over

the years, Eira had developed the ability to modulate her voice for every occasion and now she was pitching strict but slightly sexy, which added to Daf's physical discomfort.

'How old is Peredur?' Meirion asked.

'Thirteen. Why do you ask?'

Daf had to get into the meat of the matter without further delay.

'We've discovered that the people who have been selling drugs on the Maes have been using the area behind the S4C building as a drop off area. So, we installed a hidden camera and caught Norman Price leaving a bag of white powder and picking up the money.'

'Anyone could have been using a Norman Price suit. You can buy them for next to nothing on the web.'

Daf seriously doubted there was much of an international market for Norman Price suits.

'Very likely, but we need to a DNA sample from Peredur and take his fingerprints.'

Like a storm over a quiet ocean, Eira's anger broke with sudden intensity.

'You have no right to take my child's DNA, Dafydd Dafis!'

'We have every right, Eira. And if you co-operate with us, we'll be able to get to the truth, which will be the best for Peredur,' Meirion added.

'Peredur doesn't need the help of any old faggot, thank you very much, Meirion, nor of the man who has made a career out of failing at everything, Daf Dafis.'

'OK, Eira, but we're going to be making further enquiries. Has Peredur got five thousand pounds in cash, would you say?' Daf though he saw a flicker of anxiety in her blazing eyes.

'We've been putting money away for him in his bank, since he was born. I've got no idea how much is in there by now. And he gets presents from other family members. For example, Gethin's mother gave him twenty pounds after his success on the stage.'

'He must have been singing night and day to get himself five thousand pounds,' answered Meirion, with a totally straight face.

'Why are you asking about this, Dafydd?'

'Because I saw him on the Maes yesterday, determined to do something flash with his cash. Peredur told the man who was selling bikes that he could bring him another two thousand by the end of the week. How could he come across that kind of money on the Maes, Eira?' Eira took a step back in the direction of the tepee.

'I think Gethin gives him way too much money, in compensation for the fact that he left his little family for a cheap prostitute.'

'Very likely, but two thousand?'

'Well, he's got his job as Norman Price ...'

'Which won't pay anything like two thousand, will it now?'

'Perhaps he's got a separate account, from Gethin ...'

'I have to say, when I saw him, he was behaving in a very strange way, as if he had been taking something.'

'Dafydd, are you suggesting that a boy in year eight could be using drugs?'

'Yes.'

For a long moment, Eira held her perfect body perfectly still before responding, in a light tone:

'Well, why don't we just pop over and ask him if he takes and sells drugs?'

'Would you go and get him? Or perhaps, since the whole business is so sensitive, perhaps we could come into the van?'

'That would be best.'

As she led Daf and Meirion to the VW, Eira's mood changed yet again, her anger vanishing as if, perhaps, she was suddenly aware of how fragile her son's situation really was.

'He's only a little boy, Dafydd,' she whispered.

'And he can't be helped until we get to the truth.'

Eira took Daf's hand for a moment: her fingers were cool and strong.

'You're quite different from your old friend, aren't you, Dafydd?' She whispered. Daf was glad Meirion was with him: Eira's gratitude was potentially very difficult to handle, especially when she was barely dressed.

An innocent image awaited them in the camper van, a young boy playing Minecraft and drinking a smoothie. He raised his eyes courteously.

'What's occurring, Mami?' he asked. Mami. Very clever, to choose a word which underlined how young he is. Like his mother, he was a born performer.

'These gentlemen are policemen. Bad people have been selling drugs and they need to ask you some questions, sugar.' Sugar! She was at risk of overdoing it, Daf thought.

'How long will it take? Because your show is on before long, Mami, and I don't want to miss it.' Daf doubted they spoke quite so sweetly to one another when there was no audience.

'I'll call your father round, if necessary.'

'Eira,' Daf ventured, not wanting to trigger her rage again, 'we're going to have to take Peredur down to the station to take his fingerprints and so on. Someone has to go with him.'

Eira picked up her phone. She stepped out under the awning of the VW and, with the window open, she could be clearly heard inside.

'You have to come over to the caravan site at once. Peredur ... well, I don't know what's going on but Dafydd Dafis is here, in an official capacity ... No, it's not underage drinking, a lot worse than that ... Of course I can't come over and get you: I'm on stage in not much over an hour ... What about the Little Bitch, or is she too young to have a licence? Sort it, Gethin. Don't make me ring your father.'

There was no goodbye of any kind and when she returned to the VW, Eira's face was white with rage.

'The world's best father is over the limit. Too many sherbets as he was flouncing that whore of his round the Maes.' Daf noticed the impact Eira's rage had on her son and he was aware of the hatred flooding into the lad's eyes.

'Too busy for me, same as ever,' Peredur spat between clenched teeth.

'There's no reason for us to delay, Eira. Can we start by asking a few questions?'

She nodded her head but, as the conversation began, she started to brush her hair and do her make-up, preparing for the show as if nothing was happening.

Peredur stayed in character. He was a young boy enjoying the Eisteddfod with his mother, competing, socialising and earning his bit of pocket money by dancing in front of small children, dressed up as Norman Price. In the evening, he sometimes went to concerts or plays with his mother or if one of his friends had an older sibling going, he might go to the Cymdeithas gig. He didn't drink and had never taken drugs. After ten minutes, the VW was like an oven and the strong herbal scents of Eira's various skin preparations made it oppressive: Meirion suggested they should take a breath of air.

'Have you seen his septum?' Mei asked Daf, as soon as they were out of earshot.

'I thought yesterday, that if he was a year or two older, I would start to think ...'

'No, *cont*, you've been blinded by his middle-class family. It's perfectly possible to sing a folk song with a little tweed cap on your head and still snort coke, you know.'

Eira's phone rang and she answered in monosyllables before stepping out to speak to the two policemen.

'The Prof is coming over to go with you. He'll be at the main entrance in half an hour. He doesn't know anything about the drugs: I didn't want to trouble him any further than he's already been troubled by his bastard son.'

'Eira, we're very concerned about Peredur. A young boy can be very useful to people who are trading drugs – who would look twice at Norman Price? It's highly possible that Peredur has been forced to help them.'

'You're just like Carrie in *Sex and the City*, Dafydd: you're always looking for Mr Big.'

Meirion's look spoke volumes: he couldn't believe that anyone would be teasing when their child was in such difficulty. A very peculiar family.

Peredur agreed to go with them to meet the Prof. As he was leaving, Daf recalled the theatrical tradition.

'Break a leg tonight, Eira!'

In response, she gave him a lovely smile, full of intelligence and intimacy and Daf realised he had never met a woman who stirred up such contradictory emotions in him. She was cold and attractive, genuinely funny yet riddled with snobbery and Daf didn't know whether he wanted to take her in his arms or run like hell. One thing was clear: out of his mother's hearing, Peredur was a totally different boy. He even walked differently: on the balls of his feet like a boxer.

The three of them walked past a row of big motorhomes, equipped with all mod cons. On the windscreen of one of the best was a disabled badge. Peredur paused for a moment, worked his tongue around his mouth then spat on the glass.

'What do you think you're doing?' Daf demanded.

'He, the crip, caused me all this hassle because he was too tight to give me a few quid off a bike.'

'There's no connection between Garmon Jones and this case.'

'But there's a fair bit of a connection between him and your daughter, Inspector. I was going past around seven last night – they should have pulled the blinds down. I stopped for a quarter of an hour to watch: it was like a porn film. One thing for certain, the Virgin of the Vale isn't a virgin anymore.'

Daf felt a tightness in his chest as if a hand were squeezing his heart and lungs. Meirion directed a warning glance to the boy but he continued.

'I'm pissed off I didn't think of filming it on my phone: it would have been an instant YouTube sensation.'

'Like Mr Dafis said, there is no connection between Garmon Jones and this investigation.'

'But it was him put the idea in your head, that I had something to do with drugs.'

'No indeed, lad: it was your behaviour which made me concerned. I've never seen anyone more coked up.'

Daf was relieved that he had managed to shape some words because the tightness was now encompassing his whole ribcage. He decided to drink until he forgot everything that night. It was hard to ignore Peredur's thin, smirking face but Daf did manage to walk over to the main entrance without killing the little bastard. But he didn't manage to clear the images from his head and, there was an element of unhealthy curiosity involved. Sexual images involving Carys and Matt had been running through his head for months, to the extent that he'd almost got used to them, but they were pretty vanilla. But how could Carys be having a sexual relationship with a man in a wheelchair? Who did what to whom and with what, and in what order? His interest in the question brought a mouthful of sick up his throat which he swallowed with difficulty.

Standing as straight as a flagpole and wearing a jacket despite the heat, the Prof was waiting for them. He raised his hand.

'Good afternoon, Dafydd. What's the story?'

In the Prof's understanding, kindly face, Daf saw Peredur's only hope and even if he deserved to be throttled, he was only a child. In spite of his parents, Peredur might still get the guidance he needed from his grandfather.

'You take Peredur over to my car, Mei: I need a word with the Professor.'

'I don't want to be alone with him, in case he rapes me,' Peredur whined.

'Got no choice, my lad,' was Meirion's measured response. 'And you're not nearly pretty enough for me.'

For a moment, the Prof watched as if he were attending a

play but then suddenly switched into active response.

'You don't dare to speak to these police officers in that tone, Peredur Teifi. Apologise at once!'

'Sorry,' Peredur mumbled under his breath.

'I've never had any reason to talk to the police; no, that's not quite true because of the accident, but I am unfamiliar with this context. However, it's clear to me that, whatever has gone on, we need to co-operate to solve the problem. It will do no good to you at all, Peredur Mathonwy, if you decide to be insolent.'

'Sorry, Tada.'

'It's a shame we don't have time to call in to see your grandmother on the way to having your DNA test: she is very concerned about you. Now then, you settle in the back of the car and I'm certain we can sort things out. But no more cheek, you understand?'

Daf noted the impact the old man had on his grandson. Dignified, intelligent and full of love for his fellow man, the Prof was sufficiently sure of himself to set moral standards for a boy like Peredur, who had been brought up by superficial, selfish people. Daf took the old man's elbow and gently led him away from the car.

'Sir,' Daf began cautiously, unwilling to cause more pain, 'we've got one heck of a problem with this lad. We think he's got mixed up in drugs, something serious.' When speaking to those he regarded as his superiors, Daf could hear his accent thickening.

'Drugs, Dafydd? But he's only a little boy.'

'I know but we've got good reason to believe he's using.'

'It's impossible to believe that.'

'The tests will give us a definite answer, but, and I am so sorry to have to say this, I am very concerned about him.' There was no response from the old man but his head sank as if he had aged ten years. 'Come to the car. Give your keys to Meirion: he can follow behind, driving your car.'

There was little conversation on the way down to Welshpool but, in the mirror, Daf saw the Prof trying to comfort his grandson.

'Where's Dad?' Peredur asked.

'He had three pints on the Maes, in the day. He wasn't expecting to have to drive tonight.'

'I need him.'

'To be fair to him, he wasn't expecting to be called out.'

'Mum was busy as well.' His voice disappeared and Daf knew tears weren't far away.

In the station, everything was ready for them. Sheila's attitude was a big help: she behaved like a nurse, rather than a policewoman. In half an hour, they were back by the Prof's car.

'Peredur,' Daf said, 'I've been in this game twenty years and from the beginning, we've been winning the fight, step by step. DNA, blood tests, forensic techniques of all sorts. Before the middle of the day tomorrow, we will know if you've taken any illegal drug or not. And if you're prepared to tell us the whole story, we can help you.'

'Help me to do what?' A flash of the old attitude return and the Prof had to cough to warn him.

'They don't do a lot of folk singing in young offender institutions, you know. And because of the nature of the crime, the courts are right likely to say that your parents can't cope with you. And there aren't many people ready to foster kids who sell drugs. Children's home, it looks like.'

'Don't worry, Peredur, your grandmother and I will take care of you.'

'If the Court allows that, sir,' Daf explained. 'They might well ask where you were before your grandson got caught. And your age would count against you.'

'But I've never been ill in my life. Apart from a little touch of something after the accident.'

Daf was keen to hear more about this accident, as a naturally curious man as well as in his role as a policeman, because of the way in which the Prof's voice changed when he mentioned it. But there was no time for that now.

'You have a think overnight, Peredur. We can have a chat in the morning when we've got the forensic report. And, if possible, sir, can you keep an eye on him overnight? I'm not happy for him to go back to the camper van by himself.'

'You shall stay with us tonight, Peredur, with Mr Dafis just over the yard. Shall we get a take-away?'

When Peredur had climbed into the back of the car, his grandfather leant over to whisper in Daf's ear. 'What is the maximum penalty he could face, Dafydd?'

'He could face a change of Possession of Class A drugs with Intent to Supply but it doesn't make any sense to me, sir. A boy of his age can't be supplying drugs without help: if Peredur is willing to help us find who's responsible, I'm sure we can see that things are far easier for him.'

'I'll do my best to get to the bottom of this, Dafydd.'

'I feel sorry for the old boy,' remarked Meirion as Talwyn Teifi settled himself beside his grandson.

'Me too. I want to know who Peredur is protecting, and why.'

'There's an answer to every question and it comes in a bottle with a label on it saying Jamesons.'

'Thank God for that.'

'I've got a bottle up at the cottage where we're staying. Betsan will be there as a chaperone so you needn't think I'm likely to jump on your back.'

'You don't need to ask twice. The Jamesons, I mean, not the jumping.'

Chapter 6

Tuesday evening

It wasn't a cottage but a restored barn, way up in the hills, about three miles from the Maes– the perfect place to clear one's head. Betsan was sunbathing in the scrap of garden looking much younger in her summery frock. A few years earlier, safely tucked up in what he thought was a happy marriage, Daf would have been able to admire a girl like her without longing but now every woman who stirred a passing attraction had become a symbol of his captivity: with so many marvellous women in the world, why had he chosen Falmai? Then, of course, he remembered Gaenor and smiled.

'Shall I put a match to the barbeque?' Meirion asked.

'Whiskey is what's required.'

'Not on an empty stomach. That's what got us chucked out of that club in the Isle of Man, if you remember?' Meirion was laughing at the recollection as he went to fetch cans of lager.

An hour later, his second can in his hand and the aroma of sausages filling his nostrils, Daf was starting to relax.

'Can I sleep on your sofa tonight?' he asked, before pulling the ring-pull. 'Because I seriously need more than one can.'

'Why don't you ring Falmai and get her to pick you up?' Meirion suggested.

'Because we're not speaking at the moment.'

'Oh dear,' responded Meirion, without a hint of regret in his voice. 'Serious, or just a couple of days of pictures, no sound?'

'I've got no idea. And we've rented our house out, to Peredur's father, as it happens, so were stopping with Fal's brother. It's awkward beyond.'

'You're welcome to stop here but there's not much room.'

Betsan smiled and raised her eyebrows. 'Whoever it was at

HQ who booked the place seems to have got the idea that Meirion was taking me away for a bit of rumpy pumpy so there's only the one room, with a double bed. Clearly doesn't know us at all.'

'I'd be happy on the floor, just somewhere to sleep.' Before Daf had managed to drink a drop of his beer, the owner of the property appeared, walking quickly across the yard.

'Inspector Dafis? Your sister-in-law's on the phone.'

Daf was irritated as he picked up the phone but swallowed his annoyance when he heard Gaenor's voice.

'You've got to come home, Daf. All hell is breaking loose here.'

'How do you mean?'

'Some heck of a row going on in the bungalow. The old lady's run away and if that wasn't enough, Matt Blainey's sitting on my sofa crying his eyes out.'

So that was the end of Daf's sociable, relaxed evening. As he said goodbye to Meirion and Betsan, Daf couldn't help feeling low. He didn't just want to recharge his batteries, he needed to; instead, more hassle. He could agree with Mair one hundred per cent: 'Drama, we don't need no drama.'

With the window of the car open, Daf could hear Gethin's voice as he approached the yard at Neuadd. When he could see his old friend, his face was red with drink and rage.

'And who do you think phoned the pigs? Dear little Gwion. And by now, my lad has been sucked into this bloody mess with drugs.' Manon was visible, framed in the doorway, two black rivers of mascara-stained tears marring her lovely cheeks.

'But you didn't have to phone Meleri! He's been sacked now.'

'He deserved the fucking sack. He'd got the easiest job in the world but no-one can do children's programmes with half the annual output of Columbia up their nose.'

'Hallo there,' Daf called. 'Everything alright?'

Gethin directed his anger towards Daf. 'What have you done to my son?'

'Peredur's in pretty deep waters, Geth: we had no choice but to look into the matter.'

'He's thirteen, for fuck's sake, not the head of some cartel in Medellín.'

'If the forensic evidence backs up what we know already, Peredur is mixed up in drug selling. I reckon there's got to be someone putting him up to it: any idea who that could be?'

'Gwion Morgan.' Gethin did not need to think for more than a moment.

'Are you sure?'

'Yes.'

'How long has Peredur known him?'

'They've been working together since half term, since the Urdd Eisteddfod.'

'Your dad has invited Peredur to stay here tonight. He needs to be around people who are going to help him make the right choices. I'm not sticking my nose in, but arguing like this is really not going to make things easier.'

'Gwion rang you lot earlier, to say I was driving over the limit. Dad was driving, but it was still a shitty little trick.'

'You've got to put Peredur's troubles before everything else, I reckon.'

'And where's the fucking invisible mother? Giving her wonderful Saunders Lewis extracts to fifteen middle-aged Welsh teachers who are jizzing their Y-fronts at the sight of her?'

'Geth, you have got to calm down, for the sake of the lad.'

'OK, Daf, OK. Do you know where Mum's gone?'

'I've only just got here.'

'I'll go look for her. And you,' he added, turning to Manon, 'sort your fucking make-up, will you? It costs me enough.' He turned on his heel and strode off through the gate which lead down to the meadow, anger in his every movement.

'I've never seen him like that before,' whispered Manon: she was shaking.

'Nor have I. What happened?'

'On the way back from the Maes, we were stopped by the police. It was fine, because the Prof was driving but Geth's convinced himself that Gwion shopped us. So then he rang Meleri, who's the Chief Exec of S4C, to tell her about Gwion.'

'To tell her what about Gwion?'

Manon looked for several moments into Daf's eyes as if she were working out whether or not she could trust him.

'A bit of charlie, Dafydd. He's been acting daft about the stuff since form six. He started with it to get rid of his nerves when he had to perform. I remember when we got the stage in the *Ymgom*, he offered me a line. I turned it down but it certainly gave him a bit of oomph. We came first and his mother was so proud of us.'

For the first time since he had met her, Daf saw something tender in her face. 'Were you a couple since school?'

She nodded her head. 'But the trouble with the coke is, it's so bloody expensive. The two of us were working day and night to pay rent on a shithole in Riverside and, if I'm honest, I'm mad keen to have a baby. I loved Gwion but there wasn't any future for the two of us.'

'How about dealing? Would Gwion deal?'

Manon laughed and dragged the back of her hand across her face, mixing her snot and make-up.

'Gwion couldn't sell a raffle ticket. He's so hopeless.'

'And what is his relationship with Peredur like?'

'They don't know each other, apart from the two stints of Norman Pricing Peredur's done this year.'

'And what sort of a lad is he?'

'Complicated. Like his mum, he's always acting. I don't know him and he hates me because of his mother's opinion of me.'

'So, you don't think Gwion could persuade Peredur to be his runner, then?'

'Gwion hasn't got a manipulative bone in his body. He can't persuade anyone to do anything. Another difference between him and Geth.'

'I get it.' There was a silence as Manon ineffectually tried to clean her face.

'Dafydd, can you give me a lift down to Londis? There's not a drop of wine left in the house.'

'I'm not sure that's a good idea. Why not put the kettle on instead?'

Without another word, Manon turned round and retreated into the bungalow.

Daf had to smile at the irony: Falmai had been so excited about getting these respectable tenants, but instead of enjoying a leisurely barbeque with John Neuadd and praising his home-killed steaks, the family were fighting any number of demons and the bungalow had become a battle-ground.

'Thank you for coming back.' Gaenor's voice was full of genuine gratitude as she met him by the back door.

'Where's Matt?'

'Still on the sofa: I can't get any sense out of him at all, except that Carys has finished with him for no reason at all. And she has gone up to her room and won't come down to speak to him.'

In the corridor, as solid as the oak frame of the house, John was standing.

'This place has become a madhouse. You've got to do something, Dafydd.'

'OK,' Daf replied, somewhat impatient and resisting the temptation of telling his brother-in-law that Neuadd was not, in fact, a paradise on earth.

Matt was making no effort to hide his tears. He was sitting bolt upright on the sofa, weeping without shame.

'Mr Dafis, what is it?' He spoke to Daf in his halting Welsh. 'I've nothing wrong done. It is my not having the Welsh, do you think?'

'I'll have a word with her now. Blow your nose, *lanc*; it's not a good look.'

In the little back bedroom, Carys was lying on the single bed, texting. Gaenor had decorated the room for a baby girl but, after fifteen years of heartbreak, it had become the second spare room. To Daf, the room always felt sad, as if the turn of the millennium Laura Ashley floral paper had trapped the essence of all those lost children in its foliage.

'Car, you're going to have to talk to Matt.'

'I can't, Dad.'

'He deserves an explanation.'

'There's nothing to say. We've had fun together but things move on.'

'In the direction of Garmon Jones?' Carys went red but grinned from ear to ear.

'Family problem, is it, Dadi, being a love-rat?'

'What do you mean?'

'I should have spoken to Matt on Saturday because I knew, after ten minutes in Garmon's company that anything could happen.'

'Like happened in the camper van last night?'

'Have you been following me?'

'No indeed, but do remember to close the blinds next time.' Daf expected some awkwardness or embarrassment but Carys seemed very matter-of-fact about it.

'I don't give a stuff for anything any peeping Tom might say.'

'But what about Matt?'

'Right, Dadi, you've decided to interfere in my private life so I'm going to give you the truth, both barrels. I never had an orgasm with Matt. He's a nice lad but he just rolls on top of me, does a few press-ups and job's a good 'un. But Garmon ... well, Garmon has put a match to the fire. That's exactly how I feel, Dadi, like a girl on fire. And I don't know him nearly well enough to know if we've got a future as a couple but I definitely want to spend the rest of my life in his bed.' Daf had been asking for it but he was not sure he quite deserved this. 'And now you understood why I was reluctant to discuss things with Matt. He's got no technique at all and, unfortunately, his tackle's not up to much either.'

'But Carys, Garmon's had an accident and ...'

'And that's exactly why it's so awkward. I can't tell Matt that I'm having way better sex with a man who's in a wheelchair.'

'OK. I'll try to get rid of him.'

'Garmon thinks the world of you, Dadi. We'd better get Gaenor to invite him to get some supper with us before the end of the week.'

Somehow, Daf managed some sort of conversation with Matt. He asked way too many questions that were impossible to answer, but in the end, he agreed to go. The handshake on the back doorstep was awkward: Matt had grown to become a part of the family. As he left, the young man paused and gazed down over the meadows.

'We were set on having the marquee down there. Nice trees for the pics, if the weather was kind.'

Daf stood for five minutes by the gate, watching the little Suzuki vanishing into the landscape. A chapter in Carys' life had come to an end. Gaenor came out to stand by his side.

'What went wrong between them, Daf? I didn't pick up that they'd been quarrelling.'

'Carys has met someone else. Fair play to her, she's not ready to settle for second best.'

'But Matt is such a nice young man.'

'And Falmai's a very nice woman but if I don't get you on your back by midnight, I'll lose what's left of my mind.'

'Daf Dafis, what in the world can I do with you?'

'I've got several suggestions ...'

Chapter 7

Wednesday

Daf woke up in the single bed in the back bedroom. Carys was spending the night with Garmon so the bed was free for the night. It was convenient, if not exactly advisable, for Gaenor to pay a visit in the middle of the night: the shape of her head was still visible on the pillow. For the first time, at four in the morning, Gaenor had mentioned the idea of leaving John.

'Falmai could move back in to look after him, since she's always criticised how I've managed things, and the two of us could please ourselves.'

'Do you fancy living with me?'

'Well, why don't you give me the pros and cons?'

'On the plus side, we get along grand, my children dote on you and the bed side works real well. On the other hand, I haven't got much money behind me and I have promised to spend the night, or afternoon, more likely, with Chrissie Berllan.'

'Do I get a little interlude with Bryn?'

'Of course you do. Fair's fair.'

A new plan, a way forward. Daf had often dreamt of shaking the Neuadd family to its foundations: perhaps this earthquake would finally shock them out of their complacency. No, that was a fantasy; Daf was certain that, whatever else happened anywhere in the world, there would still be Joneses sitting at the broad oak table over their home-killed Sunday lunch, discussing stock prices and the poor behaviour of others, their family coldness silting their veins.

Daf was rather surprised to see Carys at the breakfast table but it was clear that she had come to make a statement.

'Some of you know already but Matt and I have split up, for lots of reasons. Anyway, I've got a new boyfriend, whose name is Garmon and it would be great if you could get a chance to meet him.'

'New boyfriend?' asked John: he hated change of any kind, no matter how slightly it affected him.

'Yes. We could sort something out on the Maes but it would be a lot nicer if, say, we were having a barbeque anyway and he could just come along ...'

'How about tomorrow night?' Gaenor offered at once.

'Great, Aunty Gae.'

'Don't say he's a vegetarian.'

'Far from it, he's a real farm boy but if we could find a plank of wood to go over the steps up onto the lawn, that would be great, because he uses a wheelchair.'

John and Falmai had a strong family resemblance anyway but in that moment of shock, when the expression on their faces was identical, they were like twins.

'Wheelchair?' Falmai exclaimed. 'Is he ill? With everything that's going on in this family at the moment, why do you have to go out and look for new problems?'

'He's perfectly well. He had an accident, that's all. He was halfway through making a film about his skills as world mountain bike champion and the director wanted him to try more and more difficult stunts, to get better footage. He broke his back.'

'It must be a lot of work looking after him, and dirty work at that, *ych a fi*!' Falmai wrinkled her nose in disgust.

Carys picked up a bottle of tomato ketchup and threw it in the direction of her mother. Unfortunately, the lid was not tightly closed.

'You look like you survived the Zombie Apocalypse, Aunty Fal,' remarked Siôn.

'I've invited Garmon here for a barbeque,' announced Gaenor, cutting across the hullaballoo, 'and like every guest who comes to this house, we will welcome him with every courtesy, if he arrives in a wheelchair or a Ferrari.'

'And talking of Ferraris, Mami,' Carys added in a bitter tone, 'he's got plenty of money, which is normally all you care about. Speaks Welsh, comes from a big farm: he'd only need to win the Blue Ribbon to be the full house in your game of Boyfriend Bingo.'

Falmai rose to her feet and walked to the door, pulling several pieces of kitchen paper from the roll on the wall as she passed. Daf reached out to touch her arm as she passed but she twitched away from his touch as if he were a stinging nettle. Full of shame, he helped Carys to clear the table.

'Years ago,' John began, in a conversational tone, as if nothing had happened, 'the Royal Welsh used to travel, like the 'Steddfod. But since it has settled on its permanent site in Builth, it's gone from strength to strength. High time the Eisteddfod did the same, in my view, high time it settled down, somewhere a long way away from us.'

No-one could find anything to say and the relief was visible on several faces when a knock on the door was heard, cutting across the awkward silence. It was Gethin, but in a very different mood than the one he had been in the previous morning: no more flirting or begging for bacon. This Gethin was like a ghost of himself, showing all the signs of a sleepless night, including yesterday's shirt.

'Sorry to interrupt. Can I have a quick word, Dafydd?'

'Of course.'

A few days earlier, Daf thought, Gethin was the epitome of the successful man, full of confidence, untouchable. Three days had changed a good deal.

'Have you managed to persuade Peredur to co-operate with us?'

'I think so. I feel like a total shit, Daf. Every time I saw him, Eira put such a positive spin on everything. I never asked him how he was feeling. Eira said she took him to a couple of counselling session after we split, just in case, but he was still playing his rugby, still enjoying going to the pictures, then, just like any lad, he developed this obsession with mountain bikes.'

'How long has he been wanting a mountain bike?'

'He's got one: you can't raise children without buying bikes. But when he worked out how often Mans and I go up north for a weekend's biking, he started looking for a much better bike.'

'Which is why he went to Garmon Jones' stand and saw that he couldn't afford the one he wanted?'

'What did you say about Garmon Jones?'

'Peredur went to his stand, kicking off. He was very abusive.'

'The effect of the coke?'

'Are you expecting a positive test result, Geth?'

'Yes, unfortunately. He's changed since yesterday, seems very low.'

'Don't tell me you can't see what's going on: coked up yesterday, on the comedown today.'

'I know, Daf, but he's so young.'

They were all sitting around the kitchen table, except Manon.

'We've asked Eira to come over to hear what Peredur has to say.' As everyone was sitting around like a committee, the Prof was in his element. 'We've prepared an outline agenda to ensure we discuss all aspects of the problem.'

'I'm not a problem,' mumbled Peredur. His skin had a greyish tinge and there were dark circles under his eyes.

'I'm happy to make a contribution but this is a family matter in the bone,' Daf clarified.

'How would it be if we discussed your points at the top of the agenda, Dafydd? We have several questions to ask about the official aspect of this business.'

'You'll have to have a cup of tea first,' the Prof's wife offered.

Daf's phone rang and he was pleased to hear Sheila's voice. He walked out into the corner of the yard where the signal was strongest.

'Forensic report for you, boss.'

'And?'

'Positive for coke in the urine and the samples from the suit are a match as well.'

'Right.'

'And the fingerprints on the Es and the coke are identical and they match.' She used the English word for fingerprints.

'Thank you very much Sheila. Just one thing.'

'What, boss?'

'The word for fingerprints in Welsh: "*olion bysedd*", OK?'

'Cheers and thanks for that.'

'No worries, Sheila.'

The family in the bungalow clearly knew what to expect but before Daf could speak, he was presented with a mug of tea. A car arrived in the yard: Eira. Without knocking or saying a word, she entered the kitchen and sat down, turning the everyday chair into a throne with her dignity.

'Where's Manon this morning?' she asked, a savage edge to her voice.

'She's in the parlour, with a book,' Gethin replied.

'Oh, Manon has a book! I do hope she's got enough felt pens to colour it with.'

'You can shut up, you sour old bitch.'

The Prof raised his voice. 'That's more than enough. Eira, Gethin, if you cannot behave properly, I will be obliged to ask you to leave this meeting. There is a good deal to discuss and Dafydd has no time to waste with your nonsense: he's not on his holidays. To begin, Dafydd, may I ask if you have received the results of the tests?'

'I have, sir, and unfortunately, there was cocaine in Peredur's water and his fingerprints on the packets of drugs we recovered, Es on Tuesday and cocaine yesterday.'

In the silence which followed, Daf could hear Peredur's shallow breathing. Then Gethin raised his head and sang an adapted version of a popular song:

'"And in summer warmth in Meifod, then cider will become cocaine."'

The original lyric spoke of cider turning to champagne.

The Prof struck his fist on the table so hard that all the mugs leapt into the air.

'I have had a bellyful of this. Your child, your only child, has been caught using cocaine and you still can't resist making your stupid little jokes. Keep your mouth shut if you haven't got anything worthwhile to say. And now, Peredur Teifi, I'm expecting to hear your story.'

It was rather a sad little tale, Daf thought. In his final year in primary school, Peredur starting losing interest in his schoolwork and his teachers were anxious about him.

'It's hard to concentrate on a project on the Romans when everyone is talking about who your dad was with in the Cameo Club last night.' He saw a doctor, who referred him: he was given a prescription for Ritalin. 'I stopped taking it because it didn't make any difference and I felt a bit sick after taking it. My friend came round, Adam, and he saw the Ritalin in the bathroom, in the cupboard. His brother would buy them off me, he said, seven pounds per tablet. There's a good market for Ritalin in Cardiff, because of all the students needing help when they pull all-nighters.'

'You never told me the doctor had put Peredur on Ritalin,' Gethin complained to Eira.

'You never asked. Besides, if you remember that time accurately, the only way of communicating with you was by writing a message on Manon's fanny and I don't know her well enough for that.'

One look from the Professor was all that was required to silence them. Peredur resumed his story.

'After that, I knew how I could make plenty of pocket money without much hard work. Bit by bit, I set up my own business, buying from people I knew, selling stuff on.'

'So no-one older than you was forcing you to sell?' Daf asked

'No. Adam's brother didn't like me doing well.'

'Are you prepared to give me the name of Adam's brother?'

Peredur looked from one face to another, as if he were checking for an answer. He found that answer in his grandfather's eyes.

'Yes.'

'Good for you.'

'On with the story,' commanded the Prof.

'There's not a lot more to say. I made the connections, so I made the money.'

'Why did you need all that money?' his grandmother asked, in a shy, quiet voice.

'To buy a mountain bike.'

'What did you say?' His grandfather could not believe what he had heard. 'You've got a perfectly satisfactory bike already.'

'But I wanted a great bike, like the Superfly. And I couldn't get a discount from Garmon Jones because everyone knows you were to blame for his accident, Dad.'

'Rubbish,' snapped Gethin, as if he had answered that question far too many times in the past. 'Garmon was always totally professional and well aware of all the risks.'

'But you made him do that last long jump because some big American company had showed interest in the film.'

'Who's filled you up with this rubbish, as if I couldn't guess?' Gethin glowered at his ex-wife, who responded in kind.

'Everybody knows, Dad. You know what it's like in my school, half the kids come from telly families.'

'Speaking of schools,' the Prof cut in, 'Derwenna and I have been considering that it might be best for Peredur to come and live with us. There's very good schooling available for him in Llandeilo.'

'Can we just stick with the official side of things for a moment please?' responded Daf. 'Since when have you been using cocaine yourself, Peredur?'

'For a few months. I needed a bit of a buzz.'

'Since your father buggered off, perhaps?' Eira suggested.

'Please, please: can you discuss your personal problems after I've finish my work? Do you take a line every day, *lanc*?'

'No. Three or four a week.'

'OK, but that's enough to create a dependency. Are you willing to start a programme to help you stop using cocaine?'

'Yes.'

'I need to decide, before I make any recommendations to the Crown Prosecution Service, if you, as a family, are going to be able to support Peredur to move on from the bad place where he is now.'

'Of course we are,' answered the Prof, who now seemed to be acknowledged by all of them as the family's spokesman.

'Fair enough, but having the responsibility for a young person who is mixed up in a business like this is a big responsibility.'

'I've never shirked a responsibility in my life.'

Eira rose to her feet. 'I can't stick any more of this. You've cast yourself as the perfect head of the family, with your wisdom, your status and your lovely, lovely Christian faith but you haven't always lived a perfect life. To start with, you've brought up a son who thinks with his cock, not his brain, and even though I've been cast as the Mother From Hell, it wasn't me who killed a boy through careless driving.'

Daf saw the impact her words had on the Prof. His face seemed to sink back into itself for a moment and he struggled to shape the words of a reply.

'It was an accident.'

'Of course it was an accident but that won't help the mother who lost her child. I've have enough of you, of all of you.'

Eira slammed the door of the bungalow so hard behind her that Daf was concerned for his door-frame. He swore under his breath: Peredur was enough of a problem as things stood, without anyone trying to undermine the one person who was likely to have a positive influence over him.

'You must do something about this poisonous atmosphere: it doesn't help the situation at all. If, and that's a big if, you are prepared to work together to help Peredur, I can recommend that he has a formal caution rather than that we prepare the paperwork for a prosecution but he's got to have some official input as well. Do you understand?'

'We understand perfectly, Dafydd. And thank you so much for your advice and for helping us in this crisis.' After formally shaking hands with the old man, Daf was glad to escape, out into the fresh air.

It was about time for Daf to catch up with the mountain of paperwork and Nia was waiting for him at the station, a rather stern expression on her face.

'I've just read the forensic report. There's an error on it.'

'What error?'

'Date of birth of the boy under suspicion. He can't be thirteen.'

'He is and he's just told me his whole story from flogging off his Ritalin tablets when he was in primary to selling coke on the Maes in his Norman Price costume.'

'Seen the Welsh news?'

'I haven't been near a telly for days.'

'S4C have sacked Hoppy the Happy Hare. Cocaine problem, they say. Was it him staying in Pandy Newydd?'

'Yes.'

'What are we going to do with all the things you've half done since the weekend?'

'If you'll help me get the paperwork sorted, I'll buy you a sandwich at dinnertime.'

'OK. But, boss?'

'What?'

'If the age of this boy is correct, we've got a humdinger of a child protection case here, haven't we?'

'Fuck. I never thought of that. The parents are fighting like I don't know what, but the grandparents are up for doing the heavy lifting.'

'A year eight boy selling cocaine? That's very serious.'

'I know. They live in Cardiff: can you get me a number for Children's Services there? And we'll have to have a key worker who speaks the language.'

'I know. Can I get Katy in to help: I won't cope with all of this on my own?'

'Knock yourself out, as the English say.'

And so the paperwork began.

Daf didn't have any time to think as he walked over to Tesco to buy his lunch. He was longing to see Rhodri, who wasn't far off the same age as Peredur. He pulled out his phone and chose from his contacts menu.

'Hi there, *cog*. How was the training session?'

'Great. Listen, Dad, the signal's crap. Ring me on the landline.'

'Where are you?'

'With Aunty Gae, of course.'

There she was again, caring for other people. Gaenor doted on Carys but perhaps even more so, on Rhodri. Falmai, on the other hand, was far more amenable with Carys, showing the best part of her nature when she was in her daughter's company. Lately, however, a gulf had opened up between mother and daughter: as Carys had developed into an independent-minded young woman, she was increasingly reluctant to even discuss the path her mother had laid out for her. Daf chose the fourth number from his contact list.

'That's better, Dad.'

'So, what are you up to today?'

'Helping Aunty Gae. I'm so stoked about this barbeque. Not that I didn't like Matt but he didn't have anything to say, apart from who'd got a grant to double glaze their windows.'

Daf laughed aloud, partly at the joke but also because his son was not Peredur. 'You're priceless, Rhodri.'

'And Gae says Meilyr can come to the barbeque as well, because he's a major fan of Garmon Jones.'

'Steady on, *lanc*: I don't know how public Carys wants things to be yet.'

'I don't care if he's dating Uncle John, the important thing is he's coming to our barbeque. He's been all around the world, you know, so we're looking for a few recipes from countries he's visited ...'

Daf was delighted just to let the tide of his son's enthusiasm wash over him. The lad was alright, would be alright, despite the tension in the family and the fact that Daf knew himself to be little short of a workaholic at times.

'D'you fancy going down to the sea for a bit of fishing?' he asked, painfully conscious how easy it was to be so absorbed in his work that he failed to spend enough time with the boy.

'That would be great.'

'Meilyr could come too, if you like. We'll go the moment this hullaballoo is over.'

'Great. Aunty Gae could do us a picnic.'

'Or she could come with us, and if we catch anything, we'll make a fire on the beach and she can cook it for us.'

'Brilliant. I've got to go now: we need to make a list for the Tesco delivery.'

Daf smiled. He was immeasurably glad that Rhodri, not Peredur, was his son and also recalled his conversation in the night. Gaenor and Rhodri were very close: if the family was to break up and re-form in a new shape, Daf couldn't see Rhodri objecting. He was also glad that, after years of trolleys and plastic bags, that food delivery vans were once more making their way through the lanes, as in his youth. Every Saturday, with his Uncle Mal driving, they would travel from house to house, sometimes stopping to talk about the weather. Daf's official role was to open the gates but in the back of the van, behind the little counter, he had to make a note of all purchases and count the change. His uncle could neither read nor write and once Daf heard a new doctor telling the nurse that Maldwyn had a mental age of six. Everyone in the village looked out for him but one evening, when Daf was ten, Maldwyn went for his usual half pint of mild in the Black. A gang of lads who were staying on a local caravan site decided to have some fun at his expense, buying him vodka until he was so drunk that he soiled himself. For six months, the big man was too ashamed to leave the house and in that time, Daf and Maldwyn spent every Saturday playing games like Ludo. Eventually, Maldwyn was ready to go out on the rounds again and every time Daf jumped down to open the gate, receiving a toot of the horn in thanks, he would remember his promise to spend his whole life fighting against the bullies of the world.

The idea of a day by the sea with Gaenor and Rhodri was dancing about in his mind and he began to seriously contemplate what life might be like with her. His visions were coloured by passion and romance, of course, but they were also very far from fantasy: he could imagine a Sunday afternoon by the fire, eating scones and playing board games. For the first time in a very long time, Daf felt as if he had a choice, the right to decide how he lived his life, and with whom.

He realised, as he was choosing a chicken wrap with low fat mayo for Nia and a BLT for himself, that there was no reason for him to go within a mile of the Maes that day. Thank God. He also remembered that he needed to keep Meirion in the loop, so he sent a text: 'Still waiting for the whiskey.' He was walking in through the door of the station when he received the reply: 'Go buy your own whiskey, you tight bastard, but come over and drink it with us.' Followed by a smiley face.

Half an hour after celebrating the fact that he did not have to go to the Maes, Daf was driving to the Eisteddfod once again, heading for the caravan site. There was no drug connection this time: the call to the station had concerned the disappearance of an expensive piece of sporting equipment. Daf felt as if he were connected to the bloody Eisteddfod with a piece of elastic: no matter how hard he pulled away, he seemed to end up back there. At least the jobsworth in the office at the caravan site had learnt his lesson: Daf was waved straight in, with directions for reaching Pitch 623.

Pitch 623: in the area where the larger, more luxurious motorhomes were parked. He had an uncomfortable feeling, which was borne out when he found the correct number: 623 was where Garmon Jones' van was parked. Daf tried to remember all the strategies, both social and professional, he had learnt over the years to help in difficult situations but he knew there was nothing he had learnt thus far in his life which could prepare him for the awkwardness of meeting a man he now knew had given his daughter her first orgasm.

'Mr Dafis, so glad it's you! I didn't think you'd bother with a bit of low-grade trouble like this.' It was impossible, even knowing all he knew, for Daf not to respond positively to the young man's honest smile.

'Everything to do with the damn 'Steddfod is potentially sensitive. What's going on?'

'I've lost my bow.'

'What?'

'Bow. As in, shooting.'

'Like a Robin Hood type of bow?'

'Exactly like Robin Hood.'

'Can I ask you why you've bought your bow to the Eisteddfod?'

'For a good while, I was known as a world champion, and that's exactly what I was. I still want to be a champion, but I need to change my event, right? I bought the bow after a training session in Stoke Mandeville Hospital with the gang from British Wheelchair Archery. My target is a place in the team for Rio and I can't stop training for ten whole days, just because I'm down here selling bikes.'

'When did you see it last?'

'Yesterday. I went for a bit of a spin, up Cader and then went down to Aberdyfi for a bite to eat. I tried to give Carys a bit of a shooting lesson on the beach. She's useless, but, fair play to her, it's a heavy bow, suitable for a man.'

'What's the difference?'

'Upper body strength. Carys has got a good eye right enough but she can't manage the bow.'

'After the trip, what happened to the bow?'

'It's the full kit, Mr Dafis. Six arrows, arm brace, the lot.'

'Worth a bit?'

'I've put it down on my insurance at a valuation of eight hundred pounds.'

Daf whistled. 'Not a kid's toy, then?'

'Far from it. And that's the thing. The box was in the boot of the car but I can't remember if I locked the boot or not.'

'What about this morning? Was it locked then?'

'I'm nearly certain I locked it, Mr Dafis. I was a bit worried about that little bastard who's been hanging about.'

'That's one problem on the way to being solved, I hope. Anyway, he wasn't here last night at all. Listen, you do know that if you admit to your insurance company that you're not sure if you locked the car or not, they won't pay you a penny?'

'I do know that, but I don't fancy telling a lie, somehow.'

'I shouldn't say this, Garmon, but in your situation, most people would say whatever gave them the best chance of making a successful claim.'

Garmon grinned and turned his hands palm upwards in a gesture which struck Daf as being vaguely French. 'I'd rather lose eight hundred quid than my self-respect.'

Daf stared at him for a moment. 'We'd better find this bow, then, save paperwork all round.'

'And if I do decide to make a claim, I'll need a Crime Reference from the police, won't I?'

'You're right. How powerful is this bow? Is it dangerous? Could you kill someone with it?'

'In a wink. Why do you ask? Anyone been shot on the Maes?'

'Not yet but, God knows, there's plenty of people there deserve shooting. I'll make a few enquiries.'

'I half think one of the kids on the site may have borrowed it. I was showing some of them how to use it and maybe one of them has decided to borrow it to have a go by themselves. That wouldn't really be stealing.'

'Check up that it hasn't been posted on eBay.'

'No-one would be that dull, to list something they've just nicked.'

'You'd be surprised.'

'I'll check when I get to the stand: no Wi-Fi here.'

Daf had to say something and this was the chance. 'And how does Carys get on without Wi-Fi?'

'She hasn't complained.' No she hasn't, Daf thought, because when she was with Garmon, checking her Instagram would be the last thing on her mind.

'You coming to the barbeque at Neuadd?'

'Of course – looking forward. I'm not a good cook and even washed down with a lot of Guinness, burnt sausages aren't so great after the third day.'

'Great, look forward to seeing you then.'

'Thanks for your help.'

'I haven't helped yet. Here's my phone number, my personal one. If you remember anything, give me a ring.'

'I will, Mr Dafis.'

'Daf, please.'

'Daf.'

For some reason, the two men shook hands as they parted. Daf walked back in the direction of the entrance to the caravan site: if he spotted any familiar faces, he could make a few enquiries about the bow.

In the caravan site shop, he came across a woman who had been at Aber at the same time as him, Tesni Waters. For some reason, her name had always made Gethin laugh: he would repeat it in the accent of one of the Gumbys from Monty Python. Daf had always found her to be a thoroughly nice person, straightforward and full of fun.

'Daf Dafis,' she began, with a grin, 'have you really arrested Hoppy the Happy Hare for possession of cocaine?'

'Tes, you know I can't say a word to you about that.'

'Look in the paper, Daf: it's the best scoop the *Daily Post* has had for years.'

'The story says he's been sacked, nothing about being arrested.'

'I'm an infants' teacher and I've got a serious question, Mr Bigshot Police Boss, who's going to be tripping through the woods on his tippy-tippy toes now, hey? If I have to tell my reception class that their favourite Happy Hoppy Hare is in gaol, they'll kill me.'

'You know what, Tes? This Eisteddfod has just been one long headache as far as I'm concerned. Latest is, I've got to find a bow.'

'To tie up a parcel?'

'No, as in a bow to shoot with. Have your kids mentioned anything like that?'

'Garmon Jones' bow, do you mean? He's been great with the kids, showing them how to hold the bow and so on. If one of the ungrateful beggars has pinched it, then I'll shoot them myself.'

'Can you do me a favour? If you hear anything about the bow, can you pick up the phone?

'No worries.'

Daf went over to Eira's VW to arrange a formal interview with Peredur and to warn her to expect contact from the Children's Services team in Cardiff. They all, especially the Prof, would need to make a good impression in order to avoid a Care Order or a Safeguarding Order being set in place for Peredur. He knocked on the little metal door and when he received no reply, Daf left Eira a brief note. As he strolled back to his car, the signal on his phone suddenly grew stronger, so he took the chance to Google the Prof's name. A story from 2013 reached the top of the results list: 'Senior Academic Guilty of Boy's Death.' Before he had the chance to read the details, the signal vanished once again, as so often happens in Mid Wales. He had almost reached his car when he was approached by a young girl, perhaps ten years old, selling the magazine *Golwg*.

'Sorry, *lodes*, but I've bought several copies already this week.'

'Please. Just one. Have you read it yet?'

'Not yet, no. But ...'

'What if you got caught in a traffic jam? You could read it whilst you were waiting.'

'That wouldn't be very safe at all but I tell you what. I'll buy a *Golwg* if you answer a couple of questions.'

'What sort of questions?'

'I'm helping Garmon Jones look for his bow which has gone missing. I'm a policeman, so I'm asking anyone if they've seen it.'

'OK. I don't know anything myself but I can ask my friends, if you like.'

'Thanks. What's your name?'

'Modlen Carter. And I know who you are: Inspector Dafis. I'm considering a career in the police myself, or journalism. I'm good at asking people things.'

'Here's my phone number and listen, Modlen, if I don't answer, it's usually because I'm somewhere where there isn't any signal. Send a text or leave a message, OK? And just so you know, I'm not interested in making a big thing out of this, but I just want to get that bow back.'

Modlen was wrong about the traffic – the system was

working perfectly. Daf parked his car for a moment when he reached the top of Cefn Llwyd Bank and looked down over the beautiful valley. On the Maes below him, people flowed like water, every drop full of hopes, anxieties and memories. He rang the station.

'Don't rush back from your jolly, boss,' Nia remarked. 'We're about to unfold the sun-loungers here because we haven't got half enough to do.'

'I need the details of an RTA which lead to a court case involving the grandfather of our Norman Price coke dealer. Professor Talwyn Teifi is his name. I need to see the Impact Statement and any reports about the defendant, OK? Carmarthen or Ceredigion area somewhere.'

'I realise you may just be setting a little task to stop me from getting bored: is there any other reason?'

'Because, in that family, which is deep in the system by now, the grandfather is probably the only person capable of being a real and consistent help to that fucked-up lad.'

'Fair point.'

'I'll be back in a minute.'

He hadn't even opened the car door when he received a call: it was as though the Maes was pulling him to it with a magnetic force. The call was from Betsan.

'Dafydd, where are you?'

'Why do you ask?'

'I've got a bit of a problem and I need help.'

'I've just left the caravan site and I'm heading back to my desk which is buried under a mountain of paperwork which has been building up all week.'

'Please, Dafydd, I really need your advice. I can't discuss this with Mei because I would never hear the end of it.'

'Personal problem?' Daf asked, thinking of his own complex situation.

'Half and half. Come and have a cup of tea with me; please Daf – I know I can depend on you.'

Daf decided to leave his car parked in the lay-by on Cefn Llwyd Bank and walk down to the Maes. He soon became uncomfortably warm which didn't help his temper. He had a mass of paperwork to get done, his family was like a little boat tossed about on a stormy sea but he couldn't turn down anyone's appeal for help. The fact that Betsan was a good-looking girl didn't really matter, because Daf liked to think of himself as ready to help anyone but her looks did make him feel self-conscious about the fact that his shirt was sticking to the flesh either side of his spine and his hair was dark with sweat, like a stoat who was having a hectic time of things. So, instead of doing as he should, and getting that paperwork done before worrying about it poisoned his waking hours, he was shambling back to the Maes to do a favour to a young woman who almost certainly would have forgotten about his existence by the beginning of the next week.

The nervous smile on Betsan's face changed his mood completely. She had walked to the main entrance to meet him.

'What's this secret you can't share with Meirion then, Bets?' Daf asked, trying to joke her out of her embarrassment.

'You'll have to promise to not hold any weird stuff my family do against me, please.'

'I've got a full set of oddbods myself and this week, they're at peak crazy so don't you worry. I'm sure it's not as bad as you think.'

'Would you like a cup of tea?'

'What about an ice-cream instead.'

Daf was rather surprise by the length of the queue, with over fifty people waiting for their 99s but before he could suggest to Betsan, who was in her uniform as always, that perhaps they should settle for a cup of tea after all, the van's proprietor called out:

'Hey guys, make some room there: the boys in blue need a break,' before offering them Mr Softees for nothing. Betsan insisted on paying and the ice-cream man was full of praises for the contribution the emergency services were making to the smooth running of the Eisteddfod.

'We don't come across a satisfied customer like that every day, Bets,' Daf remarked as they walked away, conscious that he was trying to eat his Flake in a non-suggestive manner, given that he was in the company of an attractive colleague.

'That's true. Listen, Daf, I'm supposed to be presenting a story session for children on our stand soon: can I just tell you the story?'

'Of course.'

'Mum's got a sister, older than her, well over sixty now. She was a teacher before she retired and she's ... well, she's difficult. She's single, never been with a man as far as I know, always judging everyone and thinks she's always right about everything. That's one reason why I can't discuss this with Meirion – she's so anti-gay, is Bodo Mai, she'd drive him into a rage.'

'And what's happened to Bodo Mai?'

'She conducts a small lady's choir, and a good one at that. She's not close to the rest of the family because she got a job down in Carmarthenshire years ago so after she retired, she's had nothing to fill her days except practising with Blodau Mai.'

The May Flowers: a camp title punning on the conductor's name was only to be expected.

'Are they competing?'

Betsan licked a runnel of melted ice-cream from the side of her cone so she didn't reply for a moment.

'Supposedly. But Dafydd, she came round to see me yesterday, as angry as a nest of wasps, saying that someone had poisoned her girls because all of them, apart from her, are too ill to stand, let alone sing.

'Wine flu, maybe? A pretty common ailment at the 'Steddfod.'

Betsan shook her head. 'You don't understand, Dafydd. They don't have an ounce of freedom and if one of them even dreamt of going on the lash before competing, she'd kill them. You don't know Bodo Mai: she's like the Mussolinni of the Maes, the Pol Pot of the Pavilion.'

'What if they've eaten something to make them ill? A dodgy sausage, perhaps?'

'I don't know the details but they certainly haven't been allowed to wander very far and Bodo Mai is very particular over what they eat. She takes elaborate precautions to stop anything like this from ever happening.'

Daf crunched the last of his cone. 'Bets, if she's such a bitch, why do they have anything to do with her?'

'Because they like to win. And she's shit hot, knows her stuff. To some extent, they're willing to put up with her nonsense if it's the price they have to pay for success.'

'How can I help?'

Betsan avoided Daf's eye. 'I know how busy you are, Dafydd, but could you have a word with her? I don't want her to launch an official charge because that would end up with me looking like an utter twat.' Her voice was so shy, despite the vocabulary, that Daf felt fatherly.

'Where are they staying? I'll call by now.'

Whatever else might have happened to them, the May Flowers had been lucky in terms of their accommodation. They were staying in a beautiful farmhouse in the hills above Pontrobert, only two miles from the Maes. On the lawn in front of the house, the owners had placed a vast wooden table and half a dozen chairs so their guests might enjoy the views. But the group of women Daf saw sitting around this table did not look as if they were taking any pleasure from the glorious scenery. Their ages ranged between twenty and forty and all had very difference features, but they all shared the same sallow look. Before Daf had a chance to introduce himself, the door to the house opened and a little woman stepped out into the sunshine. She was very short and, with her severe haircut, she had the look of a young boy from the 1930s. In the killing heat, she wore a tweed skirt and jacket and her formality rather reminded Daf of John Neuadd. With her thin legs and glittering tiny eyes, also reminded him of a partridge with a lot on its mind.

'Are you the policeman Betsan was supposed to be sending?' she asked Daf, without the slightest preliminary greeting.

This first sentence wasn't promising. Daf, like most people, had a tendency to start all conversations with the formal form of the word 'you' but Bodo Mai had clearly decided that he didn't warrant such politeness. He sighed and could see exactly what Betsan had to deal with.

'Inspector Dafydd Dafis, Dyfed Powys Police. How can I help you?'

By now, the women sitting around the table were all staring at him and Daf was feeling distinctly uneasy under the blank gaze of a dozen eyes.

'He was the policeman last year,' said the youngest member of the group. 'When that girl got killed.'

Bodo Mai made a rasping noise in her throat and Daf realised he had no idea of her real name: he could not dream of calling her 'Bodo' and he did not know her surname.

'Betsan said you were having a problem,' he ventured.

'Problem?' snapped Bodo Mai. 'Perhaps it is just a little problem to you, but these girls have been poisoned.'

'Are you sure of that?'

'Take a look at them, Inspector: they are really ill. Some people are willing to go to any lengths to win the prize in the Eisteddfod.'

'But couldn't they have eaten something which disagreed with them?'

The little woman almost leapt out of her shoes, ending up standing on tiptoe.

'Inspector Dafis, do you think I would let my girls come to

a place like this without taking stringent measures to ensure their bio-security? We've bought food up with us from Carmarthenshire, we're drinking nothing but Tŷ Nant bottled water and they have to use freshly boiled water to clean their teeth.'

'But in my experience,' Daf responded, ignoring her insult to his home area, 'sausages are like little terrorists: you can do your best to keep them out but just one rogue one always find its way through.'

'I have absolutely no interest in your experiences with the low-quality sausages of Mid Wales. How do you intend to catch the offender?'

'Are we sure there is an offender?'

'I know perfectly well who's responsible – Eirlys Cadwaladr from Crymych. She'd not have a canary's chance against us if the girls were well.'

'We do need proof before going around accusing people.'

'That's your job, isn't it?'

'I will be making inquiries, of course, but in the meantime it would be a great help to me if the girls could keep samples, which we could analyse.'

'What type of samples?'

Daf could not believe she had asked such a question. The little woman's eyes reminded him of the alarming headmistress in his primary school who always blamed Daf for everything, so he could not imagine how he could discuss with her the process of crapping into a yoghurt pot.

'The surgery will clarify all the details with you,' he evaded, before taking out his phone and ringing Nia.

'Don't get mad at me, Nia, but we've got another case on our hands. Six girls are sick and it's possible they have been poisoned. Can you ring the surgery and arrange an appointment with the nurse, to collect samples? It would be best if she could come up here, Bryngaled, up the back of Pont. ASAP, please, and I'm definitely heading back to the station now.'

Daf was not best pleased at the idea of leaving his phone number with Bodo Mai but he felt he had to do so. The look in her eye told him clearly that his response to her difficulty was far from adequate in her opinion and Daf was very glad to escape, even if that meant spending the rest of the sunny afternoon behind his desk.

Daf spent hours discussing the Dyfed Powys Police input into Peredur's multi-agency meeting in Cardiff, writing reports for the Crown Prosecution Service and making his contribution to the information the coroner would require for the inquest on Dewi Dolau. Files were opened and referenced, details checked, forms filled, emails sent. Nia printed out the details of the accident involving the Prof but Daf had no chance to read them. He received a text from Meirion. 'Get up here with pizzas and booze. We're nearly dead of heat and boredom.' He rang Gaenor on her mobile.

'How's things, Gae?'

'Champion, thanks. And you?'

'Drowning in paperwork. Is Carys coming back tonight?'

'Haven't heard.'

'Remember last night?'

'I remember quite a lot about last night – any bit in particular?'

'Don't talk like that on the phone: I can't breathe tidy. I mean earlier: I was just wondering how you knew where I was last night?'

'I asked Sheila.'

'Of course. Well, I fancy going up there tonight, pick up where we left off, like.'

'You deserve a drink: shall I come up and pick you up?' Her simple offer summoned an entire vision into his mind, of the two of them living contentedly together.

'Could you? Then, on the way back, we can back on the back lane over the Allt, I'll take you for a walk and fuck you under the stars.'

'You're so romantic.'

'How's Rhods?'

'Grand. We're busy making pavlovas. Sugar all over the place.' Another glimpse of how life could be, full of affection and freedom.

In the supermarket, he bought several different pizzas, a case of lager and four tubs of Ben & Jerry's. Without thinking, he selected Cookie Dough, Fal's favourite flavour. Since the mess at breakfast, he hadn't thought about her at all, as if the part of his brain which stored his knowledge of her had somehow failed. He experienced a moment of vague guilt before the ugly memories came flooding back.

Daf's priority, after arriving at the cottage, was to find a private moment to commiserate with Betsan.

'I understand the whole situation now,' he told her. 'I've never met a woman as stubborn as Bodo Mai.'

'Well, you've made a very favourable expression on her. She said you gave her no reason to doubt your competence but she was very cutting about your accent and the standard of your Welsh.' Betsan tried to choke back laughter but failed. 'She said I should be on the lookout for a man like you, who would do very well, given some intensive speech therapy and emergency grammar lessons.'

'Speech therapy?' Daf repeated.

Meirion hurried over, beer in hand. 'What's the joke?'

'Nothing,' Betsan replied, gripping her lower lip between her teeth.

'Don't tell me you've invited that lot from the CPS?'

'We all need to relax by now, Mei.'

So they didn't have a quiet night discussing police matters, but a bit of a session. The CPS gang turned up and the family from the farmhouse came over to give their guests a bottle of pear brandy. An unexpected night of fun, and when Gaenor arrived and realised that the woman who owned the holiday cottage was one of her good friends from school, Daf felt much less bad about dragging her out to fetch him. He tried to count how many years had gone by since he had enjoyed a good night out with Falmai. Every occasion had been spoiled by her snobbish and spiteful observations, reminding everyone of the importance of the Neuadd family, leaving Daf burning with shame. He realised, as they all chatted freely, how little he knew about Gaenor's life before her marriage and, as they were driving home, felt he had to mention it.

'Why don't I know anything about your family, Gae? Before tonight, I can hardly remember you saying a word about when you were young.'

She turned her head and Daf saw an unusual bitterness in her eyes. 'Because Mum and Dad – to say nothing of my brother – are not good enough to associate with the Joneses of Neuadd. So I didn't mention them, because I didn't want them to be the target for anyone's sneers.'

Daf determined, then and there, to save them all from the claws of the Neuadd clan as soon as possible: Gaenor, Carys, Rhodri and himself. In the meantime, he took Gaenor for a walk on the Allt, under the stars.

Chapter 8

Thursday

Daf had not suffered like this for ten years. His thirst woke him about four and after managing to lever himself upright, he thought for a minute that he had had a stroke. He was having difficult moving his legs but he gradually realised, through the fog in his head, that it was the effect of the whiskey. He succeeded in reaching the bathroom where he filled the tooth mug from the tap and drained its contents, time after time. He tried to vomit but failed. He went back to bed but his churning stomach stopped him sleeping. At break of day, the roses on the wallpaper started jumping up and down, making him feel yet more queasy. He shut his eyes to avoid the bloody roses and fell into a deep sleep.

'Here's your choice of remedy: a cup of tea, Panadol, a bacon sandwich or half a bottle of flat Pepsi.' Gaenor put the tray down on the little table by the bed. 'Rhod made you the sandwich, since you'd missed your breakfast.'

'Can I try them all, or is that greedy?'

'It is greedy but you look like you need all the help you can get. My brother always swore by the flat Pepsi in his party animal days.'

'Can you stay to administer the medicine, please, nurse?'

'Only for a couple of minutes: I've got mini-pizzas in the oven.'

Daf raised himself to a sitting position and Gaenor perched on the edge of the bed. He had two things inside him, both fighting to get out: the burp escaped before the emotional statement. Gaenor flinched but smiled as the sour breath reached her, and he was inspired by her amused reaction to his obnoxious morning-after state.

'Gae, I know I'm probably still pissed but I want to say

something, plump and plain. I didn't want to stop here over the 'Steddfod but right now I'm glad I did because I've seen the way you're treated, with no respect at all and I've had enough. On what I bring home, especially since I've just got my threshold payment, we could live comfortably, even without any cash behind us.'

'We could. I could easily get a job myself.'

'Rhod doesn't want to stop with Falmai so we'd be a little family. I'm sure I can raise another loan to pay back what I owe John and then, as Nelson Mandela said, we can start "the long walk to freedom".'

Money had always been a worry for Daf. He had not inherited anything and had, over the years, been obliged to meet the care costs not only of his parents but also Uncle Maldwyn. John had given them the ground on which to build the bungalow and had also provided a substantial loan when the building costs had over-run. Daf would walk out of the bungalow with no capital but that didn't worry him at all: Falmai could take the shirt off his back if he could be free to live without her. Gaenor's smile was all the answer he needed.

'I hate to cut into your practical plans,' she said, 'but I've got tell you how much I enjoyed being with you last night, meeting people, socialising. John's always so boring and, I don't know, rigid somehow: it's like going out for the evening with ... with a piece of furniture.'

'We'll have a bloody good party when we get away, even if we have to live in the Wynnstay flats.'

'Drink up your tea, Dafydd, it's getting cold.'

'Like everything else under this roof.'

About eleven, Daf was feeling well enough to fetch his car. They had to wait for what Rhodri described as 'a window in the baking schedule' so whilst the fourth batch of mini-pizzas was cooking, Daf read the court reports of the Professor's accident. The victim was fifteen years old, the only son of a widow. After her husband's death from cancer, she decided to move out of London with her son, buying a farmhouse and using her sporting expertise to create an activity centre. In its third season, the centre began to pay its way but as the holiday period was drawing to a close, Aaron was killed, not far from Newquay. After that, the mother had a nervous breakdown. The social workers reported to the court that she was judged to have 'a significant and enduring risk of self-harm.' It was certainly a sad story and a cloud on the Prof's conscience but it was still an accident, even if it had damaged a number of people. Not enough to rule out Peredur's grandfather as the key to his recovery, Daf judged, and with the smell of melting cheese filling his nostrils, it was hard not to feel positive.

When they reached the farmyard, where Daf had left his car, Gaenor pulled a little packet from her pocket.

'We had to buy a set of these when we went over to France with the car last year. It's a breathalyser. I won't have you taking any risks: Rhodri and I have got well ahead with the food for tonight so we don't mind chauffeuring you about today.' Daf blew into the tube, although he knew what the result was. He hadn't drunk nearly enough to be positive after eleven the next day and the test agreed with his assessment. 'Back to these salads then, Rhods,' Gaenor concluded.

'I'm expecting a mountain of coleslaw.'

'On the case,' replied his son.

It was his ethical standards rather than his hangover which prevented Daf from conducting Peredur's official interview, delegating the task to Darren and Nia. As an old friend of the boy's father, it wouldn't be appropriate. Daf considered that Gethin was unlikely to fulfil the role of the Appropriate Adult very well and Eira was a worse prospect. If any of their toxic spite spilled out in official circumstances, the chances of Peredur being placed with any member of his family under the terms of a Care Order would be considerably diminished. He decided to have a word with the Prof, so rang the bungalow.

'Geth, is your dad about?'

'They've gone off to the Maes early today. Some lecture or other.'

'OK. How are things?'

'Oh, I don't know, Daf. The lad's very low but fair play to Manon, she's really doing her best to raise his spirits.'

'Manon will make a good mother herself one of these days,' Daf remarked, only just succeeding in preventing himself from observing that Manon was only a few years older than Peredur.

'No way, José. I had the snip after Peri and anyway, she should be concentrating on me. That's why I pay for all her fal-di-rals.'

'I know it's not my business, Geth, but you do know she's planning on having a family, don't you? I presume she does know about your vasectomy?'

'You're right, Daf, it's not your business. I'll ring you when Dad gets back.'

Before Daf reached the main road, his phone rang: Nev.

'You know you were going on about that bow which was missing?'

'Yes?'

'I haven't found it but I have found one of the arrows.'

'You what?'

'One of the arrows. I've found one in the car park. Someone used it to trash a car.'

'Trash?'

'Words scratched in the paint, then stuck the arrow into the tyres.'

'Overnight?'

'No. I was in the car park two hours ago and it wasn't there then.

'With you in ten.'

Back to the damn Maes, Daf thought. But there was enough schadenfreude in his nature to take a certain pleasure in the turn of events: if something like this had to happen at all, it was delightful that it should happen when John Neuadd, as chief parking steward, was in some way responsible. And when he arrived in the car park, he was not surprised to see the man himself anxiously waiting for him.

'Thank God you're here, Dafydd,' he began, shaking his bulky head from side to side as if to rid himself of trouble like one of his cattle disposing of an irksome fly. 'Someone has ... has attacked a car, the car of Professor Talwyn Teifi himself. Unsuitable words, tyres destroyed: I'm at the end of my tether, I really am.'

'I'm told it didn't happen overnight, John and that's the real puzzle. How could it have happened under the eyes of your parking stewards?'

A brick-coloured flush spread over John's weathered cheeks and he shifted his weight from foot to foot like a small boy caught out in some misdemeanour.

'The team has worked that hard, and we're running a bit short of volunteers. It's late in the week so most visitors know their way about the system by now and there's next to no-one here early, so I said to my lads, the ones who've stuck at it all week, like, that they could start a bit later, kick the shift off at ten. And I had to nip down to the vet's to get some oxytetracycline so ...'

Daf cut off what was promising to be a long, farm-based explanation with a serious nod of the head.

'Oh, dear me, John. Dear, dear me.' It was a moment to savour. It was enough to repay the feeling of intense humiliation Daf had felt as he had stood, like a supplicant child, at John's desk, waiting while, fountain pen held in thick fingers, his brother-in-law filled out a cheque from the farm's account to pay the outstanding builders' bills Daf and Falmai could not meet. But the score was not yet even because this lumpish man, so discomforted now by his unwonted failure to do his duty, had accused Gaenor of not doing hers, labelling that extraordinary human being as a 'barren'.

The car was in the far corner of the field that was being used as a car park, taking advantage of the shade of a wide-crowned oak tree. On the front door letters were scratched.

'What's that word?' Nev asked. 'I thought my Welsh was up to most things but I've never seen that word before.'

'It means 'bastard' but in a literary context. Nice to see the linguistic standards of the Eisteddfod being maintained.'

'"Lamb's cock" is clear enough, but "Tadpole"?'

'Again, a literary insult, dating back to Tudor times. We'll looking for a well-educated vandal. Where's this arrow, then?'

'By the back tyre, the one that's flat.' Daf was expecting something like a prop from a film about Robin Hood, not a long shaft of smooth fibreglass, fletched with some synthetic material.

'Are we bothering with finger prints?' Nev asked.

'Of course. This is a nasty little Crim Dam and it's bound to be talked about up and down the Maes. Especially,' he added, raising his voice a little, 'when people realise how late the stewards were getting to the car park this morning.' He hoped John would have overheard.

He rang Gethin again. 'Sorry to be a pain, Geth, but someone's trashed your car, in the 'Steddfod car park.'

'Run into it, you mean?'

'Vandalised it. Scratched words into the paintwork, had a go at the tyres ...'

Gethin hissed under his breath. 'That little fucker, Gwion ...'

'We don't know who did it but you'd best sort yourself a hire car in the meantime. Gaenor can give you a lift down to Border Garage to pick one up, but phone ahead, I would.'

'No doubt about it, and I hope I don't sound rude, Daf, but we are having the holiday from hell.'

There was a very sour edge in his voice and Daf found himself alarmed at the coldness.

The lecture Talwyn Teifi attending was in the Societies

Pavilion. Daf bought a cup of coffee from a nearby van and sat down at a little table. Even as early as this, there were a few people about and Daf had to share a table with a small man, so deep in a book that he did not notice the polite question as to whether or not the seat was taken. Daf looked at his watch and, seeing that he had a good quarter of an hour before the Prof would emerge, decided to read the magazine he had bought from the girl Modlen the previous day: it was still in his jacket pocket, though somewhat crumpled. He browsed for a few minutes before coming across a familiar name: Gethin wrote a column reviewing TV programmes. On paper, Gethin's voice was as clear as it was face-to-face: witty and totally without pity. Like a big gun levelled against a doll's house, his perfect words destroyed a minor programme utterly and the piece ended with some patronising suggestions of more suitable careers for the producer of the work in question. Daf spread the magazine on the table as he read the name of the producer, Elwyn Wyn Evans: the man Gethin had been arguing with by the Food Court on Monday. Daf sighed as he finished the piece: did Gethin have to go about making quite so many enemies?

The man opposite Daf at the table put his book down suddenly, covering the magazine page.

'It's not true,' he began in a shaky voice and Daf realised that he was sitting at a table with Elwyn Wyn Evans, a man so unremarkable that, with his face hidden by his book, Daf had taken no notice of him at all.

'True or not, I was reading it and I'd like to carry on, so if you just pick up your book ...?'

Instead of moving the book, Evans wrung his small hands.

'The show wasn't that bad. He's got no right to speak about me like that. I've forgotten more about good television than he would learn if he lived to be a hundred. And I can't see that happening: someone is bound to kill the bastard before long.'

'I was walking past when you are talking with Gethin on Monday. What's going on?'

The little man flicked his eyes over Daf's face for a moment and then shrugged slightly, as if he had decided to stop trying to hide his troubles. He clearly needed to vent.

'My mother set up a very successful TV company: PlayTree Productions. It was a thriving business but when she was being treated for breast cancer, it was time to renew the lease on the studio and the landlord wanted a great deal more money to renew. Gethin offered a little investment, to tide us over and before long, he owned us. When Mum died, he just closed the business down, sacking most of the staff and taking our good ideas. He offers me work now and again but I know how he works: stripping good ideas without any proper recognition. I set up my own business, just a one-man band really, and I do get myself a commission every now and then but look what His Majesty Gethin Teifi has to say about me!' Evans pulled the book back and Daf noticed, as he stretched his arm, that there were flecks of black paint on his hands and the sleeve of his jacket. Daf pulled his phone out and rang Nev.

'Get yourself over to the Societies Pavilion right now, *lanc*.' He turned to Elwyn. 'That was a pretty dull thing to do though, wasn't it? Trashing his car like that?'

'What ...? What are you talking about?'

'I'm a policeman, Mr Evans, and one of my colleagues is going to take you down to the station. But while we're waiting for him, can you tell me where you found that arrow?'

'I tripped over it, literally, in the caravan site. I'm staying in a tent, in the far corner. It was under the hedge, as if someone had thrown it there.'

'I can see you're very angry with Gethin but you've done something really stupid, haven't you? You're not a teenage lad and you should know better.'

'I'm sick to my stomach with the system which means the few get everything and the majority are always losing out.'

'You can discuss your revolutionary ideas in the car with PC Roberts and here he is, right on cue.'

Nev face was radiant with admiration.

'Fair play to you, boss,' he whispered. 'I know there's plenty of people in our team think you are off your head completely but, off your head or not, you're still one hell of copper.'

'Less of the "off your head" business, please, Nev. This is Elwyn Wyn Evans. You can charge him right away: he's not denying anything.'

The door of the Societies' Pavilion opened and some forty people came out into the bright sunshine, blinking like middle-class moles. Daf watched for a moment: the Prof and his wife were walking, relaxed, talking to friends. They were good people, he judged, but they had somehow managed to raise a son so selfish that he injured all of those he came into contact with. Under his breath, Daf found himself humming, and it was not the sexed-up folk songs Chrissie seemed to conjure up but a gloomy, horribly apt ballad by Leonard Cohen 'Bird on the Wire'.

'Excuse me, sir, might I have a word?'

After settling his wife at the table just vacated by Daf and Elwyn Wyn Evans, the Prof readily agree to take a short walk, away from the thickening crowds where he would be greeted by every third passer-by. Daf described what had happened to the car and the old man seemed suddenly weary, as if he had been suspecting bad news of some sort. Then Daf raised the subject of the accident.

'I believe you are Peredur's best chance sir. You should come down for the interview, to be his Appropriate Adult, if you can. And I think you will stand a good chance of being allowed to help him, if you tell the social workers the truth, about everything.' There was a sceptical creasing of the Profs brow and Daf was strangely unwilling to press on but knew he must. 'What happened after the accident?'

'For the first time in my life, Dafydd,' came the response, almost as if the question had been expected, 'I fell into low spirits, a depression. I was admitted to a clinic and I stayed as an in-patient for a month. But I'm well again now and ready to give Peredur all the support he needs.' Daf had to shake his hand.

'Don't forget, sir, that even if Peredur is placed under a Care Order, you could still care for him under the terms of that order.'

'Thank you for all your help, Dafydd. Derwenna was right, it seems: she had spotted the change in the boy.'

'Then she should be well-placed to help him recover.'

Daf received three phone calls in quick succession, all from women under pressure. Gaenor was the first.

'I've just given Gethin a lift down to get his hire car and he was saying that John has invited them all to the barbeque. If they come, we've got to think again: Rhods and I would be at least two dozen profiteroles short, for example.'

'Well, John will just have to uninvite them. There's history between Gethin and Garmon and it's not going to be fair to Carys if he's there.'

'Fair play. And if the stiff-necked old bastard doesn't agree, I'll cross over the yard and do it myself.'

'Thanks, *lodes*.'

'Daf?'

'Yeah?'

'My granddad, Taid Richards, he always used to call me "*lodes*". I like it, makes me feel safe.'

'See you later, *lodes*.'

'Love you.' What a declaration!

Second phone call: Chrissie.

'Mr Dafis, there's some bit of a right odd woman here, stopping in a tent.'

'You've got to expect a few weirdos when the National Eisteddfod is in town.'

'She's English.'

'Which doesn't mean she's odd.'

'I can't put it in words, right, but she gives me a cold feeling, down my backbone.'

'What does Bryn say?'

'Nothing of any use. Can you call by for a minute?'

'Only for a minute.'

'Fine.'

The third phone call came from Nia.

'We haven't got halfway through the paperwork from the start of the week and now you bring us a Crim Dam who wants the case conducted in Welsh. He'll have to have a Welsh-speaking lawyer and all of them are on annual leave, enjoying themselves at the 'Steddfod.'

'Try Haf Wynne. She's not a big Eisteddfod-goer.'

'And when are you going to grace us with your presence, boss?'

'I'm on my way now. Just one quick call to make.'

'I've set the stopwatch.'

There was a lively scene in the field below the house at Berllan. As well as the campers who had moved from Dolau, perhaps twenty more tents and caravans had pitched up and a children's play area had been created in the centre, with the swing and slide moved down from the garden and a makeshift sand pit of breeze blocks. Bryn was busy, shirtless as usual, using a long yellow hosepipe to fill a pool constructed from square silage bales, lined with thick black plastic wrap. Some dozen children were running about in their swimming costumes, waiting for him to finish. Chrissie was making her way down from the house, dressed in a light summer dress which seemed to flow around the shape of her body. Daf realised he'd never before seen her without jeans and, despite the strength of his feelings for Gaenor, he involuntarily licked his lips.

'Thanks for coming, Mr Dafis,' she began, 'but she's not about. Gone off watching birds, seemingly.'

'I'll call by later then.'

'I've talked it over with Bryn and he reckons I'm making a sea and a mountain out of the thing.'

'Fair enough. You know how to find me, if you need to.'

'But why's she come here at 'Steddfod time, if she doesn't want to go to the 'Steddfod?'

'Perhaps she didn't know the Eisteddfod was on.'

'Maybe, before she got here; but now she's here she can't miss that fuck me pink tent, can she?'

'Fair comment.'

'She's ... well, it's like she's had her nature squeezed out of her somehow, so you can't tell who she is.'

'We're Celts, remember, Chrissie, so we tend to show our feelings to everyone on this big, round earth. Many English people are ... are quieter in their natures.'

'You could be right, Mr Dafis; we'll just have to see.'

'How's Gwawr?'

'Champion, Mr Dafis. She's a big help with all these kids about the place. She doesn't like to go out in the evenings so she spends her time with us.'

'And no other bother?'

Chrissie laughed, throwing her head back which gave Daf an unsettling view of her smooth throat.

'Look at them two, Mr Dafis.'

By the pool, in the midst of the younger children, two young people were standing. The boy was tall and remarkably handsome with a mop of thick black hair; no prizes for guessing that he was Chrissie's son Rob. Daf hadn't seen him for a few months and was shocked at the change in his appearance. Rob was in the same class as Rhodri but had grown suddenly into a young man. Nestled against him was a slender girl with red hair. Daf recalled her face: she was the eldest of Eifion Pennant's children.

'Last night, when Gwawr was up with us, the lad decided to borrow her tent for a bit of private time with this new girl of his.'

'How old are they, Chrissie?'

'He's not far off fourteen, and he's the spitting image of his dad. Not sure about her, but she's a bit older, I reckon.'

'Take care, Chrissie. Her family are...'

'I know what her family are like, Mr Dafis: her dad has been bollocksing on about one thing after another ever since they arrived. But there's nothing more natural than young people having fun together.'

Daf watched as Rob's hand meandered down the girl's back and into the waist band of her jeans, a gesture of sexual intimacy.

'Try to get them to act tidy, can you, Chrissie? The last thing we need is more hassle.' Daf was speaking as a father as much as a policeman and was preoccupied by the thought that Rob was the same age as Rhodri, who was certainly nowhere near ready to be running his hands over any girl.

Nia had exaggerated, as she often did. The paperwork was under control. Sadly, when Nia asked Elwyn Wyn if he wanted them to contact any friend or family member who might come to support him, he couldn't come up with a single name. Haf Wynne did turn out to act as his lawyer but it was clear the case didn't interest her much. As he watched her trying to escape as soon as possible from a new client who had failed to gain her sympathy, Daf asked himself if she was just frittering away her life, filling the spaces which should be filled with people with books. He felt so much older than her, particularly as seeing Rob Berllan had reminded him that his children were almost adults. He couldn't help overhearing, through the open window of his office, her half of a phone conversation accepting an invitation for supper from Mostyn Gwydir-Gwynne. He felt a strange sense of relief, as if he no longer had to concern himself about her. She would make a very good wife for the MP and perhaps that would be a life which would suit her too, graciously entertaining guests to his grand house, unconcerned about how cold this bed might be. He could not help contrasting icy, intellectual Haf with Gaenor's warmth and the memory of her voice generated a rather foolish smile which persisted on his face for hours, despite Nia and Sheila's scorn.

Before lunch he received the results of the tests on Blodau Mai: there was cause for concern. Daf phoned the surgery straight back, hoping to speak to a doctor, but had to speak to a nurse instead, who told him the samples had been forwarded to the assay lab in Birmingham City Hospital.

'Everyone one of them, Inspector Dafis, shows evidence of unusual symptoms in the liver.'

'The liver, *lodes*? It's Eisteddfod week – there's no-one for miles around with a working liver. I last caught sight of mine last night, drowning in a bottle of whiskey.' The joke wasn't a success.

'I hope we all know the difference between a hangover in the morning and liver failure, Inspector. We will need to see the results of the further tests but there's very little doubt that something has happened to these ladies.'

After the call, Daf put his head in his hands for a few moments. How on earth could a cultural festival generate so much hassle? He decided to phone his colleagues down in Brecon sometime, to see if the Hay Festival generated an equivalent quantity of crap. And now there would be a significant bill to pay for the pigging laboratory ...

The phone rang again: Carys.

'All sorted for tonight, Dad?'

'No idea. Ask Rhodri and Gae: they're in charge.'

'Can you try to stop Mum acting weird around Garmon?'

'I can try my blue best.'

'Rhods tells me you're splitting up.'

'We can't carry on like this. We're like lions in a cage, tearing lumps out of each other because we can't escape.'

'What's the plan, then?'

'After the 'Steddfod, I'll find myself a place to rent. In Llanfair, hopefully.'

'With someone?'

'What?'

'You're not planning to live alone, are you, Dad?'

'No. Rhodri's coming with me.'

'Hmm. Anyway, I haven't got enough time to discuss your romantic future just now. I am a bit surprised, mind, that with all you've had on your plate since the weekend, you've got any energy left for love-life complications.'

'You're a fine one to talk, Carys Dafis.' His daughter was a young woman now, without doubt, and a young woman full of energy and humour.

'Behave yourself tonight, Dad.'

'Of course I will.'

'Oh, and there's a story going about the Maes that some singing party from Carmarthenshire have been poisoned.'

'You know the rules. You shouldn't ask, because I'm not going to say anything.'

'Bor-ring, Dadi!'

Despite really enjoying his chat with his daughter, Daf wished he had not been reminded of his main duty for the evening, keeping Falmai in check. Daf had rapidly developed a considerable respect for Garmon, especially after their discussion about the bow, and the young man did not deserve insults or scorn. He realised that this would be the last evening overshadowed by his responsibility for his wife's unacceptable behaviour. There was some sadness mixed in with his sense of freedom but, by now, Daf had come to mourn the person he had married almost as if she were dead: she certainly didn't exist anymore.

'Nia,' he called, 'we've got to sort out interviews with this bloody singing party. Can you and Nev go up there, when you're done with Peredur Teifi?'

Nia opened the office door, looking inscrutable.

'It would deffo be overtime.'

'*Lodes*, if you listen to Councillor Bebb, which I try not to, the Eisteddfod has totally transformed our economy so you must be in line for a bit more cash in your pocket.'

'Good job my mum agreed to have Seren for the whole week.'

'I do realise that you're losing out on your chance of an Eisteddfod spree, Nia – I really appreciate that.'

A sudden smile spread over her face. 'Other way round, boss: Jack was expecting me to go to any number of shit events, especially to watch him competing in the brass band comps but thanks to all this mayhem, I've got away with avoiding them total. I'd rather be investigating a suspected poisoning than listening to him blowing his bloody trombone any day of the week.'

'Fair play to you, Nia.'

A little later, Peredur arrived with his grandfather. Daf had expected to see Eira: no sign. He rang her and got the voicemail, but also the message: she had decided to step back from the situation. Perhaps Peredur had only ever been a performance prop to her, after all.

Daf didn't find it easy to sit at his desk whilst Nev and Nia were doing the hard work in the interview room, but at least it gave him the chance to catch up on less important things such as responding to press enquiries about Gwion. In terms of Ed Mills and Peredur Teifi, Daf was pretty certain about his recommendation to the CPS: a formal caution would be enough for them, but Gwion? He would at least have to agree to a treatment package: though he was a young man, Manon had suggested that he had been using for a decade. Release on licence conditional on treatment, perhaps? He wasn't certain: he didn't want to give the CPS the idea that he was a soft touch. He forwarded the press messages to the Press Officer at Headquarters, finished Gwion's paperwork and Googled the Prof's accident once again. He wondered why it kept coming into his mind: perhaps it was because the accident was all about a momentary lapse and Talwyn Teifi was not a man known for lapses. There was an article from the *Daily Mail*: 'Double

Heartbreak for Bike Death Mum.' He read the words but didn't really need to because the pictures told a clear enough story: a happy family, a graveyard, a woman standing by the pile of flowers forming a roadside shrine.

Nev popped his head round the door. 'Got a bit stuck, boss. He's not keen on telling us where his stash is, nor the money.'

'You give the Professor this message: we're trying to do things in the best way for all of us but we can get a warrant if we have to and the lad can be remanded into a secure unit if I so much as pick up the phone. And ask if he knows anything about Garmon Jones' bow.'

'Sounds like a folk song: "Garmon Jones' Bow".'

'Just ask the question, hey?

The pressure did the trick. Ten minutes later, Daf sent Darren over to the caravan site with Sheila, to open up Peredur's hiding place. No news of the bow. The Prof asked for a word with Daf on his way out.

'Where was Eira?' he asked.

'I don't know. We tried to contact her several times.'

'I can't understand this business at all. The boy has no moral compass at all, just as if he had been raised by wolves, or by a wolf-bitch.' This apt image seemed to hang between them on the air.

'Well, once again, thank you for everything. I'll look forward to seeing you later, Dafydd.'

'Later?'

'The barbecue.'

'I'm afraid my brother-in-law made a mistake. It's only a family party.'

The Prof frowned. 'We have no intention of intruding on a private event. I am very sorry.'

Daf felt obliged to tell the truth to the old man. 'No, it's me who should apologise: Carys has invited a friend of hers and it turns out that this friend isn't exactly on good terms with Gethin ...'

The Prof sighed. 'Before too long, we won't be able to cross the threshold without tripping over someone who isn't on good terms with him. And perhaps, Dafydd, which would be perfectly understandable, you don't want your children mixing with a boy who sells drugs.'

Daf's children had never made him ashamed and he felt a profound sympathy for Talwyn Teifi.

'It's a bit of a sensitive situation, sir. Carys has got a new boyfriend and we're meeting him for the first time.' There was a gleam of jealousy in the Prof's eye, as if he would relish being preoccupied by such minor issues.

On the bench in the reception area, Elwyn Wyn was sitting alone.

'What are you doing here, Elwyn Wyn?' asked the Prof in his official voice. 'I thought you would have your head buried in your rhyming dictionary before tomorrow.'

'And what's happening tomorrow?' Daf asked. The other two men stared at him as if unable to believe what he had just said.

'Final round of the Ymryson,' the Prof responded. 'And this man is the star of the Pembrokeshire team.' Daf felt no guilt at not following the week-long poetry competition, not when his attention was so well-occupied elsewhere.

'I won't be taking part in the Ymryson tomorrow, sir,' announced Elwyn, avoiding the Prof's eye. 'Because this morning, about half past nine, I attacked your son's car. And, from the bottom of my heart, sir, I did not want to do you any harm but I couldn't live any longer with the harm he was doing to me.'

Daf saw the strength in the old man, under the lash once again. He was like an experienced boxer, taking blow after blow but staying on his feet.

'Your absence from the Ymryson will be a great loss, Elwyn Wyn,' he replied, shaking hands with the criminal.

Daf followed the Prof out to the car park where the hire car was waiting.

'Here's another life infected by us, Dafydd. What on earth have I done to deserve this?'

'Sir, if I may be cheeky enough to discuss philosophy with an expert, I don't think we get punished like that. I agree with a friend of mine who says that it is through troubles that we develop as people.'

The Prof opened his eyes a little wider as if, even in the depths of his concern, he could not resist discussing his academic specialism. 'Do you have a Catholic friend then, Dafydd?'

'I don't know about the background to ideas, sir, I just speak from experience.'

'Of course. What will become of Elwyn Wyn?'

'He's been charged. I can't see him receiving a heavy penalty.'

'But it's another great load of trouble. You must be a strong man, Dafydd, dealing with this sort of thing day after day. It's easy to see you haven't become hard hearted, so how do you cope?'

'I'm not a strong man by any means, sir, but I believe in trying my blue best. Usually, my job is just about helping people solve their own problems but now and again there is a predator about, so I have to go after them.'

Daf was rather pleased with himself for this impromptu description of his way of working but soon saw, in the Prof's eyes, that he had made a mistake.

'And I am the father of just such a predator. I remember meeting your parents on your graduation day: we were all very proud of our sons that day. And I would still be proud, if I had raised a son like you, Dafydd.'

'All I do is try to keep things running tidy in my own square mile.'

'Hmm. After all that has happened this week, I'm glad to have had the opportunity to get to know you as a grown man.'

'In the future, sir, if I can be of any help to Peredur, as a friend of the family ...?'

'Thank you.'

Peredur was sitting in the hire car, accompanied by Manon, of all people, his boyish face pulled about with tension. He reminded Daf of an illustration from a Dickens story showing a street child who has learnt too much too soon. And what was the root of his difficulty? No-one, in his clever and privileged family had given him any care or time. He was a very different boy from Rob Berllan, who had confidence in every movement and also, thankfully, different from Rhodri. Thinking of the care Rhodri had always received, Daf had to ring Gaenor.

'Need anything from Tescos?'

'A couple of bottles of soda water would be a great help and a bit more tonic.'

'Good for Coke?'

'Yes.'

They made a good team, he thought, understanding one another and offering help before it was asked for. That stage hadn't lasted long with Falmai because any attention she gave to what Daf might need was attention she had to take away from her family and the all-important obligations of being a Jones of Neuadd.

It was a fine night for the barbecue and Daf was enough of a hypocrite to feel obscurely proud of his family connection to Neuadd. Garmon was a highly successful young man and it seemed to give some balance to things for him to have a chance to see the place in all its glory. A moment later, Daf dismissed this as nonsense: Garmon liked Carys because of who she was, not what her uncle owned, or even the fact that she was the daughter of a well-known policeman. Well-known policeman? He frowned at the description. And who had the well-known policeman managed to catch lately? A children's TV presenter who liked the white stuff, a local lad who was selling 'shrooms to pay his mother's debts, a year eight boy with a nightmare family and a sad little man who had come to the end of his tether. Didn't feel much like success.

He was glad to be diverted from his tally of failure by Garmon's arrival. Falmai was standing by the front door, waiting; Daf owed it to Carys to say something.

'It's Carys' night tonight, Fal. We'll have to act tidy.'

'Look at him. His legs don't move at all. How can a person like that even consider a relationship with a heathy young girl like Carys?'

'If you're talking about the physical side of their relationship, Carys is well pleased.'

'And you discuss such things with your daughter now, Dafydd Dafis? How unsuitable! The Berllan morals are catching, as I suspected.'

'Fal, can't we just play Happy Families for one night?'

The only reply he received was the hatred in her eyes. Nothing better than damage limitation to be expected from the rest of the evening. He strolled down to the yard to greet Garmon; Carys was by his side already.

'Thanks for the invitation, Daf,' Garmon began, extending a hand to be shaken. 'I'm fair sick of the caravan site by now.'

'I'm a guest here myself, *lanc*. Gaenor sent the invitation; she's Carys' aunt.' Daf turned to see Gaenor making her way down the path to greet the guest, untying her apron as she did so, a smudge of flour on her cheek. Her smile was nearly as wide as Garmon's own and the delight in Carys' eyes made Daf grin too. Falmai was nowhere to be seen.

'Garmon, I'm Gaenor. Come up for a drink while we wait: John and Siôn have just finished milking so we don't want to see them until they've had a chance to shower.'

Daf, who prided himself on his lack of sentimentality, was taken by surprise by the emotions he felt. He'd never expected to come across a woman like Gaenor, who suited him so well, and with his happiness came a sudden fear, the fear of losing her. He knew exactly what he wanted in life now, what he needed for his 'happy ever after'.

It was clear, when Garmon met Falmai, that he had been forewarned.

'Lovely to meet you, Mrs Dafis,' he began, polite as ever.

Silence. Falmai made no reply and, as the moments dawdled past, it became awkward. Gaenor, as so often, intervened.

'What have you got in that bag of yours, Garmon? Anything in there crying out to go into the fridge?'

'I've been cheeky enough to please myself on the wine front, so I've got a few bottles of red but there's a drop of cider here as well.'

'What red wine?' Gaenor asked, taking the bag from him.

'I know I sound like an old snob when I say it but when I was travelling in South America, I picked up quite a taste for the reds they make there so ...'

The moment Garmon had been led out of earshot, Daf turned on Falmai who had been hanging back in the shadows of the pergola.

'What the hell is the matter with you, Falmai? Garmon is a very tidy young chap and you can't find a word to say to him!'

'And you are happy that your daughter, with a wonderful future ahead of her, throws herself away on some ... some cripple?'

'You know what, Fal, I heard someone insult Garmon like that on Monday, a lad who was full of cocaine. I never expected to hear words like that from my own wife.'

'So now you remember I'm your wife, do you?'

'Whatever you are, you're Carys' mother. Can't you just remember that for tonight?'

'I understand why you're such a great fan of his. Anything new gets your attention but you never stick at anything for long, always on to the next thrill. I still remember Matt, who was a lovely young man.'

'I was fond of Matt but it's Carys who makes the decision,

not us. No-one knows what's going to happen next but we have to be civil to him tonight.'

'But who's going to look twice at her after this? What kind of man would content himself with a cripple's leavings?'

'In more than twenty years, Fal, you've never really seen me lose my temper but I'm struggling now. Your daughter's got a new boyfriend: can't we just be nice to him for one evening?' Suddenly, he had a flash of inspiration. 'For generations, Neuadd has always been known for its tradition of hospitality. It would be a shame to ignore that now.' It was his last blow but it hit the target. Falmai chewed at her lip for a moment then turned and headed up to the patio beside the barbecue.

As they were waiting for John and Siôn, Gaenor's social skills and Garmon's easy warmth were enough to create a cheerful atmosphere. The only tricky note was struck by Megan, Siôn's temporary girlfriend. Having passed the week acting as the perfect girlfriend for the wealthy young man she had literally stumbled across on the Maes, her mask started to slip. A celebrity like Garmon drew her like a magnet but after half an hour of flirting and pulling her T-shirt tight over her breasts, she realised that Garmon wasn't interested in anyone but Carys. She swapped back to her previous plan then and tried to be super-helpful to Gaenor but she, an observant mother who always looked out for the interests of her son, had taken note.

Rhodri and his friend Meilyr were very taken with Garmon. Daf saw the admiration in his son's eye as Garmon discussed his travels. Rhodri was rather less mature than Meilyr, who came from Newtown and had a town boy's slickness. Thinking of Rob Berllan taking Eifion Pennant's daughter into a convenient tent, Daf was glad to see his son was still a boy.

Someone suggested a game of Frisbee on the wide lawn and in no time, all of them, expect Falmai, were running, shouting and laughing. She sat alone on an oak bench, eyes staring without seeing. Daf had to give it another go.

'Come and play with us, Fal,' he pleaded, reaching for her hand. 'We're all having a great laugh.'

'You're acting like children. I'm surprised at Gaenor, really I am. And that wheelchair will be over in a minute, you mark my words.'

'It's a sports wheelchair. He plays rugby in it, never mind a bit of Frisbee.'

Falmai turned her head and Daf returned to the game, unable to understand her. Usually, the rift in the family was between him and the Joneses but Falmai had abandoned them all, choosing isolation. She remained where she was even when her brother and nephew appeared.

Daf tried not to compare Garmon with Matt but he failed. Matt was a nice enough young man with not much to him. Daf noticed the difference as Garmon was talking to John: Matt always took great care to agree with every word John said but Garmon provoked him into enjoyable debate. John was a shy and conservative man but he warmed to Garmon at once. As he put the vast chunk of home-raised steak on Daf's plate, John remarked that Garmon was a very tidy young chap indeed and for once, Daf agreed with him. Apart from Falmai's strange silence, all was going well.

'You've got to talk to him,' Daf whispered in her ear. 'Look at the effort everyone else is making. Think about Carys.'

In response, as if she had to make some response to an irritation, Falmai rose to her feet and marched over to Garmon, cutting across a discussion between him and Siôn.

'How much medicine do you take every day?' she asked baldly. Daf saw a cloud over Carys' face but Garmon just laughed.

'Well, I needed a fair whack of Ibuprofen to get rid of my bad head this morning.'

'But you're ill, aren't you?'

'Not unless I drink a drop too much red wine.'

Having made her contribution, she returned to her place,

ignoring everyone. Daf was glad beyond words that Gaenor had made such an effort, both socially and practically. As he went back into the house to fetch another bottle of rosé from the fridge, Daf overheard Garmon say to Carys in a low, teasing voice:

'Tell me which one is your mum again? Because I can tell you which one your dad is in love with.'

Daf was startled, thinking that he was smart enough to fool everyone but Garmon was, in many ways, a remarkable young man.

Around eleven, Gaenor offered Garmon a bed for the night.

'Thank you very much, Mrs Jones but I have to get back to the van. I have my routines I stick to, every morning.'

'Physio and so on?' asked Falmai, seeing her change to steer the conversation back to Garmon's infirmity.

'Fitness, Mrs Dafis. I do an hour of weights every morning. And I do know I'm well over the limit: Josh who works for me is down in the town, on the lemonade, and he'll pick me up when I say. In fact. I'd best give him a ring now, if that's OK?'

'There's no signal this side of the house,' Carys explained. 'Dadi, can you show Garmon the hotspot?'

Daf found her choice of word rather unfortunate, given her praise for Garmon's sexual technique: he hid his smile and led Garmon down into the yard. Suddenly, the sound of an argument burst out of the bungalow.

'Noisy neighbours,' Garmon remarked.

'Only temporary. We let the place out for the 'Steddfod, to Gethin Teifi and his family.'

'And, by the sound of it, he treats his family the way he treats his colleagues. I've got three bars: I'd better text Josh.'

Daf stepped towards the bungalow, across the darkened yard, until he could make out the words of the dispute.

'Why didn't you tell me? You can't keep secrets like that.'

'It's my business.'

'But I'm the one who wants children.'

'We all want lots of things, my girl, and a sign of growing up is that we learn that we don't always get what we want.'

'But I had a right to ...'

'Oh, you sound like a little girl of ten, stamping her feet if she doesn't get her own way.'

'Will that be next, then, fancying children?'

Then, the sound of a slap.

Daf called over to Garmon:

'Excuse me a moment, *lanc*: I need to check all's well.'

'Fair enough.'

Manon was fine but there was a large red mark on Gethin's face.

'Go, if you've had enough of the lifestyle, Mans.'

'Where to? I've lost all my friends.'

'Go back to the Hoppy Happy Hare. You can go and watch him bounce about in prison.'

'That's enough,' thundered Daf. 'I'm not allowing this. You two have got a choice: either shut up at once or go back to Cardiff tonight.'

'It's the middle of the night,' Gethin protested.

'And you've broken the terms of our agreement. I'm not going to ask twice.'

Out on the yard, Garmon was applauding.

'That's the way to deal with the bastard. You know what, Daf? I've got a target for shooting at home, and to improve my aim, I've got a picture of Gethin Teifi, right in the centre.'

Chapter 9

Friday

Daf awoke with a sense of anticipation: it was the day of the Chairing ceremony. Even though he was not a great Eisteddfod-goer, he loved poetry and could not help being absorbed by the drama of the occasion. It was the greatest prize, the unique wooden chair, and at the heart of the ceremony was the moment when the pen-name of the poet was announced and spot-lights raked the crowd. One person would stand up, and so the identity of the winner be revealed. This time, his daughter was taking part in the ceremony and despite his tendency to despise all kinds of fuss, he was proud, particularly since Carys was enthusiastic about the whole thing. It might be nonsense, he thought to himself as he cleaned his teeth, but it's our own nonsense.

Thanks to the quantity and standard of the food provided, the only people suffering from post-barbecue headaches were Megan and Siôn but since they planned to start topping up very early, it hardly mattered. Carys had spent the night with Garmon but had returned for breakfast, eager to hear her family sing his praises and she wasn't disappointed.

'That's a catch worth landing, Carys,' was Gaenor's opinion. 'He's a real fine-looking piece of goods.'

'And he's got a head on his shoulders,' added John. 'About to open a shop in Dolgellau, and one in Chester, so he tells me.'

'Did you hear the story about the trip to Argentina, to the city which had been drowned? We're going to watch the film after breakfast: he sent me a link to it.' Rhodri was beaming.

'I'm so stoked to watch the film: he was telling us about how they shot some of the stunts,' his friend Meilyr added.

'I am glad you like him,' Carys began, in a shy voice Daf had never heard before. 'Because he and I ... we're ...?'

'Courting?' put in John. 'Glad to hear it. Not that Matt wasn't a very nice young man, but Garmon's got the Welsh, which does count for something.'

Falmai rose to her feet. 'I'm surprised at you, John. Daf doesn't have an ounce of common sense, never has had so I'm not surprised he's backing this business but you're usually a lot wiser than this. What's the matter with you? Don't you see that boy is after a nurse, not a girlfriend?'

'Oh, shut your mouth, Mum,' snapped Rhodri, his cheeks flaming. 'We all like Garmon. Aunty Gae, can Meilyr and I eat our toast in front of the telly please?'

'Of course you can. Shout if you want me to bring a few more slices.'

When they had gone, Carys turned to her mother in a low voice, full of menace.

'Did you have to humiliate Rhodri in front of his friend, you old bitch? I don't want you in the Pavilion this afternoon for the Chairing and if I see your face in the audience, I'll pick up the skirts of my expensive costume and, in front of the TV cameras and everything, I will piss all over the stage, so you can feel a slice of the humiliation you've heaped on us over the years. And now, since my shift doesn't start till ten and I can't bear to be in a house with you a moment longer, I think I'll nip back to the caravan site and see if I can persuade that cripple to come back to bed for an hour.'

There was perfect silence after Carys had gone, apart from the sound of John crunching his toast.

'Shame on her,' Falmai said, at length.

'No, shame on you, Fal,' answered Daf. 'You'll drive us all away, acting like that.'

'Perhaps you'd better stay out of the Pavilion anyway, Fal,' John advised her. 'It's a big day for Carys and she should have things her own way today.'

'Judas!' Falmai spat the word at her brother before rushing to the back door.

'Is Mrs Dafis having a nervous breakdown?' Megan asked in a conversational tone, sipping her tea.

Daf rang the station to confirm that he was sticking to his plan to take the day off. He'd booked the day of the Chairing off the moment Carys had been given her role, before the Chief Constable had issued his statement on cancelling leave, but he hadn't expected the week to be quite so complex so he needed to remind his team that they would have to cope without him.

'But,' Nia protested, 'we've just had the results back from the lab in Birmingham.'

'That nonsense! Those girls were hungover but couldn't face telling the old witch who conducts the choir, that's all.'

'That's not what the lab says. There's evidence of poisoning – dehydrochloric acid.'

'You're joking!'

'I am not.'

'And what the hell is dehydrochloric acid?'

'No idea. You're the one with the college education.'

'I studied literature, not chemistry. Unless R. S. Thomas wrote a poem about this acid, I'm in the dark. What did the lab say?'

'They said it is not unusual but it must have been taken in considerable quantity to produce this result.'

'How sick are they?'

'The doctor has suggested that they go up to the hospital in Wrexham, to be monitored.'

'Oh, for fuck's sake! I only wanted to take the one day off.'

'Listen, boss. I can go up to talk to them, Sheila can start the paperwork and you can go to the Maes.'

'Is there a chance they could have eaten this stuff by accident?'

'I've got on to Severn Trent about the water but the doctor from the lab has contacted the Local Authority as well; if they ate enough of this stuff to poison them on the Maes itself, then ...'

'No, Nia, don't even say it! If we have to close the Eisteddfod down for public health reasons before the Chairing, I'd have to go straight to Peru in witness protection. Anyway, these girls are supposed to only have eaten the food they bought up from Carmarthenshire with them. You'd better get in touch with the Authority and ...'

'I've already done it. An acid like this isn't normally found in the food chain and, if it was, they'd be expecting many more people to be ill.'

'So there's no reason to consider clearing the Maes?'

'Not so far.'

'Thank God for that. When you're speaking to the ladies, try to find out everything they've done since being in the area. Ask one of the lads to go up with you, Darren or Nev, because they've got the Welsh.'

'I will.'

'Thanks for this, Nia: I owe you one. I'll just be on the Maes if you need me and I'll keep my phone on.'

'It's fine, boss. Big day for Carys; give her my love, won't you?'

A little later, Daf took Rhodri and Meilyr down to the Maes; they were planning their day.

'Are you going to kick off with the climbing wall or the Science Pavilion, *cogiau*?' Daf asked.

'We've arranged to meet Rob Berllan first, with a gang of people who are staying on their campsite,' was Rhodri's reply and Daf felt nervous. The difference between Rhodri and Rob might be a few months but their families expected different thing of them. Rob was counting the days until he could leave school and start to work so perhaps it was natural that he should be starting to look around at the girls. Rhodri would still be in education, in all probability, for the next decade, then he might travel: Rob could have a child in high school before Rhodri was in a serious relationship. They were good friends but lived different lives and Daf was glad Rhodri was not one of the sort of children who ape their contemporaries or follow like sheep.

As they left the yard, all was quiet at the bungalow. Perhaps Daf's firm statement of the previous night had sobered them up somewhat. When they reached the car park, Daf resolved that, since he wasn't on duty, he wouldn't abuse his status so, for the first time that week, he joined the queue. He followed the directions of the stewards and found that John himself was indicating the precise spot where the car should be parked. The boys ran off towards the entrance but John cornered Daf for a conversation.

'I'm worried about Falmai, Dafydd,' he began, laying his heavy hand on Daf's shoulder. 'Do you reckon she is having a breakdown, like that girl said?'

'We've decided to split up, John. I can't live with her anymore and the children feel the same.'

'What?'

'Sorry, John, but this week you must have had a chance to see for yourself how she behaves. I've got to think about the children,' Daf added, less than honestly.

'Is there another woman on the scene, Dafydd?'

'I'm just talking about my relationship with Fal, nothing else.'

'But you didn't deny it, because whatever else you are, Dafydd, you're an honest man. I'm the head of the family, so I do have responsibilities towards Falmai so I have to ask: are you having a ... a relationship with Chrissie Berllan?'

'I do have a relationship with Chrissie Berllan: we're friends and I think the world of her. If you're asking me if I've jumped her, then the answer is, not yet. And, more than likely, it'll never happen.'

'I have to say, Dafydd, and I'm talking like a man of flesh and blood now, not Falmai's brother – Chrissie Berllan wouldn't have to ask me twice, indeed she wouldn't. I've never met such a sexy woman: it's like she can reach right inside you and warm you up, just with a look. That's why I won't have her come to Neuadd to scan our ewes: she makes me feel ... well, unfaithful, I suppose.' John gulped as if he were struggling to find a way to quell the images his words had summoned. 'So, you and Falmai are definitely going to split up? We've never had a divorce at Neuadd before.'

'There isn't any choice.'

'Over the years. Dafydd, I should say we've come to know each other right well, you and me.'

Daf was very doubtful of this but said nothing. 'And just lately, I've started to learn a bit about your work and how you manage to find the truth in the middle of all these complications. I'm asking for your help, not as a member of the family but as a friend, how can we manage Falmai?'

'I honestly don't know, John. If I had any strategies, I would have tried them by now. And now I've got to go: these boys are waiting by the gate. We'll talk again.'

'She can't come and live with us,' John declared, a note of panic in his voice. 'Gae wouldn't stick it, she'd go off her head.' So now you've decided to start thinking about Gaenor's feelings Daf thought, but said nothing, smiling a little to think that John did not have a faintest suspicion that his own wife was unfaithful, was about to leave him. As far as John was concerned, he was secure in his status: no woman in her right mind would leave Neuadd, especially not for a man with no financial resources but his salary.

'We'll just have to forget all about it for today, apart from making sure Fal keeps well away from the Chairing. It's a big day for Carys and nothing should spoil it, right?'

'Fair play. See you later. Oh, and Dafydd?'

'What?'

'I hope we shall still be friends when all this business has settled down, one way or the other?'

'Let's manage today first, shall we, John?' Daf was unwilling to use a flat-out lie but he really couldn't imagine having a quiet pint with the man whose wife he was about to poach, but the morning of the Chairing was not the time for any such discussions.

'See you in the Pavilion, Dafydd.'

'Right you are.'

As he walked to the entrance, Daf was feeling uneasy. He hadn't planned to discuss his marriage with John and he had come close to betraying Gaenor by accident. After paying for their tickets and seeing the boys wander away contentedly, he had to ring her.

'Thank you so much for last night.'

'It was nothing. Garmon's a lovely lad and it was a pleasure to welcome him.'

'Seen Fal at all?'

'No, but her car's not in the yard.'

'I've just been talking to John.'

'Oh.'

'I told him Fal and I were parting but didn't say anything about us. I'd like to leave that until we've got a place sorted so we can go with the minimum of fuss. I don't want to go into all that with John now, though he can see for himself how Fal's been acting.'

'You leave John to me, I can manage him. God knows I've had enough practise.'

'Just till Gethin and co are out of the bungalow and I can get a place sorted. We're talking days, Gae, not weeks but I don't want needless hassle.'

'Especially not on Carys' big day.'

'Exactly. I know she's done the other ceremonies but there's always something special about the Chairing. And I know it's nonsense but she does set great store by it.'

'And why shouldn't she? See you later, Daf.'

'I know it sounds lame, but I can't wait to see you.'

'I love you, Daf.'

'Love you, Gae.'

His hand was shaking as he put his phone back in his jacket pocket. He saw there were two missed calls from the same number, an unknown number. He was about to check his voicemail when he felt, for the second time that morning, a hand on his shoulder. He turned and saw Gethin, his face white in the fine sunshine.

'Daf, I've got to talk to you. Fancy a glass of wine?'

'Steady on Geth: it's eleven o'clock in the morning.'

'Tea, then. I've got to have a chance to apologise.'

'I'd love a coffee.'

Daf recalled something strange about Gethin: every time the two of them walked together, they fell into step, as if his feet sought to follow the pattern Gethin set. It happened again on the way to the coffee stall where the girl smiled at Gethin as she prepared their drinks; he seemed to have to force himself to smile back. Daf settled down on a bale of hay near the van: there was no shelter to be had and the sun was already strengthening. Gethin sat on the next bale, stretching like a cat on a warm window-sill.

'Daf, I am so sorry for all this crap.'

'I have to admit, we were hoping to have quiet tenants.'

'Everything seems to have happened at once this week. It's like a zit collecting pus, then bursting out all over the place.'

'That's a nice image. You ought to get back to your poetry.'

'Strange that you say that, Daf... but anyway, we can talk about poetry later on, can't we?'

'Maybe, but we're all going for a family meal after the Chairing.'

'Well after that, maybe? I'll buy a copy of the the competition verses and we can rip them all to shreds over a bottle of Rioja.'

'You're a better poet than anyone who's won lately, Geth. You should forget about your business, about women, even about your family and sit in some little cottage and write.' Daf knew he was hiding the truth behind a joking tone.

'You know what, Daf, I have got to do something to win back my father's respect.'

'The Prof thinks the world of you.'

'Sorry, Daf, but for once, you're wrong. Since I can remember, I've heard people talking about him. I remember sitting on the grass in the back garden when I was a kid, maybe three years old and he came out of the house, his shadow falling over the flowers, over the path, over the sandpit and I remember thinking that one day, I'd grow big enough to cast a shadow like that. And here I am, my old friend, grown up to be some kind of a man and I don't cast a bigger shadow than this straw.' He pulled a straw out of the bale and held it up, to emphasise the point.'

'Rubbish, Geth. You've made a lot more money than your dad, to start with.'

'But what's money matter? I've tried to enjoy what the money brings but I can't. Christ, I even bought myself a young girl to fuck and what did a get into the bargain? A son on coke, an ex-wife who is a powerful and dangerous enemy and a mother whose heart is broken. And I bet you get a hotter time in bed with that sister-in-law of yours, without having to pay a penny.'

'You can talk like that because you're loaded, Geth. If you had to struggle like all the rest of us, you'd soon realise that the English saying is true. Life is a shit sandwich and the more bread you have, the less shit you get to eat.'

'But who looks at me the way Mum looks at my dad? Who asks for my advice or values my wisdom? Even when Dad is alone, he's got his faith for company.'

'What do you mean?'

'He isn't afraid of anything. Even when he walks in the Valley of the Shadow of Death, as he would say. Five years ago, he went for tests on his heart and if the results had gone the other way, it would have been serious. He talked about it as if he was just going for a bottle of milk. And by now he's a better father to Peredur.'

'But he did have depression, quite seriously, after that accident, didn't he?'

Gethin finished his coffee before answering.

'She, the mother, was the only person I've ever seen have any effect on him. I only saw her once and she was ... Perhaps you've seen plenty of people like that, Daf, but I'd never before seen anyone like that, a woman who was talking, breathing, walking with that emptiness in her eyes. Eira reckoned it was the tranx but I think it was grief. She'd lost everything that mattered to her and why? Because of Dad. And why wasn't he driving as carefully as he usually does? He was talking on the phone at the time – hands free, of course. No, not talking: he was preaching. Some rumour had got to Llandeilo about how I had been behaving in the Cameo Club so, as he was telling me my responsibilities as a husband and father, he forgot his own responsibilities as a driver.'

'Geth, you almost sound like you're glad.'

'That's not fair, well, not totally fair. I was glad to see him, for once, tasting the bitter bread of guilt but I wasn't glad for what happened to the boy, or his mother.'

'The bitter bread of guilt? You can't stop yourself from writing poetry. Get yourself a biro and a bit of paper, Oedipus Teifi and make something worthwhile out of all your emotions.'

Gethin crushed his plastic cup. 'Just for once, just one time, I'd like to make him proud to be my father. I've tried to do something to please him but I know already that it won't be enough. I can't help thinking about our graduation day, when your dad was pleased as Punch and mine was thinking that a 2:1 just wasn't good enough.'

Daf had to laugh. 'You were jealous of me? I was the one full of envy for your welcoming home, your interesting family.'

'But every day, through every conversation, every meal, even when we played Monopoly, Dad was judging me. So, when it became clear to me that I couldn't please him, I decided to please myself instead. So here we are now.'

'Don't drown yourself in your self-pity, Geth. You've had a tough week as a family. Raising kids is hard, and harder when you split up. Peredur will come out the right side of this, don't you worry.'

'But with whose help? And I'm not sure there's much of a future for me and Manon. With Eira ... well, Eira was always acting, pretending to be a wife or a mother but Manon genuinely feels things and how can I respond?' Gethin beat his breast like a Catholic confessing. 'I'm empty, Daf. There's nothing in here. I don't love Manon. I love fucking her which is an empty pleasure, just like eating sweets. I'm not sure I love Peredur either. He's just a nuisance to me, more than anything.'

'You're bringing up a teenager: they're always a pain,' responded Daf, thinking of the warmth he felt towards his own children and the tenderness in Chrissie's eyes as she spoke about Rob. 'You should have a talk with someone outside the situation, someone who can help you see a way ahead.'

'Dafydd, my old friend, the way ahead is perfectly clear. I'm going to be making money out of creating rubbish and spending it on pleasures that don't mean anything. I haven't told you about Garmon Jones, have I?'

'No, but Garmon is close to Carys, so I don't want to hear anything ...'

'I started out loving filming with him. He enjoyed every moment on his bike and he was able to discuss every shot, a real pro. But I spent almost a month with him, filming in South America and a little seed of envy was planted then – I didn't understand how he could be genuinely enjoying every moment of his life when mine was so empty. After that trip, I started to hate him and I was longing to see him fail but every time I pushed him, he succeeded. I didn't plan his accident but I was glad to see him down on the floor. But do you know what, Daf? When they were loading him into the air ambulance and he was in terrible pain, he could still crack a joke. Now I see him, even stuck in a wheelchair and I know he has a better future than I do.'

Daf flipped. 'I've heard enough of this shit. You're trying to write a play here, a tragedy with you as the hero but all I see is a farce. You're a selfish man who has had every chance to succeed; if you're not enjoying your easy life, give everything you own to charity and try living like all the rest of us for a month, see how you like that. You'd pretty soon come to appreciate what you've got. When we were in college, we used to laugh at the losers who blamed their parents for everything and now, in your middle age, that's just what you are. Why don't you have a go at growing up, Geth? I haven't got any more time today to devote to your psychological problems.' Daf walked away quickly, not turning to see his friend sitting there quite still, the loneliest man on the Maes.

Once again, Daf had a missed call on his phone. Couldn't be anything serious – he knew the numbers of his team and the people he cared about so he was not willing to cut across what had not, so far, been a particularly restful day off.

When Daf visited Garmon on his stand, he was looking forward to the rest of the day.

'I've never been to the Chairing before, Daf,' he confessed. 'In fact, I know bugger all about anything cultural. When I was the same age as Rhodri, I spent all my time outdoors, working on the farm or on my bike so I hope you can talk me through it, so I don't make a twat of myself, for Carys' sake.'

'There's nothing for you to do, *lanc*, only sit and listen. And a bit of singing, but not much.'

'I've got to sit in a special area in the Pavilion, because of the chair, my chair I mean, not the Chair. Will you come with me, Daf?'

'What?'

'Pretend you're my carer so you can sit in the disabled area.'

'How do I do that? asked Daf, laughing.

'If I dribble a bit and you push the chair, we'll fit in with what people think of a person in a wheelchair. People like your wife, for example.'

'Garmon, I'm so sorry.'

'Nothing for you to be sorry about: she's the one who should sort herself out. If I can be cheeky for a moment, don't forget that life is short, and we're all more fragile than we think. If you get a chance at happiness, you take it, for your own sake and everybody else's.'

'Thanks, *lanc*. See you outside the Pavilion later. That's the massive pink thing in the middle of the Maes.'

On his way over the North Wales Police stall, Daf spotted Eifion Pennant. He tried to avoid him by stepping sideways into the Trinity College stand but he was a moment too late.

'Inspector Dafis? May I have a word with you, if you please?'

'I'm not working today, Mr Pennant. There are plenty of other policemen on the Maes.'

'But I need to speak with you, since you bear the responsibility for ... for what has happened.'

'What has happened?'

'It's a sensitive issue. Can we go somewhere private to discuss it?'

Even though a week in the sun had given Eifion Pennant a bit of a tan, his holiday skin was not reflective of his attitude. He did not say a word until they were on the other side of the Literature Pavilion, one of the quietest corners on the Maes.

'Regrettably, Inspector Dafis, I have to inform the police about a serious incident, a crime.'

'What kind of crime?'

Eifion Pennant was normally quick to find the right words but on this occasion, he struggled.

'My daughter is only fifteen years old, Inspector. She is a quiet, studious girl, and always has been. She is far too young to be having a ... sexual relationship.'

'Does she have a sweetheart?' Daf deliberately chose the

old-fashioned word.

'Not until this week. We are staying in the place you recommended and she is spending far too much time with the son of the people who own the place.'

'Rob? He's only thirteen.'

Eifion Pennant opened his mouth wide for a moment, like a highly cultured fish. 'Are you sure?'

'He's been in the same class as my own son, since playgroup.'

'But to tell you the truth, Inspector Dafis, that boy has taken my daughter's virginity. He will have to be punished.'

'Mr Pennant, Mr Pennant, what old-fashioned words! And what exactly are you saying has happened between them?'

'They have had ... I mean, they're ...'

'I don't want to cause embarrassment but have you discussed the matter with your daughter? And are you really sure how far things have gone between them?'

'I found a prophylactic in our Elsan.'

'A what?'

'Prophylactic. Durex, or whatever they call them.'

'Right. Not many secrets when you're camping, are there? What did your daughter say?'

'She was very stubborn. She confessed but confessed isn't the right word. She wasn't at all ashamed of what she'd done and when I tried to speak to the boy's father, he just laughed.'

'Bryn Humphries isn't Rob's dad. He's his uncle and his step-father but never mind about that. Why are you telling me all this?'

'I expect you to arrest him for having sexual relations with an underage girl.'

'But Mr Pennant, Rob's younger than her. And by a fair way.'

'What does that matter? Apart from being a sign of the immorality of his upbringing, that is.'

Daf lost the last scrap of patience. Who was Eifion Pennant to insult Chrissie, a widow who had succeeded in raising and supporting four children? Well, she had had help from Bryn but, in Daf's opinion, he was only marginally better than a household pet.

'Why is matters, Mr Pennant, is that every judge under the sun puts the majority of responsibility for the nature of a relationship on the older partner. If you're not careful, your daughter could end up in the Sex Offenders Register.'

'Are you out of your mind? She's an innocent little girl. She's studying no less than fourteen GCSE subjects, all though the medium of Welsh and she plays the oboe in the County Youth Orchestra.'

Daf had to bite his tongue because he knew perfectly well that any quip on the subject of 'blowing' would not be well received, though he decided he would share the joke with Chrissie later.

'Even if Rob had been fifteen, the CPS doesn't take much interest in cases like this.'

'CPS, Inspector Dafis? Do please try to avoid jargon.'

'Crown Prosecution Service. They decide if any case will go forward for prosecution. And in the normal run of things, they take very little interest in the sex-lives of consenting fifteen year olds.'

'My daughter does not have a "sex-life" but if what you say is true, we will have to undertake a private prosecution.'

'You stand no chance whatever of winning a private prosecution against a lad as young as Rob.'

'Then the best thing for me to do is to put it in the hands of Social Services. If he's as young as that, then he needs to be protected. It's obvious that his parents are not willing to take any steps to do so.'

Now, Mr Pennant, you're talking about protecting Rob Berllan but who from? From your daughter? I do wish you'd be a bit more careful in the way you talk, by heck I do.'

'What else can a parent do?'

'What about talking to them?'

'To the parents?'

'To Rob and your daughter.'

Without warning, two heavy tears rolled down Eifion Pennant's cheeks.

'How could I even begin such a conversation, Inspector Dafis? Would you be there with me as I have that talk?' For a moment, the expression on Pennant's face reminded Daf of Ed Mills, another person who was out of his depth. Daf sympathised with Pennant: after years of protecting children he realised the limits of what he could do. So much for a day off: first Gethin, then Eifion bloody Pennant. He had been thinking of getting a bite to eat with Meirion but it didn't look like that was going to be an option. He rang Rhodri.

'Rob Berllan with you?'

'Yes. We're in the queue for a lamb burger.'

'And his girl?'

'Ebrillwen, yes. Why?'

'Can I have a word with Rob? Pass him the phone.'

Eifion Pennant was attempting to dry his tears with the back of his hand; Daf passed him a handkerchief. Falmai had always put a fresh handkerchief in his pocket every day, just as Gaenor was expected to do for John. Those were the nice Neuadd ways but this particular handkerchief had been in Daf's pocket, unused, since Sunday.

'Mr Dafis? Rob Humphries.'

'Hello Rob. Listen, I don't want to be a pain but could you come over to have a bit of a word with me? And bring Miss Pennant with you?'

'Miss Pennant? Oh, 'Brillwen. No probs, Mr Dafis; when?'

'Do you know where the North Wales Police stand is?'

'Opposite the Principality? Yes, I know.'

'I'll meet you there in ten minutes.'

'Right you are, Mr Dafis.'

Eifion Pennant had blown his nose and wiped his face.

'They're coming to meet us now.'

With his tears, Eifion Pennant seemed to have wiped away his modesty.

'He's coming, then?'

'They're both coming. I'll ask my friends in the North Wales Police if we can use a private room they have there.'

'I see.'

'But I'm going to have a word with Rob's mother first, right?'

The little man shrugged and stepped back a little. Daf rang and Chrissie answered at once.

'Chrissie, how are things?'

'Right quiet, to tell the truth. Almost everyone's gone to the Maes, including the children. Bryn's in the silage over Pendomen so I'm all alone. Could do with some company, if I'm honest.'

Daf had to grin. 'I've got to spend the afternoon in the Pavilion, unfortunately.'

'Fair play. You don't mind me asking though, do you?'

'Not in the slightest. Listen,' he added, turning around to make sure he wasn't being overheard 'I hear you're getting a bit of hassle from our friend Mr Pennant.'

'Oh, what does the little bugger want now? His wife's a lovely woman.'

'He's ... uneasy about the relationship between his daughter and Rob.'

'Of course he is, nasty little snob. We're not good enough for people like him.'

'I agree with you, Chrissie but people like him can cause no end of hassle. He's been talking about prosecuting Rob, because of the girl's age.'

'She's a fair bit older than him – she's the cradle snatcher.'

'Have you talked about this to Rob at all?'

'Lads don't take that kind of talk too well from their mums. Bryn had a word.'

'Do you know what he said?'

Chrissie paused for a moment and replied in a lower voice which Daf found heart-stoppingly sexy.

'Bryn explained that the most important thing a man can do is please a girl and gave him a couple of tips as to how to do it. Then, he reminded him that it's no end dull to breed a child you can't afford to raise and gave him a packet of rubbers.'

'Well, at least they're taking care then. Mr Pennant wants to talk to them, give them a piece of his mind, I reckon, and he's asked me to be there. Do you want to come to hear what's said?'

'I can guess what he's got to say and it's not a good idea if I'm there to hear him say it, in case I give him the clec he deserves. I trust you anyway, Mr Dafis: no-one can do my kids down when you're about.'

'I don't think anyone would dare.'

'You're a good friend to us, Mr Dafis.'

'I do try, but remember – if I hadn't landed you with all the hassle after I had to move those people from Dolau, Rob would never have met the girl. Now, don't think I'm interfering, but isn't he a bit young for that kind of fun?'

'Some people use each other, Mr Dafis and some people enjoy each other. Rob and the girl are enjoying each other, sharing a bit of pleasure between them and as long as they recall I'm way too young to be a grandmother, what's the harm?'

Daf's duty as a policeman was to remind Chrissie about the law but he was so taken with her idea of people enjoying one another and the warm voice in which she said it that he just couldn't spoil the moment.

'Fair play, Chrissie. I'll let you know how we get on, right?'

'You know where to find me. It's a shame you're too busy to pop up to see for me.'

Even with Chrissie's voice still in his ears, Daf found that her idea of mutual enjoyment led him to thoughts of Gaenor and how much they enjoyed being together, not just in bed. Perhaps that was the definition of love.

Eifion Pennant gave a dry little cough to remind Daf of his presence and because his conversation with Chrissie had put him in such a good mood, Daf didn't even begin to be annoyed. By now, they had reached the North Wales Police stand where Meirion was giving a talk for teachers and parents on the dangers of so-called legal highs. Daf overheard a member of Meirion's audience say to his partner: 'Listen carefully, missus: we don't want our Rolant to end up like that Hoppy Happy Hare.'

Daf felt a pang of sympathy for Gwion, who had gone from being the friend of all the children of Wales to being a pariah overnight. Daf wanted to make sure Eifion Pennant understood that there were many worse things his daughter could be doing than having a bit of a holiday fling with a handsome lad but decided to save his breath. Betsan was perched on a high stool behind a counter, adding up the week's footfall: she came straight over to Daf.

'Is it true? Blodau Mai have been poisoned? Bodo Mai rang and said there was talk of their going to hospital and ...'

'We're still waiting for the full details but it's worth remembering that thousands of people every month are poisoned by what they eat.'

'Bodo Mai told me you were putting together a squad to arrest Eirlys Cadwaladr, right after the Chairing.'

'There's no such plan. "Squad", for heavens' sake! We've still got a lot of information to put together.'

'Of course, Daf. Thank you so much for helping.'

'No worries. And in the meantime, I'd like to borrow your little back room, if I may.'

'Ooh, Inspector Dafis, there's always a warm welcome for you in my little back room.'

'You need to put in for a transfer, my girl: you're spending way too much time with Meirion, and his Carry On jokes are pretty catching.' The unamused look on Eifion Pennant's face only added to the joke. 'Oh, and Bets? What's Bodo Mai's surname? You only ever call her Bodo and I wouldn't dare try that.'

'Jones.'

'Great. We're expecting a couple of young people to meet us here, Bets; can you show them where we are?'

'More young offenders?'

'Far from it. It's a private matter; sorry to disappoint you.'

Sitting at the table waiting for the children who were children no longer, Eifion was quiet. Daf felt obliged to say something.

'I know you're angry. No-one likes having to face how much their children have changed but if you can maintain a decent relationship with your daughter, that's going to be for the best all round.' Eifion nodded his head but didn't say a word.

Rob entered, hand in hand with Eifion Pennant's daughter. Daf looked from on to the other. He had noted Rob's height before: he stood over six foot, having inherited his height from his father. But until now Daf had not noticed other things about him, the dark shadow on his chin, his thickly muscled shoulders and, more than anything, his hands. The skin of his hands was stained brown and they were covered in scars and callouses. They were the hands of a working man, not a schoolboy. As for Ebrillwen? She seemed to Daf a confident girl, rather towny. Together, they seemed like any other young couple.

'Thank you for coming along,' Daf began. 'You don't know me, *lodes*: I'm Daf Dafis.'

'Ebrillwen Haf Pennant.' She extended a small hand with bright gel nails for Daf to shake.

'Nice to meet you, girl. Now then, I expect you're asking yourselves why I wanted to have a word? The truth is, *lodes*, your dad's fretting about you and he wants to talk to you.'

'Why?' Rob asked, squaring his shoulders.

'Because of Ebrillwen's age,' answered her father. 'She's way too young to have a sexual relationship.'

'Please don't, Dad,' she girl implored in a low voice.

'What's the problem, sir?' Rob asked. 'I've not done anything with 'Brillwen she wasn't keen for me to do.'

'But she's fifteen years old!'

'What odds does it make?'

'We're taking precautions, Dad. I'm not going to get pregnant.'

'But you are far too young, Ebrillwen Haf. You need to concentrate on your schoolwork, your music, the choir ...'

Ebrillwen was wearing a crop top revealing her smooth skin and as her father was listing all the respectable extra curricula activities, Rob began to stroke her stomach with his rough fingers. A visible shudder of pleasure shook her and Daf very much doubted that the most stimulating choir practice could compare with the touch of Rob's hand on her flesh.

'I'm not discussing this with you, children, I'm telling you the rules. This business is coming to an end today. I forbid any further contact of any kind between the two of you.'

'You can't Mr Pennant,' Rob answered. 'We're not living in some story book world. I like 'Brillwen and, thank goodness, she's taken a bit of a fancy to me. Words like "forbid" don't work, don't mean anything.'

'But before she met you ...'

Daf watched a slow smile spread over Rob's face, a very familiar smile. Daf had seen that smile many times on Bryn's face and it always meant some kind of sexual secret.

'You can't stop 'Brillwen doing anything she wants to,' Rob clarified, in a leisurely voice, glancing over at the girl. 'You didn't manage to before.'

'What do you mean?' Rage-induced irregular patches of red appeared on Eifion Pennant's cheeks: he was incensed by Rob's confidence.

'She's had experience before me, Mr Pennant, so your idea of keeping her under lock and key don't make no sense.'

'What?' The little man's voice rose almost to a scream.

'I wasn't the first, Mr Pennant and whatever happened

before didn't wreck her schoolwork, did it?' Ebrillwen gave Rob an encouraging smile, delighted to see him take on her father with such flair.

A heavy silence descended. Eifion Pennant was dumbstruck. Rob moved his hand from Ebrillwen's stomach to her thigh and patted her, to share his confidence with her.

'I don't suppose you two have thought that you might be wiser to wait for a bit?' Daf ventured, with very little hope of success.

'D'you remember my dad,' Mr Dafis?' Rob asked. 'And the story about the E-Type?'

'Your mum told me, a couple of years back.'

'I'm going to tell Mr Pennant the story, right?' Daf nodded. 'My dad, he loved cars and my mum is a top mechanic. They saw an ad for an old E-Type, restoration job, over Telford way. They went to see it then had a chat. They'd got the cash saved to buy it but they decided to invest it in a new bale-wrapper instead, put the money into the business. They'd been to Telford on the Saturday, ordered the bale-wrapper on the Monday and on the Tuesday, Dad was killed. Accident. I've learnt the lesson, and I'm not waiting for what I want out of life because if you wait, you may never come to enjoy it. Sorry that you don't like it, Mr Pennant, but I've inherited this from my dad: I'm living for today and stuff tomorrow.'

'And,' added Ebrillwen, dropping the level of emotional charge, 'I just don't want to wait. I'll turn sixteen in November and if I like, I can leave home then. I quite fancy going to live at Berllan. At the moment, Dada, I'm doing everything you expect me to do, working hard at school, planning to stop on for sixth form, then off to college. But if you try to take over any more of my life, I'll pack up and go, as soon as I can.'

Daf tried not to enjoy Eifion Pennant's defeat at the hands of a couple of adolescents, but failed: it was priceless.

'I know my family's not smart enough for you, Mr Pennant,' Rob said. 'We're just everyday sort of working people, but we can all try to get on. Why don't you come up and have a barbecue with us tonight? There's always plenty of burgers in the freezer, and our own lamb chops too.'

'I'm not giving my seal of approval to this relationship,' Eifion Pennant mumbled under his breath.

'No-one's asking you to do anything of the sort,' retorted his daughter. 'Just try to act like a normal dad, that's all.'

No-one could describe them as a happy family as they made their way out of the North Wales Police stand but at least the awkward conversation was over. Fair play to the young ones, Daf thought, they had answered very well and it was clear that Rob's maturity wasn't just physical. But then, he'd grown up in the shadow of his father's death, totally different to Rhodri who was still keen on Lego, albeit Technics. Daf decided he would celebrate the end of the week in which he had seen more than enough of other people's children by getting presents for his own two, a box of Technics for Rhodri and something nice, to be selected after a consultation with Gaenor, for Carys.

'Setting yourself up as a family therapist now, are you?' Meirion asked. 'There's no end to this bugger's talents, Bets.'

'That lad reminds me of someone I've seen on the telly: is he another one of your media types?' Betsan asked.

'That's not very observant for a police officer, Bets: he even walks like a farmer.'

'I know who it is: the man who was a suspect in the Jacinta Mytton case.'

'His uncle.'

'Oh, you're all related round her,' complained Meirion. 'I can't wait to get back to cosmopolitan Caernarfon.'

'I can't wait for all this shit to be over either,' Daf agreed. 'We normally live steady round here and I don't see why we have to go and import trouble from every corner of Wales.'

'That's a fine welcome!'

'I meant to say, thank you for all your help. It's all sorted now, I reckon.'

I still can't get my head around a kid that age dealing coke,' Betsan remarked. 'How's he doing?'

'Still on the comedown so he's a bit low.'

What did you expect, you Mid-Walian cockwomble? A year eight kid gets busted dealing drugs and you describe him as "a bit low"!'

'You know what, Meirion Martin, it's my day off today, which means I don't have to put up with any of your crap. Thanks again for everything: I'll come up north and buy you a drink one of these days.'

As he left them, Daf checked the time on his phone: an hour and a half before he was due to meet Garmon to go to the Pavilion. He was highly tempted to check out those missed calls but he knew all too well how much time could be taken up even solving the smallest problems. For the rest of the day, he was not going to concentrate on anything but supporting Carys. Except, naturally, he did have to ring Chrissie.

'It all went well enough with our little friend Mr Pennant. His daughter's as stubborn as he is and Rob answered him right well'

'He's a tidy lad, is Rob. He's been through a fair bit in his life, Mr Dafis and if anyone deserves a bit of fun, it's him.'

'Fair play, Chrissie.'

'With all due respect to his education and what have you, Mr Dafis, but that little bantam cock knows fuck all about us. Rob's up before five every morning so he can get his work done before he goes to school. You know what he had for his birthday last year? An arc welder from Bryn and me and the kids clubbed together to get him a torch, one of those you can wear on your head, a right useful bit of kit it is. Since then, he's taken to working late as well, doesn't come in till after ten some nights. And in the time … well, the time after we lost his dad, what with him doing all the jobs he could and caring for the little ones when I was on the yard, I wouldn't have kept things running without him, honest truth, Mr Dafis.'

'I know. Rob did give Mr Pennant a bit of the story.'

'Good for him. Anyway, thanks again, Mr Dafis and don't forget what you promised me, will you?'

'Cheers, Chrissie.'

His phone rang before he could put it into his pocket. Nia.

'You've got to come up to talk to them, boss. They're acting so odd. They're refusing to go to the hospital for observations and when the nurse came up to repeat the liver function tests, they were really savage with her.'

'What about the old lady?'

'Well, she's obviously a few tenors short of a choir, isn't she? We're just not getting anywhere with any of them.'

'I'm on my way, don't worry.'

Once again, Daf could enjoy the unfolding view, the outlines of the distant mountains and the green hills nearer at hand. Through the open window, he could hear the song thrush, several blackbirds and a robin, all singing songs with the same meaning: 'This is my territory.' Daf gave a rueful grin as he recognised his own attitude to the Eisteddfod visitors in the robin's tune: it was his patch and he had had enough of strangers coming in and causing bother. Then, of course, he recalled that at least two of the most serious offenders of the week were local: Dewi Dolau and Ed Mills, and it occurred to him that he should have evolved beyond the territorial attitudes of song birds with brains the size of a lump of sugar.

A Severn Trent van was parked in the yard outside the farmhouse. A young woman in overalls was packing her tools into the back. Daf greeted her in both languages: she replied in Welsh.

'Afternoon, Inspector. We'll have to send everything off for a full analysis but from the tests we've made already, just on simple pH readings, there is no sign of any unusual acid in the water.'

'OK. Thank you, *lodes*.'

'It's worth saying that, if the build-up of acid was in the

water supply, it would have affected the other houses fed off this branch from the reservoir. There are fifteen houses off this pipe: we've contacted them all and there is nothing wrong, no-one reporting symptoms.'

'Right.'

'And I know we're only the simple people from the water board and we don't have all the technical forensic resources of the police but we know we can depend on our little litmus strips, you know.'

'Yes, great, thank you for all the information.'

'People take water for granted but you'd die of thirst a lot faster than you'd starve. And think of all the illnesses, things like cholera and typhoid: if our water supply wasn't secure, we'd be facing a plague of some kind every summer. You see our vans going about from day to day and you never think twice about it, but, Inspector, we're working to keep our residents safe, just like you guys in the police. We're the biological safety police and no-one gives us a *smic* of respect.'

'Speaking personally, I value your contribution very highly but if the water in this case isn't the problem, I'm going to have to make some more enquiries. Thanks again, but I have to go.'

Of course the girl's passion for her job was ludicrous but Daf recognised her attitude. He could bore for Britain about Dyfed Powys Police in exactly the same way as she could about the water board. Nia appeared from the back of the house and her expression told him that she was relieved to see him.

'We can't get any sense out of them at all, not even a few scrappy bits of a story.'

'What does the old lady do when you're asking questions of her singers?'

'Just hangs about, her face like thunder.'

'That's your first step, then. You take her off into another room while I take a turn at the girls.'

Nia laughed. 'That sounds like the perfect plot for the first ever Welsh porn film: a policeman taking a turn at a ladies' choir. We'll have to cast someone who looks better than you in the buff as the policeman, mind: how about Bryn Gwaun?'

'Do shut your mouth, Nia: I've only got an hour.'

In the sitting room of the farmhouse, Bodo Mai and her Flowers were sitting in silence. There was a shade more of colour in their cheeks but the fury in Mai's eyes had thrown them into a paralysis of fear.

'Good afternoon, all,' Daf opened, not expecting any reply.

'Good afternoon, Mr Dafis,' the girls responded in a monotone, like primary school children greeting a teacher. Very odd, from grown women.

'Right then, ladies, we've got to try to solve this mystery without delay. My daughter's taking part in the Chairing ceremony and I'm not going to miss it, do you understand?'

'Our competition starts in half an hour,' said Bodo Mai, in a bitter tone.

'You will have to forget about that. There is a chance that nothing further at all, including the Chairing may take place on the Maes today. If we can't discover the source of the substance which has made you ill, the County Council will have no choice but to close the site entirely and bring the Eisteddfod to an end.' He paused and observed the effect his words had on the women. Their fear was visible, which had been his idea: they needed to realise that this wasn't some kind of game.

'So, Nia is going to take you into the kitchen, Miss Jones, to ask for a full and detailed history of the party whilst I have a chat with the rest of you. Nia, have you managed to get another member of the team up here to help?'

On cue, a car drew up in the yard and, half a minute later, Nev was at the door. Daf stepped out into the hallway to speak to him.'

'How are you, *cog*? Something odd going on here.'

'I heard.'

'It seems clear that they're trying to hide something so we

need to have some solid evidence to go with whatever we've got from the test results. So you need to go through the bins and the recycling boxes.'

'That's not fair at all, boss. Why don't you do the rubbish and I talk to the girls?'

'I haven't got any time to waste with your nonsense today, Nev: you'll find some gloves in the boot of my car.'

Daf's conversation with the members of Blodau Mai was pretty fruitless. Even without Bodo Mai looming over them, they were reluctant to say anything much at all. They had travelled up together from Llandeilo and had, so far, been down to the Maes only twice.

'And what did you have to eat the last time you were down on the Maes, on the Wednesday?' he asked.

'I had an ice-cream,' answered the youngest member.

'Nothing but a cup of tea in the Churches Together area.'

'I had a fruit salad, in a big plastic cup.' And so on. Every one of them had chosen something different to eat or drink, and nothing they had chosen had not also been consumed by hundreds of other Eisteddfod goers who had not then displayed any symptoms.

'What about in the evenings? Don't tell me that the buzz of the Eisteddfod hasn't tempted you ladies down to Meifod, to the Rugby Club or even over the hill to Llanfair Caereinion?'

'We've been being sensible, Inspector,' replied a short, round-faced woman … We're not to go out until after we've competed.'

'I get the situation, girls. Miss Jones thinks you've all gone to bed with a mug of cocoa but when she's sleeping, you sneak downstairs and away for a bit of a spree?'

'No, Inspector, really.'

The door opened and Nev entered.

'Excuse me, boss, but can I have a quick word?' Nev scanned the ladies of the party as if assessing their potential as girlfriends but Daf wasn't observant enough to work out which, if any, of them had caught the young man's eye. Daf stepped back out into the hallway. Nev grinned at him, offering him an evidence bag full of little cardboard boxes. Handkerchief over his fingers, Daf pulled one box out and read the label.

'Laxatives. Lots of them. And look here on the label: 'contains dehydrochloric acid.' Bingo, *lanc*, bingo.'

'But boss, there are dozens of these boxes.'

'And they're all empty. Looks like the girls of Blodau Mai have been caught out doing something dull, but nothing more than that.'

'Do people ... abuse this kind of tablet? I've never heard of it before.'

'Only to lose weight.'

Daf's phone rang.

'Inspector Dafis? Derek Gwilym, from Powys County Council. I've heard there's been a case of poisoning at the Eisteddfod so I've contacted the regional emergency team. We've got people in place ready to shut the Eisteddfod down and clear the Maes.'

'You don't need to even think about doing any such thing. It was an accident, totally unconnected with the Maes.'

'Are you sure?'

'One hundred per cent. I've got the solid evidence in my hand at this moment.'

'I'll need the details to be confirmed on paper, Inspector.'

'The station in Welshpool will get that to you within the hour. And Mr Gwilym, there is no need for any action of any kind from the regional team, right?'

As he put his phone away, Daf noticed the time. He was going to have to hurry his interview with the ladies if he was to get to the Maes in time to see Carys at the Chairing.

'Right Nev, you make sure Nia keeps the old trout busy for another ten minutes while I see how these girls respond to seeing these boxes.'

When Daf put the boxes, in their transparent bag, down on

the coffee table, all the members of the party began to jabber on at once.

'I've got no time for this babble. I need to get this straight, from just one of you, OK?'

Their spokeswoman was the oldest member of the group, a copper-haired alto in her forties.

'We know we've been stupid, Inspector, but you've got to understand, this singing party is Miss Jones' life. Over the years, we've let her and ourselves down time after time but this year, we were going for it flat out. Mai decided to order expensive frocks for us from a swanky shop in Llandeilo but they weren't ready until Monday.' Another of the party members opened the door of a cupboard: a row of identical smart dresses was hanging inside it. 'One for each of us but ...' she blushed as she got to the kernel of the story, 'but every one of us told a few fibs when Miss Jones asked us for our measurements to have the frocks made. We told her the sizes we hoped we would be by August but it didn't work out that well. They're a very fitted style.'

The youngest member put in: 'It was my idea to lose weight quickly before we performed but we went over the top. The tablets were much stronger than we thought and when we didn't see immediate results, we took some more. Please don't tell Miss Jones. We've let her down.'

Daf smiled at them. 'Don't you worry, ladies, I'm an expert in keeping secrets.'

It took less than five minutes to cobble together a story which was good enough to convince Bodo Mai, with vague talk of second tests and a peculiar strain of gastric flu which affects the liver. Then Daf could return to the Maes.

He only had a few minutes to spare before meeting Garmon but Daf decided he needed to do something to check if Falmai was going to keep away, as Carys wanted. He saw her from a distance, wiping tables and could not see much to gain from approaching her.

Amongst a group coming out of the Faith Pavilion, he spotted an old friend of his, the Catholic priest of the Welshpool parish, Father Joe Hogan. He was a generous and caring man who understood Daf's work perfectly. Daf noticed that, yet again, he was wearing charity shop trainers, which meant he must have, yet again, given his good shoes to some homeless person who knocked on his door. Daf had no interest in any form of religion and tended to be highly suspicious of any man who gave his whole life up to preaching unbelievable tales to the ignorant but the two men had worked together often and had become friends. Daf could not have thought of anyone better to help him in current circumstances.

'Joe?'

'Dafydd! How's things?'

'Listen Joe, are you going into the Chairing?'

'Hadn't planned to.'

'Then can you help me out? I've got to go into the Pavilion in a minute to support Carys in the Chairing and she's had a heck of a row with her mum, in fact, we're all on bad terms. Carys doesn't want Fal to come to the Chairing.'

'Is that fair on Falmai? She sets such great store by these things.'

'Please don't be so fucking reasonable, Joe. I'm ninety per cent certain Fal will just stay here for the rest of the afternoon but if she looks like leaving, could you hold her up for ten minutes or so? Just until the doors are shut, then she won't be able to get in anyway.'

'OK, but I'm doing it for Carys, not you.'

'Thanks for this, Joe. I don't want it to be awkward for the girl.'

As Daf turned to head for the vast pink tent, he heard a familiar voice greeting Joe.

'Father Hogan, good to see you.'

'Professor Teifi, how are you? And who's this lad here? Your grandson?'

'Indeed, Father Hogan. Peredur is my grandson and I would be delighted if you could light a candle for him, and for the whole family, when you next have a chance.'

Daf turned to look but they had disappeared back into the Faith Pavilion. It was pleasure to forget about them by talking to Garmon.

'No sign of the bow, I suppose, Dafydd?'

'Not yet. Listen, I don't think I really apologised properly for Falmai's attitude last night.'

'Carys and I have talked it over. Your wife's certainly not going to win prizes for her attitude to people with disabilities.'

'I'm not making excuses but she's under a lot of stress at the moment.'

'I know. Living a perfect life with everything being given to you on a plate is a heck of a strain. Being privileged is very stressful.'

'We don't see eye to eye like a husband and wife should.'

'Can anyone see eye to eye with a woman like that, Daf? I've learnt a bit since being in this chair. To me, there's only two kinds of people, those who live life and those who moan on the sidelines. Carys tells me you're leaving your wife: best of luck to you.'

'We'll see.'

They did not have to join the queue, because of the wheelchair, but they passed John, Gaenor, Rhodri, Siôn and Megan who had clearly been waiting for some time. At once, Daf saw that something was troubling Gaenor. As the others spoke to Garmon, he asked her:

'Are you OK?'

'I need to talk to you, as soon as possible.'

'Straight after the ceremony, right?'

'Great. I've got something important to say to you.'

There was concern in her face but also such kindness that Daf felt as though, together, they could manage any difficulties.

'We're going in through the special crips door,' Garmon

explained to Rhodri, taking the sting from the vile word by using it. 'Saves us having to wait.'

'I'd better wait here with Aunty Gaenor and Uncle John. It's bad enough Dad queue jumping, let alone two of us.'

'I'm helping not queue jumping. Be good then and I'll see you later.'

As they circumnavigated the Pavilion to reach the disabled entrance, Garmon couldn't believe how many people were prepared to queue for hours for the result of a poetry competition.

'It's the tradition of the thing, more than anything,' Daf explained. 'Besides, as you know yourself, everyone loves award ceremonies. And there's all the drama because we don't even have a shortlist to go on: the winner could be anybody. Even the judges don't know because of all the entries using pen-names.'

In the distance, behind the Pavilion, on the hill over the hedge from the field where Ed Mills got his 'shrooms, a woman was walking alone, a large bag in her hand. She reminded Daf of Breugel's painting, *The Fall of Icarus*: everyone busy about their daily tasks, attending the Chairing in this case, not seeing what might be happening away in the distance. She seemed to be a million miles from the hectic Maes.

As Garmon had predicted, the stewards were very accommodating, leading them to a reserved section in the centre of the audience.

'The procession will come right past us,' Daf confirmed.

'Carys looks amazing in her robes. She's like a princess off *Game of Thrones*.'

The place was full and the stewards were working hard to ensure that every available seat was filled. Daf heard a dispute breaking out behind him.

'I'm keeping this seat for my partner and I won't give it up. I've been waiting here for two hours for him and it's very important that he has a seat.' It was a familiar voice: Manon.

'I can't turn round to check: was that Gethin Teifi's piece of stuff kicking off?' Garmon asked, not lowering his voice.

'It was Manon, yes.'

'He's expecting to walk in late so everyone gets a chance to bow and scrape before him.'

Daf didn't see the result of the dispute between Manon and the steward because the ceremony was beginning. Carys swept past them, walking in a stately style: Garmon's eyes were wide and glittering. As was the tradition every year, a great sword was held up and half drawn. The question was then asked of the assembly, three times: 'Does peace reign here?' Three times, the crowd bellowed out: 'Peace.' A chance of a bit of peace would be a fine thing, Daf thought, as the judges took their places. Perhaps it was because his daughter was taking part or because the Eisteddfod was in his square mile but Daf thought the ceremony was special, full of grace and meaning. The judges also expressed their opinion that the poetry too had reached new heights.

'I can't follow everything they're saying, Daf,' Garmon admitted. 'This literary Welsh is too complicated for a bike boy.'

'I'll give you evening classes when the weather shuts in, *lanc*.'

The judges were heaping praise on the poet who had chosen to use the pen-name 'Prodigal Son' for the skill he, or she, had shown in his, or her, poem. 'Family' was the topic set and Prodigal Son had described the relationship between a father and son. The father in the poem was a good man, dignified, kindly and wise but his son was a selfish bully. The closing section, which was read aloud, was the son's promise to change, to follow his father's example in the future. Ranged along the back of the stage, rows of poets and other worthy citizens waited and Daf was certain that he could see an unusual shine in Talwyn Teifi's eyes, as if he were holding back tears. Everyone was waiting for the result.

'Therefore, on the sound of the trumpet, will Prodigal Son

and Prodigal Son only, stand to his or her feet.'

The trumpet sounded and the searchlights flickered over the audience, looking for the successful poet. No-one had moved. They searched again – nothing. The Archdruid called the pen-name again: no response.

'Wow, someone likes a bit of drama,' observed Garmon.

The stewards hastily flung the doors open in case they had been barring the door against the winner but there was no poet hammering and demanding admittance. Daf noted that the seat beside Manon was still empty, confirming a suspicion which was growing in his mind. After some discussion with the other officials, the Archdruid announced that the ceremony would continue without a poet, as it did in the years when no poet was deemed worthy of winning the Chair.

'So, where's the Prodigal Son then, Daf?' Garmon asked.

'Hard to know, without a real name.'

Then, just before they all sang the national anthem, the Archdruid made an unscheduled declaration.

'The name of the winning poet in the Meifod Eisteddfod 2015 is Gethin Teifi.'

Daf saw the Prof's shoulders start to shake. His son had been good enough to win but not courteous enough to accept his prize.

'There he is again, Daf, creating a fuss and letting everyone down,' Garmon remarked.

Outside the Pavilion, there was a very uneasy atmosphere, as if nothing would ever be the same again. Small groups of people were discussing the ceremony in low voices. Daf's phone rang: Nev.

'There's something on the ground, behind the Art Pavilion.'

'Leave it alone, it'll be an installation.'

'It's not art, it's a corpse.'

'A corpse?'

'Yes. The body of a man who's been shot.'

'Shot?'

'Yes, but not with a gun. He's got an arrow a yard long sticking out of his throat.'

'I'll be with you now.' He was unwilling to give any explanation to Garmon who might, if Daf's hunch was proved right, be a suspect. 'Listen, *lanc*, I've got to go. Yet another work crisis.'

'No worries, Daf and thanks for the company. See you later.'

There was no sign of guilt or anxiety in his open face but he had lost his bow. And he knew how to shoot accurately. And Daf only had Garmon's word for the fact that the bow had ever been lost at all.

It was Gethin, of course, who had been killed before he could receive his Chair. The blood of 'Prodigal Son' was spreading on the dry grass. He lay on his back, arms spread wide.

'OK, Nev, here we go. First, phone the reception area and get the gates closed, there and around the whole site: get the Maes sealed tight. Then, get me all our boys and any members of other forces. We need SOCOs and tape to keep people away: this is a crime scene. Right?'

'Right, boss.'

'Make sure Nia gets here straight away, and Sheila. I'm going to stay here until there's someone else available to keep an eye on the body then I will be opening a temporary incident room in the North Wales Police stand.'

For several minutes, perhaps almost ten, Daf was alone with the body of his friend. The greatest irony, he felt was that Gethin had just won his Chair for a poem promising to change his behaviour but he never had time to make that change. His phone rang.

'Mr Dafis? It's Modlen here, Modlen Carter.' I sold you a copy of *Golwg*? You told me to ring you if...'

'I'm sorry, sweetheart, but I can't talk now.'

'But it's important.'

'Ring me later then, OK, *lodes*?'

Nev ran up with a couple of stewards who had thin metal poles under their arms. Nev had found some tape and the first perimeter was established, turning that corner of the Eisteddfod Field into an official crime scene. Daf ran as fast as he could, looking for the Professor and found him, just emerging for the robing room.

'I've got terrible news, sir. Gethin has ...'

'Taken his own life?'

'Has been killed sir.'

'Which is why he didn't accept his Chair?'

'Yes. He's been shot by an arrow, from a bow.'

'Thank you for breaking this news yourself, Dafydd. I must go to find Derwenna and Peredur.' There was a weary acceptance in the old man's face as if his worst fears had been realised.

On his way over to the North Wales Police stand, Eira stopped him, gripping his forearm.

'Is it true, that someone has killed the bastard?'

'Don't talk like that. But it is true.'

'Oh, hip hip hooray.'

'He was the father of your son, remember, Eira.'

He broke out of her grip and hurried around the corner into the buzz of the new incident room. Of course it was a tragedy, especially to the Prof and his family, but it was also a chance for Daf to show his team what leadership looked like.

'OK, we need statements from anyone who was in the area of the Art Pavilion, anyone who spoke to Gethin Teifi today or saw him. We're looking at a list of people who had good reason to kill Gethin Teifi. Got a marker pen, Bets? Write these on the white board. In his family, we've got his ex-wife Eira Owen Edwards and, yes, she was on Corrie, his thirteen-year-old son, Peredur Teifi and his parents Professor Talwyn and Mrs Derwenna Teifi. Then we've got his new lover, Manon, don't know her surname, and her ex, Gwion Morgan who was until recently TV favourite Happy Hoppy Hare. Then there's the man we arrested for trashing Gethin's car, Elwyn Wyn Evans. Better add Garmon Jones. Or Garmon Mountain Bike, as they call him. We haven't got time to go into all the motives but that's where we start. Time of death is going to be crucial because, if he was killed during the Chairing ceremony, the Prof was visible on the stage all though, Garmon Jones was sitting beside me and Manon was behind us. I want you to check on Gethin's car, not the one which got trashed yesterday but the replacement he hired from Border Garage yesterday morning and I want a search made on the place he was staying during the Eisteddfod, which just happens to be my home. Oh, and the victim just won the Chair, so poetic jealousy may be a factor so we need to know who knew the identity of the rivals of 'Prodigal Son' which was the pen-name he used for the competition, other poets who felt they deserved to win.'

'Hells bells, boss,' Nev called out. 'Talk about hitting the ground running.'

'Get in touch with Children's Services in Cardiff to keep them in the loop: there's a live case affecting the son.' He took a breath. 'Don't stand there like blocks of wood; there's work to be done.'

Meirion was staring at him. 'That's a bit of a speech, *cont*.'

'Can you nip down to the main entrance, Mei? Everyone's got to be kept on the Maes so we could do with someone down there with a bit of authority.'

'Fair enough, boss.'

'How many phone lines do you need?' Betsan asked.

'Four. And the fastest Wi-Fi we can get.

'Councillor Gwilym Bebb's outside: he wants a word.'

'Please go and tell Councillor Bebb to go and do something mediaeval to himself with a ceremonial sword, Betsan. I'm busy.'

Daf sat down heavily on a foldaway chair behind a broad table. He didn't notice Modlen Carter arriving, rubbish bag in her hand.

'You've got to see this, Mr Dafis. It's important.' She emptied the contents of the bag onto the table. A peculiar object made of fibreglass fell onto the table in front of him, together with some strips of carbon.

'I'm so busy, Modlen.'

'Not too busy for this. This is Garmon Jones' bow. I found it last night and rang you time and again, but you weren't answering your phone.'

'Last night?'

'Last night. I went for a walk down by the river last night and I found this stuff chucked into the hedge, not far from the caravan site.'

Daf counted the arrows. Five. Garmon had lost six but one had been used by Elwyn to scratch the paint on Gethin's car. He remembered something. It was a black arrow. Everything which had fallen out of Modlen's bin bag had been black, the bow, the arm brace, every arrow. It was a white arrow sticking out of Gethin's throat.

'Thank you very much for this, Modlen and please forgive me for not answering the phone before. We don't get any signal at all in the house.'

'Hmm. Well, I've made sure I haven't destroyed any finger print evidence and I'm willing to give evidence in court. You won't need to bother with any video link for me: I'd be fine in the court.'

'Thank you so much, Modlen. When I get a map of the site, can you show me where you found the bow? And when Sergeant Francis arrives, she'll take your fingerprints for elimination purposes, OK?'

'No problems. Any time. And I tend to answer the phone when it rings, Mr Dafis; you should give it a try.'

Daf looked at the equipment on the table in front of him. It looked as if it was not Garmon Jones' bow which killed Gethin. He rang Betsan.

'I need a detailed map of the site, including the caravan site and surrounding area. And I've got some stuff here which need to go to forensics ASAP.'

'OK, Dafydd. Meirion's on the phone and he's sounding seriously stressed. And victim's family have arrived. Do you want to crack on with the statements straight away?'

'If you think they're up to it.'

'And thanks again for dealing with Bodo Mai: she tells me it was a rare form of gastric flu in the end.'

Betsan came in with her phone, which she handed to Daf, mouthing Meirion's name silently.

'Listen, Daf, there's some young lad here wants to speak to you urgently.' In the background, Daf could make out Ed Mills' voice.

'They're not letting me onto the Maes, Mr Dafis, and there's a woman gone and hanged herself in our covert.'

'On my way.'

The best place to eat on the Maes, *Pl@tiad*, was between the incident room and the main entrance and it was there that the family had agreed to meet to celebrate Carys' successful completion of her ceremonial role. All the family, except Falmai, were standing outside and Daf took Carys to one side.

'I'm sorry, *lodes*, but there's no way I can make it here for the meal.'

'I've heard. Gethin Teifi's been killed.'

'Yes, and I'm so sorry to let you down.'

'Is Garmon a suspect?'

'Way too early to say.'

'Well, that's the perfect end to the perfect day for the Virgin of the Vale. Is it true that Gethin was shot with an arrow from a bow?'

'You know the rules, Carys: I can't discuss a case.'

Carys turned back to the rest of the group and, as he was turning to go, Gaenor came up to him.

'What's the matter, Daf?' she asked, in her tender voice.

'Gethin Teifi's been shot. There's a long list of people with a reason to kill him but only one of them can use a bow, and that's Garmon.'

'Poor Carys.'

'I'm not sure I can continue with the investigation. It's never a good thing to investigate the death of a friend and Garmon's position make it even more of a mess.' There was so much comfort in Gaenor's eyes that she didn't need to speak.

'I've got a more personal announcement to make to you, Daf.'

'Won't it wait?' She smiled at him and his heart leapt. 'You're not carrying, are you?'

'You just told me to wait before I told you.'

'Are you sure?'

'Yes. I did a test the day before yesterday and I went to the doctor today, after I spoke to you. I felt so guilty about the session I had on Monday but the doctor told me not to worry, unless I did it every day.'

Despite all the crap, the death of his friend and family tangles, Daf had to celebrate. It was like a blessing on their relationship.

'And before you ask, I'm sure it's yours not John's. He hasn't had much interest since he started calling me a barren but anyway, this little one started when he was up in Kelso at the ram sales.'

'I'll get everything sorted. And in the meantime, for God's sake, Gae, take care, won't you?'

It was hard but not impossible not to kiss her, the mother of his new child. He tried to empty his mind of all things personal as he turned to walk to the main entrance but he failed miserably. The baby changed everything, made it all alright, somehow. In the middle of all the crap and confusion, a new life was developing. He tried not to think about all the children Gaenor had lost and knew that it was futile to think his sperm would be better than John's in creating what she wanted so much, a viable child. She might lose their child; she wasn't young any more. Whatever happened, Daf was determined to support her every way he could: he wouldn't be calling her barren, whatever happened to their baby. Barren! What a disgusting word for a man to use about his wife.

He hadn't gone more than a few yards when Falmai came into sight, a determined look on her face.

'Well, I hope you've learnt your lesson, Carys Dafis. What a disgraceful ceremony! You're courting a murderer and your father has dragged his filthy work onto the Maes to spoil everything for everyone.'

'That's enough, Falmai,' her brother thundered. 'We know nothing about Garmon in this business and it's totally unfair to blame Dafydd for everything.'

'But who let our home to that sort of people?' Her words were still flowing like a millrace when Daf turned again and walked away.

In the reception area, Meirion had managed to set up some kind of system, supported by the stewards. It was clear that everyone had heard the story of the empty Chair and there was a peculiar, muted atmosphere, as if everyone was aware that a new and sinister chapter in the history of the Eisteddfod was being created. No-one was challenging Meirion's authority like Eifion Pennant had done on Monday at Dolau, thank goodness. On the far side of the building, Ed Mills was standing in the sun, wearing working clothes.

'I know you're beyond busy, Mr Dafis, but I didn't know who else to turn to.'

'It may just be a co-incidence but two corpses within half a mile on the same afternoon is pretty unusual.' Ed jumped up into his Land Rover and Daf scrambled into the passenger seat, wishing he had chosen darker-coloured trousers.

'It was like a nightmare, Mr Dafis. I saw the crows were gathering and I thought it must be a ewe dead there, under the trees ...'

'Don't try to describe it, Ed: take me to see for myself.' His phone rang yet again: Sheila.

There's a girl here says I'm to do her fingerprints: Modlen Carter, is that right?'

'Yes.'

'And she showed me on the map where she found this missing bow: hidden in the hedge right by Elwyn Wyn's tent. His name is on your white board.'

'Find him, Sheila.'

Just as the birds of prey had come to drink Dewi Dolau's blood, there was a cloud of birds over the little strip of woodland. When he opened the Land Rover door, Daf could smell death.

'She's here. On the ash tree above the stile. I think she must have climbed to the top of the stile and then ...'

'Ed, we'll have forensic people up here soon to find out exactly what happened so you don't need to create your own theories.'

She was in the shade. It took a moment for Daf's eyes to become accustomed to the darkness. In that moment, Daf tried to count how often he had seen corpses of people who had hanged themselves. Over a dozen farmers, three, or was it four, young men under the influence of drugs and one old woman who had hanged her Labrador before hanging herself. Every one had been a tragedy, the end of a life which had run out of hope.

Despite her face being distorted by the rope, Daf knew her at once, from the pictures in the papers and because he had seen her walking on the slope before the Chairing ceremony. On the ground under the ash tree was a large sports bag. The zip was open and inside Daf could see a large bow and several white arrows. He rang Chrissie at once.

'You know that odd woman you were telling me about, where is she now?'

'Gone out somewhere but before she went, she gave us an

envelope. She asked us not to open it until seven tonight but Bryn opened it the moment she was gone. There wasn't any name on the envelope and I thought someone might come to call for it. Inside, there was a piece of nice paper and just one sentence, no address or "Dear So-and-so", nothing like that.'

'What did it say, Chrissie?'

'In English, it was: "For him to feel as I have felt." And that was it. Bryn reckoned it must be a message to some boyfriend or something.'

'What was she wearing, do you remember?'

'Dark blue track trousers and a light little coat, a cagoule-type thing. Black I think that was.'

Daf did not need to glance up for confirmation.

'So, was there some chap she sent that message to, do you reckon, Mr Dafis?'

'It's not about love this time, Chrissie, but about loss. Her only son was killed in a car accident and it broke her heart. She decided to even up the score with the person who killed her son by killing his and now she's taken her own life. Can you make sure no-one interferes with her things until we get over to you?'

'Of course. Fucking hell, Mr Dafis.'

'I'll see you later, *lodes*.'

From the top of the slope, Daf looked down at the Maes, thinking of the events of the week. He could see Dolau silent and empty, Berllan tranquil under the late sun. He thought about his old friend, a man full of talent and potential who had lost his way and of the woman the *Daily Mail* had described as a 'former Commonwealth Games archery medallist': she had lost all that mattered to her in seconds. Gethin was an utter bastard, using people and discarding them yet he had been killed because of mistake his father had made. So many victims and no-one left to hold to account. Perhaps we're all victims one way or another, Daf thought, as he rang for the ambulance.